RICOCHET

"Mix Craig Johnson's Longmire and Lee Child's Reacher with a humongous dollop of pure, high-powered originality and you get Taylor Moore's Garrett Kohl. It's the mark of a great thriller when you can't put it down until the end. Ricochet not only takes care of that, but leaves you breathlessly hanging on for Kohl's next adventure."

—Jerome Preisler, *New York Times* bestselling author of Tom Clancy's Power Plays series

"Moore may not have invented the modern take on this tried and true genre, but he displays a mastery of it here on par with Lee Child's similarly protective figure, Jack Reacher. To that, he adds a dash of Brad Thor to the mix in fashioning a tale that will leave you longing for the next entry in the series."

—BookTrib

"Muscular but heartfelt, *Ricochet* is an adrenaline-fueled nail-biter. Riveting, propulsive, and timely, *Ricochet* is the rare thriller that fires fast on all cylinders."

—J. Todd Scott, author of *The Far Empty*

PRAISE FOR
FIRESTORM

"Diverse characterization, exciting scenes, and great world-building details also helped pull this reader into the conflicts in the novel. The author captures the characters, as well as the cultural lifestyles and traditions, and brings them to life. Fluid writing and fantastic world building, as well as an excellent, fast-paced plot, will keep readers engaged. The well-plotted story stays at a high level of intensity throughout most of the novel."

—Mystery and Suspense Magazine

"*Firestorm* is a great addition to the Garrett Kohl series. If you like fast-paced thrillers, this is a great read."

—Thoughts from a Page

"*Firestorm* is a story of love, land, and loyalty. Blurring the historical lines of fictional genres, Taylor Moore intertwines components of the timeless Old West tales and current elite operator action thrillers. This book is what I would define as a "modern western," examining the changing landscape (both physical and political) and the individuals who continue to try to hold back the tide of change and modernity in an environment that measures time in decades, not days."

—Best Thriller Books

PRAISE FOR
DOWN RANGE

"*Down Range* fuses the classic Western with the modern thriller. DEA operator Garrett Kohl has big skills and an even bigger heart that drives him to a pulse-pounding showdown as good as anything you'll read this year—and maybe ever."

—Mike Maden, author of *Tom Clancy's Firing Point*

"Having lived it, Taylor Moore hits every bit of the cost of counterterrorism in *Down Range*, but this story is much more. It's a riveting thriller with a family in crisis at the core. It's my kind of book."

—Brad Taylor, author of *American Traitor*

"Taylor Moore's *Down Range* is an intense, authentic, and spellbinding powerhouse that pulls no punches. With high-octane action as well as genuine Texas lore and bravado, readers will be wanting more from hero Garrett Kohl and author Taylor Moore, and soon!"

—Mark Greaney, author of *Relentless*

"A stunning debut, as wild and beautiful as the Texas High Plains in which it's set, *Down Range* turns the thriller genre on its head. Stretching from Kabul to Amarillo, Moore's yarn is chock-full of gripping action, white-knuckled suspense, and, most important, heart."

—Don Bentley, author of *Tom Clancy's Target Acquired*

"Combining the suspense and intrigue of a Tom Clancy thriller with the action and grit of a hard-hitting western, Taylor Moore's *Down Range* is sure to entice fans of both genres, as he weaves a wild tale of betrayal, vengeance, and death on the Texas High Plains."

—Philipp Meyer, author of *The Son*

"[A] strong debut. . . . Things culminate in an exciting, Texas-style showdown between Kohl's family, cartel sicarios, and a host of other bad actors. Fans of J. Todd Scott and C. J. Box will want to check out this propulsive, character-driven thriller."

—*Publishers Weekly*

"Delivers both a compelling story and a vivid portrait of the landscape of the High Plains of Texas. . . . Moore has written a tense and irresistible thriller that fans of C. J. Box and the military action novels of Brad Taylor will savor. The chaos mixes well with a stellar panorama."

—*Library Journal* (starred review)

"Debut author Moore's hold-your-breath thriller introduces DEA agent Garrett Kohl. . . . Though our hero's outnumbered, he's able to lead the brutal criminals into the Texas High Plains for a wild Western showdown. Moore's previous experience as a CIA intelligence officer and deep Texas roots bring authenticity to this action-packed tale."

—AARP

RICOCHET

BY TAYLOR MOORE

Down Range

Firestorm

Ricochet

RICOCHET

A NOVEL

TAYLOR MOORE

WILLIAM MORROW

An Imprint of HarperCollins*Publishers*

RICOCHET. Copyright © 2023 by Robert Taylor Moore. All rights reserved. Printed in the United States of America. No part of this book may be used or reproduced in any manner whatsoever without written permission except in the case of brief quotations embodied in critical articles and reviews. For information, address HarperCollins Publishers, 195 Broadway, New York, NY 10007.

First William Morrow premium printing: July 2024
First William Morrow hardcover printing: August 2023

Print Edition ISBN: 978-0-06-329239-0
Digital Edition ISBN: 978-0-06-329240-6

Image credit: Pages vii, 1, 105, 211, 273: Shutterstock/CreativeOasis

William Morrow and HarperCollins are registered trademarks of HarperCollins Publishers in the United States of America and other countries.

24 25 26 27 28   BVGM   10 9 8 7 6 5 4 3 2 1

To the unsung, unseen, and unknown covert warriors who've fought the wicked and stood up for the oppressed: no monuments mark your battlefields, but your sacrifice is not forgotten. It is to these brave souls that I dedicate this novel.

PART ONE

If you do not change direction, you
may end up where you are heading.

—Lao Tzu

Chapter 1

Mustang Island, Texas
Gulf of Mexico

Garrett Kohl had lived most of his life *head underwater* and he was definitely there in more ways than one. As a former Green Beret turned deep cover counternarcotics agent, he'd thrown up his hand for more than a few risky assignments, but this latest black bag operation with the CIA was one for the books. Of course, tabula rasa was the end goal—a blank slate that would clear his debts, expunge his record, and put him back on the path to living in peace.

The only obstacle in his way was the last High Value Individual (HVI) on the target deck, a final checkbox on the mission to locate seven American traitors who had scattered to the four corners of the earth. In order for Garrett to hang up his guns for good, he had joined a specialized counterintelligence task force made up of paramilitary gunslingers.

The mission objective was to deliver swift, but most importantly *quiet* justice. And like the ancient apostles, they were given their own version of the Great Commission, an assignment to convey a clear and distinct message to the fugitives and their Russian handlers. *You can run. You can hide. But no matter where you go, we will hunt you down.*

Former CIA operations officer Bill Watson, a turncoat of the worst kind, had been hustled from safe house to safe house until reaching his final departure point in the Lone Star State. He was smuggled aboard a trawler in Port Aransas and given over to mercenaries manning an oligarch's superyacht. They were making a beeline for Havana Harbor when NSA cyber-induced *technical difficulties* killed their engine and left them stranded off the Texas coast.

Nearby and ready to pounce, Garrett waited in the belly of a Mark 11 SEAL Delivery Vehicle (SDV), a twenty-two-foot-long submersible that looked like a cross between a torpedo and the Little Boy atomic bomb. He saw nothing but pitch-blackness and heard only the humming whir of the electric motor—focusing on the rhythmic cadence of his respiration as it cycled through the closed-circuit rebreather.

To keep his mind occupied for the last two hours, Garrett recited the lyrics to Robert Earl Keen's "Corpus Christi Bay" and pondered whether they should eat at Snoopy's Pier or the Black Diamond Oyster Bar once they were back on the Texas Riviera. Either was a winner, but since it was his mission partner's turn to buy, there were multiple factors at play. And sticking one another with a hefty tab had become somewhat of a costly, albeit time-honored tradition.

Garrett strained his eyes in vain to locate Mario

Contreras inside the murky bowels of the mini-sub. Although only fifteen feet below the surface of the Gulf waters, it felt like the dark side of the moon. And it contributed to his growing unease. In any direct-action operation there are a million things that can go wrong. But in a subsea assault, multiply that by a factor of ten.

As a graduate of the Army's Combat Diver Qual-ification Course (CDQC), Garrett was comfortable in the water and could hold his own among most Ranger Regiment and Special Forces frogmen. But the training he'd gone through in Key West, Flor-ida, was a lifetime ago. And there was a hell of a big difference between simulation and real-world op-erations. Sneaking aboard a heavily guarded yacht to kidnap Watson was about as real-world as it gets.

The thought of drowning or being shot had cer-tainly crossed Garrett's mind, but the bulk of his worry was for the ones he'd leave behind. All he wanted to do was return to his ranch in the Texas Panhandle and spend the rest of his life training horses, raising cattle, and, if Lacey would accept his marriage proposal, grow their blended families with a baby or two.

Garrett made a concerted effort to fret over some-thing more relevant to the mission, like whether he'd changed the batteries in his night-vision gog-gles (NVGs). He'd just begun another mental check of his equipment when a light flashed—the signal given by either their pilot or navigator to let them know they'd arrived. Pulse racing, Garrett reached up and slid open the door in preparation to exit the sub. Despite the warmth of the water, he was feeling the chill of the lengthy submersion, and welcomed the chance to get moving.

It was a hundred-yard swim in the early morning darkness—no small task strapped down with gear. In addition to primary and secondary weapons, which included his DEA-issued LWRCI SIX8 rifle and a silenced Glock 17, Garrett would take an extra dive helmet and rebreather for the traitor Watson, whom they were bringing to justice. This spy gone awry was behind the brutal interrogation of another CIA operations officer named Kim Manning, their mission commander and Garrett's dear friend. For this reason, and a whole host of others, Watson wouldn't get off easy with a bullet to the head. He'd answer to Kim face-to-face.

Hatch doors open, Garrett grabbed his rifle and latched it to his chest with a carabiner. Armed and ready, he rose to a crouch and followed Mario's lead, pushing off the floor to the outside. But the relief he gained by fleeing the metal coffin was short-lived, as claustrophobia gave way to the chilling naked exposure in the vastness of the black ocean.

Garrett flutter-kicked away and caught up with Mario, who was already a few yards ahead. He focused on the good weather, which included low illumination due to a brewing storm, and an unusually rough sea state. While the chop would make boarding the vessel trickier, the clap of waves on the hull would provide terrific sound cover to mask their assault.

In and out as quickly and quietly as possible was the key to their plan. They'd rehearsed it over and over with every contingency imaginable. But as they used to say back in Iraq and Afghanistan, *the enemy gets a vote, too*. Given their CIA team's success in tracking down the other American defectors, there was no doubt the Russians would be prepared.

Garrett found himself winded at about fifty yards. Of course, he'd never let Mario know he'd struggled to keep up. As a former Green Beret, there were few things worse than admitting that to a SEAL.

When they reached the transom, Mario pulled his secondary weapon first, a silenced SIG Sauer P226. Pointing it up at the swim platform at the aft of the boat, the frogman gave a couple of flutter kicks to break the surface and held steady aim.

Garrett followed suit, sliding the Glock from his holster and aiming at the great unknown. Rising above the waves into the balmy air, he found what Mario had already discovered. *Nothing.* At least nothing that posed an immediate threat. Garrett covered his partner, who heaved himself onto the transom.

Cleared of any visible danger, Mario turned and offered a hand. A clasp of his wrist and a swift tug put them both on board. After slipping off his dive helmet and rebreather, Garrett removed his fins, secured them to a carabiner, and tossed them over his right shoulder.

Met by the pungent stench of wet cigarette ash, Garrett sucked in a couple of big breaths through his mouth and glanced around. The glint of at least a dozen crushed beer cans and a couple of rum bottles littered the aft deck.

Given the engine troubles, Garrett had fully prepared for the mercenaries to be on full alert. But in the small hours and pitch-blackness of the empty ocean, Watson and his minders had already let down their guard. In what they must've assumed would be smooth sailing to the friendly shores of Cuba, the celebration had already started with a helluva lot of booze.

Following his partner's lead, Garrett grabbed the NVGs from his kit and secured them over his eyes. The immediate gray glow in the goggles' illumination brought a sense of relief—the advantage of a predator who owned the night. Mario shouldered his primary, a short-barreled Noveske Mk18 rifle, and brought it to the low ready. Creeping methodically atop the teak deck, the former SEAL moved along the wall on the port side. Before passing each window of the main salon, he would halt for a peek, and then quicken his pace as he snuck by the opening.

Garrett trailed close behind, having memorized the number of steps it would take until reaching the side entry. With access to the yacht's blueprints, and an exact replica at their disposal, they knew the boat inside and out. The problem was finding their HVI. The guest of honor should be enjoying the luxury of the primary suite, but if the guards were feeling extra cautious, then Watson might be sleeping on a bedroll down in the engine room.

As Garrett followed his CIA counterpart along the deck, he couldn't help but be aware of each squishy tap of his wet dive booties. To mask the noise, he tried to keep in step with the lapping waves, a system that worked until they ducked into the side access door.

Transitioning from the low ready to ready to rock 'n' roll, Garrett cleared the left side of the room as his partner swept right. In the grayish glow of his NVGs, he painted anything suspicious with the bright splotch of his infrared laser. Thankfully, other than a mess of tequila, gin, and vodka bottles atop the dining room table, there was nothing much to see.

Skulking through the salon, Garrett couldn't help but wonder how the yacht's owner could have so much money and such bad taste. As if the gold and burgundy color scheme and floor-to-ceiling tapestries weren't bad enough, they'd hung a disco ball from the ceiling. The décor could be described as Eurotrash chic, a visual abomination made worse by the walloping stank of cologne, cigars, and sweat that lingered heavy in the air.

Mario pushed ahead to the galley, just as practiced with perfect efficiency of motion. Fortunately, the area was clear. But a crew member on anchor watch or rummaging for a midnight snack had always been their biggest concern. With a vessel that could sleep up to two dozen, there was a damn good chance that someone was going to get the munchies.

Putting a bullet in one of the mercenaries didn't faze Garrett a bit. They were former Spetsnaz—Russian special operators, who willingly joined and knew exactly what they'd signed up for. Smoking some poor stewardess who was just trying to feed her family back home, on the other hand, wasn't an option. But he wasn't so sure about his CIA partner, who was more accustomed to shooting first and forgetting to ask any questions later.

Mario cleared the cabin like the old-school pipe hitter that he was, keeping an even pace and perfect balance as he made a level sweep of the area, lighting every possible hide with his laser. He shuffled around a corner to clear a dinette space, a blind spot they'd highlighted from schematics, and thankfully kept moving.

Garrett gave a silent word of thanks to the Almighty as they passed a stairwell to the berth, where the crew was hopefully sleeping, and then trailed Mario into the hallway to the primary suite. Stacked single file as they moved forward, rifles at the ready, Garrett made a quick turn behind his mission partner and then a hard left down a pitch-black corridor.

Ten steps. Five steps. Three steps. One. Mario halted at the entrance to the main cabin. It had probably only been a couple of seconds for confirmation, but it felt like a lifetime to learn that Watson was where he was supposed to be. As practiced a million times before, Mario broke right and turned to cover the door while Garrett passed on through.

As Garrett pulled out the zip tie, he couldn't help but smile. For the millions of dollars spent getting to this point, the final leg of the journey involved a tool of the trade that cost less than a few cents. Not only was Garrett about to capture the most destructive traitor in U.S. history, but his debt to the CIA would finally be paid off and he could get back to his family. It wasn't even a toss-up as to which gave him more joy. All he could think about was home.

With only one obstacle to that in his way, Garrett darted to the bed, flipped Watson over, and had his wrists shackled before the scumbag knew what hit him. The turncoat opened his mouth to yell for help but clamped it shut when he saw Mario's rifle pointing at his face. Watson searched for answers, which he found in Garrett's whispered explanation.

"They want you dead or alive, Bill." Garrett tilted his head at his partner, who pressed the muzzle of his rifle to Watson's forehead. "Move nice and quiet, and you'll at least get a trial."

The prisoner didn't say a word—just nodded vigorously.

Although they'd only met once, Garrett had been wearing his usual attire—faded Wranglers, a Howler Brothers pearl snap, and Twisted X moccasins. In his black camo wet suit, he probably looked less like a human and more like a creature from the deep. It took a moment, but it was clear that Watson recognized him.

If the long, dark hair and heavy beard wasn't a dead giveaway, then the thick Texas accent must've done the trick. Garrett grabbed Watson's forearm, yanked him out of bed, and looked him over. No comms devices or weapons, just a pair of black skivvies. *Safe to move.*

Garrett couldn't help but grin as he offered a little nugget of their exfil plan. "Gonna be a cold-ass trip in the back of that sub."

A bewildered expression preceded Watson's whispered response. "*Sub?*"

Garrett didn't explain. The prisoner would get the picture soon enough when they shoved a dive helmet over his head and yanked him into the ocean. With Mario through the doorway, Garrett jabbed his rifle's muzzle between Watson's shoulder blades. They followed Mario's lead, tiptoeing down the dark hallway. A right turn past a descending stairwell then a sharp left into the crew mess got them halfway back to freedom and safety.

Garrett was just starting to rest a little easier when a light flicked on from behind. A quick pivot and his laser found the silent prowler center mass. A squeeze of the trigger would've neutralized the threat, but the desperate eyes of this young brunette in a fuzzy pink bathrobe kept Garrett from firing. Shuffling backward as she began to hyperventilate, her bare feet *tap-tap-tapped* on the vinyl floor until her back slammed against the massive Sub-Zero refrigerator to her rear.

Lowering his barrel, Garrett flipped up his NVGs and put a finger to his lips. As he smiled his gentlest smile and pushed the air with an open palm, the girl seemed to calm after a few deep breaths. She eased her hands up and gave a slight nod, conveying her compliance.

Turning to Mario, Garrett pointed at the exit ahead and jabbed his finger at the door. It took his partner an uncomfortably long time to shift aim, but he eventually made a quick pivot and moved into the main salon. Of course, Garrett knew that once she sounded the alarm, they'd have about thirty seconds to get to the platform where their gear was tethered to the transom.

If a shoot-out erupted, the chaos of the moment would buy them enough time to get off the back of the boat, but not much else. As soon as they hit the water they'd be shredded by gunfire.

Garrett nudged Watson with the muzzle and the turncoat dutifully marched forward. They trailed Mario around the dining table, between two leather sofas and through the side door. As they stepped outside, Garrett lofted up a quiet *Praise Jesus* that there were no screams, no sirens, and no frantic footsteps of rushing guards. There was only the howl of the ocean wind, the lap of waves on the hull, and then the *check-check* of Mario's suppressed rifle.

The Russian sentry on his early morning rounds never even saw it coming. He just crumpled where he stood at the top of the stairwell, dropping his Brügger & Thomet MP9 submachine gun, which slid across the teak and dinged against a railing. Mario engaged the twitching body twice more as he glided past—head on a swivel in search of the next threat.

Garrett jammed the end of his suppressor at his prisoner's back and gave it some pressure, a tacit clue to pick up the pace as they moved down the stairs. Now compromised, every step along the deck seemed amplified. With Watson clomping alongside them, they had all the stealth and sub-tlety of a stumbling drunk teenager banging on bongos.

Once they'd reached the transom at the back of the yacht, Garrett clipped his primary on to the carabiner and drew his Glock to cover Mario.

They'd rehearsed the drill a million times before, but there's nothing like game day. Every action was labored—his movements jerky—even flipping the selector switch on his rifle had taken a couple of clumsy tries.

As his partner brought their dive equipment onto the deck, Garrett kept one eye on the prisoner, the other on the long stretch of balcony behind them. With his sights drifting left to right and back again, he took in the scene in the gray glow of his night vision, wondering why in the hell the girl in the galley had not roused the guards.

Was she too scared? Did she hate them? Had she been in a sleepwalking haze and gone back to bed thinking it was all a bad dream?

About halfway through this wishful thinking the lights flicked on and bathed the transom in a yellowish glow. Garrett flipped his NVGs up and saw a shirtless mercenary leaning over the rail. Finding the guy's face in his sights, he pulled slack out of the trigger and squeezed. The guard's body spasmed as it rocked backward and dropped out of sight behind the stainless-steel barrier. Garrett turned to find Mario securing a dive helmet onto a frantic-faced Watson. Ready to exfil, the former SEAL drew his sidearm and provided security just as rehearsed.

After holstering his pistol, Garrett strapped on his rebreather, just as the rattle of machine guns came from behind. Mario unloaded on the shooter with his SIG, and its rounds *tinged* and sparked off the brass handrail. The gunman ducked, hung his arm over, and fired blindly, splintering the deck below until his ammo was spent. With a mag change in progress, Mario jumped into the black water, prisoner in tow, and submerged beneath the waves.

Garrett turned back for one last look just as a blast struck him center mass. The *whap* of the buckshot met his chest with the force of a Louisville Slugger. The body armor saved his life, but the shrill *hiss* from his mangled rebreather told him everything he needed to know. He would not be departing the same way he'd arrived.

Garrett dashed across the transom and threw his back against the hull, finding minimal cover behind the stairs. He knew that Mario would return for him. They'd planned for every eventuality, and there was no circumstance where either would be left behind. But he'd have to buddy-breathe to the sub—doable but not easy—especially when huffing in air after a firefight.

Garrett dropped an empty mag, popped in a fresh one, and hit the bolt release. In a lull in the shooting, he leaned left and peered around the edge to get an eye on the enemy. But the calm was soon broken by another spray of buckshot that clipped his left shoulder. Jerking back for cover, Garrett instinctively mashed his palm down on the stinging flesh wound.

Zeroed in by the shooter, Garrett raised his rifle and swore that he'd get the bastard who'd blasted him twice. The guys with automatic weapons seemed to fire blindly but the one with the 12-gauge was a hunter, picking his shots with patience and care.

Rising to a crouch, Garrett moved to the low

ready and strained his thigh muscles as he eased upward at a glacial pace, back flush with the wall. Head still below cover, he stopped short of the threshold and readied himself for a move. Spotting his new hidey-hole in the underbelly of a set of stairs on the starboard side, Garrett sprinted across the deck.

Gunfire erupted into a cacophony of *cracks* and *snaps*, but the gamble paid off. With the boat lights blazing, the gunmen became silhouetted in his optics. Leaning over the rail they were wide-open. Starting on the left, Garrett set his red dot on the dark mass and fired three times. With the shadow gone, he slid right and found the next in line. Ducking as a blast of buckshot peppered the iron stairs above his head, he drew up his barrel in a hasty search.

As the hunter with the shotgun was ejecting a shell, Garrett found his target and landed a double tap to the chest. The *check-check* of his suppressed rifle preceded a spray of glimmering crimson. The shooter slumped over the rail, somersaulted midair, and slammed face-first onto the teak with a mushy thud. With the 12-gauge out of commission, Garrett locked on to the next target who was firing down from above. The gunman had just polished off a mag and turned to run when Garrett found his mark. He squeezed twice and the bad guy smacked the deck.

Grabbing a spare dive mask from his pouch, Garrett couldn't help but remember the immortal words of his old DEA mentor. Joe Bob Dawson used to say that *two is one and one is none*. And damned if that hadn't proved to be true. With reinforcements on the way, Garrett dove into the water and crammed under the yacht's transom overhang, just as a hail of bullets rained down from above, pecking the water all around him.

Diving beneath the boat brought about a feeling of both dread and reprieve. The first minute of submersion was tranquil considering his position. And that wasn't by accident. Combat diving was as mental as it was physical. He'd managed to occupy his mind until something grazed his thigh, and he became suddenly aware of his bleeding shoulder and the kind of sea critters in the Gulf that might take interest. Having missed a good breath, his lungs were on fire. But it wasn't a mind-over-matter kind of pain. It was the electric throb of a body depleted of oxygen and the flashing red alarm that he was about to drown.

Kicking back to the surface, Garrett banged his head on the hull and gulped in a mouthful of salt water. He hacked out the caustic brine that spewed from his nostrils and fought to suck in air between each bone-jarring cough. Nowhere to go but down, Garrett grabbed his detector to locate the SDV's internal beacon. The handheld device gave a digital reading of the vessel's location. He had just activated it when machine-gun fire unleashed from the deck.

Ducking beneath the water, Garrett swam beneath the yacht and came up gasping on the other side. Met with another hail of bullets, he resubmerged and pulled up his gauge to locate the sub. He was completely spent, but there was no going back to the surface. Garrett tried to resist the temptation to gulp in air, but his body was starving for oxygen. Light-headed and nauseous, he rolled forward and flutter-kicked into the black abyss below.

A quick glance at the detector showed the bar turning from orange to yellow to green. He was at least headed toward the sub. With adrenaline racing and the hope of rescue, the first thirty feet of his descent was a breeze until that voice in the back of his mind chimed in—the one that asks, *What if it's too far?* It was in that moment of doubt when he felt the burn—not only from his shredded lungs, but in the panic-stricken terror that he wasn't going to make it.

Body quaking, neck tightening, Garrett fought the irrational urge to open his mouth and breathe. It was then that he realized there was no turning back. A couple more labored kicks got him into a free fall to the ocean floor, but he was no closer to salvation. He came to the grim conclusion that he'd never see his loved ones again.

Praying as desperate a prayer as he'd ever prayed, Garrett grasped for something—anything—a shred of hope that this wasn't the end. In that moment, he saw the glimmer of light, a pulsing glow just a few feet ahead. Whether it was bioluminescence, an oxygen-deprived hallucination, or one of God's holy angels beckoning him to Glory, Garrett wasn't sure. He only knew that it was *something*, which was exactly what he'd asked for.

Two more kicks, then a regulator was shoved in his mouth so suddenly it didn't seem real. The sub's auxiliary air given to him by Mario was pumping the sweetest oxygen he'd ever breathed. A lot of things should've captured his focus but all he could think of was one—an orphan from Afghanistan—his son. *Asadi* was all that mattered now. Garrett vowed right then and there that when he returned home, he was never going to leave again.

Chapter 2

Asadi Saleem Kohl stood in line at the middle school cafeteria watching a fistful of french fries drop next to the pizza on his tray. It was a culinary combo that he loved but didn't quite understand. Since his arrival in America, he'd experienced a few challenges in his transition from life in Afghanistan. Adapting to the local fare had *not* been one of them. He could happily dine on barbecued brisket, chicken fried steak, and Blue Bell ice cream for the rest of his life.

Shuffling right for his chocolate milk, he glanced down to admire his new Twisted X cowboy boots—the same exact style that his dad wore. Even better, they'd caught the eye of his girlfriend. And impressing her was right up there with earning approval from his grandpa, Butch.

Asadi had just sidled up to the milk cooler to find there was nothing left but *skim*. Deflated at the thought of having to suffer through that, he glanced at the lunch lady for help. Mrs. Lupe had taken a liking to him early on because of his accent, which fell somewhere between his choppy village Pashto and a relaxed Texas twang that he'd picked up on the ranch.

He'd just mustered the right words to make his request when she dropped her tongs and a hand flew to her chest. Jaw slack, Mrs. Lupe turned and bolted through the kitchen, out of a side door, and into the hallway. Dying to know what startled her, Asadi turned back to the dining area, just as the in-unison *oooohhhh* that usually followed a solid putdown or preceded a fistfight echoed through the cafeteria.

Hoping not to miss all the action, Asadi strained his eyes and focused on a narrow opening in the crowd of gawkers. He was dismayed to discover his girlfriend, Savanah, was holding the smashed remains of a piece of chocolate sheet cake in her hand. He was even more distressed to find that the rest of it was smeared across the face of the new kid named Sam, a hulking seventh grader who was roundly feared by even a few of the more delicate teachers.

A slow-motion swipe of a hand across his lips and Sam shook his fingers, slinging icing onto the linoleum. Hushed whispers and the low rumble of students shifting uncomfortably followed the whining screech of a few chairs, as those near the skirmish made a hasty getaway. Sam's cheeks, usually a bit rosy, darkened to beet red as he pinched the frosting-covered pecans from his face, one by one, and flicked them away.

Asadi had just willed himself to run over to Savanah when the bully clutched her wrist and jerked her out of the chair. Asadi thought he couldn't have been any more shocked by the spectacle until she pushed the mousy ringlets from her eyes with her free hand, and reared back to swing. It was a solid attempt, but Sam saw it coming. Before she connected, he blocked her arm, clutched her elbow, and yanked her close. She struggled to break free, but the bully had Savanah in his iron grip.

Bolting to her, Asadi searched the room for a teacher but there were none to be found. Garrett had once told him that schoolyard tussles were just part of growing up. And so long as he didn't start it, he'd never get in trouble at home. Thinking this was more of a *just in case* than a *when this happens* sort of deal, Asadi hadn't paid that close attention, but now he wished he had.

The low murmur of students, who ranged from roundly disgusted to thoroughly entertained, gave way to a deafening silence. Stopping short of the struggle, Asadi mustered his bravest voice, but it came out as more of a squeak than a growl. "Leave her alone!"

Sam glanced back at him, seemingly amused by the challenge. "Or what?"

Great question. Asadi looked around again to find there were still no teachers. His lunch lady pal who'd bolted from the assembly line was hopefully getting some help. But without an adult around, the cafeteria was as lawless as the old frontier that he had learned about in Texas history. In the world of might makes right, the good guy didn't always win.

When Asadi provided no answer, Sam's lips curled into a cruel grin. His protruding canines made him look a bit wolfish. "Yeah. That's what I thought."

Never one to cower, Savanah doubled down with an insult. "Get your fat, *booger-picking hands* off me!"

As quickly as he had snatched Savanah from the chair, he shoved her back into it. Asadi was moving to Savanah when Sam turned his sights on him and closed the distance. He thrust out his frosting-laced palm, grabbed Asadi's shirt collar, and yanked him so hard he was nearly jerked off his feet.

An attempt to break loose was met with a tightened grip, another swift tug, and the loud rip of Asadi's pearl-snap denim shirt. Only inches from Sam's icing-streaked face, the bully became a single blurred mass of glaring eyes and flared nostrils. He squinted and leaned in.

"Where do you think you're going?" Sam turned to Savanah, wearing a look of disgust. "Why you even with this kid anyhow?"

The sting of embarrassment and betrayal followed her long silence. Asadi knew Savanah was scared, but he couldn't help but think that maybe she was wondering why she was with him herself. After all, Savanah was the prettiest girl in their grade. Maybe it wasn't enough to be neighbors and share a love of horses. *Maybe* she was looking for a tough guy like Sam.

As this sad realization was playing out in his mind, the bully snatched a carton of milk from the table and held it over Asadi's head. Deep down, he knew what was coming. But before Asadi could move, the container was upturned, the contents gurgled out, and they trickled down the bridge of his nose, splattering across the once-shiny toes of his brand-new cowboy boots.

The familiar harmony of *oooohhhhs* sprang from the lips of his classmates again and doused the fire of his billowing anger with the gasoline of embarrassment. Unfortunately, his response didn't match that of his rival. There were no menacing one-liners, squared-off shoulders, or any shred of bravado. Asadi's reaction was the one he feared most. *Tears.*

A quick glance at Savanah made the situation worse. Her face radiated pity. The mocking laughter that filled the cafeteria was nothing compared to losing her respect. With that added insult to injury, Asadi gathered every bit of raw-nerved humiliation, curled his fingers, and let loose with a wide right hook that landed knuckles to jaw.

The *clack* of Sam's teeth sent the throng of jeering students into a shocked silence that seemed to last an eternity. The look on the bully's stunned face was etched on Asadi's brain. But what came next was all a blur. Asadi had no idea how it happened, only that he went from upright to horizontal in a bone-jarring crash on the floor.

Wind knocked from his lungs, Asadi gasped for air, rose to sit, but was met with a furious fist to the side of the head. The second slammed his right cheek, and the third struck the other. But it was the straight-on punch that really took out his starch. The only thing nice about the ringing in his ears was that it drowned out the echoing chatter that came from the crowd.

Most begged Sam to stop, while others egged him on. But the only voice that really mattered was Savanah's—the one screaming for help.

Although surrounded by onlookers, Asadi had never felt more alone. He didn't know where the coach came from, only that he arrived before things got a whole lot worse. Wiping the milk from his forehead, Asadi scrambled to his feet and fled the scene. It was the worst of all options, especially when making sure Savanah was okay should've been his first priority.

Asadi wanted to be brave. And wanted to be tough. But he'd been none of those things. He'd been thoroughly humiliated. And the only one he could bear the thought of talking about it with was Garrett—the only one who knew just what to say to make things right. Of course, he was gone again—leaving Asadi to wonder if his dad was ever really coming home for good.

Chapter 3

Garrett's road trip across Texas was just what the doctor ordered. After handing the traitor over to Kim, he'd done the requisite after-action review and debrief, then moseyed down the road. It wasn't that he didn't care. It was just time to move on. The Drug Enforcement Administration's Field Division in Dallas had reassigned him to Amarillo's Resident Office, which meant he could finally put down some roots and build back the ranch after a wildfire had ravaged it nine months earlier.

His end goal was a life suited to getting married and raising a family, not one where he was shot up or drowned down on the coastline near Mustang Island. But there was a burden of guilt that stings every soldier's conscience when they drop out of the fight. Fortunately, his self-flagellation was quickly alleviated by a quick trip over to Lawton, Oklahoma, to visit a few aunts, uncles, and cousins on the maternal side of his family.

They were the last tie to his Native American heritage—a lineage he'd gravitated to at an early age, and held near to his heart, especially after his mother died. It was fun to catch up on the latest gossip, which only took a few minutes. But glancing over the old photos on the wall at his aunt's house there was something that struck him in a way that it never had before.

His great-uncle had landed on the beaches of Normandy on D-Day, fought in Europe until the war was over, and then moved back home, where he lived the rest of his days as a high school football coach and volunteer firefighter. He'd served his country, his community, and his family with honor and distinction before passing through the pearly gates or moving on to the happy hunting grounds, wherever Comanche Reformed Church members go when they say their final farewells on earth and enter the afterlife.

Garrett wasn't ready to take up the rocker or the grave just yet, but he was looking forward to returning home. And there was something about those old pictures that gave him a sense of peace, permission to turn the page and start anew. He was fairly certain that his mother and her favorite uncle were conspiring in heaven, hatching some scheme that would allow him to cast off the burden of warrior and finally enter the next phase of his life.

GARRETT DROVE INTO CANADIAN AFTER taking the scenic route home. It was a meandering ramble of red dirt back roads through rural Oklahoma that had given him a little extra time to think. The visit with his Comanche relatives had opened his eyes in a way that it never had before. Whether they knew it or not, their DNA was built for survival. But it wasn't just in the physical sense, as would be expected of the tribes who had ranged America's Great Plains.

His kin were uniquely geared to weather storms in a way that was difficult for most living in modern society to understand. *Wanting more* for these historical nomads was a foreign concept. It wasn't about the accumulation of things. It was about *having just what you need*. Sometimes there was a little more in life. Sometimes a little less.

Garrett had never put much focus on acquiring possessions, but he certainly wanted to hang on to what he had. And keeping the ranch intact to pass down to Asadi was his number one goal. The wildfire that ravaged it had left him in a state of near financial ruin. Insurance had fortunately covered most of the damage, but the destruction of his center-pivot irrigation system meant there'd be no hay crop, nor a way to continue his stocker-steer feeding operation through the winter. His hopes of making the farm profitable were dashed.

Squaring the banknote for the new equipment and expansion to ranch was contingent on having a few money-generating enterprises. The lenders had been lenient to a point, but that would only last for so long. With their homeplace and the ranch as collateral, it certainly turned up the heat. Something big needed to happen. And it needed to happen fast.

Garrett turned his black three-quarter-ton GMC off the highway at the Oasis Truck Stop on the outskirts of town and pulled up next to a fuel pump. Distracted by his problems, he had only just remembered that he hadn't eaten all day. Stomach rumbling and slightly irritable, he donned his Lone Star Dry Goods cap, jumped out of the truck, and got the diesel flowing. Pondering in his mind which preservative-filled culinary abomination he'd purchase as he marched up to the store, Garrett hadn't even noticed that his archrival was walking out the double doors.

If Bo Clevenger had been any closer, he could've bitten him. And knowing the psycho criminal the way he did, Garrett wouldn't have been at all surprised. Instinctively, he took a few hasty steps back, grabbed the front of his shirt with the left hand to yank it up, and readied his right to draw. With the Nighthawk 1911 in his belt, Garrett wasn't too worried. But with this behemoth, it'd take more than a couple of rounds to do the trick.

Bo smirked, then took a couple of lumbering steps forward. "No need for that, Kohl. Ain't got no weapons."

Garrett felt a bit foolish. To this point there'd been no threat. But the assurance from Bo that he was unarmed meant little. The man, himself, *was* a weapon. Back in his rodeo days, he'd been a champion bulldogger, but had ultimately been banned from the sport after snapping the necks of more than a few steers. And that was just the least of his many offenses.

"Surprised to see you out." Garrett dropped the front of his shirt but kept his distance. "Third time's a charm, right? Thought they'd have thrown away the key."

"Oh, you know what they say. Can't keep a good man down."

"Known you to be a lot of things, Bo. But a good man isn't one of them."

Bo chuckled. "People change, you know."

"*People* do. You don't."

Bo looked off into the distance. "What about your buddy, Ray?"

The smug grin that followed the question told Garrett everything he needed to know. This wasn't a casual conversation. It was a threat. Bo had been doing some snooping around. The question was how much he knew. Garrett was fairly certain that his DEA cover was still protected, but Ray Smitty's status as a confidential informant (CI) for the Texas Rangers could very well be compromised. If so, that meant he and his family were in danger.

Both the Garza Cartel and the Kaiser clan, for whom Bo had worked, had powerful connections, lots of money, and an extensive network of spies on both sides of the law. Which meant there was a solid chance someone had tipped Bo off to who was responsible for putting him behind bars. The out-of-the-blue mention of Smitty didn't sit well.

"Ray Smitty is the rare exception," Garrett countered. "Got a second chance and done something with it. Can't blame a man for doing what's right by his family."

"I *don't* blame him."

"Then why'd you bring it up?"

"Because all I want is what he got." Bo looked Garrett in the eye. "A second chance."

"Nothing stopping you from making a change."

"No. I reckon there's not." Bo held up a finger

and wagged it. "But . . . there's just one thing I still can't figure out."

Garrett already knew where this was going, but figured he'd play along. "What's that?"

"Can't help but wonder how Smitty got out clean. I had to sit my ass in the pen for two years while he was getting his life back. I got a kid to look after, too. *Almost* don't seem fair."

That comment was a clear message. Bo knew something was off. He might not know everything, but he at least suspected that Smitty had cooperated with law enforcement in some capacity. Now he was fishing for answers.

Before Bo could continue, Garrett cut him off. "You just passing through?"

Bo shook his head. "Here to stay. So, you might as well get used to seeing me around."

Garrett heard the diesel pump click behind him but kept a careful eye on Bo. "Well, it looks like I'm done here."

"Yep. Looks like you are." Bo smirked again. "*Done.*"

"If you're waiting around for a welcome home fruit basket or something, I think you're gonna be real disappointed."

Seconds later, Bo cleared his throat and flashed a smug grin. It was the kind of look that says *I know something you don't know.* "Next time you see *her*, please give Lacey my best."

The mention of her name sent Garrett's pulse racing, and an unbearable heat flashing on the back of his neck. Threats against him, or even Smitty, were one thing, but bringing up the love of his life was quite another. This thug had put her in danger before. He would not do it again.

Done with the games, Garrett sprinted forward and launched a boot into Bo's chest. Colossus or not, the man stumbled backward and slammed into the store's double doors. Despite the jarring crash that shattered the safety glass, he appeared to be unhurt and for the most part unfazed. Only thing different was that the smirk was gone.

Garrett had just cocked a fist and taken a step toward Bo when a siren chirped from behind. He turned to find the Hemphill County sheriff's F-250 creeping up across the parking lot until it came to a lazy stop midway between the pumps and the store.

Ted Crowley got out, marched around the front bumper, stopped short, and rested his palm on the pistol grip. "What the hell's going on here?" He lifted the cowboy hat and wiped his brow with a sleeve. "What'd you do to that door?"

Crowley was the kind of guy who always seemed to be everywhere and nowhere at the same time— just in time to take the credit or cast the blame. And it didn't take long for the sheriff to side with the ex-con. Not surprising given his hatred of the Kohls. He had close ties to the Kaisers, who had backed his campaign for years in exchange for him turning a *very* blind eye.

"You all right, Clevenger?" The sheriff stepped up to Bo and gave him a close inspection. "Got a bit of blood there on your neck."

Bo wiped his palm across the back of his head and

stared at it. "I'm good." He looked back at Crowley. "No big deal."

"Positive?" The sheriff eyed Garrett, clearly aching to catch him in the wrong. "Looks like something is off here."

Bo shook off the suggestion. "Just an accident." He looked to Garrett. "Ain't that right, Kohl?"

What could Garrett say? He'd physically assaulted Bo because of a vague comment that nobody but him would consider a threat. "If you're good, I'm good."

Bo gave a nod, which seemed to suffice, then Crowley gave the requisite *free to go* response, disappointment written all over his face. With that nasty and somewhat confusing business concluded, Garrett took his leave. As he eased back into the driver's seat of his pickup and cranked the engine, he kept a careful eye on Bo, who was staring right back at him.

It wasn't too big a mystery why Bo hadn't ratted him out. He wanted no official record of the altercation that could be used in a court of law. After all, if some clash did come about, it would trace right back, making him a prime suspect. What the criminal was cooking up this time, Garrett hadn't a clue. But one thing was certain. It was all going to culminate in a violent end.

Chapter 4

Liam Bayat became suddenly aware that he was being followed. At a facility responsible for servicing the most destructive weapons on earth, it wasn't a surprise. On top of the team of paramilitary officers, many of whom were former U.S. special operations forces, there was an internal security team keeping an eye on everyone.

The Security Police Officers (SPOs) fell under the National Nuclear Security Administration (NNSA), which coordinates with the DIA, CIA, and NSA, not to mention the watchers watching the watchers from the FBI. It was the Bureau's special agents focusing on counterintelligence that Liam worried about most.

The Pantex nuclear weapons facility, located on the most barren plains that the Texas Panhandle has to offer, is seventeen miles northeast of Amarillo. It is an ominous fortress of barbed wire, bunkers, and hardened structures—the look of a top-secret military test site crossed with a federal supermax prison.

Its perimeter is guarded by roving sentries in 4x4s and monitored by every type of advanced electronic surveillance equipment known to man. But the real key to safeguarding the nukes is the barren sixteen thousand acres of wasteland surrounding the complex. A surprise attack would be nearly impossible. The prairieland is so pancake flat you can spot a centipede on the approach from ten miles away.

Liam made a quick right turn past the cafeteria into the men's room of the Administrative Support Complex, a building that despite its foreboding exterior looked like any other government structure on the inside. He moved to the sink and washed his hands for no reason other than to try to look natural. A glance in the mirror revealed bloodshot eyes and beads of sweat clinging to his brow.

Noticing a few new strands of silver added into his formerly jet-black hair, he wondered how things could've ever gone so wrong. With the entrance of another employee, Liam dragged the back of his hand across his forehead and flew out the door. He'd made it no more than a few feet when he heard the call of a female voice from behind.

Liam was tempted to pretend he didn't hear her, but it was obvious by the shudder of his body that he had. Ducking the polygraph for too long had put him on the head of Pantex security's radar. He liked Beth Madison, but she could be a little too no-nonsense, having yet to shed the stiff demeanor from her time in the military. She still wore her auburn hair in a bob cut, and rarely deviated from a charcoal suit. At least today there were pinstripes.

Liam tried to look pleasantly surprised. "Oh, hey there, Beth! How are you?"

She smiled but looked genuinely pained. "Be a whole lot better when we can close out your file. Any chance I can get you in for that poly?"

Liam waggled the empty folder he'd been carrying around for show. "Got a couple of meetings this afternoon, but I can swing by your office and set something up."

It wasn't a lie. He'd leave a note on her door after hours. Like a lot of government workers, most Pantex employees didn't hang around a second longer than required unless there was an emergency. And his overdue security screening didn't count as a crisis. At least not yet.

Beth winced. "You're gonna get me in big trouble. You know that, don't you?"

After passing the rigorous background check at the start of the hiring process, plant employees were largely left alone—no different than any other military or intelligence job out there. They were on the honor system, a method of self-monitoring dependent upon patriotism and morality. There were periodic reinvestigations to keep his security clearances active and unfortunately his had just popped up again.

With the best *I'm so sorry* expression Liam could muster, one that must've made him look like a cowering dog, he raised his wrist and tapped his watch. "Really, I'm going to be late."

Liam had just spun on a heel and hightailed it when he heard her steps behind him. He fought the urge to turn back and moved quicker to gain some distance but hopefully not enough to arouse suspicion. Her steps quickened as she caught up with him. With a tap on the shoulder, Liam stopped and turned around. *This was it. He was caught.*

Beth thrust out a business card. "New office and extension." She flipped it over to show him where she'd written down the information in blue ink. "Didn't want you getting lost."

Liam stared at it blankly, too nervous to even comment, then took the handoff and shoved it into his front pocket. "Where?"

Beth's look of amusement turned to puzzlement. "It's on the card."

Liam let loose a nervous laugh that sounded as guilty as he felt. "Yeah, of course."

"You feeling okay?" Beth was clearly studying him. "You look a little flush."

Like him, she had served in the Army and completed a tour in Mosul, Iraq, around the same time. As a Human Intelligence Collector, Beth had done her fair share of interrogations and it showed in her personality. There was a combination of assertiveness and suspicion, even in casual conversations, that set more than a few around Pantex needlessly on edge.

Liam raised the empty folder again to emphasize the point. "Just under pressure, that's all." This wasn't a lie, either. "A lot going on with a new contract. Changing the specs on me every damn day. We're over budget. And now someone in Washington wants to push up the timeline. All to get a photo op for some high-level visitors. And nobody will confirm when or even *if* they're really coming."

At a place like Pantex, there were always a million projects going on at any one time. But the projects he worked on were as sensitive as it gets. It was the reason that everyone involved was back under the microscope. As a structural engineer and project manager, he was critical to most of the teams implementing new programs. His delay in completing his security screening and odd behavior had likely put him on a watch list. He wouldn't be surprised if he was being monitored at his desk and followed outside work.

Fortunately, Beth's demeanor shifted once again, from concern to condolence. Anyone who'd been in the military or worked in government long enough knew the drill. Chain of command, bureaucracy, and unreasonable expectations from people who didn't have to do the job was part of the beatdown, a universal language in federal contracting that would explain everything from a case of the Mondays to setting yourself on fire and driving your car off a cliff.

She'd understand. But her sympathy wouldn't last long. Someone up the chain would start asking questions. Before he could go on, Beth waved him off.

"Don't sweat it for now. We've got until next week before I have to get your pack submitted. Give me a call when you're caught up."

Liam fought every instinct to exhale and wipe off the sweat that had reappeared on his forehead. Instead, he pressed his palms together in front of his chest in a comical sign of gratitude. "Thank you, Beth. Really appreciate it."

The gesture got a grin and a finger wag from

her in return. "You owe me one. You know that, right?"

As Beth turned to walk away, his heart sank at the thought of his betrayal. But it wasn't only the guilt of his disloyalty to the country. His heart ached for the ones who trusted him, the ones who'd risked their careers just to do him a favor. Despite all the efforts to safeguard the world's deadliest weapons, the security officers charged with protecting them could be fooled with a couple of lies, some pathetic whining, and a folder full of nothing.

No matter how Liam tried to justify his actions, he was a filthy, dirty traitor—the linchpin for subverting a country that welcomed his Iranian immigrant father with open arms, and which Liam himself had once defended in uniform. His world, yet again, was burning down around him. And there wasn't a damn thing he could do to stop it.

Chapter 5

As Garrett turned off the highway onto the gravel road leading up to his brother Bridger's house, he decided not to mention the Bo Clevenger altercation lest it put a damper on his long-awaited return. There would be time for dealing with that later, along with his other major problems like financial ruin. For now, he just wanted to savor the moment.

Of all the many homecomings over the years, this one might be his best. Because it would hopefully be his last. Since Asadi came to live with them, Garrett had longed to be a rock-solid presence in the boy's life. And now he had that chance.

Not that Garrett needed it, but seeing his son sitting proudly atop a sorrel mare named Sioux was the extra dollop of proof that it was good to be back. The boy had taken to team roping, which was Bridger's specialty. Garrett's brother, who'd once been a collegiate rodeo champion at Tarleton, declared Asadi a natural after the first lesson and had been coaching him ever since.

Garrett pulled up to the side of the roping arena,

put the truck in park, and shut off the diesel engine. There was a time when his son would've dropped whatever he was doing and met Garrett in a full sprint. But not today. A young man in the making, Asadi would wait until the job was done—just like Butch had taught him. Garrett's father had been a surrogate grandpa since the day he arrived.

Garrett hung his head out the truck window and called up to his dad, who was perched on the top rail. "I've seen undertakers who don't wash their hands get a warmer reception than this. What's a guy gotta do to get a *welcome home* around here?"

Butch lifted the straw Resistol from his head, wiped the sweat from his brow, and glanced back. "Boy is in training. Can't be distracted by every little thing." He dropped the hat back onto his mess of curly white hair, grabbed the brim between his thumb and index finger, and pulled it low on his forehead. "You back for good now, or what?"

Thinking back on his last mission down in the Gulf of Mexico, Garrett had to laugh, wondering if his dad would be as gruff if he knew that his youngest son had nearly just been killed by Russian thugs. Of course, gruff was Butch's default temperament. Had the old man shown any concern, Garrett would've expected the old coot had six months to live.

"Done what I need to do, I guess." Garrett opened his truck door, hopped out into the grass, and walked the few feet over to the arena. "Looks like you're stuck with me from here on out." He climbed to the top of the fence, took a seat next to his father, and watched Asadi as he tossed the loop of his lariat onto a mechanical dummy steer and dallied off on the saddle horn.

Butch tipped his brim. Just barely. Even slighter an expression was the tightening of his cheeks, which was about as close as he got to a smile. "Asadi will be glad to hear it."

While Garrett and his dad still had their issues, his return to the ranch with Asadi had been a turning point in their relationship. They weren't just building the business. They were building back their family after years of neglect.

At risk of saying something meaningful and getting Butch riled, Garrett focused on Asadi, who had brought his sorrel to a halt as he took a little calf-roping instruction from Bridger. With the boy now sitting still, Garrett noticed what he had thought was a smudge of dirt above Asadi's left cheek was actually a black eye.

"Wait a minute." Garrett turned to his dad, who seemed to be awaiting the inquiry. "What the hell happened to him?"

Butch winced, and for the first time since Garrett arrived, turned, and looked him dead-on. "Might've been a scrape while you were gone."

"A *scrape*?" Garrett leaned forward to survey Asadi a little closer. "He all right?"

"Yeah . . . boy's fine. Just one of them schoolyard things, you know."

Garrett had been in plenty of *schoolyard things* when he was a kid. Mostly with Bridger. Had it been anyone else other than Asadi, Garrett would've shaken it off and laughed, chalking it up to a *boys will be boys* sort of deal. But this was his own son. Aside from that, Asadi wasn't a scrapper. He was a gentle soul, a sweet kid with a big heart. There was someone else at fault.

Garrett could feel his blood starting to boil at the thought of some kid laying a finger on Asadi. "Well, what happened, Daddy? Who hit him?"

"Big butterball named Sam Clevenger."

"*Clevenger?*" Garrett railed. "That's not—?"

"Yep." Butch spat out the rest like sour milk. "Bo Clevenger's boy."

Damned if that wasn't a coincidence. Or maybe it wasn't one at all. From their earlier run-in, it was clear that the ex-con had something on his mind. *Was it revenge?*

Garrett once had the chance to take Bo out of the food chain but had taken the high road instead. After seeing him again today, and hearing this disturbing news, it made him wonder if he'd made a mistake. Some men needed killing. Bo was one of them.

Garrett shook his head. "Should've offed that sumbitch when I had the chance."

Butch looked at Garrett askance. "*Sam?*"

"Of course not, Daddy. I'm talking about Bo."

"Well, *he* ain't the problem for once. It's his ruddy-faced little pup stirring up trouble."

Garrett recounted the whole earlier episode at the Oasis Truck Stop, then launched into a diatribe about what he was going to do to Bo when he found him. He had just begun to lay down the list of tortures that would curl the hair of a medieval dungeon master when Butch held up his hand and pushed the air.

"Now, hold on, Garrett. Whatever's going on with Bo is between the two of you. Don't you go interfering in this situation. It's Asadi's problem and he's gotta handle it. Bullies are a part of life and he's going to have to deal with them at some point. Earlier the better, I say."

That was the kind of nonsense Garrett used to believe before it was his own kid getting picked on. Now he wanted to shove this Sam Clevenger's head into a pile of fire ants. Asadi *was* tough, but his heart was as kind as any God ever forged. Of course, Garrett knew that his dad was highly protective when it came to Asadi. If Butch wasn't worried, then he'd try not to be either.

"All right then, I'll leave it alone. But I want to make sure this is over." Garrett was wound up all over again. "Clevengers aren't your run-of-the-mill bullies. I mean, you know as well as I do that Bo is a damn sociopath. A killer. He's just never been held accountable."

"I'm not arguing with you on that one. But this is his son we're talking about. Just a boy. School put Sam in detention for a week. So, he's out of the picture. At least for now."

"And when he returns?" Garrett shot back. "Then what?"

"Like I said. Asadi has to handle it. He won't be a kid much longer."

If Asadi was up against a Clevenger, then Garrett was going to make sure the boy was locked and loaded—metaphorically speaking. He was about to dig a little further when Asadi slid down from the saddle and marched right up. His cowboy bravado dissipated with each step, and the boy looked powerless to bridle his delight in seeing his dad.

As Garrett eased off the top rail and dropped into the arena, his own joy was no better masked. He was home forever and there was no better feeling. Both he and Asadi held their swaggering gait until they met in the middle and then all bets were off. The kid wrapped his arms around him and latched on. After about a half-minute embrace, Garrett let loose of Asadi, put his hands on his shoulders, and maneuvered him out front to get a good look.

"Missed you, Outlaw." He took a step back and eyed the boy from head to toe. "Believe you grew an inch while I was gone. Thought I told you not to do that."

Asadi shrugged. "Not my fault."

Garrett did his best to pretend he didn't notice the bruises. He tilted his head at his brother, who was riding over. "Your uncle Bridger know anything worth learning?"

Bridger leaned back in the saddle. "What can I say, Bucky? With this kid under my wing, he may win more buckles than the both of us." He cocked an eye. "How many you have again?"

The only thing that surpassed his roping skills was his trash talk. As close as they were, Garrett and his brother couldn't have been more different. Growing up, Bridger lived for the limelight of rodeo and football, while Garrett was always searching for the perfect hunting spot or secret fishing hole. But they'd always had each other's backs.

Garrett ignored the question and looked to Asadi. He could tell the kid was a bit sheepish because of the fight. Of course, there was no point pretending it didn't happen. A Kohl family tradition was ignoring the obvious and Garrett had been trying desperately to break that custom.

"Looks like you got into a scuffle?" Garrett mustered up a big grin to let Asadi know everything was okay. "What happened, man?"

Asadi looked down and shuffled his feet. "I . . . I don't know."

Garrett kneeled and put his index finger under Asadi's chin and gently brought his face up to where they were eye to eye. "Told you before. So long as you don't start the fight, you'll never be in trouble with me." He winked to lighten the mood. "Can't guarantee anything with the principal, though. For that you might need a lawyer."

"Don't worry." Bridger grinned wide. "You'll get the family discount."

Asadi looked back to Garrett, a little misty-eyed. He cleared his throat, but his voice was still a bit froggy. "It Savanah. I worried she—" Stopping short, he looked away and kicked at the dirt with the toe of his boot.

Bridger, who'd been waiting patiently nearby, turned his horse's reins and rode over to Butch, who was still perched on the fence. They were dealing with a *girl* issue, which called for privacy. Another family tradition was avoiding conversations relating to *matters of the heart*.

Garrett ducked under the brim of Asadi's Catalena cowboy hat and locked eyes. "Okay, spill it. What's going on?" When Asadi still didn't answer, he pulled out his cell phone and waggled it. "I can always call Lacey. You know that *Savanah* is her favorite subject."

Asadi fought not to grin but couldn't contain it. "No call Lacey. *Please*."

"Then you better start talking." Garrett grinned, too. "Or you'll leave me no choice."

Asadi looked back up, the Lacey joke seeming to have raised his spirits. "Savanah think I'm not tough now. She think I'm a wimp."

The very idea was laughable. Asadi had helped save Savanah's life not nine months before, and there was nothing but admiration for him in her eyes. But preteen insecurity was what it was and there'd be no convincing him otherwise. Asadi wasn't as big and strong as the corn-fed locals who were gearing up for football. And that had bothered him for a while.

Garrett wished he could've told him that it didn't matter, but it was yet another one of the many hard-fought battles to come. It was right up there with bullies. As much as he hated to admit it, Butch was right. Asadi had to start facing these problems on his own.

"Asadi, I'm sorry about what happened at school, and we're going to fix it. And I can also tell you for certain that Savanah doesn't think you're a wimp. I promise you that."

"How *you* know?" Asadi's response seemed more skeptical than curious. Kid was getting a little more attitude the older he got.

"Because I've seen how she looks at you. When you two are out at the ranch with the horses, she hangs on your every word."

Asadi's attitude mellowed a little with news he was eager to hear. "Really? That true?"

Garrett had witnessed it firsthand. The boy was a natural horseman and Savanah loved horses. Asadi wasn't a brute like Sam, and he might not be a starter on the football team, but he was a helluva rider and a damn fine cowboy in the making. Savanah could see it, too.

"Listen to me, Outlaw. I've whupped my share of bullies." Garrett gestured at his brother, who was off his horse and leaning against the fence. "Your uncle Bridger is just one of many." After a hearty gut laugh from Asadi, he continued. "And one thing I can tell you is that those guys never win. Eventually the good guy gets the girl. You know how I know this?"

Asadi rolled his eyes. "Because you get Lacey?"

Garrett shook his head and chuckled. "Take it I've told you that story before." He was about to tell it again when Asadi interrupted with a question that threw him off a bit.

"How you going fix Sam Clevenger?"

Garrett racked his brain to understand what Asadi was talking about. The kid had come a long way with his English, but it was still lacking at times. Then it dawned on him that he'd said they would fix what happened at school. Obviously, he'd be on the phone with the principal as soon as possible, but the bottom line was that Asadi needed to know how to defend himself.

"Going to have to give you a little instruction." Garrett put up his fists in case Asadi didn't fully understand. "Show you a few tricks I've learned over the years."

"*Tricks?*" Asadi was somewhere between nervous and curious. "What tricks you know?"

"Enough to teach Sam Clevenger to stay clear of you from here on out." As a student of Pat Mc-Namara, another former Green Beret, Garrett *did* know a few things. And they were battle-tested. "Why don't you finish up with Bridger and we'll start training when we get home."

The idea of a few new tricks to handle Sam was just what the doctor ordered. Asadi made his way back to his horse with a lot more swagger.

Butch sauntered up from behind. "Everything okay now?"

Since his dad had been watching Asadi while he'd been gone, Garrett didn't want to act like everything had gone to hell when he wasn't around. "Ah yeah, he'll be all right." Throwing his dukes up, Garrett shot a couple of faux jabs at Butch. "Gonna hang up that old punching bag we got in the barn and show him what I know."

The old man didn't miss a beat. "That'll keep him upright for about two seconds. Then what?"

Garrett ignored the barb. "He just needs a little confidence. That's all."

"Needs more than that."

The old man was salty as a pirate and full of menacing one-liners. But his comment had more of a judgmental tone. It wasn't like him. Something was off.

Garrett dished it right back. "What the hell is that supposed to mean?"

"Means you're his dad now. Need to be around for things like this."

With Bridger and Asadi back on their horses, Garrett felt a little freer to let loose of his temper, which was getting more irritable by the second. "You think I don't want that?"

"I don't know what you want. Just know that being a father comes with responsibilities. And a big one is being around when he needs you."

"What would you know about it? After Mama died, I remember you spending more time with Jim Beam than you did with me and Bridger."

Garrett immediately felt guilty for that, but Butch was the last one who needed to be throwing any shade when it came to parenting. There were a couple of years when he and his brother had felt pretty alone. His dad didn't recoil at the insult, nor did he come back swinging. He was uncharacteristically even-keeled.

"Wasn't *father of the year* but never claimed to be. *Was* around, and you know it."

That was true. For better or worse, Butch had always been a steady presence in their lives. They could always count on him being there. "So, what's your point, Daddy?"

"My point is that it's time to back off with work and be around some. You said this was the last one and you need to mean it."

"This *was* the last time," Garrett conceded.

"Until it's not."

There was a part of Garrett that wanted to argue but he knew Butch was right. It had always been that way in special operations. One more mission. One more battle. One more war. Sometimes you just have to know when to say enough is enough. As if on cue, the cell phone in his front pocket buzzed. He took it and checked the screen to find it was Kim Manning.

Having seen it, too, Butch launched in: "You know I love Kim to death, but she's always got something cooking. Some life-or-death matter that can't be handled without you. At some point, you're going to have to just say *no*."

Garrett thumbed the side button on his phone and let it go to voice mail. He didn't need the next mission, the next battle, or even the next war. All he needed was right there in front of him. He had his family, his horses, and the clear blue Texas sky above. If the biggest problem was a middle school bully, he could handle it. He just wanted to live the rest of his life in peace.

Chapter 6

CIA Operations Officer Kim Manning had just emptied a carafe of lukewarm coffee into her green Dartmouth mug when she glanced over to find Deputy National Security Advisor Conner Murray sauntering through the door. It was the first time he'd ever set foot inside the Agency's headquarters—at least as far as she knew. And for this reason, his sudden appearance was a bit unnerving, especially in the evening hours when nobody else was around.

Discussions regarding the hunt for the worst traitors in American history had typically required her to take a trip over to the Old Executive Office Building, just a stone's throw from the White House. She waved him over to the conference table in her makeshift operations center on the sixth floor of the Original Headquarters Building (OHB).

Despite Kim's unease, she kept it light. "Guess they'll let anyone in here these days."

Murray smirked. "Got some nasty looks from

the guards when I was climbing over the fence, but we got it all straightened out."

Murray had the look of a frat boy turned Beltway bandit, with the untenable cockiness of a Georgetown grad. He'd come dressed for battle in a Nantucket red Johnnie-O polo, khaki pants, and a pair of Gucci loafers. Of course, Kim never judged a book by its cover. As a petite blonde who'd made her bones fighting the global war on terror, Kim had been underestimated a time or two. But that's exactly how she liked it.

Because of the compartmented nature of their assignment, Kim's counterintelligence operation was spearheaded from a vault within a vault—taking *need-to-know* to the next level. Her phantom base was little more than a few computers, some maps on the walls, and a silver coffeemaker that never stopped percolating. But her strength wasn't capacity. It was capability.

"Don't let the Agency police officers hear you calling them *guards*," Kim chided. "That's a greater offense than breaking into the building."

"Noted." Murray gripped the back of the chair, rolled it over, and sat. "So, this is the Death Star, huh?" He looked around the room and scrunched his nose, clearly unimpressed. "Always wondered where Darth Vader hung her helmet when she wasn't traveling around with her storm troopers making trouble for me."

"Pretty sure that if I'm Vader, *you're* the Emperor." Kim cut eyes at Murray. "And it's the other way around. We're the ones keeping you out of the media's spotlight."

Although she liked him, Kim had no doubt that Murray would've had no problem joining the dark side of the Force. In fact, he was probably the only kid on the block who volunteered to be Dr. No when everybody else wanted to be James Bond. But he'd turned out to be a fervent ally in tracking down the American turncoats. More importantly, he'd kept his promise to fast-track Asadi's U.S. citizenship and the adoption process for Garrett.

Kim was expecting another bad *Star Wars* joke out of Murray when his brow furrowed and he got down to business. "Any news out of our friend Watson?"

Murray always liked to remind her that the traitor was a mutual acquaintance, possibly his way of sharing the culpability of knowing someone they both should have caught. In Washington, nobody wants to go down with the ship alone.

"Not much yet." Kim gave a shake of the head. "Mario said he's talking just enough to keep us coming back for more."

"Anything my people should know about?"

By *people*, Kim knew that he meant the national security advisor and the president. Because of the many gray areas in which her counterintelligence unit was operating, Murray preferred there to be a couple of firewalls between him and them in case of blowback.

"Confirmed what we suspected." Kim shook her head in disgust. "He was working with the Russians on the rare earth minerals deal. In exchange for hiding Moscow's hand, he was awarded with all the perks. Money and power. Usual incentives for people like Watson, who feel they've always deserved more."

"Anything on a Chinese connection to the Russian mining operation?"

"Still working on that one, but I have a good feeling that the *bear* and *dragon* are in cahoots. I'll have Mario lean on him a bit harder in the next interrogation if that's something you want us to work on first."

"Not too hard." A look of unease spread across Murray's face. "Just don't touch him. Okay?"

It was obvious he was worried about this backfiring on the administration. In his position, it was sometimes better not to know all the details.

"Don't worry." Kim raised her eyebrows. "*We* won't."

Murray groaned, looking more uneasy. "What'd you do with ol' Billy boy, anyhow?"

"Just gave him what he wanted from the Russians in the first place."

He looked at her quizzically. "And what was that?"

"A place to retire on a tropical island." With Murray still bewildered, Kim clarified. "Detention center in Guantanamo Bay, Cuba, to be more precise." She grinned. "He probably envisioned his Caribbean getaway with a lot more mojitos and island girls than razor wire and jihadists. But I thought it was a fair compromise given the blood on his hands." Kim had expected Murray to be a little squeamish, but he seemed preoccupied.

"He mention anything about what's happening in Tehran?"

The mention of Iran took Kim off guard. That'd never been brought up once in relation to Watson. "Didn't know there was a connection. But I can pass it on to Mario. Why?"

"Something else is going on." After a pregnant pause, Murray added, "Something big."

"Bigger than this?" Kim couldn't help but be curious, but the truth of the matter was that she was looking forward to a little downtime. She'd even considered a trip out to Texas to see how Asadi was settling in. "Please don't tell me there's another rogue intel officer out there."

Murray narrowed his gaze. "No, but we think it might be related to the damage done by Watson and the others. Might be the reason CIA assets are dropping like flies."

Kim wondered how in the hell Murray knew something she didn't. "Watson didn't have access to the ones we're losing. Hard to believe Moscow would—"

"Not the Russians. It's Iran."

Kim pondered the logistics of it all for a moment. Intelligence operations within the Islamic Revolutionary Guard Corps (IRGC) were largely spearheaded by Quds Force, a group of paramilitary fighters that was somewhat of a cross between the CIA and Army Special Forces. The spy organization had a global reach, in part due to the widely dispersed Persian diaspora around the world. But assassinating over a dozen Agency assets would be a hell of a feat for any country, no matter how robust the resources at their disposal.

"Certain it's the Iranians, Conner? That'd stretch their capabilities pretty thin."

"It's them all right. And we've responded in kind."

Kim would've asked *what'd you do* but that operation would be highly compartmented. He wouldn't answer unless she was read into the program. The closest she might get was *how do we know*. "We have an asset inside the IRGC? I mean, where's the proof? If you slap the Iranians upside the head, better be damn sure it's warranted. They're gonna hit back."

"A slap was warranted and then some. And to answer your question, we know it was them because we've traced it back to a cyber intrusion in your classified network. Their hackers have been creeping around in the system undetected for months. Looks like they had some technical support from the Russians, but we can't prove it yet. IOC and NSA are all over it. They're running a joint operation that includes a counteroffensive over at Fort Meade."

Now it all made sense. The Information Operations Center (IOC) was the cyber arm of the CIA. Something this devastating would be kept extremely *close hold*. Not only that, but the task was also being run in coordination with the National Security Agency over in Maryland. That would take spooky to the next level. The big question was, what did it have to do with her?

"I can do a lot of things, Conner, but cyber isn't really in my wheelhouse."

"South Asia, however, is. And there's a good chance this Iran deal could go to the next level. If it does, we'll need allies on the ground. Just like we did after 9/11."

Kim didn't even have to ask. She already knew what that meant. It was no secret the exodus of American and coalition forces from Afghanistan had left the Sunni Taliban at odds with the wealthier and militarily superior Shia of Iran. Where there was jealousy there was opportunity. And Kim knew just the right tribal chieftain in Waziristan to spearhead a war.

This was the kind of operation Kim once lived for, but so much had changed over the last couple of years. Witnessing what Garrett had with Asadi opened her eyes to a world that offered so much more. She wanted someone to miss her. She wanted someone to celebrate her return. In other words, she wanted a family. But none of that was on the horizon—at least for now.

Murray slid his palm across the table and nudged her hand. "What's the saying here, Kim? You want to make your career, you gotta *run to the guns.*"

If it came to blows with Iran, even in a shadow war, Kim knew her name would go down with legends like Gary Schroen, Bob Baer, Gust Avrakotos. She didn't crave the limelight brought about by movies like *Zero Dark Thirty*, *Syriana*, and *Charlie Wilson's War*, but any intelligence officer who said they didn't want their career immortalized was full of it.

The problem was that Kim had run to the guns her whole career and was on the verge of burnout. But devoted CIA operations officers never admit their limitations. They accept their next assignment like a dutiful soldier. For better or worse, the Agency *was* her family.

A shrug and a smile, and Kim was on board. "Iraq. Afghanistan. Syria. Why not Iran?"

Murray was clearly pleased with her response. "Assuming you'll want to get the old band together? You, Mario, and Kohl have made quite a trio."

It was true. They *had* made a great team in bringing down the Russian spy ring. But all good things must come to an end. Garrett, her conscripted DEA special agent, had fulfilled his obligation to the CIA, and she had turned him back to his family, namely Asadi.

"Mario will be on board, no question about it. But I can't ask Garrett for any more than he's already given. He's paid back his debt to us with interest."

Her first run-in with Garrett in Afghanistan a couple of years earlier had not been a pleasant one. The DEA agent heading a counternarcotics task force in the Hindu Kush mountains had somehow turned a reconnaissance mission into an international incident. On top of being in an area designated off-limits, he broke every rule of engagement. But when Asadi's village was razed by Taliban thugs, Garrett couldn't stand by. He rescued the boy and brought him back to base.

Directed on a protective custody assignment by Kim, Garrett took Asadi back home to Texas to lie low, until things got further complicated when Garrett got entangled with a Mexican cartel and a gang of local criminals who were trafficking heroin through his ranch. Executing his signature move to tackle his foes, Garrett left another trail of dead bodies in his wake.

In exchange for cleaning up yet another of his messes, Kim did what CIA operations officers do—look for leverage. As recompense, Garrett had taken on the role of her off-the-books black bag operator—a part he was born to play. With his help in the rendition of a major kingpin named Emilio Garza, and by tracking down the traitor spy, Bill Watson, Garrett had more than fulfilled the terms of the agreement. It wasn't until Murray brought up the next part of her deal with him that she remembered Garrett wasn't quite done.

"What about Faraz?" Murray asked. "Didn't think he'd let that one go without a fight."

Months ago, before agreeing to tracking down the traitors, Kim had set some specific terms on the deal. In addition to granting Asadi U.S. citizenship, she asked for permission to go back to Afghanistan to bargain for his brother. Thought to have been slaughtered in the attack, reports arose that Faraz Saleem had been conscripted into a warlord's army and was now working on the eastern border for an Iranian drug trafficker named Naji Zindashti.

Kim took a moment to think things through. "Haven't mentioned any of that to Garrett yet." She was beginning to wonder if going into a Taliban-controlled country to search for someone who may or may not still be alive was starting to sound like a suicide mission.

"Why not?" Murray looked surprised. "Thought you said he would be all over this."

"He would be," Kim admitted. "It's just that he has Asadi now. He has his life back. I don't know. Maybe there's such a thing as good enough."

"And this is what *good enough* looks like? Garrett and the kid as father and son." Murray nodded, seeming to understand. "That's fine. But Asadi has no idea his brother might be alive?"

Kim shook her head. "No reason to bring it up unless I knew something for sure."

Murray smirked. "Okay."

"*What?* You don't think I'm doing the right thing?"

"Didn't say that." Murray winced as he took a sip of his coffee, then set it down disgusted and pushed it away. "Just think Asadi deserves to know the truth."

Kim couldn't believe a political hack like Murray was lecturing her on *the truth.* "And what if this leads to a dead end?" Before he could answer, she interjected, "He'd be crushed. Or what if Garrett goes over and never makes it back? Asadi's orphaned twice. Have you thought about that? Yeah, maybe this *is* good enough. They at least have each other. Why push it?"

Murray seemed amused by her passion. "Hey, you're the one who brought Faraz up when we made the agreement. Don't fault me for holding up my end of the bargain."

"So, you think I'm welshing on the deal?"

"Didn't say that, either."

"Then what are you saying, Conner?"

"I'm saying that the kid has a right to know. To make that decision. If you had a sibling that was presumed dead but wasn't, wouldn't you want to find them?"

There was a part of Kim that wanted to lash out

at Murray. She wanted to ask what *he* was willing to risk. But it hadn't been him who'd thrown that Faraz card on the table. And as much as she hated to admit it, this political operative was right. Asadi should know the truth about his brother and Garrett should be the one to tell him. It was a family decision.

Realizing the futility of arguing, Kim turned to the wall and stared. Once again, she'd put her loved ones in danger. Whether she wanted to or not, it was time to make that phone call to Garrett. It'd be up to *him* to determine if what they had out there on the Texas High Plains was *good enough*. It was up to *her* to start preparing for war with Iran.

Chapter 7

Garrett found the heavy punching bag exactly where they'd left it. The old Everlast had probably sat in the tack room inside the barn for at least twenty years. Despite a thick coating of dust, which would get knocked off the canvas within the first few punches, it was in perfect condition, as well it should be, given that the thing had never really taken more than a few solid licks.

Boxing lessons had been Butch's bright idea for Bridger, who had a bit too much unbridled testosterone back in those teenage years. After a bout of pasture party *fisticuffs* landed him in *handcuffs*, their dad thought it might be worth enlisting the help of their next-door neighbor Kate Shanessy's now-deceased husband to direct Bridger's restless energy into Golden Gloves instead of battling it out with football rivals from Perryton or Spearman.

Well, *A for effort*. The old man had tried. But Bridger, being Bridger, took the skills he learned and parlayed them into a professional ass whupping for anyone who dared talk trash about Canadian, Texas, or the mighty black and gold. Preferring a moving target to the stationary punching bag,

Garrett had become his brother's primary sparring partner. It was a fun family activity until it went too far, which it always did, and the boxing turned to brawling.

Garrett dragged the bag across the barn floor, hoisted it up to the hook on the beam where it hung years ago, and looped a link of the chain to where it hovered a couple of feet above the concrete floor. He wanted to keep it low enough to teach Asadi how to disable someone's legs. A boot to the knee-cap had proved highly effective in getting himself out of a few bad jams.

At the sound of Asadi's footsteps, Garrett turned around and flashed a smile. "Well, what do you think, Rocky?"

Garrett's spirits rose at the thought of the marathon of movies they'd need to watch together to get the boy up to speed. In fact, he wondered if maybe they should've done that first before putting him on the bag. With "Eye of the Tiger" playing in his head, Garrett put up his dukes and rocked the white and blue Everlast with a left-right combo. Without any gloves on, he felt a burn as the canvas skinned his knuckles.

Asadi's face turned quizzical. "Who Rocky?"

"Glad you asked. I've found that Rocky and Rambo can teach you just about everything you'll need to know to get through life."

Asadi stopped midstride. "*Rambo?*"

Garrett didn't know why he brought up Rambo, since it had nothing to do with boxing. Maybe it was just the Sylvester Stallone connection. Or maybe it was because there were values to be gleaned. Mental toughness. Survival skills. Self-reliance. All were traits that had kept Garrett alive and thriving during his Army Special Forces and DEA career.

Garrett batted the air. "Don't worry. That's advanced-level stuff. For now, we're starting with the basics. Like learning how to deal with a punk like Sam Clevenger."

Asadi seemed to shrink, and his facial expression went from confounded to fearful in the blink of an eye. It was clear the incident had taken an emotional toll on the boy as well as a physical one. The thought of him going through any more grief tore Garrett up inside. He'd see to it Asadi never had to experience that kind of pain and humiliation again.

Figuring it was best not to dwell on what happened in the school cafeteria, Garrett decided to get right to the lesson. "Got your gloves?"

Asadi pulled a pair of leather work gloves from his back pocket. "What we gone do?"

Garrett chuckled to himself. The kid probably figured he'd been summoned to the barn for farm chores. "Gloves are so you don't hurt your hands."

Asadi eyed the swinging Everlast as if it were a swaying cobra. The kid had adapted so well to life in America that at times, Garrett forgot many things were still brand-new. Clearly, he had never seen a punching bag in the small mountain village where he grew up. And the idea that it could somehow hurt him had clearly thrown the boy for a loop.

"Don't worry. You'll be driving a hole through this thing in no time." When Asadi didn't budge, Garrett moved around behind him, gripped his shoulders, and eased him closer. "Now this right here is a safe distance."

They were still about five feet away, but Garrett wanted to teach him about *zone awareness*. "If it looks like you're about to mix it up, you need to keep a little room between you and your opponent. About your height is a good rule of thumb." He moved back in front of Asadi and looked him in the eye. "Do you know why?"

Asadi peered around him and stared at the bag. "Enough room run away?"

Garrett stifled a laugh. "Well, that's not a bad idea if the guy has a knife or a gun. But I'm hoping that from here on out, the worst you'll have to deal with is an oversized bully. Real reason is so you can see what's coming. Guy makes a move then you're ready for it."

Garrett took Asadi's hands into his own and raised them level with his chest. "Now turn your palms out."

Asadi did as he was instructed and then curled his hands into fists. "Like this?"

"I like your instincts, Outlaw. But for now, I want them open. Like you're pushing the guy away. You see, the best fight is no fight. And we want to try to talk our way out of it first."

Asadi looked skeptical as he unclenched. "What I supposed say?"

"Guess that all depends. But try to get the guy to cool down if you can. Something to let him know that you're not looking for things to get any worse. But if he wants to take it up a notch, you'll be happy to oblige."

Garrett knew his explanation was only making things more complicated, and it was unlikely that anyone with the last name Clevenger would ever back away from violence. With the *turn the other cheek* speech box checked, they could move on to more important steps.

Garrett reached out again, hooked Asadi's bony forearms, and raised his limbs a couple of inches. "You've got a little distance to see what's happening and you've done your best to talk your way out of it. But this clown decides to make a move. This is why your hands are already up. Now make a fist."

Asadi curled his little hands into tight balls. "He in big trouble."

"Darn right he's in trouble."

Over the years, Garrett had gleaned a little about pretty much every fighting technique known to man. And when it all came down to it, he was a big believer in mixed martial arts. From jujitsu to Muay Thai there was something to be learned. But as his old DEA mentor, Joe Bob Dawson, used to say, there's not a style in the world that beats a solid first punch. No matter how big or strong an opponent is, if you can ring his bell and get him on wobbly knees then it's *good night, nurse* for the son of a bitch who wanted to throw down.

Garrett turned to the bag and gave it another one-two punch to demonstrate. This time he dialed it back to save his knuckles. "Like that. Left jab to the nose to stun him. Then you follow up with a solid right." He turned to find Asadi repeating the drill in slow motion. "Perfect. Now try it on the bag."

Asadi moved closer, dukes in the air, and gave it the old one-two, just as instructed. But unlike Garrett's punches, the boy's produced no jarring thuds, clink of the chain, or squeal of metal-on-metal friction from the link and the hook above. There was only the melodic *tap-tap* of leather on canvas. It was as gentle as morning rain.

Garrett was about to jump into the subject of hip rotation when Butch ambled through the barn's front door. Asadi turned back briefly but kept focused on the task at hand. The old man stood shoulder to shoulder with Garrett and watched.

"Well, you got a Mike Tyson in the making yet?"

Garrett chuckled. "Maybe in spirit." He turned to his dad. "You know him as well as I do. He doesn't have that killer instinct. Just not in his DNA."

"Neither did you at that age. You got it along the way, though."

"Maybe so. Just not sure if I want that for him."

Butch turned with a curious expression. "Why is that?"

Garrett didn't regret his years overseas with the Army or doing undercover counternarcotics work, but there was a part of him that wondered if he had squandered precious time. He'd never been happier than he was right there on the ranch.

"Just wonder if it was all worth it. Being gone all these years. What was it all for?"

Butch looked back at Asadi. "Sounds like you're dipping into matters that are none of your business."

"How are the choices I've made in life none of my business?"

"Because making sense of the universe is up to God. You want to know answers that you're never going to get here on earth. Foolish waste of time. If you'd done this thing or that thing, would your life be better or worse. Doesn't work that way."

Garrett could feel himself getting roped into one of the old man's aggravating philosophical debates. He knew he should avoid it, but it was already too late. Curiosity had gotten the better of him. "Then how does it work, Daddy? Enlighten me."

"Life isn't about choosing your own fate. It's about your reaction to what gets thrown at you. How you handle it. What you do with a surprise."

Garrett couldn't help but think about the unexpected death of his mother when he was a kid. Nobody would ever choose that path. Butch had taken to the bottle, while Garrett and his siblings, Bridger and Grace, each checked out in their own way. They'd fallen apart as a family and hadn't been right until an orphan boy from Afghanistan came into their lives. He was a missing puzzle piece from another box that somehow fit just right.

Garrett focused on Asadi. "You mean him?"

"Everything in your life led to that boy. And him to us. So, before you go questioning the man upstairs, maybe you ought to just say thanks. Be grateful for what you got. The past is the past. Leave it where it belongs. Took me too many years to learn that lesson."

Garrett took a moment to process. He hated to admit it, but his dad was a hundred percent right. "Okay, if we don't have any real say in the future and it's all just a big gamble, then how do I move forward knowing there's no certainty? How do I guide my son?"

"You can't avoid life's problems." There was a rare look of softness in the old man's eyes. "Just teach the boy how to respond when they come up."

There was a temptation for Garrett to argue. Given his line of work, he had become an expert in contingency planning. But the last thing he ever planned for was Asadi. And it had been the best thing that ever happened to him. Maybe it *was* time to quit questioning God's will and just say thank you. Before Garrett could admit there was truth in his father's words, Butch had already moved on.

"What did the spymaster have to say?"

Garrett had hoped Butch had forgotten about Kim's phone call. He had been trying to forget about it himself. "Well, you were right. She wants me on another mission. Is that what you wanted to hear?"

"Always like to hear that *I'm right*. But I'm more curious about your answer."

"Told her I'd have to think about it."

Any kindness Butch had held in his gaze was lost at that moment. "Dammit! Didn't I tell you she'd suck you back in."

Asadi turned from his vigorous bag workout a bit startled by Butch's outburst. He wiped a few beads of sweat from his forehead. "I do okay?"

"Yeah, you're doing great, sonny." Butch took a deep breath and tried to calm down. "Why don't you take a quick break. Go grab a drink of water from the hose round back." Asadi looked thankful for the reprieve, jogging to the door. When he was outside and around the corner, the old man got back on a roll.

"What's the matter with you, Garrett? You got the whole world right in front of you and it's like you don't even see it. Don't even care."

"It's *not* that I don't care." Garrett took his own deep breath and lowered his voice for a conversation he especially didn't want Asadi to hear. At least not yet. "There's something I haven't told you yet."

Butch looked at the door to make sure Asadi was out of earshot. "What's going on?"

"Asadi had an older brother. Kid named Faraz."

"Yeah, you told me. Killed with his folks when the Taliban raided the village."

"*Suspected* he was killed," Garrett clarified. "Then we got word that the raiders had taken some prisoners. Teenage boys that they could use as soldiers."

"And Faraz was one of them?"

"We think so. I mean, nothing is certain over there when it comes to intelligence. But Kim is pretty sure that it's him."

Butch looked skeptical. "*Pretty* sure?"

"She's taking a trip out there to address some other stuff I can't get into, but while she's there, she's going to try to broker a deal for Faraz. Asked if I wanted to help."

"A trip *where*?"

Garrett reluctantly confessed, "Afghanistan."

"Well, last I heard, the Taliban wasn't exactly throwing out the welcome mat for American soldiers." Butch shot a disapproving glare. "And what's this *other stuff* she's talking about?"

"Kim couldn't tell me over the phone. But I get the impression that it ain't gonna be a picnic in the Hindu Kush. Sounds like she needs me there for protection."

"Like I said before, Garrett, I love that girl to death. But she's got a way of pulling you back in. And I have a feeling this Faraz business might just be an excuse."

"Kim wouldn't lie about that."

"Not saying she's lying." Butch shook his head. "But have you seen the proof yourself?"

"No. According to her source, there's a kid named Faraz, who is the right age and from the same village as Asadi. It all adds up. Kim's pretty sure it's him."

"If it's certain, that's one thing. You better be sure it's worth the risk." Butch glanced around to make sure they were still alone. "Because this is a big-ass gamble if you ask me."

"If Asadi has family out there who are still alive then it's worth the risk."

"*You* are his family now."

Garrett took his dad's words to heart. But it would be hard to live with the guilt of inaction if there was a chance that Faraz could be saved. "I get that. I really do. Just don't see how can I look Asadi in the eye if I know I could've done something?"

Butch's softened expression registered his understanding. "You can look him in the eye as his father. The man who has to make the hard calls, even when it hurts." He again looked to the door to make sure they were speaking in private. "If you really have heartburn over this then maybe you should tell him."

"I can't put that on him, Daddy. He's just a boy."

"That's true. But you made him a promise the last time you left that this was it. That you were done. You willing to break that vow when he needs you most?"

Garrett sighed. "It's not fair to put that kind of pressure on him. To make him choose between me or his brother."

"It isn't fair. That's true. Of course, life isn't always fair. We both know that. It's full of difficult choices. And this is just the first of many to come. Asadi has a right to weigh in on this one."

"That kind of decision can haunt you forever."

"No arguing that," Butch conceded. "But there's a moment of truth that everyone faces at least once in their lives. *His* might've just come a little earlier than most folks."

Garrett couldn't disagree; however, it was too early to heap that on top of everything else. He was wondering how he would even begin to broach the subject when Asadi came jogging back inside the barn. With gloved fists guarding his chin, he gave a one-two jab every few steps, looking less like a little boy who needed to be protected, and more like a young man who was ready to take on the world, and possibly face the most difficult decision of his entire life.

Chapter 8

Liam stared out at the open plains behind his ranch home thinking another man's thoughts. Growing up with a Persian father, he had heard the term *inshallah* so often it had almost become a verbal filler like *um*, or *you know*. The translation *if God wills it* had over time morphed into slang. He never uttered the expression, seeing it as little more than a way to assign order to chaos—a made-up magic phrase with no more spiritual significance than Murphy's law.

What had once seemed like deference to the Almighty felt more like a cop-out for hunting up real answers. To this point, his treachery could almost be excused given the circumstances. But with every day that passed, Liam was becoming less the victim and more the accomplice. Several sleepless nights in desperate prayer had yielded no solutions. In fact, it had only raised more problems. Even in death his children would suffer. His blackmailer had assured him of that.

Liam moved to the top rail of the backyard deck and surveyed fifty head of registered Charolais cattle gathered at the windmill by a dilapidated set of working pens. Despite a rainy spring that had left the pasture behind the house emerald green and the stock tank full, the cattle preferred fresh water and would hike a mile out of their way to get to it.

There was nothing more desirable than purity, Liam surmised. His soul ached for it.

Watching the cattle drift up to the trough to get their fill after an afternoon graze had become his end-of-the-workday routine. Just twenty minutes with the cows, a can of Pondaseta beer, and all was right with the world. The ranch was a blank slate, an opportunity for him to do things right. *How did it go so wrong?*

The move from the upscale La Paloma neighborhood in Amarillo to a farm near the small community of Lefors was a bit of a gamble. With the exception of holiday visits to see his maternal grandparents, Liam hadn't spent much time there at all. In fact, his ranching and maintenance skills probably fell somewhere between Billy Crystal's character from *City Slickers* and Eugene Levy's from *Schitt's Creek*. But the transition had been a good one. And the hardships of ranching life had been eased by some very helpful neighbors.

A radical change in both venue and lifestyle had been necessary—a way to hit reset after his wife's unsuccessful bout with pancreatic cancer. Three tumultuous years fighting an invisible enemy had left him and his children physically, mentally, and spiritually exhausted. The move to the country with its fresh air, boundless blue skies, and God-breathed sunsets had renewed his family's spirits.

The endless chores that came with the territory were a much-needed distraction.

His family had been on the path to healing. At least until now.

Tempted to sink lower at the thought of his dire predicament, Liam turned to find his son walking up from behind. "Hey, buddy boy. Didn't hear you pull up. How was practice?"

Wade rolled his eyes as he leaned against the porch rail. He'd already made it clear that at sixteen, he was too old for *champ*, *sport*, or *pardner*. If those were a no-go, then *buddy boy* was certainly non grata. Liam was about to correct his earlier mistake when Wade moved on to a topic even more pressing than nomenclature.

"What's for dinner, Dad?"

Liam furrowed his brow. "Well, hello to you, too."

The kid tried to look tough but broke into a grin. "Sorry. Hit the weights and now I'm starving."

As the younger of the two siblings, Wade had taken things harder, and had become withdrawn. But his school in Lefors had a decent six-man football team. He'd found himself a new set of friends, and a special calling for farm life. He even had the hearty look of a plowboy. Unlike Liam's daughter, Robin, an olive complected brunette, Wade had curly blond hair and freckles like his mother's family. For a *variety* of reasons, people thought he was adopted.

Liam rested the crook of his arm on the back of Wade's neck and squeezed. "Yeah, I know. Gotta bulk up for next season, right?"

Wade flexed and broke away. "Do if we're gonna beat Wildorado."

It hit Liam that he might not be there to see it and he felt the lump rise in his throat. Rather than let his son see his anguish, he pivoted fast, walked over to the picnic table, and picked up the faded blue Nerf football that was there when they moved in. There were a few hunks missing, but it still flew straight as an arrow.

Liam tossed the ball to Wade, who took a few steps back until he was up against the rail. "Heard from your sister yet?"

Wade pursed his lips as if he didn't care. "They made it to College Station."

The school had taken a group of college-bound seniors over to visit Texas A&M University for a couple of days. Liam knew that Robin's boyfriend was on the trip, and Wade couldn't stand him. He wasn't a fan of the smug little bastard himself. But he also knew that too much pressure would send her further into his arms. Keeping quiet hadn't been easy.

"Cody looking at going to A&M next year, too?"

The look on Wade's face said it all. "I don't know. Maybe."

"And you don't like this guy?" Liam already knew the answer, but he wanted to know why. "He doesn't mess with you or anything, does he?"

"*Mess* with me?"

"Yeah, tease you. Sometimes older kids do that."

Wade laughed off the notion. "Not to me, they don't."

His son was back to his tough-guy routine, but

Liam didn't care. He wanted to get to the bottom of what was going on. There was a part of him that found his fatherly concern a bit ridiculous given his other problems. And he wondered if it was merely a way to focus on something that he could actually control. Of course, there was another part of him that speculated it was his subconscious egging him on to settle his affairs, to right any wrongs before the end.

Liam and his son, the rough-and-tumble cowboy, had never been close, not like he and his daughter, who was more of an academic. Robin was his STEM kid, the science and math geek who spent hours watching documentaries on black holes and string theory, while Wade longed for the rancher's life. The differences had never bothered Liam, but it was obvious they'd bothered Wade.

Liam tossed the ball back. "So, what's the deal? He rubs you the wrong way?"

"Not sure, Dad." Another shake of the head. "Just don't trust him, that's all."

"Sounds like you know something I don't."

Wade was about to throw the football but held on. "He said some stuff that got to me. Something he told one of his friends."

Liam opened his hands for a catch. He was finally getting some information and didn't want to break the momentum. "What's that?"

Wade threw the ball, broke eye contact, and turned toward the cattle. "Dad, I don't want to talk about that kind of stuff."

"What stuff?"

"You know." Wade hemmed and hawed a moment. "Things you don't want to hear as a brother."

Or a father, Liam thought but didn't say. There was no need for his son to go any further. He knew what Wade was getting at and it didn't surprise him. Robin had been dating this boy for eight months, and he suspected things were getting serious. There was a part of him that hoped and prayed it wasn't *that* serious. With all the information he needed to get himself sufficiently worried, Liam held the ball in his grip and dug his fingers into the soft foam.

"Son, why don't you go set the table? I'll be there in a minute."

Wade turned back looking nervous. "You're not going to say anything? Because I—"

"I know." Liam threw up a palm. "Don't worry. We never had this conversation."

Wade moved to the sliding glass door and opened it. Before going inside, he turned back and mumbled a *thanks*, *Dad* before stepping inside the house.

Wade's revelation was neither that unexpected nor even that alarming in the grand scheme of life and the tragedies that come. Every father of a teenage daughter in the history of mankind had faced that awful prospect. What tortured Liam was that all options for dealing with his problems at Pantex separated him from his children's lives forever.

Someway, somehow, Liam had to deny his extortionists what they wanted without putting more lives at risk. And he had to do it all without landing himself in prison for the rest of his life. There was only one man he knew who successfully lived a life that fell somewhere between black and white and got away with it. If Ike Hodges couldn't help him then nobody could.

Chapter 9

Alibates Flint Quarries National Monument
Potter County, Texas

Garrett had called in a favor from a park ranger friend. For the conversation he was about to have with Asadi he wanted some alone time, a moment for him and his son to connect over a mutually shared passion. Since his arrival, Asadi had taken to bow hunting with as much fervor as he had for horses. The past winter had been a good season. Asadi had gotten a mule deer buck and a whitetail doe—enough meat to stock the freezer and keep them eating well through spring.

The hunting ritual was more than a form of entertainment, or even a means to put something on the dinner plate. It was an important rite of passage for boys on the road to manhood. Like Garrett, who appreciated the spiritual side of the endeavor, Asadi treated it as sacred. And there were few places more hallowed than the Alibates Quarries, which were located on the Canadian River, west of the Kohl Ranch.

At the top of the ridge, Garrett halted midstride, turned back, and surveyed the valley behind him.

The vast and unforgiving High Plains topography was nearly forty thousand square miles, a seemingly endless stretch of grassland that was as sprawling as the ocean. The emptiness of the region was as much a part of its character as the never-ceasing winds. Its most significant feature was the Caprock Escarpment, a caliche ridge running some two hundred miles across Texas from New Mexico to Oklahoma.

Garrett looked to Asadi, who was devouring the landscape with wide eyes hungry for adventure. The boy, like him, let his imagination run wild. They didn't see empty prairies. They saw a valley full of teepees, tens of thousands of bison, and maybe even a brontosaurus or two depending on how far you wanted to let your mind roam back in time.

Asadi turned back grinning ear to ear. "We almost there?"

Garrett knew Asadi was under the impression they'd be collecting arrowheads, another of their favorite pastimes. The truth was this quarry had probably been picked over a long time ago. Archaeologists believed the area had been actively mined going back around thirteen thousand years, used by mammoth hunters, and other early indigenous clans, to include the Antelope Creek people, who set up a partially agrarian civilization there in the mid-twelfth century.

"Well, we're at a decent spot for a talk." Garrett had planned to wait but he wanted to get it over with. He would not be able to enjoy the day until he got the news about Asadi's brother, Faraz, off his chest. "Why don't we take a seat here?"

Looking a little disappointed that they had to stop before reaching the top, Asadi found a wooded step jutting out of the trail, plopped down, and glanced up. "What you want talk about?"

Not nearly as agile, Garrett took a little longer to take his seat on the stoop and nestle in beside the boy. Now that he had, he wished he'd kicked the can down the road a little more. How do you broach a subject as delicate as this one?

"Well, Outlaw, what I wanted to talk about is something kind of serious."

Asadi cowed a little. "About what happen at school?"

"No. Nothing to do with that. It's just that I might need to go away again for a while." Garrett was winding up to give the reason when Asadi cut him short.

"But you promise stay."

"Yeah, I know what I promised. But something's come up and—"

Asadi seemed more panicked than angry. "You said same last time."

"Last time was different."

Asadi looked off into the distance. "It *always* different."

Garrett put his hand on Asadi's shoulder, but he yanked away. "Come on. Look at me."

The anger in the kid's eyes gave way to sadness. "You promised."

"I know I did. But there's something I haven't told you. And I really don't know how to say it, other than just to come out and tell you."

Asadi turned back. There were tears in his eyes. "Tell me what?"

"It's about your brother. It's about Faraz."

Asadi's expression went from crushed to curious. "What about him?"

"We have some information. Nothing for sure yet. But there's a chance he's still alive."

Asadi's face didn't change. "Alive?"

Garrett nodded. "We think. I mean . . . we hope."

"*Not* dead?" Asadi pressed, clearly searching for clarification.

"We think maybe he was captured when the Taliban came to your village. Might a took a few other boys, too. Some friends of yours possibly. I don't know."

The bittersweet news took a moment to soak in. But once it did, Asadi seemed to understand. "Faraz can come here? He live with us?"

"If we can find him, then yes. He'd have a home here with us on the ranch."

Asadi turned back to the valley, seemingly staring out at nothing, clearly in a daze. "The other boys? They coming, too?" He turned back smiling. "They live in Texas like me?"

"I don't know about the others, Asadi. They might have families that want them home. And quite honestly, I don't know if we can get them back, even if we wanted them."

Asadi's smile went wide, and Garrett knew exactly what he was thinking. It was written all over his face. In the boy's mind, he was already teaching his brother how to ride a horse, how to string a bow, how to let your mind run limitless in a place that wasn't that different than it had been in the Old West. Asadi was imagining a life here that included Faraz.

For Garrett, it was a beautiful thing but exceedingly dangerous. If left unbridled, hope could destroy your soul. "Now, I just want to remind you that this ain't a done deal yet. This is what we *hope* can happen."

Asadi's face screwed together. "What I need do?"

It was obvious to Garrett that Asadi was still a bit confused. If he was telling him, there was a reason. Which he might as well get to. "Well, the thing about it is, and the reason I needed to tell you all this is because I might be gone for a real long time. And like you brought up, I promised I wouldn't leave you again."

The kid was informed and bright, so the grim reality of what an American mission into Afghanistan would look like wasn't lost on him. He witnessed the razing of his village by the Taliban firsthand and knew the kind of murderous butchers Garrett would be up against.

Asadi turned a bit gloomy again. "It dangerous?"

Garrett wanted to brush it off, to act like it wasn't a big deal, but this was that *moment of truth* Butch was talking about. "Yeah, to be honest with you, it would be risky. But in my opinion, it'd be worth the risk if Faraz is still alive."

Asadi looked down at his boots. "It my choice."

"Well, it'll be *our* choice. And we'll make it as a family. But I made a promise that I wouldn't leave you again. So, if I did, I wanted you to know the reason why. And I wanted your blessing to do it." Garrett hesitated to add the next part but felt it necessary. "Just in case."

The boy needed no further explanation. Garrett

had used the words *just in case* in many conversations on emergency preparedness. In survival situations, that expression usually falls into the realm of *life and death*. It carried the gravity of the situation that Garrett had hoped.

Asadi looked back. "If I say, you no go, then you stay here. Right?"

"Like I said, we're a family. We make these decisions together. For better or worse. Through thick and thin, we're a team."

Asadi gave a solemn nod, rose to his feet, turned up the trail, and kept hiking without a word. It wasn't a yes. It wasn't a no. It was the reaction of someone who fully understands the dire consequences of a decision. It was exactly what it looks like when a boy becomes a man.

Chapter 10

As Liam walked into Crippled Crows he was struck with the godawful smell of some damn good memories. It was amazing what fun times the stench of stale beer and cigarettes could conjure up in the mind. The dive bar owner, Ike Hodges, was the big brother he'd never had, an old-world cowboy with a horseshoe mustache, and an easygoing yet stoic deportment of some bygone era gunslinger like Wild Bill Hickok or Wyatt Earp.

Growing up in Stinnett, near the barman's home around Adobe Walls, Liam had always looked up to Ike. In fact, he had been influential in directing Liam toward military service. He wanted to follow Ike's footsteps into the service as a helicopter pilot, particularly after hearing his exploits in the Army's 160th Special Operations Aviation Regiment, better known as the Night Stalkers. But Liam's eyesight had kept him out of flight school.

Given his proclivity for math and science, Ike directed him toward the Sappers, an elite cadre of combat engineers. They had their own intensive and highly difficult training course, which also served to weed out any soldiers unprepared for the rigors of operating in war zones, behind enemy lines. On top of explosives training, the course focuses on mountaineering, airborne and water operations, breaching skills, and small-unit tactics.

Liam's specialty had been demolitions, a job that had led him to combat deployments in Iraq and Afghanistan, and eventually opened him up for his current job at Pantex. All he had to do was swap out C-4 and TNT for uranium and plutonium. It was a relatively smooth transition.

Liam stood in the middle of Ike's bar and studied a pool table. The felt was so faded it had turned a sickly color of aqua. Feeling like he was trespassing, he called out, "Hey, Ike! You around?" When he got no response, he called again. "Ike! It's—"

Liam was cut off by the barkeep who sauntered out of the men's restroom, wiping his hands with some crumpled paper towels. "Can't a man sit in peace without a *damn* interruption?" He balled up what was left, tossed it into a fifty-gallon drum used as a trash can, and squinted at Liam through the neon glow. "Guess I just ought to be glad you didn't roll a stick of dynamite under the door."

Liam knew Ike could be prickly, but the joke was a good sign. "Wanted to catch you in between shifts. Figured you'd be in high spirits after hiding last night's earnings from the IRS."

The tall and lanky barman strolled up to Liam. "Oh, I pay just enough to keep the jackboots at bay." He thrust out a hand. "Come at a perfect time, my friend."

Liam took his hand and Ike pulled him into a hug. He let loose after a solid squeeze and looked around. Although no one was there, a smoky haze still floated in the air. Reflecting the pastel fluorescents, it bathed the corrugated tin and particleboard walls in various shades of pink and blue. There was a yellowing poster of the Budweiser girls that, judging by their hairstyles, had to have been hanging there since Ronald Reagan was commander in chief.

"Didn't expect it to be *totally* empty," Liam teased. "Place losing its charm?"

Ike looked around, too, and shook off the notion. "Nah, we cater to more of a church crowd. Pews will empty out in a couple of hours and this place will be hopping."

Despite the seriousness with which he said it, it couldn't have been further from the truth. Ike's *crowd* was made up of oil-field hands, cowboys, and truckers, many of whom had either never attended church, or only went for some much-needed confession. Aside from that, it was only Saturday. But in a windowless place like Crippled Crows, time had no meaning. Ike marched to the beat of his own drum, taking laws as mere *suggestions*, which probably included adhering to a standard *days of the week* calendar like the rest of the world.

Knowing better than to even ask, Liam moved on. "Well, can you take a break from your *rat killin'* and visit a minute?"

The quip struck a chord with Ike, who grinned. "Who says I can't do both?" He turned to the pool table behind him and swept a few balls out of the way that clacked together as they careened off the bumpers. "Pull up a seat."

Liam followed Ike's lead and leaned against the

rail. "Got something I wanted to talk to you about. Something I don't know how to handle and you're the only one I know that can help."

"Figured as much. That's why I suggested we get right down to it."

Liam looked at him, curious. "How did you know?"

"When people stop by off-hours there's usually a reason. And given the fact I haven't seen or heard from you in a couple of years tells me there's something you need."

Although it wasn't said with any tone of hostility, Liam received the message loud and clear. His long absence hadn't gone unnoticed. "Yeah, I'm sorry about that. It's just that after the funeral. The move. And starting over. Seems there's always something that—"

Ike raised a hand. "Forget it. You're here now. And I'm glad of it." He cocked an eyebrow. "But I've known you long enough to tell that something's wrong. When people come to me, they're either looking for some dirt on somebody or a way to dig themselves out of a mess. Guess I've grown used to being the redneck mafia don around these parts."

Liam chuckled, relieved that his friend wasn't carrying a grudge. "Well, Godfather, it's the latter. I've gotten myself into some serious trouble. And I'm not sure there's a way out."

"There's always a way out. Doesn't mean it won't hurt like hell."

"Not as worried about me as I am about my dad."

Like the two of them, Ike and his dad always had a special bond. When no one in their small community had understood a thirst for adventure beyond the borders of Hutchinson County, Reza Bayat had been a source of advice and encouragement. In fact, it had been his recommendation to join the Army and fly helicopters. It was an opportunity for a poor farm boy to get out, learn a skill set, and leverage that talent to see the world.

Ike's eyes narrowed. "Now you got me worried. What's going on?"

Liam hesitated, knowing Ike would not be happy with the answer. "A few months ago . . . Dad decided to go back to Iran."

There was a delayed response before Ike's outburst. "Has he gone *crazy* or what?"

"I begged him not to go but he wouldn't be stopped."

Ike put his fist to his forehead. "What the hell was he thinking?"

"He was thinking about a brother with Alzheimer's, for one. And he wanted to see him while he still could. He wanted to apologize when it meant something. While he understood. Do what he wanted to do for him all these years but couldn't. Dad took a gamble and lost."

Ike knew the whole story, about how Liam's father had aided the American government after religious radicals tortured and executed his fiancée. When caught, Reza Bayat had barely gotten out of the country alive, leaving everything behind, including his parents and a sibling. While his intentions had been good, they hadn't been without consequences. And abandoning his family left him riddled with a burden of enormous guilt.

"Guess I understand," Ike conceded, "but it was still a damn foolish thing to do."

"He thought that enough time had passed, and he wouldn't be on anyone's radar. Everything was fine until he tried to leave. They caught him at the border. I probably wouldn't have even known any of this, but I was approached with this information."

"*Approached?* What do you mean approached? By who?"

Liam thought a moment, wondering if there was any detail he missed. "I don't know, but he was Persian. Had no detectable accent in English. But he spoke to me in fluent Farsi once."

"What did he want?"

"At first, nothing," Liam explained. "He showed me photos of my father. He's being held in Evin Prison. Where they house political dissidents."

Ike looked genuinely pained at the report. "Yeah, I know of it. They say it makes the old Tower of London look like the Ritz-Carlton. Is he okay?"

"No. He's emaciated and pale. A shell of who he was." Liam could barely get out the words, nearly choking up as he remembered the images shown to him on the screen. "Cuts and bruises all over his face and neck. His eyes were glassy and unfocused, like he was drugged. He was barely recognizable as the man who'd left here three months ago."

"*Ah hell.* And you're sure it's him? You're absolutely positive it's your dad?"

"Wouldn't you know your own father?"

Ike nodded. "If you haven't already, you've got to tell someone who can help. I would never suggest this unless it was absolutely necessary. But you've gotta go to the feds."

"The Iranian who found me said they'd know if I told someone, and they'd torture him for it. Then he'll be hanged as a traitor for his crimes."

"They're just trying to scare you. Get their bluff in. They couldn't know what—"

"They'll know, Ike. They know everything. There's a spy. Or spies. Somewhere in our government. No one can be trusted."

Ike looked puzzled. "What makes you think that?"

"Because they showed me my father's own file from the CIA. One from years ago. They showed me other documents on other Iranian informants as well. Ones who they claimed spied for America. All executed. They have proof and they're using it against him. And me."

"What do you mean, and *you*? They want something in exchange?" Before Liam could answer, Ike pieced it together. "Pantex."

"They know everything about me. Things my father didn't know. Things I'd done in the Army. My job now. My access. Coworkers. Supervisors. Everything about my children. Where I live. When I explained I didn't work on nuclear technology, they already knew that. They said they just wanted help in hardening their infrastructure to protect their own nuclear program. They said once they had that they'd let my father return and they'd leave me alone."

Ike shook his head. "And now they're backing out on the deal?"

"They said they need more."

Ike looked at him askance. "So, your treachery goes only so far?"

Liam felt the sting of guilt and deserved it. But he always rationalized that he was putting no lives in danger. Their follow-up request could put everyone in the world at risk. He hated the idea of his father's suffering, but he had to draw the line somewhere.

"Ike, I never intended to provide anything beyond what was commercially available. I thought I could appease them with a few outdated documents stamped SECRET. I'm not saying that was right. But I couldn't deny them that. Not until my father was safe."

Ike's accusatory tone softened. "That's the oldest spy trick in the book. Been more than a few get roped in by that one."

"What are you talking about?"

"They never even wanted what they asked for the first time," Ike explained. "They just threw something easy at you. Something that wouldn't be hard to get. Once you were in, you were in. And you would be in way too much trouble to report it. They take it up a notch until you're delivering what they really wanted."

Liam's heart sank. That was *exactly* what happened. The people with whom he was dealing were morally bankrupt but that didn't mean they were stupid. He had been the one to fall for their ploy. It was too good to be true. He'd been played from the start.

"I don't know what to do. If I don't do what they want they'll kill my father. If I turn myself in the results are the same." Liam put his head in his hands. "I'll die if I have to. But I just can't risk subjecting my father to more torture. I can't be the reason for his suffering. And I can't put my children's lives in jeopardy. I won't do it. Period."

Ike stared at Liam a moment, seemingly deep in thought. "Well, I don't know how to fix this problem. But I have a friend who just might."

"Can he do this without the Iranians knowing? Quietly?"

"This guy defines the expression *under the radar*." Ike smiled. "Let me grab my phone from the back and I'll give Garrett a call."

Chapter 11

Garrett eased up beside Lacey and took in the view. Atop the Caprock Escarpment was his favorite place in the world—had been since he was a kid. He never dreamed it could get better until he stood there taking it all in with the woman he loved. If Garrett could go back and tell his teenage self he'd be planning a future with his high school crush one day, he wouldn't have believed it. But here they were lockstep in life, just looking for the right spot to build a home.

Of course, it was all hypothetical at this point. Lacey would never get too serious about discussing next steps until he officially popped the big question, which he respected and understood. But he'd not wanted to take their relationship any further until his obligation to the CIA was behind him. While most of that was settled, the question of what to do about Asadi's brother still remained. He had no idea what he was going to do about that one.

Since bringing up the situation during their morning hike out at the Alibates Quarries, Asadi had not said a word about it. Garrett figured the boy would need a little time to process the information.

That was to be expected. But Asadi seemed largely unfazed by the news, leading Garrett to wonder if he fully understood, given the language barrier.

Deep in thought and distracted, Garrett repeated the question back to Lacey to buy some time. "Above or below?"

"Yeah, I mean you've probably thought about this a million times before. Right?" Lacey was still staring out over the ranch, her eyes taking in the green expanse of prairie that extended to the far horizon. "I think I'm leaning toward a view."

"Oh, yeah, well it certainly has its advantages."

Garrett couldn't believe how far the ranch had come since the wildfire. Of course, he, Asadi, and Butch had worked like hell to get it there. They'd cleared a lot of dead brush and hauled off tons of charred debris. But the truth was that the remarkable transformation was by God's healing touch. Abundant moisture from snow and rain had made the place flourish. At the moment, they had more grass than their cattle could handle.

"What about below?" Lacey turned to him. "That's how you grew up. Guessing you loved waking up every morning and seeing the Caprock off your back porch."

Garrett thought it silly, but the view of the ranch had less to do with his preference and more to do with the fact that they'd be looking over his dad's old farmhouse. Butch was getting on in years and his age was starting to show. The only way the fiercely independent old man would allow himself to be looked after is if Garrett did it on the sly.

"That was nice, too," Garrett agreed. "Not being

belted by a cold north wind when I was working in the barn at five A.M. before school was probably the biggest advantage."

"Good point. Now that Asadi has taken on that job, I'm sure he'd appreciate that." Lacey turned to Garrett. "How did your talk go today? He feeling okay after the fight?"

Garrett had only been partially honest with Lacey. He had wanted to check in on the bully incident, but the Faraz situation was the thrust of the *big talk*. He dreaded telling her about it even worse than Asadi. But it was time to rip off the Band-Aid.

"So . . . there was something else we discussed. Something I didn't tell you about."

Lacey paused and turned, looking mortified. "Nothing to do with him and Savanah, I hope. About you know . . . something . . . physical."

It took Garrett a second to realize what she was talking about. "No way! Asadi's just a kid. How could you even think that?"

"He's in middle school, Garrett. And kids are growing up faster than we did. You know, they have all these weird chemicals in plastics now. Chicken hormones. Times are different and so are our children. Trust me, I don't like the idea any more than you do. But I'm getting questions from my own about all sorts of things. Some of it I even had to google."

"Well, not Asadi. He's different than other kids. Innocent."

Lacey chuckled. "Every parent says that about their own. Until—"

"Until what?" Garrett shook off the suggestion.

"No. It's not that. Trust me. He's barely beyond the puppy love stage. If even that."

"Then what is it?"

Garrett stared out over the horizon. For news this bad he couldn't look her in the eye. "It's something that involves me."

"Please don't tell me you're leaving." Any semblance of amusement Lacey had gained from Garrett's discomfort over discussing the kids was lost in an instant. "You promised."

"Well, something's come up."

"Something *always* comes up."

"This is different," Garrett countered.

"It's *always* different."

The exchange was uncannily similar to his conversations with Butch and Asadi. Garrett figured he better just get it on the table, lest he relive them. "Faraz is still alive."

"*What?*" The news stopped Lacey in her tracks. "Asadi's brother? I thought you saw him murdered right in front of you."

"I saw a lot of people murdered that day. Men, women, and children. But I can't say specifically who they were or if someone got away."

"How are you just hearing about this now?" Before he could answer, she filled in her answer. "No, wait. Let me guess. *Her?*"

There had always been a little jealousy and Garrett understood why. It wasn't just that Kim was beautiful, educated, and worldly. It was that she always seemed to win him over, to commandeer his time and attention. If Butch had noticed this, then certainly Lacey had, too. Even his old Texas Ranger buddy Trip Davis had suggested Kim might've had a *thing* for him. But none of that had anything to do with this. Why couldn't anyone understand that?

"It was Kim who found out," Garrett admitted. "And she'd be the one leading the mission to get Faraz back."

"*Mission?*"

Oops. Wishing he had phrased it more casually, Garrett tried to put it in less alarming terms. "The *effort*, I should've said. She's the one with the contacts over there."

"Over where?"

Garrett hesitated, already anticipating her response. "Afghanistan."

Another wrong answer and Lacey's face showed it. "You mean the place run by the Taliban? The place where Americans are strictly forbidden? The place where they would lop off your head for even stepping foot inside?"

Garrett threw up his hands, palms out, to stop the rapid-fire assault. "Nothing's decided yet. It's just out there and it had to be discussed."

Lacey looked dumfounded. "With Asadi?"

"Well, of course, it's his brother. Had to let him know. Give him a choice."

Lacey crossed her arms. "He's way too young to face that much responsibility. That's not right to put a burden like that on a young boy. To have to choose between his brother and you."

"But Daddy said that this was just one of a million tough decisions he'd have to make in life, and he deserves to have a say in it."

As soon as the words came out of his mouth,

Garrett already knew Lacey's response. And she would be a hundred percent right. Taking parenting advice from Butch was like having the Zodiac Killer as your spirit guide. And it was one of the many reasons Garrett needed Lacey. She was a maternal voice of reason, countering his dad's *feelings are for sissies* philosophy.

"Garrett, didn't you once tell me that Butch had you operating a backhoe at the age of seven?" Lacey's face softened a little. "Your father is a good and wise man but he's still a frontier cowboy. And he thinks like one. It's just who he is, and I love him for it. But *you* are Asadi's dad now. As difficult as they may be, you have to make these decisions on your own."

Garrett was kicking himself for listening to Butch. The old cob had lived his life from one hardship to the next. Just because the previous Kohls bypassed childhood didn't mean Asadi had to do it as well. This was too much to handle.

Suddenly, Garrett didn't feel worthy to be the kid's father. His first big test had come, and he'd failed. "What do I do now, Lace? Asadi already knows."

"What did he say?"

Garrett shrugged. "Didn't really say anything."

She didn't seem surprised. "Give him some time then. Let him process the news. But don't wait too long. Talk to him tonight, maybe. Eventually, you might have to give him an out."

"An out? What do you mean?"

Lacey looked a little sheepish. "You might have to lie to him." Before Garrett could argue, she continued: "If you can see this is killing him, then you have to take away that burden. Tell him you were wrong, maybe. That they thought it was his brother, but it was someone else."

"That would kill him, too," Garrett argued.

"Would it be worse than being the reason for your death?"

The answer was a resounding *no*. It wouldn't. Him being wrong about Faraz would be heart-wrenching but it in no way compared to Asadi thinking he was responsible for that. Garrett had lived with the crippling guilt of thinking he had been a contributing factor to his mother's car accident when he was about the boy's age. Nothing was worse than that torment.

Garrett smiled. "Why do I ever do anything without consulting you in the first place?"

Lacey returned the gesture. "You know, I ask myself that question all the time."

Garrett was leaning in for a kiss as the cell phone buzzed in his pocket. He would've ignored it but with everything going on with the Faraz situation, his instinct was to be on the safe side. Thanking his lucky stars it wasn't Kim, Garrett showed Lacey the screen so she could see it was their mutual friend Ike, possibly wondering why the bottle of 13 Arrows bourbon he kept hidden behind the bar just for him was starting to collect dust. But truth be told, Ike wasn't a casual-call kind of guy. If he was reaching out, it was probably important.

When Ike led off with *we've got a big problem*, Garrett's face must have shown his dread. The barman wasn't unnerved easily, if ever at all. Given the fact he skipped past the usual ball-breaking and launched straight in set Garrett on edge. With everything on his plate, he would've put it off if humanly possible. But while his obligation to Kim and the CIA was paid back, Garrett's debt to Ike for rescuing both Butch and Asadi had yet to be touched.

Hearing the news, Lacey was clearly annoyed. Their leisurely afternoon of strolling atop the Caprock, sipping on a bottle of Sauvignon John, would have to wait. Even more importantly, their planning for their future would once again be put on the back burner. But Garrett had made a promise, months back, that he would not shut her out of *his world*. For their relationship to work, she needed to be a part of it.

That meant that if Ike had a problem, Lacey would be part of the solution. A partner for life, she reminded him, meant *for better, for worse*. Garrett just hoped the words *till death do us part* were a promise for way on down the line.

PART TWO

. . . the wicked shall be cut off from the land. And the treacherous uprooted . . .

—Proverbs 2:22

Chapter 12

As Liam made his way down the county road to the ranch, he noticed that he was being followed. Or at least *suspected* that he was being followed. Since taking on the role of reluctant spy, he lived his life in the rearview mirror—both literally and figuratively. Of course, a treachery-induced guilty conscience had sent his imagination into overdrive. Now every conversation at Pantex was scrutinized, and every coworker a potential threat.

Were they reporting to the FBI? Or worse yet, *Were they spying for Iran?* He couldn't help but wonder who else was on the take. After all, if they got to him, then they could get to anyone. And when it was all said and done, government employees, with the world-ending knowledge in their brains, were essentially on the honor system.

As Liam made the final curve to the entrance of the ranch, whoever he had suspected was trailing him at some point had disappeared. They'd either pulled off the road or turned around and gone the opposite way. It was certainly strange, but still didn't prove anything. There was no law against taking a leisurely country drive, going only so far, and then deciding to turn back.

It wasn't until he saw the silver Chevy Trailblazer, parked out front of the entrance to his ranch, that his worry really kicked in. Three vehicles on the same deserted country road, at any one time, qualified as an anomaly in his book. If he was suspicious before, then seeing his son, Wade, standing out next to the passenger side of the vehicle sent a chill down his spine.

Liam jammed the accelerator of his black Toyota Sequoia and pulled up by the Chevy in a screeching halt. He rolled down the window and called out to his son. "Everything okay?"

Wade was in his running shorts and tank top, clearly out on a jog. It was a daily routine. Anyone who'd been watching the place would know when and where to find him.

"Yeah, Dad. These guys are just lost. Helping them find their way back to I-40."

Complete garbage. They were thirty miles north of the interstate. There were two middle-aged men, both of whom were dark-haired and olive-skinned. Just like him. It didn't necessarily mean they were Persians. But it didn't mean they weren't. Could just as easily be federal agents, trying to get information from Wade that they could use against him.

Liam craned his neck out the window for a better look. "Can I help you gentlemen?"

The passenger tilted his head at Wade. "Like your boy said, just a bit lost. Much gratitude to your kid here getting us back on the right track."

There was no accent, at least as far as Liam could tell. "Where you headed?"

The driver spoke up. "Looking for a historical marker. World War Two POW camp."

There were numerous Texas historical markers in the area, one of which designated the location of a German internment facility for Rommel's Africa Korps. It was a plausible excuse for driving around out there. And again, no crime. But talking to his teenage son, no matter who they were, was crossing the line in a major way. Time for them to move on.

"Not even close." Liam thumbed back in the opposite direction. "Turn around here and go back to the highway. Go right on your first paved road and head south until the interstate. Once you're there, get on it." He wanted to make sure they got the point. "And don't come back."

A look of anger flashed in the passenger's eyes, but he didn't address the comment. He just repeated Liam's instructions, and then added with a hint of sarcasm, "*Grateful* for the help."

Notwithstanding the mocking tone, it was said with a level of professionalism. Any real tourists would've been pissed. Whether these guys were FBI agents or Iranian operatives Liam didn't know, but he was certain that this was by no means a friendly visit.

As the silver Chevy executed a three-point turn in the middle of the gravel road, Liam waved his son over. "Jump on in, kiddo."

There was that look of teenage disgust again. Partially due to *kiddo* and partially because of the interruption. Grumbling to himself, Wade made his way around the hood and popped into the passenger side. He slammed the door shut and sat in a huff. Liam checked the rearview and watched as the Chevy pulled away. He knew it was foolish but made the snap decision to pursue.

Wade, not knowing what was going on, had his objections. "Why were you so rude, Dad?" He glanced around in confusion. "And why are you following them?"

"Just making sure they get to the highway all right."

Wade was clearly weirded out. "But they're going to think you're some hillbilly psycho."

Good. Let them think that. Liam was about to add more nonsensical reassurance for his son's benefit when the Chevy's red taillights flashed and they stopped in the middle of the road.

"Get down, son. Head below the console."

"*Why?*"

"Just do it," Liam commanded. "Right now."

Despite clear reservations, Wade partially obliged. He scrunched low in his seat but kept high enough where he could still see over the dash. "What's going on?"

"Haven't you been hearing the stories? Watching the local news?"

"*Stories?*" Wade looked skeptical. "What news? What are you talking about?"

"Meth cookers. Looking for a place to hide. They're cracking down in Donley County. Maybe they're moving over here?"

"Are you kidding me?" Wade rolled his eyes.

"That wasn't Walter White and Jesse Pinkman. Just some lost business dudes, looking for a Civil War sign or something."

Liam was too focused on the Chevy to worry about his son's terrible grasp of basic American history. But they'd definitely come back to that one later. He reached beneath the driver's seat and pulled up the Beretta pistol he kept stashed there since he was first approached. He placed it on the console and put his hand back on the steering wheel.

Wade's eyes went wide. "Whoa. Why do you have your gun in here?"

"Like I said, I saw on the news that there's an increase in drug trafficking in rural areas. Just wanted to be prepared."

"But *here*?" Wade eased up a little and stared at the Chevy, which was still going, albeit very slow. *Oddly* slow. "Nothing interesting ever happens out in these boonies."

"Better safe than sorry."

"Wait a minute." Wade turned and eyed Liam skeptically. "This have something to do with your work? With the nukes?"

"No." Liam gave a playful wink. Maybe he had underestimated his son. His knowledge of historical events might be off, but his instincts were dead-on. "It's probably nothing."

"But what if they—"

"They won't. You were right the first time. Probably just some lost tourists." Liam grabbed the pistol from the console and brought it over the steering wheel. He wanted them to see it—to really get the message. "They'll move on. Don't worry."

No sooner had Liam given this reassurance to his son than the Chevy's left door flew open. The left leg of the driver extended out onto the gravel road. It sat there for only a few seconds, then it eased back in. The door shut, the brake lights came on, and they pulled away.

Liam's confidence suddenly dissipated, as the fact that he and his son could've been gunned down became all too real. Whoever was after him posed a real threat, and the sooner it was dealt with the better. Liam couldn't believe that it had come to this. His fate now rested in the hands of a derelict barman like Ike, and some mysterious cowboy named Garrett Kohl.

Chapter 13

Asadi looked across the Canadian Rodeo Arena and saw Savanah riding toward him on a bay Quarter Horse named Eazy Day, which had morphed into Eazy for short. The laid-back gelding was an early birthday gift from Butch. Asadi pretended not to notice her, keeping rigid in the saddle atop Sioux and maintaining a steady eye on the others on the roping team.

Asadi hadn't responded to any of Savanah's phone calls since the beatdown in the cafeteria. The whole ordeal wasn't her fault, of course. Sam Clevenger had deserved that cake in the face and a whole lot worse. She stood up for herself and Asadi didn't blame her. But somehow, it'd been him who was punished. He wasn't mad. Just embarrassed. How do you get your butt kicked in front of your girlfriend and not act like something was wrong?

Savanah eased up and looked out at the arena as she spoke. "Glad you showed. Didn't know if you still wanted to be my header since you never returned any of my *five* phone calls."

Asadi wanted to respond with something cool,

something tough, but all he could muster was something dumb. "Been busy. Too much work in barn."

"Too much work, huh?" She rolled her eyes. "That never stopped you before."

Asadi kept his gaze on the duo of twin brothers out in the arena. "Sorry. I forget."

That *really* set her off. "So, you were busy, or you forgot? Which was it?"

Savanah had been nothing but kind to him since the day they'd met. She'd taken him under her wing at school, been his English tutor, his roping partner, and now his girlfriend. She had done nothing but help him make the transition from new kid to local and he was repaying that debt by acting like a jerk. For the life of him though, he couldn't get his emotions under control.

Savanah gave Eazy a little kick and positioned her horse in front of Sioux, blocking Asadi's view of the roping duo out in front of him. "You gonna ignore me or what?"

Asadi leaned to the left and looked beyond her. "I just watching."

Asadi wanted to spill his heart to her, to relay his fears that she would forget all about him and move on. He wanted to address his humiliation over his tears in the cafeteria. And most importantly, he wanted to tell her about Faraz, and the awful choice he had to make about giving Garrett the go-ahead for a mission to Afghanistan.

Savanah circled around and pulled up parallel, saddle to saddle, and her voice softened. "Talk to me. What's going on?" A gentle smile crept onto her face. "You know I'm not going to leave you alone until you tell me what's up."

Asadi turned and locked eyes. Her face was as welcoming as it always was when he confided his most precious and hidden thoughts. It surprised even him when the first thing he blurted out was, "Faraz still alive."

Savanah was stunned. "*Faraz?* Like your *brother* Faraz?"

Asadi could feel all sorts of emotions welling up inside, emotions he didn't even know he had. Excitement of the possibility he could be reunited with Faraz battled the fear over what could happen to Garrett. All he could do was nod, lest he burst into tears. Again.

Savanah looked around to see if anyone was in earshot. She didn't know everything but knew enough to know that what he was telling her was privileged information. Lowering her voice, she asked, "How do you know?"

"Garrett tell me today."

Savanah's face brightened. "That's great news, right? If he's still alive you can finally be brothers again."

"That the problem. Garrett would have to go get him. Back home. In Afghanistan."

It was clear from Savanah's grim expression that he didn't have to explain. She knew how dangerous it would be for an American over there. "Is he gonna do it?"

"If I say yes, then he go. If not—" Asadi shook his head.

"Oh. Now I get it. It's all on you."

"I have to pick Garrett or Faraz. Feel guilty no matter what."

Savanah looked sympathetic. "What's your gut telling you to do?"

"I don't know. I not want mess anything up. My life here good." He rubbed the side of his face where it was still a little bruised and chuckled. "Well. Pretty good."

"It *is* good." Savanah giggled and reached out to him. "First of all, you got me as a girlfriend. And you know what else?"

Asadi took her hand into his. "What?"

"You're my hero."

Feeling like a lot of things, but certainly not a hero, Asadi's cheeks burned with embarrassment. He was about to argue until Savanah followed up with an explanation.

"When everyone else just sat around doing nothing, you were the only one who came to help. Nobody stands up to Sam because they're terrified of him. But you weren't. He might've gotten the best of you but at least you tried. Better than any of them other boys who didn't do a gosh-darn thing but sit there and pray that he didn't come after them next."

It *was* true. Everyone was scared to death of Sam. Of course, getting humiliated again had no appeal. What Savanah didn't know was that he was learning to fight. In fact, he punched that old Everlast bag so hard and so long that his knuckles bled. And with Savanah's vote of confidence Asadi's whole attitude changed. Somewhere in this understanding, he made the decision about his brother. Once he was ready, he would go after Faraz himself.

At that very moment, Sam heaved his hulking body to the top rail of the fence, directly across the arena. The move was no accident. He did it for intimidation, blaming them both for getting in trouble at school. The bully scowled, and Asadi glared right back. He had fled when the marauders came to his village, and he had fled in the cafeteria. But those days were over. From this day forward, he would never run away again.

Chapter 14

Ray Smitty sat at a table at the Crossroads Market, wondering where the waitress, who was supposed to fetch his mint chocolate chip double scoop, had run off to again. After a thorough search of the little grocery store that tripled as a deli, burger joint, and ice-cream parlor, he turned to his wife, Crystal, who didn't seem to be as annoyed.

The weekend was his only time off from the Mescalero Ranch, and Smitty suspected that with a promotion to foreman his free time would whittle down even more. He kept that news hidden from Crystal, who was highly skeptical of the affluent new owner. Vicky Kaiser had returned to run the family business after her murdering, kidnapping, friend-of-a-drug-cartel brother Preston met his end at the hands of Garrett and his High Plains version of *The Wild Bunch*.

Smitty did battle with the negatives and focused on the positives. He couldn't look too far in the future, and he couldn't dwell on thoughts from the past. His drug-running days with Vicky's brother had nearly cost him everything, which included his wife, daughter, and damn near his life. Had it not been for Garrett, he'd either be back in prison or dead.

His existence had been in a constant state of flux since childhood, group home to group home, foster family to foster family, and because of this he was never settled. Here today, gone tomorrow had been his life for so long that everything seemed destined to collapse. If things ever got too good, too secure, you could bet your ass the world was about to fall apart.

It was why Smitty felt an odd satisfaction when even their basic needs were met. It was a game he played in his head since he was a kid. If the world went to pot, right then and there, would he be fine? Smitty looked around the empty store and turned back to Crystal. "Reckon we could make a go of it if things turned *Walking Dead* on us all of a sudden?"

"*Walking Dead*?" Crystal glanced over her shoulder confused. "Talking about zombies?"

"Well, symbolic ones, anyhow. If something cataclysmic happened, could we survive?"

Crystal scrunched her nose. "What about Savanah? We would want her with us, too."

"*Yes*. Of course, we'd have our *darlin' girl*. I'm just saying *hypothetically*. Could we fend off the bad guys? Live off the land? Not starve to death and all that?"

"Nope." Crystal shook her head. "I don't think so."

Smitty's aggravation grew with every second that passed, and his ice-cream cone didn't arrive. "I got skills. Why the hell not?"

"Ain't no beer in this town." She shot him a playful smile. "You wouldn't last a week."

It was true, he did like his Pearl. And falling victim to Armageddon in Miami, Texas, would add a heap of calamity on top of the brain-starved zombies. Roberts County was one of only a few in the state that was still dry. With less than eight hundred people there to begin with, it was likely beer supplies would run out pretty damn fast.

Smitty conceded with a solemn nod. "This place is less hospitable than most, I suppose. But assuming we already had a solid stash set aside for emergencies—what about then?"

"Why are you asking me all this?" Crystal's face fell in clear disappointment. "You didn't lose your job, did you?"

She knew him too well. It was obvious he was trying to distract himself from the news he'd eventually have to divulge. "No, the opposite."

"The opposite would be you got another job. And you already have one. That mean you're leaving the job you got?"

Dammit! The guessing games put him on edge. "It means I'm up for a promotion. Ranch foreman at the Mescalero."

Crystal looked at him blankly. "Congratulations, I guess."

"You could be a little happier for me. It's a big deal."

"Big deal as in . . . ?"

"More responsibility." Smitty let out a huff. "And a nice little pay raise. Does that help?"

"*What* responsibilities?"

Crystal had breezed past the good part, as usual. She still didn't trust the Kaisers and was right not to.

Since returning to Texas, Vicky had assembled her brother's old henchmen for reasons uncertain—a gang of worker bees that included rodeo cowboys and oilfield hands on the wrong side of the law. Riding herd over them was the Hemphill County sheriff, Ted Crowley, who was more crooked than all of them put together. He just never got caught.

Smitty was fairly certain he was being groomed for something. That was for sure. But he couldn't let Crystal know that until he was certain. Last thing he wanted to do was blow an opportunity. That had always been his MO and he aimed to break his failure streak.

"All this means is a few more responsibilities around the ranch. Making decisions about the cattle and horses. Hiring and firing. Keeping up with the budget. That sort of thing."

Crystal looked kind of impressed, which was rare. "Sounds like good news then."

"It *is* good news, but there's a small downside, I suppose."

"Of course there is." An exhale from Crystal. "What now?"

"If I'm running the place, Vicky would want us out there to keep an eye on things."

Crystal crossed her arms. "You mean we'd have to move?"

"It's a great house. Twice as big as what we got now. And there'd be horses to ride. Hunting. Fishing. You name it. They got it."

Smitty knew she'd never been happier than out on Garrett Kohl's property, but what he was talking about was career progression. On top of that, it would be a helluva nice place to live. The Mescalero was just shy of seventy thousand acres, roughly a hundred square miles. There was even a runway out there capable of landing a 727. It wasn't just a ranch. It was a dream resort.

Crystal pursed her lips, wheels in her head turning. "What about Savanah?"

Smitty knew this was coming. "We'd be in Gray County, which means she'd move here to Miami for middle school."

A Canadian High School alum, and a die-hard Wildcat to the bone, Crystal's face registered her disappointment. "A *Warrior*?" She shook her head. "No way."

Smitty might as well have suggested their daughter drop out of the sixth grade and become a stripper. His plan was flying off the rails and he needed to get it under control fast.

"Hold on now." Smitty held up his hands and pushed the air. "I've done some investigating. And Miami ISD has a wonderful reputation. They've got—"

"They don't even have real football, Ray. It's just six-man. I want to follow a *real team* with a shot at the state championships. Is that too much to ask?"

Before he could recount any tidbits gleaned from the school's home page, Crystal had already moved on. "And what about my job at Henry's? You know Lacey's mom isn't doing well. We'd be all the way out at the Mescalero. What if she needs me to open up the café early? Like last week. Remember she—"

"I hear what you're saying. But none of that would change. Just some earlier mornings, and a few more miles on the road. Savanah could help you get the kitchen going before school."

Crystal seemed to calm a little. "Everything's perfect. Savanah and Asadi are such close friends. She's got a part-time job helping the Kohls train horses. She's even on the rodeo team. Just don't see why we'd want to mess it up. We got it good."

"What do we really got, though, Crystal? A favor, that's all. Garrett is nice enough to let us stay on the ranch, but he doesn't need me. With his place burnt up from the wildfire, it's going to take another year or two to get the stocker cattle and hay operation back in full swing. And I've got an opportunity *now* at the Mescalero."

"But you're not a cowboy, Ray. Not a real one anyhow."

"I'll *try* not to be offended."

Crystal chuckled. "You know what I mean. Oil and gas have been your life as long as I've known you." Her expression soured. "That and *other* things."

"Vicky sees potential in me."

Crystal didn't hesitate in her response. "That's exactly what I'm afraid of."

A couple of times Crystal had made accusations that Vicky was being a bit flirtatious, charges Smitty found absurd. His boss was a beautiful blond socialite, not the type to lower herself to the likes of someone like him. That said, she wouldn't be the first among the upper crust to forsake those stuffy sycophants and social climbers to go after *the help*.

As a rough-and-tumble oil-field hand, former

drug smuggler, and ex-con, Smitty brought an element of danger to the table. He'd never had what might be described as traditional good looks, but he did have a certain redneck charm. Crystal had said his looks and personality fell somewhere between a rail-thin version of Jethro Bodine on *Beverly Hillbillies* and George Clooney's character in *O Brother, Where Art Thou?* But he hated to think that Vicky's interest in him had nothing to do with his work ethic and job performance on the ranch.

Smitty had worked hard to dig himself out of a whole lot of trouble and the Kaiser family had a way of stirring up more of it than most law-abiding folks could handle. He knew it was a risk. But it seemed like a risk worth taking. Guys like him didn't get many chances.

"Well, just think about it, Crystal. Keep an open mind. What Vicky is offering here is an opportunity. I wouldn't just be a hired hand anymore. I'd be *management*."

For people like them, a lifetime of taking orders from someone else was as natural as walking, talking, and breathing in air. The idea that someone in their social standing could be in charge of anything was tantamount to a miracle. Had he told her he was accepted into Harvard Law School, his wife couldn't have been more impressed.

It looked as though she was trying to wrestle back how proud she was of him, but it ultimately busted through. "Ray, I want the best for our family. And you've come a long way. Worked real hard. You deserve this promotion." A smidgen of doubt on her face preceded her words of warning. "Just be sure of what you're getting into. We can't take another disaster."

Remembering back to the wildfire that savaged the Kohl Ranch and nearly killed him and Savanah, Smitty couldn't agree more. But it wasn't an act of God that had him worried. It was what he saw at the Mescalero. The zombies weren't banging on his door just yet, but with Garrett's report of a freshly paroled Bo Clevenger skulking around town, he wondered if this was a *too good to be true* opportunity and a recipe for a *Walking Dead*–style cataclysmic end.

Chapter 15

Lacey Capshaw had cleared what she hoped was the last of the tables for the evening. It'd been a bit slow for a Saturday night. But slow wasn't always a bad thing, especially when she was eager to close up the café and meet Garrett for a beer up at the Stumblin' Goat before he went back to the ranch. Given their earlier conversation on the Caprock, there was an irresistible urge to talk more about their future. Of course, talking to a man about that was like stalking wild game. Any movements too sudden or aggressive could send them darting into the brush.

There was a part of Lacey that wished she'd kept Crystal around to help clean up, but it seemed that she and Ray were seeing less and less of each other lately given the piling workload at the Mescalero. But in an isolated place like the Texas Panhandle, you took gainful employment where you could and you didn't look back.

Lacey had just gathered the last of the dirty dishes and placed them in the sink when the bells jangled on the front door. *Damn. Should've locked up when there was a chance.* With a swipe of her hair back behind the ear, she tried to mask her regret. The chance to leave was gone.

As Lacey moved back into the dining area, she stopped dead in her tracks at the sight of her old best friend from high school. Vicky Kaiser was waiting patiently in front of the PLEASE SEAT YOURSELF sign by the front booth.

"Well, hey there, Vick! Long time no see." Lacey immediately wished she'd come up with something better. Her *salutation* sounded more like an *accusation*. And she didn't want it to seem like she was waiting around for Vicky to rekindle the friendship.

"Hi, girl!" Vicky was all smiles. "Sorry to show up so late."

"No, you're fine. Let me grab a menu."

"Not staying for dinner, Lace. Just wanted to see if you could chat a sec."

"Sure, have a seat." Despite the fact that she was missing an opportunity to see Garrett, Lacey was dying to know what Vicky could want, having finally stopped by after being back in town for several months. She gestured at the booth. "Want a Coke or something?"

Vicky took a look at the table then back to Lacey and shook her head. It looked as though she had considered it for a millisecond, then changed her mind. "No, I can't stay long." She batted off the offer with a wave of the hand. "Need to get out to the ranch. Just saw the light on and thought I'd stop by."

Apparently, sitting at a greasy spoon diner like Henry's was beneath a Kaiser. Lacey was tempted to levy the accusation but quickly recognized the large chip on her own shoulder and reminded herself that she had no idea what Vicky was thinking. It just seemed that her old cheerleading pal always caught her at her worst.

Lacey was sporting blue jeans and a food-splattered pink and white gingham apron while her friend was decked out in Chanel, carrying the most beautiful Hermès Birkin handbag that Lacey had ever seen. As usual, she was straight off the fashion pages of *Vogue*.

Lacey forced herself not to look disappointed. "Glad for the visit. Even a short one."

Vicky looked a little sheepish. "Look, I know when I came back I said we'd get together. And I really meant that. You've always been a real friend. Even when I didn't deserve one. But I've just been busy, you know. Trying to get the business back together. And quite honestly, it's been a bit of a disaster."

"I totally get it, Vick. I've had to rebuild my life several times. Kind of still doing it."

"Then you understand?"

"I do," Lacey admitted. "But I also know that it's a lot better if you don't have to do it alone. When you're ripped down to the studs you need people who care about you the most. Happy to be a shoulder to lean on. *If* you want one?"

"Depending on others for support isn't exactly in the Kaiser DNA."

"Oh, I know that." Lacey chuckled. "All too well. The Capshaws aren't that different than the Kaisers. Fiercely independent. But it's what ultimately led my dad to take his own life. Trust me, it's a lonely road. And it's worse on the ones you leave behind."

Vicky winced. "I didn't mean to bring up any bad memories."

"Anything that close to your heart isn't ever a memory. When you lose someone special in such a senseless way, you'll relive it every damn day for the rest of your life."

"I understand." Vicky gave a nod. "Feel like if I was here for Preston, maybe I could've kept him out of trouble. Things wouldn't have ended the way they did."

Any outcome for her brother would've been better. But he was bad news. Even for a Kaiser. Lacey doubted that anyone but Jesus on steroids could've saved Preston's dark criminal soul. But rather than dredge all that up, she moved on to what she could do something about.

"What's done is done. And there's no going back. I think what you're doing is fantastic. Trying to build back the business is good for the community." Lacey held her hands out and made an exaggerated show of looking around the empty restaurant. "Trust me when I say, we all want to see Mescalero Exploration succeed. I'm not the only business around that could use a shot in the arm by another oil boom."

Vicky narrowed her gaze. "Well, that's what I wanted to talk to you about."

Oh boy. Lacey knew this couldn't have just been a social call. Her knee-jerk reaction was to shut Vicky down before she even started, but her interest was piqued. It hadn't been that long ago when she mentioned some big plan involving the Capshaws and the Kohls. *Was this it?*

"Okay, what's on your mind?"

"Expansion." Vicky's demeanor changed from casual to career driven. "I don't just want to pick up where Preston left off. I want to grow Mescalero into something bigger. Not just a company. An empire."

"Well, you're straightforward. I'll give you that."

"Why wouldn't I be?" Vicky didn't wait for an answer. "I have every opportunity to create something lasting here. To continue what my great-grandfather started."

"Some might be content with a successful company. Which you have. I for one, just want enough customers so that Mom can work a few less hours and not have to worry about what we owe the bank."

"That's exactly why I'm here."

It was clear by the fire in Vicky's eyes that Lacey had struck a chord. "About our loans?"

"Not just yours. The whole community. And more specifically, Garrett's. I mean, it's no secret that he's in financial trouble. Insurance covered most of the damage done to his irrigation and hay equipment but he's no better off than before he bought Kate Shanessy's land. And the fact that he's missed an alfalfa crop already puts him further in the hole. Without that center-pivot watering system, he's just another poor dirt farmer trying to squeak by."

Lacey did her best to hide her emotions, but she

could already feel her face turning flush. "Sounds like you spot an opportunity in his hardship."

"As a matter of fact, I do," Vicky admitted unapologetically. "An opportunity to help."

"Oh really? I also remember the Kaiser DNA was never too keen to *help* unless there was something to be gained by it."

"And there is."

"Then get to it, Vicky. What does all this have to do with me and Garrett?"

"I'd be willing to pay off his land notes."

"Why would you do this?"

"Just as I said. To help."

Lacey followed her incredulous glare with the same question. "*Why?*"

"I want unfettered access to drill across the Kohl place."

"Mescalero already has that right with your mineral lease." Before Vicky could come up with a lie, Lacey decided to give her old friend a little friendly reminder. "You might remember, I grew up in the oil business. My dad made a career doing exactly what you're talking about now. And I was by his side for a lot of it. If you want my help, then be straight with me."

A short pause from Vicky as it was clear she was contemplating her options. "Okay, I want access to Garrett's water for fracking."

"You already have access to underground water through your surface lease with the Kohls. Try again. This time with the truth."

Vicky smiled, seemingly to enjoy the spirited

exchange. "Okay, I want *all* their water and I want it for free. The existing contract limits the use to their property. I want it for every oil well Mescalero drills in the area."

Lacey shook her head. "You want to take advantage of Garrett while he's down?"

"Lacey, the best water source within thirty miles is on the Kohl Ranch. And now that Garrett has new deeper wells dug for his hayfields, it can supply almost everything I need."

Lacey had her beat. "And paying for that water would cost you a fortune."

"I don't just want the water. I want caliche, gravel, and sand. Everything Mescalero requires for drilling operations and to complete our wells. Garrett's ranch has it all in spades. We get a carte blanche surface lease on the property, and we wouldn't have to buy anything. Paying off his land note would cost me pennies on the dollar in comparison to what I'd gain in resources. And it would give us a leg up on my biggest competitors. They wouldn't stand a chance."

"Your plan is to exploit Garrett's ranch? You know I'm going to let him know the second I get the chance. Why are you telling me this?"

"Because I'm *trying* to be honest about it. To be up front so there's no confusion."

"But you're not being up front, Vicky. If you just pay for all those things you mentioned, then Garrett could take care of the loans. He wouldn't need this horrible deal."

"Doesn't work like that. Garrett needs the money right now. Not over the course of years. I write him a check now and he can pay off all debts. Gets the creditors off his ass immediately."

"And you get a sizable addition to the Mescalero Ranch?"

"It would be a purchase of resources only. Garrett can keep running his cattle and training horses on the land. None of that would change. All I want is what I need for oil and gas production. He gets what he wants, and I get what I want. Win-win."

It didn't sound win-win to Lacey. It sounded shady as hell. "What's my role in all this?"

"I want *you* to convince Garrett to do it."

The laugh came out before Lacey could stop it. "You have to be kidding me."

"I never joke about business."

"And I'd do this because . . . ?"

"Because you're reasonable, Lacey. You love him. And you know what's best for him."

"And *you know* he hates your family. He'd never consider this otherwise."

"He's going to lose everything. And I'm the only one offering a lifeline."

Lacey shook her head. "There's *always* another way."

"It doesn't take a genius to figure out that you guys are getting serious. And I expect a marriage proposal is in the works. My guess is that you already have a nice little spot picked out on the ranch to settle down."

Lacey had to wonder if Vicky had been spying on them earlier. "What if we do?"

"Then that's great. Nothing has to change. We do our thing. And you do yours." Vicky took on a rare look of genuine gladness. "Whether you believe this or not, I'd be ecstatic for you to find love and contentment. Hell, I want that for myself. But I'm not a dreamer. I'm a realist. And I'm here to preach some damn hard reality. Without me, Kohl Ranch is gone forever."

It wasn't easy for Lacey to hear those words. Her family had lost everything when her dad went broke. And taking their land was the beginning of the end for her father. Garrett wasn't the type to resort to such drastic measures. Of course, losing the ranch would take a notch out of his soul. But the last time Lacey meddled on Vicky's behalf it put a dark cloud over their relationship. The consequences for *not* intervening, however, were possibly even worse.

Chapter 16

Garrett took a seat in the Stumblin' Goat Saloon at the far end of the room. He'd been craving ribs, blue cheese coleslaw, and banana pudding for the past three days and needed to get his fix. Whoever Ike's friend was that needed help had fortunately come around dinnertime. Between the music and the crowd at the bar, there was enough sound cover to mask anything that shouldn't be heard by prying ears.

Opting to hide in plain sight versus suggesting a backroad meeting, Garrett waved over Liam Bayat, suspecting this Pantex engineer had information on a drug ring, which wasn't as uncommon in government installations as the average taxpayer would hope. Military, intelligence, and law enforcement organizations weren't immune to bad seeds coming together in the unlikeliest places, to include bases, prisons, and even the odd nuclear weapons facility.

Usually, it was nothing too serious—knuckleheads smoking weed on their lunch break. But every now and then, real-deal criminals were involved. That's when things got interesting.

Garrett threw up two fingers to the waitress, who gave a nod as she set a couple of burgers down in front of two cowboys up at the bar. "You're the only one in here I haven't known since kindergarten, so I suspect you must be Liam."

The newcomer stood politely, waiting to be invited to join before taking a seat. "Thank you for seeing me on such short notice."

Wearing boat shoes, chinos, and a blue-check button-down, the guy looked better suited for brunch at Amarillo Country Club than beers and barbecue at the Goat. With his curiosity piqued, Garrett gestured at the chair across from him. "Friend of Ike's is a friend of mine. What can I do for you?"

Liam looked around the room before sitting. He scooted closer to the wall and kept his head trained at the door. "Ike tell you why I'm here?"

"Didn't say much. Warned it was best not to talk over the phone. Didn't really surprise me since you work out at Pantex." Garrett lowered his voice. "I've worked with some tight-lipped folks throughout my life, but you guys take the cake."

"Well, there's secrets and then there's secrets." Liam seemed to brighten, as he took it as a high compliment. "What we're doing out there could end human civilization. Kind of takes things to the next level."

"That it does. Exactly why I wanted to meet with you right away. The fact that this human-civilization-ending technology is only a few miles from my ranch and my family makes it a particular concern to me."

"Same here," Liam shot back.

Garrett didn't take his new lunch companion for the ranching sort. "Whereabouts?"

"Over by Lefors. Inherited some land from my mom's parents near McClellan Creek."

Garrett knew the area and thought of it fondly. Not only was it beautiful, but it was steeped in history. He specifically remembered the Battle of North Fork, which took place in the early 1870s. It was the first major strike by the U.S. cavalry and their scouts against the Comanche. The battle, won by the federal troops, preceded the Red River War, a campaign against the roving tribes, which also included the Kiowa, Southern Cheyenne, and Arapaho.

"You're like me then. Got enough on your plate with wildfires, flash floods, and tornadoes to worry about any man-made disasters. Guess that's what brings you up for a visit."

Liam jerked around as the waitress came up from behind and dropped off two Shiner Bock beers. Fortunately, she hadn't noticed his skittishness. He looked up and thanked her, in a way that seemed robotic. It was clear the guy was under some severe stress.

"Well, you already know what I want," Garrett told the waitress, then turned to Liam. "Barbecue can't be beat."

"Sounds good." Liam flashed a casual smile at the waitress. "Whatever he's having."

As she made her way back to the kitchen, Garrett figured he'd better get right to it. His guest looked ready to bust. "Ike give you my background?"

"Said you were in 10th Special Forces Group. Served around the same time I did. Probably some of the same places, I'd guess."

Garrett perked up. "What branch?"

"Army. Combat engineer."

"Had a couple of buddies who went to Sapper school. Skills came in handy a time or two."

Liam seemed to calm a little. "Knowing how to blow things up had its advantages in places like Iraq and Afghanistan. Worked with a few guys from Nineteenth Group but spent most of my time with the Rangers. Those guys could always find a reason to make things go boom. Got me shot at a lot more than your average Twelve Bravo."

"I don't doubt that." Garrett chuckled and then took a sip of his Shiner. "Look, I'll swap war stories with you all evening long. One of my favorite pastimes. But Ike made this sound kind of pressing. Want to get down to business?"

Liam took a sip of his own beer, set it back on the table, and stared at the bottle. "How do I know I can trust you?"

"You don't," Garrett replied flatly. "But Ike does. And it sounds like you two go way back. Guessing that's why you're sitting here with me now."

Liam was quiet a moment. "Ike said you know people in our government who can do things through unofficial channels. *Quietly*."

Everything Garrett had done since he started working with Kim and the CIA had been bullets and bombs. Nothing quiet about that. She was certainly able to cover it all up, though, or at the very least deflect attention from the massive craters and body count. "I don't know anyone as off the books as Ike. But if you've got a problem, I might know someone who can help."

Liam shook his head. "I don't even know where to begin."

"Most folks say start from the beginning," Garrett explained. "But I've learned over the years, particularly in combat, that sometimes it's better to go with the bottom line up front. Get the problem out on the table and we can dissect it from there."

"Okay, then. Well, I guess the bottom line is that I'm providing classified information on one of our country's most sensitive nuclear installations to an Iranian spy."

If there was ever a mic drop, then this was it. Garrett couldn't have been any more shocked had the guy pulled out a pocket full of spent uranium and dropped it on the table. Maybe this should've been a backroad meeting after all. It took a second to gather his composure and come back with what he hoped wasn't a look of panic.

"All right then. That's about as up front and direct as it gets." Garrett leaned back in his chair as the waitress set down their barbecue. After she was back at the bar, he continued, "Well, you're obviously not doing it willingly or you wouldn't be telling me."

Liam proceeded to relay the information he'd told to Ike earlier, that his father's care and safety all rested upon his cooperation. Garrett hated to think of a family member suffering at the hands of these sadists at Evin Prison. That said, providing information to the enemy couldn't continue, even if it was mostly benign. Garrett agreed with Ike's assessment that the Iranians were buttering Liam up for something.

Garrett put on his DEA thinking cap to work

through the next steps. Sure, they could find the extortionist and arrest him, but what good would that really do? There had to be others out there, a network of Iranian spies doing the exact same thing all over the country. They had to see where it led. Of course, finding answers would require the CIA, the Department of Energy (DOE), and FBI, all working together. And apparently there was a mole somewhere inside the lines of communication. Any operation launched would be over before it began.

"Listen, Garrett, I'll do whatever I can to help. And I'll take whatever punishment I have coming. But I just can't do anything to jeopardize my father's life. I know his going back over there was stupid. I also know why he did it. When he escaped from Iran, the government punished his family. Severely. He gained everything moving to America and they lost it all. The guilt he's carried all these years nearly destroyed him."

If anyone knew that same exact guilt, it was Garrett. He fought down the lump in his throat. For nearly his entire life he felt like those around him were doomed. In fact, it was a driving factor that kept him working undercover solo operations over the last few years. You can't lose what you don't have. But his deep love for Asadi and Lacey had changed his perspective.

"I get it, Liam. But I can't make any promises about anything other than I'll try my best to get your dad home safe. He's in a tight spot. The only thing I *can* guarantee is what you're doing with the Iranians ends right now."

Liam's chin slowly lowered to his chest. "I know. I just thought if I gave them something that would be enough. But what they want me to do now compromises everything."

It was clear now that Liam had been holding back. Garrett leaned forward again. "What are you talking about?"

Liam looked up. "I'm supposed to carry a device inside the SCIF at Pantex and connect it to our system. Somehow, it's supposed to download what they're looking for and store it on a drive. They said if I do this *one* thing, they'll let my father go."

This was information Garrett could work with. He was no computer expert, but he was certain that one of Kim's CIA techno geeks could handle the job. He'd heard of cyber ops like these in the DEA, and had once handed off a laptop to a cartel boss that made it look like he was getting millions of dollars when his accounts were drained.

The idea could potentially work the same way. Give the Iranians something that looks real enough to make them happy but altered enough that it's useless. It just had to buy enough time to convince them they'd tapped Liam for all the intel he was worth, and to let his father go free. Whether or not you could trust them to do that was the big question. But that was tomorrow's problem. Today's issue was getting his hands on that device.

Garrett spoke a little slower, working through a plan in his mind. "All right, I've got an idea. I'm going to need some help. When will you meet the Iranian again?"

"Don't know. About a week usually passes before I hear from him. It's always a text message. And always from a different phone number."

Garrett thought a moment on how to proceed. "How long has it been since the last time?"

"Three days. He's supposed to hand off the device to me at some point before work. But I don't know any more than that."

Damn. Garrett was worried this wouldn't give them enough time. "Okay, then we need to move fast. Tell me what they're after and I'll get someone working on it."

Liam gave a sheepish smile. "I know it seems crazy after everything I told you. But I can't talk about it."

"I'm not asking for the nitty-gritty details on nuclear bombs. But I can't get someone working on this unless I know what the Iranians are expecting."

Liam exhaled. "Weapons transport and storage. Bunker-buster design and missile placement facilities around the country. I work on the most sensitive security projects in the world. Technologies our adversaries have dreamt about getting their hands on for decades."

Garrett wasn't all that surprised. He had no clue of everything going on out at Pantex, but knew it had a tight partnership with its neighbors to the west, Sandia National Laboratories, and Los Alamos. If Tehran, Moscow, Beijing, or any other enemy of the state were looking for a way to hit the U.S. where it hurt, the opportunity was sitting right there in his backyard.

Chapter 17

The last time Smitty had been in the main office of the Mescalero Ranch headquarters his drug-running partner had been gutted like a fish by a cartel hit man. Needless to say, even after a year, his sense of dread was fresh enough to get a good sweat going. Of course, all that had taken place under the reign of Preston Kaiser. Vicky's deceased older brother was a narcissist to the nth degree and a kidnapping murderer to boot.

Vicky exhibited her sibling's ruthlessness in business and his unquenchable thirst for power, but she hadn't demonstrated his penchant for criminal behavior. At least not yet. Since she was working with the feds to pay back taxes and right the wrongs of her sibling's past indiscretions, Smitty figured his boss would be on the straight and narrow. But that wasn't how the Kaiser family operated. Half-shady had always been a hallmark of their operations.

Since Vicky had taken over Mescalero months before, all of their dealings had been conducted at her home in Canadian, not out on the ranch. It made Smitty wonder if she hadn't been out there until now because it was where Preston died in a helicopter crash. Officially, it was an accident. Unofficially, his death had Garrett Kohl written all over it.

As Smitty walked down the hall and turned into the office, his stomach was twisted into knots. He felt like he could hurl at any moment. Vicky, on the other hand, sitting at the desk at the far wall of the room, looked as fresh as a daisy, seeming not to have a care in the world.

"In here, Ray!" Vicky glanced up from the notepad she was scribbling on, waved him over, and then went back to her furious writing. "Have a seat."

Smitty walked in and sat in one of the plush leather chairs before her desk. While she finished up whatever she was working on, he glanced around at all the mounted trophy game. There were mule deer, whitetail, and exotics of every kind. The biggest elk he'd ever seen was on the wall behind her. Where Smitty wouldn't turn was to the back of the room where the grizzly stood. Its bared teeth, outstretched arms, and claws grasping for invisible prey made it a ghastly sight. Right there before it was the place where his old partner, Boggs, was sliced wide open and drained of his blood. Ever since then that damn-ass bear had haunted Smitty's dreams.

Vicky began so suddenly that it almost startled him. "Want to add a little fun to that coffee?" She gestured at the bar to her left. "Got about anything you could want over there."

There wasn't a single brand of liquor he recognized, but that wasn't a surprise. The Kaisers, particularly Preston, didn't just like the *finer* things, they liked *exclusive* things, the kind of things only inordinate amounts of money can buy. Smitty would've actually loved a Pearl. His favorite beer hit the spot just about any time of day. But despite her boast of having *anything you could want* he doubted his brand met her sophisticated palate.

"No, ma'am, got to get a saddle on Mae West today. She handles like a Quarter Horse but is as high-spirited as a Thoroughbred." Smitty chuckled. "Better have my wits about me, I reckon."

Vicky rose from her high-backed chair and slinked over to the bar. The tall blonde, with sharp, blue-blooded features, an heiress to the Kaiser fortune, had a style that fell somewhere between her old life in Manhattan and her new one in Texas. It meant nothing to him, but Crystal was green with envy. His boss smelled like a million bucks, too. He kept that nugget to himself.

Vicky splashed a little Garrison Brothers into her coffee mug, then grabbed the bottle and walked back over to Smitty. "Balmorhea. The only bourbon my brother ever used to drink." She gave a little smirk, then poured at least two fingers into Smitty's open thermos. "Pretty much the *only* thing he used to drink."

Smitty took a sip to be polite, remembering his old boss's love of whiskey and all the bad decisions Preston made while drinking it. "Much appreciated. Thanks." He felt a bit stupid for basically saying the same thing twice, but she was making him nervous.

Vicky moved to her desk, turned around, and leaned into it. "Can't recall my daddy once riding sober and he was the best horseman I ever knew." She took a seductive sip. "And don't worry about

Mae West. I've got something else for you to do today."

Smitty gave a nod. "What's on the docket, boss?"

"Want you to pick up a package at the Mescalero office over in Borger. Our old carbon black plant west of town. Know it?"

Who didn't? It had been the talk of the Texas Panhandle after a big shoot-out where Garrett's crew and Vicky's henchmen, unlikely bedfellows, had teamed up against a hit squad of Russian mercenaries running security for an illicit rare earth mineral mining operation.

Smitty was a bit confused. "If it's a simple delivery, I can have one of the boys run over and fetch it. Larry's free after he finishes up feeding the horses."

Vicky shook her head. "You're going to get something in return. Something important that needs to go back to Canadian. Hand delivered by you."

Smitty couldn't imagine Vicky would be in the drug-running game like her brother, but he wasn't going to take any chances. He was about to inquire as to who he would be making the delivery to when she moved on to the next subject.

"Ray, there will be quite a few more *responsibilities* around here that I want you to take the lead on. Understand?"

Not really. And Smitty was scared to ask. He just knew she'd thrown out that word again. *Responsibilities.* Maybe Crystal was right. Maybe Vicky had questionable motives. Not only that, but Smitty couldn't help but notice she was looking at him a bit longingly. Either this wasn't her first drink of the day, or she really did have a thing for *the help.*

Smitty figured he'd better nip it in the bud. "Happy to load up my plate with more work, so long as it don't keep me out too late. Family and all, you know."

"Of course, I know." Vicky moved around the desk and eased back into her leather chair. "Your wife, Crystal, and I are old friends."

Old friends? They'd met only once. But that wasn't worth mentioning.

"Yeah, she told me that. But with my girl in school and Crystal working—"

"For Lacey," Vicky interrupted.

"Yes, ma'am, for Lacey."

"Ray, you don't have to worry. I know all about what's going on in your life. About Savanah. About your relationship with the Kohls."

Smitty thought he detected some disdain in her voice. "Is that a problem?"

"Only in where your loyalties lie."

"Kohls have been real supportive of me and my family, you see."

Vicky looked offended. "And I haven't?"

Smitty cleared his throat for no other reason than to buy some time. There was an unmistakable edge to her voice, and he wanted to tread carefully. "No, you've been great. Gave me a job when I needed one. And an opportunity for more. Nobody does that for a guy like me."

"What's the problem then?"

"Problem is I got it made, and don't want to mess nothin' up." Smitty didn't want to tell her about the zombies, but they were always on his mind. "I kind of like how things are."

"I get it, Ray. But you have to understand that I need a man out here full-time. Someone keeping an eye on things. A man I can depend on."

"Really think I can do all that with the setup we got going. Still just a phone call away if you need me." Now Smitty felt like *he* was hitting on *her*. "I mean to say, if you want me." Somehow his second try sounded even dirtier.

Vicky smiled, but it looked forced. "I'll have to go with someone else for the job then."

"Someone else?" Smitty's heart sank. He'd come to be thought of as boss around the ranch and didn't fancy the idea of answering to anyone else but Vicky. "Like who?"

No sooner had the words left Smitty's mouth than he heard the heavy steps coming down the hall from behind. It was a slow, dragging gait that was oddly familiar.

"An old friend of yours." Vicky's eyes brightened with a look of mischief. "Another of my brother's most trusted men."

Smitty racked his brain. Everyone, other than him, was either in prison or dead. He'd just come to the only awful conclusion when a voice boomed from behind.

"Well, if it ain't . . . Ray . . . Smitty."

That growling voice was both unmistakable and unforgettable. Bo Clevenger was as big as the grizzly and just as mean. He was scary enough before Smitty became a CI for the Texas Rangers and helped to put the lunatic behind bars. Fortunately, Bo didn't know that. At least Smitty hoped he didn't know. But even before the bust, Preston's key henchman had suspected him of working with rival drug traffickers.

Garrett had warned him Bo was in town. But he'd damn sure never expected to see him out at the Mescalero again. It would take some fancy maneuvering to talk himself out of this one.

Smitty turned to find the massive Bo more colossal than ever. Muscular and towering before his incarceration, this former bulldogging rodeo champion must've found the prison weight room. That and a tattoo artist. Three crosses jutted up from his collar, along his bull neck, to just below the jawline. The cold-blooded killer had either found religion or joined some sort of cult.

Smitty willed himself to speak as if there was no bad blood between them, which wasn't easy by a long shot. "Well, hey there, Bo. Didn't expect to see you out here."

What Smitty had wanted to say was *at all*. Bo had been sent up on drug trafficking charges. The countryside wasn't safe with a derelict like him released into the wild. He shouldn't have been out until he was long in the rocker. Maybe not even then. But apparently, Vicky had hired him some *rolling ball of butcher knives* appellate lawyer who did a helluva number on the parole board. How he convinced them to release a killer like Bo was anybody's guess.

Smitty tried his best to sound enthusiastic, but it was damn near impossible. "That's a stroke of good luck."

"Don't believe in luck." Bo dipped his shaved head at Vicky. "Got me a guardian angel. Gave me a job and a place to stay." His eyes drifted back and rested on Smitty and an unsettlingly cold glare. "On account of my loyalty."

There was that word again. Now Smitty was convinced there was scheming afoot.

Vicky chimed in and broke the awkward stare-down between him and Bo. "Worked for us for years. Started with my father out of high school. Isn't that right, Bo?"

"That's right," Bo confirmed, looking extra gracious. "Hooked me up with a job when nobody else would give me the time of day. Fine man, your daddy."

Smitty was starting to see a pattern here. Vicky's family was like the Statue of Liberty for criminals. But instead of *Give us your tired, your poor, your huddled masses, yearning to breathe freely*, the Kaisers wanted the panhandle's *young, hungry, and desperate for anything, willing to break the law in exchange for a place at the table*. Mescalero, both the ranch and the oil company, gifted an identity and a purpose to wayward cowboy delinquents who had none.

Vicky looked as magnanimous as a saint on the church house wall. "Everybody deserves a second chance." She turned to Smitty. "Wouldn't you agree?"

What could he say? This was probably his twenty-third second chance. Of course, there was no way in hell he was going to work for Bo Clevenger—the same psycho that would have thrown him off the Canadian River Wagon Bridge two years earlier had Garrett not been there to save his ass. The best way to keep an eye on Bo was to make sure he was in charge of him and not the other way around.

"What we were talking about earlier, Vicky. About the manager job."

Vicky perked up as if she already knew the answer, as if the whole point of Bo showing up was to put on the pressure. She didn't speak, just waited for him in half-hearted anticipation.

Smitty cleared his throat. "Guess I'm your man."

Vicky stood and threw out her hand to lock in the deal. "Knew you'd come around."

Before Smitty could rethink it, his hand was in Vicky's shockingly tight grip. She shot a glance at Bo, slow enough to be detected but quick enough that it was meant not to be seen. One thing for certain, they were up to no good. Smitty didn't know why she was putting two ex-cons together. He only knew that he was playing right into her hands.

Chapter 18

As usual, Kim waited in Conner Murray's office for at least fifteen minutes before she heard him talking to his assistant outside the door. She always assumed his habitual lateness was a power play, a way to make her aware of who was *really* in charge. CIA case officers were masters of leverage, using mind tricks to assert control of both friend and foe. But she'd yet to see anyone outdo some of the political operatives at the White House.

Murray scrambled from one meeting to the next in a perpetual state of shell shock, given a never-ending slough of hair-on-fire foreign policy emergencies. Not only did he have to maintain an in-depth understanding of global issues, but he also had the challenge of dealing with the optics, in terms of American voters.

It wasn't enough to address the issues or advise the president on what to do next. Shielding his boss from the repercussions was a big part of the job, if not the biggest. It was the kind of work that Kim, who to her own career detriment *called the ugly baby as she saw it*, never could or would do in a million years.

Murray breezed in, shut the door behind him, and moved around his desk. With a heavy sigh, he collapsed into his chair and flashed her a remorseful look.

Before he could launch into what Kim expected was a big apology, she shut him down. "Don't even worry about it. I know you have a lot on your plate."

Murray steepled his hands and tipped them at her in gratitude. "Oh, you have no idea."

"I'll get right down to it, then. Got a call from Garrett and there's a problem at Pantex."

It was obvious Murray was accessing the Google search engine of his mind to pair Garrett and the nuclear weapons site down in Texas, and gotten the *Sorry, no results found* message. "What relationship is there between Garrett and Pantex, other than neighbors?"

"None, really. But he was introduced to someone who works there. A project manager."

Murray's eyes narrowed with interest. "Go on."

Kim relayed all that Garrett told her. Essentially, everything starting with the imprisonment of a former CIA asset in Iran and the extortion of a Pantex employee. But her follow-up with cyber experts and compartmented files revealed much more. "Liam Bayat's father, Reza, wasn't just any clandestine asset. He was one of our very best sources of intel on Iran in the late eighties. Back during the Tanker War."

During the Iran-Iraq War in the 1980s, both countries began launching attacks against pipelines and facilities, causing a disturbance in the world's petroleum supply, which was exacerbated by assaults on each other's oil tankers in the Persian Gulf. With over one hundred vessels either hit or destroyed, the West took notice and got involved.

It was clear by Murray's delayed response that he was thinking of a way to turn this into a positive. "What was Reza Bayat's motivation? Had to be good to take that kind of risk."

"According to our files, Reza was nonpolitical and already part of Tehran's educated upper class. He had an affinity for the U.S. after receiving a PhD in petroleum engineering from Stanford. He hoped to see his country advance, to transition into the twenty-first century as a global power. A beacon for technological innovation in the Middle East."

Murray shook his head. "Hope is a dangerous thing."

"Reza had a dream of what his country could be and made that very clear. After all, he was an engineer. And he knew his Persian history. His people had mastered water supply systems, batteries, the first freaking refrigerator for crying out loud. But that wasn't what brought him over to our side."

Murray leaned in, thirsty for more. "Revenge. Best motivating factor known to man."

"Reza couldn't stand to see what they were doing. The prisons. Torture. Executions. All of it. But when his fiancée was taken by the secret police and never returned home, he lost all faith in his country. Through a trusted Canadian friend who he worked with at the Imam Khomeini Port, Reza offered to help. And we gladly accepted."

"And now he's suffering through imprisonment and torture himself." Murray shook his head, clearly saddened by the ordeal. "What can we do to get him out?"

"That's what I'm working on now. My cyber team at IOC tells me that it sounds like what the Iranians are passing on to Liam is something our tech ops guys call a *stinger*. Basically, it's like an electronic vacuum that can tap into the classified system." Before she could convey the next part, Murray had figured it out.

"The CIA assets who were murdered. This is how they were compromised."

"Possibly. You asked if there was a connection between Watson and Iran, and maybe there was. Could've been him who brought a device like that into headquarters, passed it on to the Russians, who in turn passed it on to Iran. Still piecing it all together."

Murray looked skeptical. "Think Russian intel would let loose of something that good?"

"They would if it was mutually beneficial. If the Iranians could do something they couldn't. Something that would really make us hurt and give them plausible deniability. Then I think there's no limit to what Moscow would do."

"So, this is a joint op? Iran and the Russkies in cahoots?"

Kim raised her hands and pushed the air. "Not saying that. At least not yet. Not until we know more. It's just *one* theory. But that would mean we have another mole hunt on our hands. The Counterintelligence Center is all over it. And we're trying to sort that out."

Murray seemed to process for a moment, as if weighing his options, and considering the political fallout. "How do we handle Pantex?"

"My cyber team has the idea of creating a dummy download. Give the Iranians what they *think* they want. It'll all be bogus, but by the time they figure that out, Reza Bayat will be back home, safe in Texas."

"What makes you think Iran will keep its word with Liam and let his father go?"

"Nothing. But to get what they want, then we'll have to get what we want. A swap. The device for the hostage. Liam will just have to make sure they know these terms are nonnegotiable."

Murray was clearly unsettled. "Don't know about all this. Seems too easy."

"Nothing easy about it, Conner. This is as risky at it gets."

As someone who'd been the victim of a failed exchange, Kim knew all too well the dangers. But she was also well aware that doing nothing at all meant the sure death of a former asset. Selfishly, from an operational perspective, her CIA cyber team would be working on a way to turn their collection device against the Iranians. They'd also run a surveillance program against the foreign operatives and take down the entire cell.

"The key to all this," Kim added, "is running the operation offline. We're clearly hacked. We know that much. So, all this will have to be done somehow without tipping our hat. Like we're doing now. Everything must be in person until we know exactly how and where we're exposed. That takes a lot more time and limits who we can trust to bring on board."

"Enter Garrett Kohl." Murray smiled. "That cowboy's about as off the grid as it gets."

"We use Garrett to run Liam until we can get our own team in place."

"How long do we have until Liam meets with his handler and gets the device?"

Kim shrugged. "Less than a week, probably. So, that doesn't give us much time. My guys are working on it round the clock."

Murray let out a bigger sigh than before. "You know what I'm going to say next."

"Of course I do. You want to know what the blowback is going to look like for the president if this doesn't work."

"We are talking about a *nuclear* facility here, after all. Kind of gotta ask."

Kim knew that was coming and had already prepared. There was a time when it would have pissed her off if someone was worried about the optics when a man's life was at stake. But sadly she'd spent enough time over at the White House to know it was inevitable. Kim had learned to pick her battles, and the public relations fight politicians lived for wasn't one of them. She stuck to the fight she knew and understood—winning the war.

"Conner, none of this will ever go public. If the Iranian operation to collect sensitive data at Pantex fails, which it will because we already know about it, they'll keep that to themselves. The obvious awful downside is that we lose a loyal former asset. They may claim to have killed a CIA spy, which we will disavow. Just more ravings by a fanatical regime who murdered a political dissident. Our fingerprints are nowhere to be found on Reza Bayat."

Murray narrowed his eyes again, this time focusing on her in a look of disbelief. He was probably wondering how anyone could be so cold and calculating. There were times when she even surprised herself.

"Okay, Kim, sounds like you've got a plan in motion. What do you need from me?"

Smart boy. Like the covert operation against the traitors she'd just wrapped up, Kim would need a presidential finding to embark on what might ultimately be a mission to snuff out the man exploiting Liam Bayat. Essentially, she needed permission from the Oval Office to eliminate a Quds Force operative if the circumstances called for it.

Kim raised her eyebrows, a playful way of letting Murray know that a victory like this was going to cost him. "Just need the go-ahead from your bosses to get this under way. Way I see it, we're already looking at a potential war with Iran. It just happens to be kicking off on American soil. Which isn't a problem with Garrett, a DEA special agent, leading the charge. But I'll need money, resources, and assurances for the people I involve in this operation."

Murray looked sick again. "What kind of assurances?"

"Same deal I got before. Ability to expunge records. Make problems disappear."

A single nod from Murray. "Then I want assurances as well."

"And what might those be?"

"That if this thing blows up, it doesn't involve the administration. It'll have nothing but Kim Manning and the CIA written all over it."

Providing a guarantee that could doom her career and mar the Agency forever, Kim wasn't just gambling with her own fate, but with the life of an American patriot named Reza Bayat, held captive over six thousand miles away. While her confidence had been the bedrock of her success, she also knew there was a damn good chance that it would ultimately be her demise.

Chapter 19

Asadi looked around the Cat's Paw, a little burger shack across from the school, to find it empty of patrons. Garrett had dropped him off earlier than usual, needing to get up to the bank first thing to discuss an extension on his loans. Doing his best to put that out of his mind, Asadi focused on the bacon, egg, and cheese taco that was burning the palm of his hand.

Asadi thanked the cook and headed out the front door to enjoy his breakfast in the cool morning air. He had just rounded the corner of the building when an all-too-familiar voice stopped him dead in his tracks.

"What are *you* doing here?"

Coming from Sam Clevenger, it sounded more like a threat than a question.

Startled, Asadi could muster no better response than the obvious one. "Taco."

It was the part of the nightmare when he normally woke up, but this time his enemy didn't disappear. He sat right there at the picnic table, his husky shapeless body, like a mound of smushed clay. Sam's expression was of equal surprise, a clear sign that the bully wasn't lying in wait. It was a chance encounter of the most unfortunate kind.

Asadi was even more caught off guard by his own reaction, which centered on what to do with his breakfast. The decision was made for him when Sam rose from his bench, lumbered over, and slapped it out of his hand.

Asadi had just begun to backpedal when Sam reached out and grabbed him by the collar. A brief moment of panic mixed with anger preceded a calm from the memory of Garrett's earlier instruction. *Move left. And keep moving left.*

It was an odd but useful fighting tactic that his dad assured him would throw an opponent off kilter. With that simple mantra playing out in his mind, Asadi broke the bully's grip with a sweep of his forearm and spun out of reach. Sam grasped for him and took three powerful swings but none found their target. After a couple of counterclockwise circles, Asadi made a sudden pivot and glided in the opposite direction.

Futile punches kept on coming, but eventually a dazed and disoriented Sam started huffing and puffing. His vicious frontal assault devolved into a staggering sideways limp. Frustrated with Asadi's circular bob-and-weave technique, the bully ducked and charged. But dizzy and out of breath, he tripped over his own feet and plowed face-first into the grass.

Sam had just risen to a knee when Asadi moved in and let her rip. His punches weren't *powerful*, but they were *plentiful*. The first found the bully's cheek, and the second bloodied his nose. But it was the third on the lip that knocked Sam flat on his back. Asadi followed up with a flurry of fists, a left-right combo that jackhammered Sam until he threw up arms in defeat.

Remembering Garrett's lesson on graciousness in victory, Asadi rose and offered a hand. But the pounding steps closing in from behind cut short his kindly gesture. He had just turned to see what all the commotion was about when he was slammed in the back. Asadi caught himself before falling, but his circumstances couldn't have been worse.

Sam was standing side by side with his buddy, Craig Gunderson, who looked equally eager for a fight. Quickly realizing that Garrett had never given him a Plan B, Asadi grasped for one on his own. Unable to flee, and finding two bigger fighters bearing down on him, he grabbed the only weapon he could find—a discarded broom leaning wonkily against the wall. Although he felt a bit ridiculous, Asadi wielded it with no less ferocity than a Roman gladiator.

Unintimidated, his attackers pursued, a decision they would come to regret. Even Asadi was amazed what the broom could do. Craig was the first to get a face full of stiff bristles and immediately went down. The sight of it must've done a number on Sam, who stopped in his tracks but didn't move out of the way. Asadi launched another jab that caught the bully beneath the chin and sent him staggering backward. In pursuit, he cocked his fist, and was just about to launch it when halted by the booming command from an authoritative voice.

Asadi hoped that Sheriff Crowley had witnessed

more than the last few seconds of the fight. But it became very obvious when the lawman grabbed his sleeve and yanked him toward his truck that he either hadn't, or just didn't care. Asadi hadn't just made things worse with Sam. He had somehow managed to create yet another adversary in Craig Gunderson. And if that wasn't bad enough, it was starting to look a whole heck of a lot like he was getting hauled off to jail.

Chapter 20

The sudden text message Liam received from his Iranian handler had made for a slight deviation from his morning commute to work. Instead of going north on the highway, he was instructed to go south. It was the first time his directions to the rendezvous location were ever given piecemeal. He suspected the reason might be because they knew he'd talked.

Liam tapped the brakes at the end of the highway and slowed his Toyota Sequoia to a crawl as he wove through the tiny town of McLean. There wasn't much left behind from its glory days off the old historic Route 66, with the exception of the Devil's Rope Barbed Wire Museum and the Red River Steakhouse. Just off the feeder road on Interstate 40 sat the Cactus Inn Motel, a little motor lodge that probably looked exactly like it did when it was built in the 1950s.

Despite the fact that the name was laughably redundant, it was a nice little motel, and the perfect spot for a surreptitious meeting with his Iranian handler. There were enough strangers passing through not to raise any suspicions, but it was vacant enough for some privacy. Beyond this advantage, there was no indication of where Liam's Iranian handler came from or where he went when he left. Oklahoma City was a three-hour drive to the east—Albuquerque five hours to the west. And there wasn't much in between but hinterland hidey-holes and vast swaths of endless rangeland along the way. Few better places existed to drop right off the face of the earth.

Liam was driving in the fog of his own mind, the result of days on end of turbulent sleep. He had almost breathed easier after his meeting with Garrett, until his brain moved from one problem to another. There was certainly some relief in confessing his crimes, but it did little to assuage his concerns over what would happen next. The fate of his father was his first priority, followed by a close second, which was how to provide for his children when this was all over.

It was unlikely he would get the death penalty, even though that was still technically an option for treason. But a lengthy incarceration was as bad as execution. Maybe even worse. He'd rather die and let his children move on than have them live the rest of their lives in limbo while he rotted away in jail.

As emotional darkness was setting in over his situation, Liam rounded the corner by the motel office and drove across the parking lot to where his contact sat in his car. Per usual, the vehicle was nondescript, looked like a rental, usually something like an Impala or Malibu. It was a white Nissan Versa this time. License plates, likely fake, were from Arkansas.

Liam parked alongside it, got out of his Sequoia, and eased to the driver's-side window. The Iranian operative was as forgettable as his car. In black Oakleys, khaki pants, and a starched white shirt, he looked as common as any of the business travelers on the interstate. There was even a coiled-up necktie in the passenger seat, a few crumpled McDonald's bags in the back, and Starbucks in the cupholder. He even wore the weary look of a salesman, a bedraggled sort of countenance that fell between homesickness and exhaustion.

The operative turned to him and rolled down the window as casually as if he were ordering a burger and fries. But instead of yelling into the clown's mouth, he just smiled. It was a gesture that came across more menacing than kind. "Ready to be done with all this?"

Liam felt the burn of insecurity, as if his treachery to this spy was somehow written all over his face. "This is it, right?" He asked in a way that was less like a question and more like he was solidifying the terms of a contract. "I do this, and we're done for good."

The operative answered his question with a question. "Don't we have a deal?"

"I want assurances my father will be safe." Liam knew he would get no such thing. His bluster was all for show. He didn't want to make it look too easy, lest the Iranian get suspicious. "If I'm going to do this then I want proof you'll keep your word. You'll let him go."

"The proof you will get is when the *traitor* is back here at home."

It was the first time that the spy's demeanor had ever been anything other than nonchalant. Stressing the word *traitor* worried Liam tremendously. This was clearly personal. "How do I know you won't back out? What if I do all this and you kill him anyway?"

The operative pushed the wraparound sunglasses up to his forehead. "We won't."

"And if I—"

"*You* will do exactly as I say, or your father will suffer for it. And I'll make sure that you watch and listen to every agonizing moment."

Showing his eyes was another first. It made Liam suspicious. "You have to see this from my perspective. How do I know that what I'm doing will matter?"

A heavy sigh preceded the Iranian's glance to the right as a U-Haul van pulled into a parking spot. What looked to be a father with his college-aged daughter scooted along the bench seat and filed out of the vehicle to stretch their legs. Liam couldn't help but think of Robin. If he hadn't screwed things up, this would be them. If he did everything right, maybe it still could be?

The spy moved the wraparound shades back to his eyes and keyed the ignition. "It *will* matter. Trust me." He reached into the backseat and pulled up a black Adidas backpack from the floorboard. "The device is in here."

Liam looked around before taking the handoff. "What do I do with it?"

"Nothing." The Iranian shook his head. "Just carry it in with you and set it as close as you can to your computer. It's on a timer. Will turn on by itself."

"Then what?"

"Then you bring it back."

Liam began to panic. He had assumed it was something that would be left permanently. For Garrett's plan to work, they would need more time. "Bring it back? When?"

"End of the day." The Iranian glanced around nervously at the sound of a slamming door. "Meet me here after work."

"What if I can't do it? What if someone is watching? Or gets suspicious?"

A flash of anger spread across the spy's face. "*Why* would anyone get suspicious? If you've been doing exactly what I told you there should be no problems."

With some strange version of the Shakespearean line *doth protest too much* playing out in real time, Liam shut up. "There aren't any problems. I'm just nervous. That's all."

The Iranian smiled as he shifted the car into drive. "Don't be worried. By the end of the day, I'll have everything I need, you'll be done, and your father will come home."

Liam let the bag dangle by his side. "So, I'll see you here later then?"

The spy gave a nod, pressed the accelerator and the Nissan lurched forward. After a quick U-turn, he skidded out of the parking lot and sped down the road. Liam wasn't sure exactly what had just gone down. He only knew that the man he'd just met with was lying through his teeth.

Chapter 21

Garrett paced back and forth inside the waiting room of the Hemphill County Sheriff's Office, racked with anxiety over a landslide of problems that hit nearly all at once. The decision from the bank that there would be no more extensions on his loan payments struck hard. And the news of Asadi's arrest certainly splashed gasoline on the fire. But the call from Liam about his meeting drenched Garrett's angst with enough rocket fuel to launch him into orbit.

Too far away to take the handoff, he made a snap decision that he prayed he'd not regret by involving Lacey. Picking up supplies for the café in Pampa, she was the only one close enough to retrieve the device. Had it been almost any other scenario, Garrett wouldn't have done it. But with Reza Bayat's life at stake, and the obvious threat involving nukes, it certainly fell into the desperate times calling for desperate measures category.

Inviting Lacey into his world was exactly what she asked him to do. And the simple transfer with Liam was as safe a way to dip her toe into clandestine operations as any.

Garrett had just coordinated the meeting location between Lacey and Liam on a back road west of Lefors when Crowley marched out with Asadi's shirtsleeve gripped in a tight fist. It was an unnecessarily aggressive act that Garrett knew was meant to get him riled. And it worked.

"Let loose of him, Crowley. Right now."

"You want to make a move?" The sheriff stopped midstride. "Go for it. I've got room enough in here for you both."

Since kicking Crowley's ass would only make matters worse, Garrett calmed himself down. "Just let him go and we'll be on our way."

The sheriff kept ahold of Asadi's shirt, clearly an overt move to let Garrett know that he wouldn't be bossed around. He smiled his campaign smile, unclenched his fist, and patted him on the shoulder. "Free to go, son. At least for now."

As Asadi moved to him, Garrett processed the comment. "What do you mean *for now*?"

Crowley was looking a bit coy. "Who knows? Parents may want to press charges."

Garrett laughed. "You can't be serious? Did you even talk to the school about what happened the other day? The Clevenger kid came after Asadi. Even got detention for it."

"In fact, I *did* talk to the school, and they mentioned a scuffle."

"A scuffle, huh?" Garrett draped his arm over Asadi's neck and pulled him close. "That damn Sam Clevenger started all the trouble. Kid needs to be dealt with."

"Oh, you mean the way you came after Bo at the

Oasis?" Crowley wagged a stubby finger at Garrett. "Makes me think you got an axe to grind. And might be that your boy here wants to settle his daddy's scores." The sheriff tsk-tsked and shook his head. "Eye for an eye makes the whole world blind, I say."

Garrett wanted to throttle Crowley even more than he did Bo or Sam. The sheriff lived from one vendetta to the next, abusing his position in law enforcement to get even with his foes. This had nothing to do with Asadi and everything to do with the Kohl family's long-standing feud with the Kaisers. Crowley had run interference for them as far back as Garrett could remember.

"Look, you got a problem with me then let's talk. But you're gonna leave my son out of it."

"Nothing but trouble has followed you home, Kohl. Ever think about that?"

Having been convinced he was snakebit, the comment hit Garrett hard. It was true that calamity had struck since he returned. The ricochet effect was something he couldn't ignore. When bullets missed him, they always landed somewhere. And at times, it had been loved ones who'd suffered. But suggesting this had to do with anything other than a schoolyard bully was absurd.

"Hemphill County is *your* responsibility, Crowley. And from what I can see you've done a piss-poor job of minding the store while I was gone."

"I do my part around here." The sheriff's face reddened. "Now, *you* do yours."

"And what exactly is my share of responsibility?"

"Simple. Get your boy under control." Crowley

pointed in the direction of the school, which was less than a half mile away. "Got two kids being patched up by the nurse after Asadi took a broom to their face. Glad I got there or who knows what damage he might've done."

Broom? Garrett resisted the urge to laugh. He would've loved to see these two bullies get a face full of spiny bristles. That said, he knew this could get twisted and didn't want to get Asadi into any more trouble than he was already in. Fortunately, Bridger walked in the door. He called his lawyer brother to come over the second he heard what happened.

Bridger stood in the foyer for a moment, surveying the scene. "Everything okay?"

Garrett looked to Crowley. "You tell us."

Bridger's mere presence immediately changed the tone. The sheriff had lost enough legal battles with him over the years to know when to back down.

Disappointment was written all over Crowley's face. "You can run him up to class, I suppose. Since the incident didn't take place on school property, principal can't do anything."

Garrett figured he'd better hightail it before he said or did something he'd regret. He needed to get to Lacey as fast as he could. There'd be time for dealing with the sheriff and his nonsense later. Especially with a pro like Bridger on their side.

As they walked through the door and out onto the sidewalk, Garrett turned to his brother. "Think you can get Asadi to school for me? I've got some things I need to tend to."

Bridger looked a little confused. "I don't mind, of course, but I'm thinking the school is going to want to talk to his dad about all this. Not his attorney."

Garrett glanced down at Asadi, who seemed equally confused, if not saddened that he was about to be pawned off so soon. It was a natural reaction. The poor kid had just been through something traumatic and would likely want to talk about it. And here Garrett was leaving him to again fend for himself.

A shock wave of guilt hit Garrett at once. He turned back to his brother. "Yeah, you're right. That's my job."

"Anything else I can do?" Bridger asked. "No appointments until afternoon."

The last time Garrett had asked for a favor, his brother had wound up in the hospital. There was nothing to be done at the moment anyhow, so he decided to take Asadi with him to the café and get the backpack. It would give them a chance to talk.

"Don't sweat it, Bridger. Just need to push a couple things back but I'll be fine."

"Sure about that?" It was clear from Bridger's skeptical glare he wasn't buying it. "I can adjust my schedule if you need me to."

"Yeah, I'm positive." Garrett wasn't just thinking about the handoff, he was thinking about Butch's words from two days before. These were the *exact* kind of circumstances for which a father needed to be around. "It'll be fine. All under control."

For some reason, though, Garrett had a sinking feeling. Maybe it was because for the first time ever the mission was taking a backseat to his personal life. Or maybe it was due to Crowley's parting words. The *for now* comment regarding Asadi's troubles didn't sit well.

Garrett couldn't help but think it stemmed back to Liam and the device. There was something too easy about the Iranian's plan. And nothing in the world of espionage was ever without a little pain. He just prayed Lacey wasn't on the receiving end of it.

Chapter 22

Lacey had just pulled her maroon Ford Explorer over on the side of a white caliche road and looked in the rearview mirror. She rolled down the window and exhaled a sigh of relief when she saw a black Toyota Sequoia pulling up from behind. As Liam pulled up and parked just a few feet behind, Lacey donned her ROKA aviators, feeling a bit silly, as if she were wearing a costume for the part. But the glare from the morning sun was levitating at just the right angle, making it almost impossible to see without awkwardly shielding her eyes with her hand.

Pulse racing, heart thumping out of her chest, Lacey had to grin. In her faded Levi's, New Balance running shoes, and white T-shirt, she still wasn't quite ready for the Monte Carlo Casino. But she'd at least crumpled the gingham apron into a ball and pitched it into the backseat. In the history of undercover operations, her errand to pick up a backpack on an old dusty farm road didn't count for much.

It wasn't the mission, though, that got her excited. It was the fact that Garrett had finally let her into his world. There would always be hidden aspects of his past life, and that was fine. But moving forward as a couple, Lacey wanted as few barriers between them as possible. She just wanted to be a part of his world and contribute to something special.

Honorable motives aside, Lacey had to admit it was a thrill, and certainly better than refilling coffee cups and wiping down tables at the café. It didn't classify her as a Bond girl just yet, but she could only hope this was just the first of many top-secret excursions that would bridge the gap between Garrett's mysterious realm and her own.

As Liam Bayat stepped out of his black Toyota Sequoia, Lacey was relieved to see him wearing his sunglasses also. But he wasn't at all what she imagined. He was of medium height and slender, dressed in a blue blazer, khakis, and a yellow button-down dress shirt. *Not the look of an underworld informant.* Liam looked like a regular dad on his morning commute to the office. But for the black backpack, contents unknown, there was nothing mysterious about him.

He stopped at her window, shooting her a nervous grin. "You must be Lacey."

She glanced around at the nothingness of their surroundings. "Guess you're Liam."

"Garrett tell you anything about what's going on?"

Lacey shook her head. "Just said to get this bag and take it right back to him."

Liam stammered a little, as if he felt like there should be more of a conversation but didn't know what to say. "Well, I guess there's nothing left to do but to hand it over then." He lifted the bag and passed it to her through the window.

Lacey took the backpack, eased it over the console, and gingerly placed it in the passenger seat. "This okay?" She took a stab at a joke to lighten the mood. "Need to be buckled in?"

"No, that's fine like that." Liam chuckled. "At least, I think."

Lacey was struggling to come up with some meaningful thing to say when Liam took off his sunglasses and leaned in. The softness of his blue eyes matched his gentle smile.

"Lacey, please tell Garrett thank you for this. And no matter what happens, I appreciate what's he's done for me and my family."

Lacey didn't quite know how to answer, having not a clue as to what was going on. She decided to wing it with something generic. "Well, I'll be sure and tell him. I know he was happy to help. All part of the job, you know." Her response was so ridiculous she wanted to kick herself. But Liam seemed not to notice. He just turned and walked away.

Lacey was wondering what the etiquette was at this point. Did he leave first? Did she? Do they go opposite ways? Deciding to make the first move, Lacey put her Explorer in drive and headed back the way she came. She had just executed a three-point turn when a white Chevy Suburban with dark-tinted windows roared up behind Liam's Sequoia and skidded to a halt.

The SUV had government-issue written all over it. Knowing Garrett could straighten out the matter, Lacey didn't worry. Her only concern was that she'd messed up—maybe even been followed. She had just tapped the brakes and pulled to the side of the road when three men, who she suspected were plainclothes federal agents, piled out of the SUV, pistols at the ready, and crept up on either side of the Sequoia.

Her mind's eye played out the rest of the scene like a cop show, with Liam yanked from his vehicle, shoved to the ground, and wrestled into handcuffs. But to her shock and horror, it didn't end how she'd imagined. Wincing first, then reeling back at the unexpected bang of gunfire, Lacey mashed the accelerator to veer clear of the lead barrage that ripped into Liam's Toyota. Seconds later, bullets shattered her back window and punched holes into the dash.

Lacey jerked the steering wheel hard to the left, fishtailing out of the ditch until she was back on the caliche road. Pedal to the floorboard, her four-cylinder engine whined into an angry groan as she grabbed her cell phone from the passenger seat. Lacey swiped the screen and jabbed Garrett's contact number. Before he even answered, she had launched into a plea for help.

"Garrett! Garrett! Something's wrong!"

A brief pause on Garrett's end. "What—? What happened?"

"They're shooting! Outta nowhere! Just started shooting!"

"Wait! Slow down. *Who's* shooting?"

"Them! Whoever! I don't know!"

"Wait, Lacey. Slow down. Tell me exactly what happened."

Lacey gulped in a breath before she began. "Took the bag from Liam. Then some guys pulled up. Government vehicle, I thought. Then they just shot him."

"*What* government vehicle?" Garrett fumbled with the next part. "From—from where?"

"I don't know! Pantex, I guess. I stopped to tell them what was going on. To explain. But then they shot at me, too!"

"You okay? You hit?"

Lacey patted herself down, not really sure if she was or not. "I'm fine, I think."

"Thank God! Where are you now?"

"Not far from where you told us to meet." Lacey leaned a little farther out and looked ahead. "Farm-to-market. Just west of Lefors."

"Okay, just keep going to town and don't stop until you get there. Whatever happens. No matter what. Do. Not. Stop. Go to the school. Fire department. Anywhere there's people around. I'm coming your way right now. Keep on the move until we meet."

Lacey looked up and discovered in her rearview that the white Suburban was about two hundred yards behind. "Garrett, they're behind me now! They're following!"

"Keep driving," Garrett coached. "Safe as you can. But fast as you can. Keep. Going."

"What's happening?" Lacey stifled a sob. "I don't understand. Why are they after me?"

"I don't know just yet. But I'm going to find out." Another brief pause from Garrett. "What about Liam? Do you know what happened to him?"

Even though Lacey didn't know him, she felt moved to tears. She'd only just met Liam Bayat, but she could tell he was a good soul. His eyes revealed genuine appreciation, the gratitude one parent shares with another. He wasn't a professional spy, just a man in desperation.

"Garrett, I don't know. But he couldn't have made it. There's just no way—" Lacey caught herself before she broke down. "I'm so sorry."

"Nothing to be sorry about, Lacey. Just keep on the move and I'll handle it. Can you stay away from these guys until I get there?"

Lacey choked up a little getting out her next words. She thought about her children. She thought about everything that was at stake. "Yeah, I can do that."

"Great. I'll see you in a few minutes. I promise."

The line went dead as Lacey traveled farther east. She looked back again to find the Suburban closing the distance. There was no doubt Garrett could handle any danger. The only real question was if he would make it there in time.

Chapter 23

As Smitty drove around the outskirts of Pampa, he stared out at the ranch country in silence. He had a sinking feeling that Vicky Kaiser was up to something bad and he should've turned down her offer. Of course, she wasn't a woman who was accustomed to hearing the word *no*, particularly from a subordinate. But he couldn't help but think she was sending him down a dangerous path, and a major clue was this mysterious mission.

Bo was riding shotgun—probably along as Vicky's spy—to see how Smitty handled what was adding up to be a sketchy assignment. It'd be no surprise to find out there was no real exchange and the whole thing was just a test. The *loyalty* conversation had been playing out in his mind since he walked out the front door. Smitty was ginning up some lame small talk, dithering between the weather and the Dallas Cowboys, when Bo beat him to the punch.

"So, what do you think about it all, Ray?"

Smitty knew exactly what his passenger was getting at but felt the need to buy a little time to get his messaging straight. "About what? You mean, what's going on at the ranch?"

Bo cut eyes at him. "What the hell else would I mean?"

As a new boss, Smitty realized he should set Bo straight on talking to him like that. But when conversing with a violent thug you had to tread lightly. "Think that Vicky has some good ideas about getting the business back on track after some hard times."

Bo let out a laugh. "You mean after Preston turned you and me into drug mules for that damn Garza Cartel and nearly got us killed."

Smitty had hoped to just move on past all that. "Vicky wants to keep everything on the up-and-up, so that's what I aim to do." He hesitated before adding the next part but felt it necessary. "Hope you're on board."

Bo laughed again, a little louder. "*Up-and-up*. If that's how you want to look at it?"

"Well, that's how she explained it to me."

"I'm fine with that." Bo turned to Smitty. "I'm a reformed man, case you hadn't heard."

"Hadn't, but glad of it. Been down the road to hell and back myself. Ain't an easy one."

"Yeah, I got my boy to look after now. Just me and him these days. Gonna do it right."

Smitty knew that scenario all too well. Locked up twice in the state pen had kept him from his wife and daughter for long enough. He'd had a lot of help getting back on his feet. And most of that came from Garrett. But if Bo was genuinely serious about a fresh start, then Smitty would do all he could to assist. The big question was if this was for real, or just another con.

In order to find out, Smitty decided to dig a little. "What about your boy's momma? She worth a damn?"

"Nah. Ain't seen her since Sam was in kindergarten. And he's in middle school now. She took off with some surveyor outta Elk City and moved to the Everglades, last I heard."

"Who watched after the kid when you was locked up?"

The question seemed to hit Bo the wrong way. He didn't make a face or anything, but he went dead quiet and just stared out the window. In prison, Smitty had found that inmates tended to talk about everything, even when there was nothing much to say. But if someone went quiet all of a sudden you could bet your ass there was a reason. And it was one that you probably didn't want to know about. His guess was that the kid had ended up in the child welfare system, like himself. Which could be a real bad ordeal, depending on where you got plunked.

Smitty changed the subject. "How was it down there in Navasota? Knew a couple of guys who transferred over to Wynne from the Wallace Pack Unit. Said the warden was a jackass."

"Same as the rest, I suppose." Bo perked up. "At least we had the prison farm to keep us busy. Scorcher in the summer, though. *Damn* was it hot and humid."

Smitty felt pretty good that he had Bo talking. "Take any classes?"

"Nah, but I found a higher calling, you could

say. Even read the Bible. Cover to cover. Twice, in fact."

Smitty was genuinely happy about the news, even if his new partner looked less like Jesus and more like Goliath. He just hoped the reading wasn't done as initiation into a Charles Manson–style religious murder cult. "Took to the scriptures, did ya?"

Bo gave a solid nod. "Like a hooker to crank."

Smitty was impressed. Beyond the Lord's Prayer, which his foster mother said to him every night before bed, he was out of luck. "Anything worth a damn?"

"A chunk of it, I'd say. But I'm partial to the Old Testament." Bo's eyebrows rose with his next question. "You know the Psalms?"

"Know *of* them. Don't reckon I could point to one though if you put a gun to my head." Smitty turned to Bo. "Got any you're partial to?"

Bo gazed out over the prairie and cleared his throat. "Praise be to the Lord my rock, who trains my hands for war and my fingers for battle. Part your heavens and come down. Touch the mountains and make them smoke. Send forth lightning and scatter the enemy." He turned back to Smitty, looking proud of his performance. "Can keep going if you like?"

Smitty swallowed hard. "Maybe later. Don't want to wear you out." The truth of the matter was that Bo's menacing recitation of God's word made him even scarier. "For now, I want to talk about the ranch. You know, what we got going for the future."

Bo looked a little disappointed to be shut down. "Well, I suppose we are on the company dime. What you thinking?"

"Thinking there's about to be some big changes, and I want to make sure you're on board with what I got planned. You see, them boys we got here look up to you. Especially the ones into rodeo. You still got a reputation around here. If I get the Bo Clevenger seal of approval then we got buy-in."

Bo beamed with the compliment. "I'll do my part if you do yours." He glanced over. "Think you're up for the job?"

Smitty was tempted to dig into what job Bo was referring to, but he knew not to reveal his hand. "You got any ideas about next steps?" It was an open-ended question meant to further stroke Bo's ego. He was clearly clued into something.

Bo locked eyes. "Hell yeah, I got ideas. Lots of them." He didn't wait for the go-ahead. "I say we can make way more money in oil and gas than we did in the damn drug game."

Smitty perked up with talk of the energy business. That was *his* world. The world that he loved. If there was a way to earn big, he was all ears. "What makes you say that?"

"Pure and simple," Bo explained, "it's all about supply and demand. Not everybody wants dope. But there ain't a damn soul out there that don't have to fill up their ride. Not only that, but everything in the world is also made of plastic, which comes from hydrocarbons." He reached up and slammed his palm on the dashboard to emphasize his point. "Hell, even them little wind-up cars running on Duracell get their go-juice from natural gas. No matter what they say, the world needs oil. And we got a whole damn ocean of it right under our feet."

This is where Smitty had Bo whipped in the intellect department. "I don't disagree. But the problem is that oil and natural gas are out in the open for anyone to buy and sell. That's where the black market comes in handy for making a profit. Dope running is all about risk."

"That's why Vicky's plan is perfect." Bo smiled wide. "She adds a little risk into the oil and gas game. Makes it a gamble *not* to go the Mescalero way."

"A gamble?" Smitty turned to Bo, especially curious to know what Vicky had up her sleeve. "What kind of gamble? Other than the fluctuation in price or investing big money in a dry hole, risk in the energy sector is pretty straightforward. Like any other business, I guess."

"Yeah, but with *my help*, folks around here will find out what the downside might be to going with the competition. Particularly when siding with one of them big corporate outfits that don't belong here. And with *your help* they'll find out what they're missing out on."

It took a second of racking his brain, but Smitty pieced it together. As an experienced oil and gas pumper on the Texas High Plains, he had a damn good awareness of the area. He knew all the producing wells, how much they were yielding, and for how long they were profitable. Having worked only for Mescalero, though, his knowledge was limited, and it hit him that Vicky was grooming him to be an oil scout, essentially a spy for the oil and gas industry, tasked with monitoring drilling activity and keeping tabs on the competition.

The job can be as innocent as tracking oil trucks, or as illicit as sneaking onto private property to check well logs. He even heard stories of scouts breaking into competitors' offices to steal their seismic data. As a former oil-field lease operator, Smitty had a lot of know-how on the technical side of petroleum operations, and he knew the Panhandle like the back of his hand. Which meant he had an idea what Vicky wanted him to do. If he was the brains, then Bo must be the brawn. And that was a damn scary thought.

Smitty was about to dig further when the call came in from Garrett. Knowing it would throw his friend into a tailspin to hear that Bo was in the truck, he was tempted to let it go to voice mail. But a call like this during work hours was rare. He worried it might have something to do with Crystal or Savanah.

Shifting his cell phone to the left side of his head so that his riding companion couldn't hear, Smitty answered the call. "What can I do for you, sir?"

Garrett launched in. "You near Lefors by chance?"

"Few minutes north." Smitty glanced at his watch. "Why? What's up?"

"Need you to get over there quick as you can."

Hearing the panic in Garrett's voice, Smitty

jammed his foot on the accelerator until it hit the floor. "Everything okay?"

Bo perked up and stared at the speedometer. "What the hell, man?"

Garrett spoke up. "Who's with you?"

"No one," Smitty shot back. "Everything all right?"

Thankfully, Garrett pressed on. "You got a gun, Ray?"

Of course he did. It *was* Texas, after all. Smitty popped open the console and pulled out the Cabot Diablo 1911 he'd commandeered from a drug lord down in Mexico. He turned to Bo, who was eyeing the semiautomatic pistol. "Change of plans. Gotta make a detour."

"What about Borger?" Bo argued. "You heard the boss."

"We'll go afterward," Smitty assured him. He turned his attention back to Garrett. "What's going on?"

"Don't know for sure. Just know Lacey's got some real dangerous folks following her, and I don't want them anywhere close. Understand?"

"Yep. Where's she at now?"

"Driving down a farm-to-market, just west of Lefors. You know that area?"

"Like the back of my hand." Smitty eyed the pistol. "We'll be there as soon as we can."

"*We?*" Garrett shot back.

"Me and Bo Clevenger." Smitty clicked off the phone and tossed it on the dash, knowing Garrett would balk at the idea of having an adversary along for the ride. But short of kicking the ex-con's ass out on the side of the road, there wasn't much else he could do about it. And if there *was* trouble, Bo might just come in handy. It wasn't every day that you'd want the guy around. But sometimes it paid to have a stone-cold killer on your side.

Chapter 24

Asadi kept looking over from the passenger seat of Garrett's pickup to try to figure out what was going on. Since leaving the sheriff's office, his dad had been on his phone, preoccupied with the emergency that was playing out in real time as they drove. Part of Asadi was grateful for the disruption, knowing there was a good chance he might be in trouble for getting into a fight. But most of him was just worried about what on earth was going on.

During a break in the marathon of phone calls, Asadi dared ask, "Lacey? She okay?"

"Hope so, buddy." Garrett kept his focus on the highway, hands white-knuckled on the steering wheel. "Might've made a bad call." He shook his head, eyes still focused on the road. "Gotten her involved in something I shouldn't have. Pray to God I'm wrong."

Asadi strained his eyes but could see nothing before them. "Where we going?"

No sooner had the words left his mouth than a call came in from Butch. Fortunately, he hadn't left the house, or he'd be damn near impossible to reach. The old man had sworn off cell phones and seat belts, claiming people lived for millennia perfectly fine without them.

Garrett answered, "Need a little help, Daddy. How soon could you get over to the café?"

"Can be there in half an hour. Why?"

"Have to tend to some work stuff but I got Asadi. Need to drop him off if I can."

"Yeah, that'd be fine." A pause on Butch's end. "Why's he not at school?"

"Long story. I'll let him off at the café as I pass through. Crystal's there now."

"Where's Lacey?"

"That's who I'm going to check on."

"Everything okay?" Butch shot back.

"For now it is. She was helping me out with something, and I need to get to her pronto."

"Say no more. Be there as quick as I can."

Garrett ended the call and tried Lacey again. It rang and rang then went to voice mail.

Asadi could see the worry etched on Garrett's face. "Where is she?"

Garrett turned and smiled, which Asadi could tell was purely to put him at ease. "About to meet her in a few minutes. That's why I got Butch coming over to fetch you at Henry's."

Asadi was about to follow up when Garrett picked up his phone and made a call. A single ring and Ray Smitty's frantic-sounding voice came over the speaker.

"We're northeast of Lefors, Garrett. You close yet?"

"Nah, I'm just now at Miami. You'll reach her before I do."

"Heard anything at all?"

Garrett grimaced. "No. She's not picking up."

"Don't sweat it." Smitty's voice softened, sounding a bit insecure. "Cell service ain't worth a damn out in the sticks. Probably all it is."

"How long until you get there?" Garrett asked.

There was some muffled conversation and then Smitty spoke again. "We're hauling ass. So, about fifteen minutes. Will give you a shout soon as we spot her."

"Really appreciate it." Garrett tapped the end-call button and mashed on the gas. Under his breath he added, "More than you'll ever know."

LACEY LOOKED BACK AGAIN TO find that the white Chevy Suburban was nearly on her tailgate. She'd kept a fair distance on the caliche road, the massive white dust plume in her wake acting as a smoke screen to keep the attackers at bay. But turning onto the asphalt highway had proved to be a bad move. Her little four-cylinder was no contest for the massive V-8 roaring up behind. She had just looked back when the SUV rammed her bumper and she nearly lost control.

Fortunately, Lacey found her grip on the wheel and straightened out before swerving into the bar ditch. A jerk to the left got her straightened out, but a second jolt sent her into the culvert. The *thunk*, *clunk*, and *swish* of clods, pebbles, and tall weeds beneath the undercarriage overtook the whine of her engine. With the Chevy pulling up on the driver's side, Lacey reached blindly for her phone, patting at the passenger seat, and finding nothing. She glanced right and caught a glimpse of her phone on the floorboard. The screen was glowing with an incoming call.

Do-or-die, Lacey leaned across the console and grasped for it. Her first swipe yielded only air, but in a second attempt her fingernails caught the edge of the case. She was dragging it toward her when the SUV rammed again from behind, knocking the phone just out of reach. Lacey looked up, just in time to spot a concrete draining pipe only thirty yards ahead.

Slamming on the brakes, she skidded a good fifty feet across the tall grass, watching the Suburban as it flew by. Lacey reached over the console again and grabbed her phone with the right hand, then popped back up and yanked the steering wheel with her left. A punch of her foot on the accelerator and she was fishtailing out of the trench and back onto the road.

A glance in the rearview revealed she'd gained a little distance from her pursuers, who had stopped in the middle of the road. A quick check of the screen showed over a dozen missed calls, a couple from Smitty, the rest from Garrett. She swiped it open and jabbed his contact number.

Barely a ring and Garrett answered, "Praise Jesus! Are you okay?"

Lacey nearly burst into tears at the sound of his voice. "Garrett, where are you?"

"About fifteen minutes away. Coming as fast as I can."

Lacey's heart sank. He was farther away than she thought. "You gotta get here!" She glanced in the rearview and found that her pursuers were gaining ground again. "They're trying to ram me off the road!"

"What road? Exactly where are you right now?"

"Right past Cabin Creek, I think. Why are they doing this, Garrett?"

"I don't know. But just keep on the move and everything will be okay. Smitty will get to you quicker than I will. Watch for him. He's in one of the Mescalero trucks."

Lacey looked back again to find the Suburban nearly on her tail again. "Hurry, Garrett! They're back!"

"Okay, I need to let Smitty know where you are. I'm going to—"

"No! Don't hang up!" Lacey knew it was irrational but as long as she could hear his voice, she felt safe. "Please don't leave me."

"I'm *not* leaving you, Lace. I'll never leave you. But I gotta let Smitty know where you are so he can find you. I'll call right back. I promise."

With no other real choice, Lacey relented. "Garrett. Please hurry."

"I am. I promise. I love you."

Lacey had waited a long time to hear those three words from Garrett. And she never got tired of hearing them. "Love you, too."

All her life, Lacey had been a scrapper. It had started with the tragic loss of her father that left her mother penniless, the battle with her ex-husband, and the process of rebuilding her life from scratch. She had survived blizzards, wildfires, cartel assassins, and mercenaries. But this time was different. For some reason, deep down, it really felt like this could actually be the end.

Chapter 25

Smitty turned to Bo, who was wearing a wide grin. If riding along in a pickup going over ninety miles an hour bothered him, he certainly didn't show it. In fact, he seemed to relish in the thrill. The former drug runner had a penchant for risk. Which was probably why he could never make a break from the Kaisers, who seemed to live from one calamity to the next.

Bo turned to Smitty and asked again, "What the hell is this about anyhow?"

Needing to cover, Smitty ginned up a good lie. "Ain't for sure. Just know it has something to do with Ike. Think maybe Garrett owes somebody money from Crippled Crows."

It was a plausible excuse. The mere mention of Ike Hodges and his notorious dive bar could explain any dealings that would involve bad blood, a car chase, or gunplay. And it made its way around Canadian that Garrett had gotten himself into financial troubles.

Bo donned a look of satisfaction. "Well . . . well . . . the perfect Kohls ain't so perfect."

The comment didn't sit well with Smitty. "What's your problem with the Kohls?"

"Just get sick of seeing them act all *holier*-than-thou."

"Thought you was a holy roller now." Smitty shot Bo a side glance. "What's your problem with them living by a different standard?"

"Nothing. When it's gen-u-ine. But the Kohls act like they're better than everyone else."

"And the Kaisers don't?"

Bo shook his head. "Just richer, that's all. But they're crooks like the rest of us. And they don't pretend they're not. What you see is what you get with them folks."

Smitty couldn't disagree. The Kaisers cared little about what anybody thought of them. Money and power bought allegiance. *Loyalty*. Their code of ethics shifted like the desert sand.

"Maybe you're right about the Kaisers," Smitty admitted. "But the Kohls have treated me and my family right. And whatever damn code Garrett lives by, he's stuck with it for as long as I've known him. He's as devoted a friend as I've ever known. So, thick or thin, I'm on *his* side."

Bo cut eyes at Smitty. "Doesn't seem to fit the oath of allegiance the queen is after."

Smitty suddenly remembered his earlier conversation with Vicky Kaiser, about his serving two masters. One word from Bo to her could wreck everything. He wouldn't just lose his promotion. He'd likely lose his job. "You gonna say anything to her about it?"

Bo shook his head. "Nah, might as well let things play out." He chuckled in a way that seemed a bit menacing. "You're as good a foreman as any, I guess."

Smitty wondered if Bo knew that he was next in line for the job. But rather than dig further, he changed the subject. "Worried what we're doing might get you in trouble. Maybe I ought to let you out here. A rancher will be along shortly, and you can hitch a ride back to town."

Bo batted off the notion of trouble. "Keep a-going. Worse things in the world than Garrett Kohl owing me a big-ass favor."

Smitty didn't reveal it, but that was certainly true. Garrett had paid him back in a major way. He was just about to ask what his passenger had in mind when they came over a hill and saw the back of a white Chevy Suburban. SUVs of that make and color were common but given the high rate of speed it had to be them.

Bo perked up, too. "That's our guys right there. Guaran-damn-tee-it."

Smitty tapped the brakes just a little and brought it down to eighty since he didn't really have a plan. "Better call Garrett and see what he wants us to do."

Within the first ring, Garrett answered, "Found them?"

"Spotted the Suburban at least. Haven't seen Lacey's Explorer yet. But we're on a flat straightaway right now. Hard to see what's ahead."

"Sure it's them?" Garrett pressed, a little skepticism in his voice. "Running out of time."

The fact of the matter was that Smitty wasn't certain. And this was too dire a situation to jump the gun. Lot of people traveled damn fast on these lonesome country roads. He was going to have to get a better angle, which meant getting around the side to see what was ahead.

Smitty pulled into the opposite lane, jammed his foot on the accelerator, and got it back over ninety. He was pulling up around the side of the Suburban when he saw Lacey's maroon Explorer right in front of their grille. "Found her, Garrett! We found her!"

"Okay, great." A pause from Garrett. "Whatever you do, don't let them out of your sight. They won't try anything with witnesses around."

"Don't worry." Smitty looked down at his boot, which held steady on the gas. "We're on it. They're not going anywhere without us."

"Where you at now?" Garrett pressed.

Bo chimed in. "County road outside of Lefors, but we're about to get on the highway. They'll have to slow down at a sharp turn ahead. We can move in and knock them off her ass."

"I know the place," Garrett answered. "If you can cut them off and let Lacey get away, then do it. But remember these guys are armed. So, keep a little distance."

Smitty was just wondering how in the hell he was going to do that when he saw the sharp turn in the road. A tap of the brakes turned into a full-on stomp when the Suburban's taillights lit up, and its tires left a trail of smoke and rubber as it skidded across the asphalt. Just ahead of the Chevy, Lacey's

Explorer made a hard right but hadn't slowed down near enough.

In the blink of an eye, her Ford flipped sideways and became a whirling blur of maroon. It hit the culvert, smashed through a barbed-wire fence, and flipped end over end until landing upside down in a cloud of dust in the pasture. Smitty didn't know how many times it spun, only that when it finally stopped, there was nothing left but a pile of debris. In shock at the horrific sight, he fumbled to get the words out: "She—she wrecked."

There was an unmistakable fear in Garrett's voice. "You said she wrecked?"

Bo, equally horrified, muttered out, "Flipped off the road."

"Is it bad?" Garrett shot back.

Smitty knew that the answer was *yes* but didn't dare say it. "Don't know yet."

"What's going on?" Garrett's voice rose. "Is she—?"

"Just get here quick as you can." Smitty ended the call as he eased up behind the Suburban, which had just pulled over on the shoulder. "What do you think, Bo?"

Bo grabbed the pistol from the console. "Think I'm going to ask a few questions." He reached for the handle, opened the door, and stepped outside.

"Ah, dammit!" Smitty yelled to Bo, "Gimme that gun! You're in enough trouble as it is."

Whether Bo heard him or not, Smitty wasn't sure. But he had no time to argue. Lacey Capshaw was likely in the fight of her life. Whoever was in that Suburban was Bo's problem now. His only thoughts were of what he might find inside that Explorer.

Throwing open the door and jumping out of the seat, Smitty dashed from his truck to the mangled SUV. Leaping over a piece of wreckage that was possibly the bumper, he tripped when his foot hit a side mirror and tumbled to a knee in some churned-up dirt. Smitty scrambled to his feet and sprinted until he got to the open driver's-side window and dove inside. He didn't know if Lacey had been thrown out of her seat belt or if it had never been buckled in the first place, but she was lying unconscious on the roof of the cab. In her tight grasp was the strap of a backpack.

Figuring it might be important, Smitty ripped it away and tossed it through the window. He knew never to move someone who'd been injured, but the leaking fuel tank changed the rules. And he'd rather take that risk than leave her there to be burned alive. Given the acrid chemical smell of melting plastic overtaking the odor of gasoline, it was only a matter of time.

Gently as he could, Smitty rolled Lacey over and grabbed her under the arms. A couple of solid tugs and he had her clear of the wreck and into the pasture. He knelt beside her and brushed the hair from her face to find her cut, scraped, and bloody. If she was still alive, it wouldn't be for long. Realizing he left his cell phone in the truck, Smitty glanced around, just as the sound of gunshots reported from the rear. Two men fired pistols from behind the Suburban's hood.

Bo stood smack-dab in the middle of the road,

shooting right back at them. As calm and cool as Jesus atop the Sea of Galilee, he marched forward, cracking off round after round from the Cabot Diablo. The old outlaw wore a wide grin, loving every moment of his return to the fight.

Spooked by the brazen and somewhat psychotic display, the shooters moved back around to the driver's side. One jumped into the front seat, the other in the back. But their hasty retreat didn't slow Bo down one single bit. He kept moving forward, banging away with his pistol as the Suburban spun out, the wheels caught hold, and the vehicle careened down the road.

The immediate threat now speeding around the corner and nearly out of view, Smitty turned his attention back to Lacey. She hadn't moved a muscle since he found her, and the truth of the matter was that he didn't know if she was even breathing. With Bo running up, cell phone to ear, talking to the 911 dispatcher, Smitty squeezed her hand, leaned in, and whispered the Lord's Prayer. It was a desperate and hopeless act, but at the moment, it was all he had to offer.

Chapter 26

Garrett marched into the waiting room at Pampa Regional Medical Center on a hunt for answers. Arriving at the crash site after Lacey was life-flighted to the hospital, he'd had only minutes to get the rundown from Smitty and Bo. Of course, they knew little more than he did. According to a Texas state trooper at the crash, a dead body was found on the side of the road several miles away.

The victim either wasn't carrying an ID or it had been stolen during the incident. The trooper had described the victim as a middle-aged man with a medium build and dark complexion. That could've been a lot of people, but it sadly fit Liam Bayat's description to a tee. Given Lacey's accounting of what happened, there was no way he could've survived.

Spotting Garrett from across the room, Butch stopped his pacing and walked over. "Damn sure glad you're here. Maybe you can get more information than I can."

His dad must've assumed that because of Garrett's romantic status with Lacey he'd get more answers. But the truth of the matter was he'd yield no better treatment as a boyfriend. It was an unexpected sting that made him even more sorrowful. He wondered if his caution in taking the next steps in their relationship was a decision he'd come to regret.

Garrett looked down at Asadi, who was nearly in tears. "She's gonna be all right, Outlaw. I promise." He pulled his son close, wondering if those words of assurance were more for himself. "She's the toughest girl I've ever known. So, don't you worry. Okay?"

Butch paused before speaking. It was as if he didn't know how much to reveal in front of Asadi. "Doctor doesn't know much yet. Said it's going to be tricky."

The vague explanation made Garrett more pissed than worried. "What does that mean?"

"Head trauma is complicated." Butch gestured at the ER nurse behind the counter. "She said they probably should've taken Lacey to Amarillo but needed to get her into surgery immediately. Had to relieve the swelling on her brain."

Ah hell. Garrett didn't know much about medical issues, but he'd seen enough head trauma in Iraq and Afghanistan to know that everything that Butch said was true. Lacey could wake up fine or die on the table. The brain was a mystery, even to some of the best neurosurgeons in the world. What would happen next was anybody's guess.

Understanding the need to keep calm and collected for Asadi's sake, Garrett kept an even voice. "She's in surgery now?"

Butch gave a nod. "Should be in there for a few hours."

"I guess we just have to wait and pray then."

Garrett looked down at Asadi. "Why don't you go ahead and take him back to the ranch," he said to Butch. "Get some lunch and tend to the horses. It'll take his mind off all this a little. Anything happens, I'm just a phone call away."

Butch seemed to acknowledge that it was better *not* to be around. If bad news came, Garrett didn't want it delivered from some nurse or doctor. He wanted to do it himself.

Butch tilted his head at the exit. "Come on, sonny. Gonna be a spell before we get an update." He looked up to Garrett. "Can I get you anything? Pick up some lunch?"

Garrett forced a smile. "Appreciate that, but I'm all right." He knew he wouldn't be able to even look at food without getting sick. "Might grab something from the vending machine later."

Asadi leaned in and gave Garrett a hug. "Sure you not want me stay?"

"Appreciate it, Outlaw, but there ain't nothing to do for now but wait. Y'all get back to the ranch and take care of your chores. I'll call when I have some news."

As almost an afterthought, Butch turned around and picked up the backpack under his seat. "Ray said she was gripped on to this like it was the map to Solomon's gold."

With all that had happened, Garrett had almost forgotten the whole damn reason Lacey had gotten involved in the first place. It hurt to know that even on the brink of death she was clutching on to the bag. She didn't even know what was inside. But if it was important to him, it was important to her. Lacey was as faithful a warrior as God ever made.

Garrett was about to take the handoff when he changed his mind. "Actually, do me a favor and take it back to the house. Kim will be down shortly. She'll know what to do."

Anybody else would've had a million questions, but with the CIA involved, Butch simply agreed. He pulled Asadi to his side and the two walked out together. Both were putting on brave faces, but Garrett knew exactly what they were thinking. Because he was thinking it, too. *What on earth would they do without her?*

Garrett looked around the empty waiting room and a flood of memories came rushing back. The most prominent on his mind was of Lacey there with Butch. She'd risked her life to save him. It was just the kind of woman she was—loyal to a fault.

Running his fingers through his hair, Garrett let out a big exhale. There was no way around the fact that he caused all this. Because of his stupid plan Lacey was in emergency surgery, and by the sound of it, Liam had been gunned down and left for dead on the side of the road. His kids were probably just now getting the horrible news.

Garrett rolled his forearm to the left, opened the palm of his hand, and stared down at the tattoo on his wrist. The block letters beneath the skull and crossbones spelled *Memento Mori*. The Latin phrase, literally translated, "remember you will die," meant many things to many people. To some, it was a reminder of mortality; to others it was *seize the day*. For him, it was about making your life count for something bigger than yourself. And to this point, he'd done just that. But *his* axiom was now responsible for the death and sorrow of innocents.

There was a temptation to sink low on the thought of what *he* might've caused. But wallowing wouldn't save Lacey, nor would it get him a step closer to catching the men who did this. At the very least he had the cyber collection device, thanks to her, which would thwart the Quds Force operation. Unfortunately, it would do nothing to save Liam's father.

A quick glance at the television to find Doppler Dan tracking a thunderstorm on the local news, and Garrett moved to the exit, then stepped outside to give Kim the horrible update. Marching across visitor parking, Garrett donned his Ray-Bans and moved to the far end of the lot where his truck was parked. He had just reached for his phone when he heard rapid footsteps from behind.

Spinning in a full circle, Garrett scanned row upon row of vehicles in search of the culprit but came up empty. He stilled himself and listened, but there was nothing to hear but the sound of the west wind as it whipped through the narrow corridors of parked cars. He was about to chalk up the hallucination to raw nerves, a sensory overload in the wake of tragedy, but then the sound was back again. It was followed by a flash in the corner of his eye.

Garrett looked left through the labyrinth of vehicles, just as a figure darted from behind a yellow Jeep to the cover of a gray minivan. He reached back, grabbed the pistol from his belt, and ducked low. With his fingertip grazing the trigger, Garrett stalked his adversary, inch by inch, row after row, pistol at the ready for whoever was on the approach. He'd just begun to wonder if his pursuer had fled when the grind of pebbles confirmed that someone was nearby.

As the barrel of a Beretta poked out from behind the taillights of a black Ford Bronco, Garrett dashed forward and grasped for the pistol. Whether it was the *startle* or the *struggle* that sent the weapon flying, Garrett didn't know. But it twirled out of the gunman's hand and clacked on the ground. Had the would-be assassin been a half-second faster, then he might've recovered. But Garrett had already jammed the muzzle of his Nighthawk into the nape of his pursuer's neck.

A glance around to make sure they were alone, then Garrett took a couple of steps back and gave the command, "Hands up. Nice and slow. Then turn around." Craving answers more than revenge, he elected to keep the stalker alive. At least for now.

Before federal agents arrived and extended a *right to remain silent*, Garrett wanted to exercise his own *special right* as a man who was contemplating the loss of a loved one. He'd be asking a few questions and he'd not be asking them nicely.

Upon the measured turn of his captive to face him, Garrett couldn't help but believe he was experiencing yet another raw-nerved delusion. The murdered man he'd been trying to help was not only alive, but for some reason, sneaking up with a gun. Liam Bayat owed him a detailed explanation. And for both their sakes, it had better come fast. And it better be good.

PART THREE

Why do you seek the living
among the dead?

—Luke 24:5

Chapter 27

Smitty had been so preoccupied with what happened to Lacey he'd forgotten about all the other problems weighing heavy on his mind. Garrett assured him an explanation as to what went down with the gunmen was forthcoming, but Smitty doubted he'd actually get one. His friend's secrets usually traced back to the CIA.

Smitty had learned over time that there were some things better left in the dark. Anything that had to do with Kim Manning usually fell into that category.

Fortunately, there was little to answer for at the scene of the wreck. The state troopers, first to arrive at the scene, were so busy tending to Lacey's injuries they hadn't bothered to ask about much else. Per Garrett's instruction, Smitty and Bo kept the shoot-out all to themselves.

As they drove the dip-diving hills into Canadian, Smitty turned to his passenger, who'd been notably quieter. "Doing all right? Haven't said much since—" He paused, not really knowing how to describe the incident with Lacey. "You know. All what happened."

Bo kept his eyes forward and took his time answering. "Just makes you think, I guess."

Smitty had seen the look in Bo's eyes as he stood in the middle of the road drilling .45 rounds at whoever was in that white Suburban. It was clear the old dope-smuggling rodeo star had enjoyed a taste of the action. But his sudden sullen demeanor was unexpected.

It wasn't wise to prod a killer like Bo, but Smitty did it anyhow. "Think about *what*, exactly?"

"About life, and what we do with it." Bo seemed to be grasping for something in his mind. "Says in Exodus that whoever strikes someone, and they die, shall be put to death."

Smitty figured he'd better get his partner in a better mood. Last thing he needed was the maniac in his passenger seat trolling for vengeance. "Well, Lacey's hanging in there for now. Besides, don't the Bible say something about turning away wrath? Offer the other cheek?"

"Mentions it," Bo admitted, albeit a little reluctantly. "But it also says there's a time for war. 'Do not think I have come to bring peace to earth. I have come to bring the sword.'" Turning to Smitty he added, "Them are Jesus's words. Don't get no clearer than that."

"And the part about forgiving your neighbor?" Smitty countered.

"Folks doing the shooting ain't my neighbor," Bo corrected. "Never seen them sons a bitches a damn day in my life."

Smitty sighed in defeat. So much for the scriptures. Bo had him whupped. "Well, like I said before, Garrett will call if he needs us. For now, we just gotta finish the job for Vicky and get back out to the ranch."

Smitty turned the Mescalero pickup into Canadian and made his way to the Kaiser compound. He always had a sense of dread as he pulled into the circle drive. It was a distinct vibe that poor folks get when they know they don't belong. He felt guilty in its presence.

After parking his truck in front, Smitty grabbed their delivery, which was a long cardboard tube typically used to store maps or blueprints. He turned to Bo, who was sitting like stone, staring at the mansion. "You coming or what?"

It was obvious Bo felt uncomfortable, too. But he finally gave a nod and stepped outside. They made their way to the wraparound porch and looked at each other like kids on a dare. Knowing he was in charge, Smitty took the lead. And per Vicky's instructions, he opened the door and marched right in.

Bo followed him inside, looking dumbfounded. "Damned if this don't impress."

That was an understatement. The multimillion-dollar lodgings at the Mescalero Ranch were a sight to behold, but the rustic western theme and mounted wild game gave it more of a down-home vibe. It was a motif that made him feel comfortable. In his element. The Kaiser mansion in town, on the other hand, was pure opulence. It was how Smitty imagined old families like the Rockefellers once lived. *Look, but don't touch.*

His taking in of the scene was interrupted by a

familiar male voice, apparently on a phone call in a room at the back of the house. Smitty and Bo again looked at each other before proceeding through the living room, down a dark hallway where the corridor opened up into a large office. Unlike Vicky's setup at the ranch, which looked like it was purely for show, this one was all business—*oil* business from the looks of it.

There were maps pinned to the walls, mostly of the Texas Panhandle, broken down by county, section, and mineral leaseholder. They were color-coded by energy operator, indicating areas where companies held wide swaths of territory under oil and gas production. Sheriff Crowley was focused on a flowchart unfurled across the desk.

After finishing up his call, Crowley dropped the phone in his shirt pocket and looked up at Smitty. "You got it?"

Smitty held up the canister. "Guess so."

The sheriff made a beeline over, took the hand-off, and pulled out the contents. Once unfurled he spread it out on the table and used a couple of paperweights to hold down the corners. The flowchart highlighted every oil producer, service company, and driller in the area and showed their interconnectivity, to include an estimation of their financial engagements.

Crowley's eyes lit up like sparklers. "Money well spent, my boy." He pulled a second document from behind that one and studied it intently for a few seconds before taking his hands off the ends and letting it roll back together. He moved quickly to an open safe across the room and stashed it inside.

Smitty didn't know exactly what it was but recognized it as some sort of seismic data—the kind
most oil companies heavily guarded. The Black-
jack Petroleum logo in the top left corner was suspicious. Of course, there was always the chance it
was purchased legally. But given all the cloak-and-
dagger, Smitty suspected otherwise.

Crowley gave a nod. "There'll be more where
this came from."

Smitty knew he shouldn't ask but wanted to get
to the bottom of things before he dug himself into
a deeper hole. "More of what?"

Crowley looked to Bo before turning back to
Smitty and narrowing his gaze. "You know what
we're trying to accomplish here, don't you?"

Suddenly, Smitty felt out of the loop. "Grow
Mescalero Exploration. Best way we can."

"That's right." Crowley looked pleased. "And the
best way to do it is with good information. Quicker
we figure out where to start, the quicker we can get
you out there on the hunt. Be sure we're making
all the right moves when we start acquiring more
leases and get to drilling."

That confirmed Smitty's suspicion that he was
being groomed to be an oil scout. But it still didn't
mean they were doing anything wrong. The energy
sector was as sneaky as it gets and protected their
secrets like plans for the D-Day invasion. That
would explain the cagey nature of his cohorts, who
apparently included Crowley. But it didn't explain
why a law enforcement officer would be involved in
an oil and gas operation.

"I get my role here, Sheriff. I've been in the oil

business for a while now. Know this country like the back of my hand. But ain't exactly figured what you bring to the table."

"Well, I'm a consultant, you see."

"Consulting on what exactly?"

Crowley looked as though he was searching for the right words. "Legal. Matters."

Smitty grinned. "Thinking a lawyer is better suited for that. Am I right?"

The sheriff kept his composure, but his face tightened. It was clear he didn't like to be questioned, particularly by a former ex-con. "Well, that's where this gets a bit over your head, son. Upper-management decisions you've not encountered on an oil rig or out servicing wells."

Smitty fought to keep cool. "Fair enough. Still doesn't explain how you fit in."

"I *fit in* because it's my job to uphold the law. And there's a lot of people who don't respect it. Particularly folks from out of town. Folks who use up resources. Pilfer our water and road material supplies. Suck up our oil and gas, then take the money and run."

"Way of the oil and gas world, Sheriff. Don't see how you can stop anyone from doing that."

"Well, you can't, really. But you can remind them this is a place that plays by the rules. And as the man in charge of enforcing said rules, I'll make it clear that it's better to do business with locals. People around here who respect the place. Folks like you, who need the work."

Now it was all too clear. Crowley's job was to make life hell for anyone who *wasn't* Mescalero

Exploration. It also explained why Vicky had been buying up oil field service companies over the past few months. With the sheriff making trouble for outsiders, it would force them right into her hands. In some ways, it was exactly how the mafia works. Even if she couldn't get every single lease as a producer, she could make money in a hundred other ways.

Smitty had to marvel at his boss's ingenuity. She was as ruthless as her brother, Preston, without *technically* breaking the law. And the sheriff was just as wily. He gets to earn on the side consulting for Mescalero, while gouging the competition and filling the county's coffers with money from fines and penalties. He would look like a hero to his constituents. No doubt he'd be sure to publicize his efforts in protecting the community from outsiders.

As a beneficiary of the plan, it was hard for Smitty not to jump on board. Still, though, he was suspicious of Crowley's motives for revealing the upper-management crap to lowly serfs. "Just as soon keep what we got here, so long as everything is on the up-and-up."

"Oh, it's on the up-and-up," Crowley assured.

The sheriff said it in a way that was unconvincing, but Smitty didn't care. As long as they weren't doing something dangerous, that was fine. It was the next topic that made him queasy.

Crowley's eyes narrowed. "Got a deputy friend down in Gray County that tells me you two boys were the first on the scene at the accident near Lefors. Said you pulled poor Lacey out of the wreck and held her hand until the ambulance got there."

Of course, Smitty knew that he and Bo had done nothing wrong, other than veer off course from Vicky's mission at Garrett's request. But Crowley's tone and stare were accusatory. He even looked back and forth between them as if looking for someone to crack.

Smitty answered, "Yeah, we were there. Wish we could've done something to stop it."

Crowley looked puzzled. "What was there to stop?"

Damn. Wrong answer. Smitty stuttered out the next part, "Well, I just meant the wreck, you know. Wish I could've slowed her down, I guess."

Crowley perked up. "So, she was speeding, was she?"

Smitty could kick himself. He was just digging a deeper hole. "Hard to gauge. We were a bit behind her. Looked like she just took the curve too fast."

"She's got a couple of small kids, you know." Crowley frowned. "Just thankful they weren't with her if she was driving reckless, like you say."

"Never said that," Smitty corrected, a bit testily. "Was just an accident. Can happen to anyone."

Crowley seemed pleased at having gotten a heated reaction. "And what were you two doing out there? Vicky said you were on your way to Borger."

Thinking quick on his feet, Smitty mustered up a lie. "Well, we were but then I remembered that I had a saddle to pick up in Lefors."

"For the Mescalero?" Crowley squinted. "Vicky didn't mention anything about that."

"No, it was a personal matter. Picked it up as a favor to Butch Kohl."

"For *Butch*?" Crowley spit out the name like rotten garbage. "And you did this favor while you were on the clock for Mescalero?"

The only good thing about this interaction was Bo's silence on the subject. He'd figured him for Vicky's stooge, which in turn meant he was a stoolie for the sheriff. But so far, he hadn't contradicted a single word. *Maybe he really had changed?*

"Sheriff, I made a mistake. Shouldn't have done that on company time. But I'm glad I did, so I could be there." Smitty looked up to Bo and then back again. "Now, if this is all the business we've got here, then we need to get back to work."

Crowley's demeanor softened. "Guess it's just my nature to be curious, even about matters that are none of my affair." He held up a finger. "Before I let you go, there is one thing that does concern your friend, and a little situation we've got out at the Kohl Ranch."

Smitty didn't know what that entailed but knew it would be bad. It was almost certain given the earlier conversation with Vicky that they were pitting him against the Kohls.

Chapter 28

Kim drove her silver Chevy Tahoe up the highway after touching down in Amarillo, feeling guilty about not stopping by the hospital to see Lacey. But there was nothing she could do there. Her energy would be better spent hunting down the bad guys who did this rather than sitting around worrying. As her mind raced, she gazed out at the rolling plains just south of Pampa.

On Kim's last visit, the place had been scorched by drought. But almost miraculously everything changed. A snowy winter and a rainy spring had turned the brown prairie wasteland to a lush Irish green. The endless clear sky she remembered was now dark and foreboding, with billowy gray clouds that descended from the heavens and appeared close enough to touch.

Expecting an update from Garrett, Kim was surprised to discover that the incoming call was from Conner Murray, who was likely seeking a report of his own for the president. She swiped the screen and hit the speaker button. "Nothing new since last time we spoke. Headed to the ranch to retrieve the device. Will fly it back to headquarters as soon as I have it."

"Well, there's news on my end," Murray offered. "More to the story than we thought."

Kim hated surprises, and they just kept coming. "Please tell me it isn't something bad."

"Just found out that Shepard made an unannounced trip to Pantex today."

Kim had never met Secretary of Defense (SECDEF) Randall Shepard, but he had a damn good reputation. The farm boy from South Dakota was a two-term congressman and former Marine Corps colonel, horribly injured in an IED explosion in Afghanistan. Fitted with prosthetic legs, he went back home to Sioux Falls after a long recovery at Walter Reed National Military Medical Center in Bethesda, Maryland, to found and run a highly successful commodity trading firm. His return to military service as SECDEF had nothing to do with a lust for war, and everything to do with being a soldier's advocate.

Although he'd swapped his iconic olive-green service dress uniform for a dark pinstripe, Shepard was a Devil Dog to the bone, who still wore his thick silver hair high and tight. He was also just as trim and fit as he was in the Corps. Roundly respected by politicians on both sides of the aisle and adored by almost everyone in the armed forces, he would make a hell of a prize for the Iranians—a nice reprisal after the assassination of their cherished General Soleimani.

"What's the purpose of Shepard's trip?" Kim asked.

Murray seemed to be reading as he explained, "Looks like he's inspecting a joint program between

Department of Defense (DOD) and Department of Energy (DOE). Pantex, Sandia, and Lawrence Livermore are on the itinerary. Can't get into those details but the stop in Texas was part of some big tour across the country. All I can say is—"

"Liam Bayat," Kim interrupted. "Anything to do with him?"

"That was the first thing I checked. Bayat has no part in this meeting. Only upper echelon. So, it's unlikely he knew any of the specifics, like when and where. Security detail keeps all that close hold for the purposes of OPSEC. Shepard was scheduled to visit Liam's department head. But that's just a coincidence."

Kim had been in the intel world long enough not to believe in coincidences. Chances were slim to none that those two events lined up by accident. Operational security, or OPSEC, would be tight for the SECDEF. It wasn't unheard-of for a high-level official to make an unannounced stop, particularly when inspecting a highly sensitive project. And anything involving a nuclear weapons facility and national laboratories was as sensitive as it gets.

Something was off, though, and Kim could feel it down deep. "Okay, I really need a look at that device then." She said the next part more to herself. "Sooner the better."

Murray narrowed his eyes. "What makes you say that?"

"Timing is just too perfect. I don't think Liam was involved in an intel collection op."

There was a brief pause on Murray's end. "Some

sort of malware maybe? A worm or virus that could damage the plant?"

"Not that, either. Liam was directed to take the device into the building. Nothing to hurt in there like centrifuges or radioactive material. Anything destroyed could easily be replaced. And everything on their servers is backed up. For all the effort, it wouldn't do that much damage."

Of course, Murray's suggestion was certainly worth consideration. The Iranians had wanted retribution for the Stuxnet cyberattack that damaged centrifuges at their Natanz nuclear enrichment facility. Sabotaging a place like Pantex would be a coup for sure, but an unequal reprisal. Using operatives to attack an American nuclear target directly was a declaration of war.

Kim felt the sting of exclusion. "What are you *not* telling me, Conner?"

A clearing of the throat followed a brief pause. "Not sure what you mean?"

"I mean Tehran wouldn't go beyond a collection op without a good reason."

"They don't need a reason. They've wanted to annihilate the 'Great Satan' for decades."

Kim was scanning her brain for the root cause; the first incident coming to mind was the assassination of Quds Force commander Qasem Soleimani in 2020. But the Iranians had already retaliated with a missile attack against an American military base in Iraq. That could be part of the reason, but all of a sudden, Kim remembered her *slap upside the head* comment from days before. Iran was retaliating because we'd already struck a major blow.

"You're holding back." Kim's tone was accusatory, just as intended. "What did we do?"

"I beg your pardon."

Kim's patience was wearing thin, but she wanted to keep her composure. "I'm not an idiot. Don't treat me like one."

"I know you're not an idiot, Kim. That's not what's going on here."

"Then what is going on?"

There was an edge to Murray's voice she'd never heard before. "You don't *need to know* everything at this point."

"I *do* need to know if you want my help."

A sigh preceded Murray's response. "It's compartmented. Joint program I told you about with NSA. Only a few of your colleagues, mostly leadership, and a few top dogs on the seventh floor have been read in on it. You of all people should appreciate limiting the distribution."

"I appreciate that when it's none of my business. But the deeper we dig, the uglier this gets. And right now, I have a front-row seat for something that I feel is about to get worse."

"I told you we should be preparing for all-out war. What more do you need to know?"

"I need to know *why*," Kim stated flatly. "Until I know the lengths to which Tehran is willing to go, I won't know where they'll draw the line. Or if they'll even draw one."

Murray let out a groan. "Listen, here's what you need to know. In coordination with the Israelis, we hit a couple of key Iranian nuclear military targets about six months ago. Turns out that two of the Iranian Supreme Leader's sons happened to be there as part of a visiting delegation. Some sort of state visit. It was just a wrong-place-at-the-wrong-time kind of fiasco."

For the sake of operational security, Murray shouldn't be sharing this information over an open line. But given the situation on the ground, Kim considered it worth the risk. The consequences of not getting the full picture could make matters even worse.

"Why haven't I heard anything about this, Conner? Why hasn't *the world* heard about it? I'm shocked Tehran didn't go straight to the UN."

"And say what? 'The U.S. and Israel blew up our secret nuclear weapons base we weren't supposed to have, and we're pissed about it'?"

It wasn't all that shocking. Something similar had happened back in 2007, when the Israelis took out Syria's bourgeoning nuclear weapons program. Damascus moaned for about five seconds and then let it all pass. It was about the time Britney Spears had a meltdown and shaved her hair off, which meant the world had more important things to discuss. But there was still more to this Iranian story that Murray wasn't sharing.

"What else, Conner? No shame in us publicizing something like that. There's a reason *we're* not talking about it internally, either."

A pause and a huff from Murray. "Women and kids were there, too. Families of the delegation. The Supreme Leader's grandchildren. Obviously, he's pissed and out for blood."

Kim didn't know if she could rest any easier

knowing why Tehran had taken the gloves off. But at least now it made sense why Iranian operatives were in America's heartland. It wasn't about stealing secrets, or even sabotage. It was about getting revenge. And assassinating a high-level U.S. official was a good way to start. What Garrett had in his possession wasn't a collection device or malware. It was most certainly a bomb meant for the secretary of defense.

Chapter 29

Garrett's first few minutes with Liam had been awkward to say the least. Seeing a man, who was supposed to be dead, sneaking up behind him with a gun had painted an automatic ugly picture of what might've gone down. But a quick debrief inside the cab of his truck revealed what Garrett already knew earlier from Smitty's report of a hit squad in the white Suburban. This Iranian operation was way bigger than a one-man show. Liam's follow-up confirmed it.

Not surprisingly, he immediately insisted they check on his son, Wade, before doing anything else. Given the circumstances, Garrett would've done no differently. Of course, more than likely the Quds Force operatives were either on the run or hunkered down in a safe house but the fact that they'd come after Lacey meant they could still turn up the heat.

As they drove up to the ranch, Liam leaned forward, his worried eyes trained ahead in search of his son, who was usually out for a run this time every day after school. Several vain attempts to reach him by phone had ratcheted up his father's anxiety, which would not be tempered until Wade was safe and sound.

Garrett looked over at the Beretta semiautomatic pistol in Liam's shaky grip. "Dead guy they found on the side of the road out there. That your first?"

Although Liam was a combat engineer and had been deployed to Iraq and Afghanistan, it didn't necessarily mean he'd ever taken a life. Most veterans hadn't. It was more than likely that on top of everything else, he was processing the life altering fact that he had just killed a man.

Liam looked down at the gun and stared at it as if he were seeing it for the very first time. "Had this thing for years but never thought I'd use it. Hell, I didn't even know if I'd have the guts to pull the trigger if it came to that."

"But you did," Garrett confirmed.

Liam shook his head. "Too late for Lacey, it seems."

There was a temptation for Garrett to really let him have it. Maybe if Liam had acted sooner, she would be okay. Or maybe if he'd watched his six a little closer, he would've known he was followed. But in the *what-if* game everyone's a loser. Garrett had learned that the hard way. Aside from that, he couldn't say he wouldn't have done the same. If someone in his family was imprisoned and tortured, nothing would stop him from getting them back. As much as he wanted to blame Liam for what happened to Lacey, the reality was that the man sitting beside him was struggling with the harsh reality that his father would be executed.

"Nothing's too late yet," Garrett assured. "Lacey's in surgery, and she's in great hands. I've learned over the years not to waste time on things you can't control. Focus on what you can. And right now, we can make sure your son is safe and then hunt down the ones who did this."

Liam's face brightened. "You're going to let me help?"

"So far, you're the only one who knows what they look like. We may even need you to draw them out."

Liam paused, as if contemplating what those words actually meant. "Like bait?"

"I don't like to think of it that way." Garrett shrugged. "But there's a possibility they're going to want to retaliate for the betrayal. Or they might just want to shut you up."

Liam gave a solemn nod. "I'll put myself out there if it means bringing them down."

"Well, I don't plan to risk any more lives if I can help it. But I'm definitely going to need you on my team."

"What about the cops?" Liam asked. "I can give a description of the guys I saw. What they were driving and all that. Maybe there were cameras around or something? Ways to track their vehicles? I'm pretty sure they were rentals."

"We have to keep law enforcement in the dark for now. At this point, they don't know any more than that some guy was shot and left for dead. It'll cause a stir, but they'll suspect it was drug related. Deal gone bad on a backcountry road. That sort of thing."

Liam turned back again, looking a bit shocked.

"But shouldn't we get everyone we can out looking for them? Get word out to the media. Broadcast it all over."

"That'd be fine if this was a missing persons case, or even a regular manhunt. But this is something else completely. First of all, these guys are extremely dangerous, and we don't want just anyone engaging them, especially some well-meaning yokels. And the people I'm working with believe that a big public manhunt will just push them further beneath the radar."

"So, we're just going to do nothing?"

"Not nothing. My friend at the CIA is coming down here now. She has all the right contacts at the FBI and will know just what to do. But that means we need to bring these guys out into the open. Make them show their faces."

Liam pointed to the entrance of his property on the left side of the road. "Over there. That's my place."

Garrett tapped the brake, crossed over a culvert, then rolled over the cattle guard that rattled his GMC for an instant. With no sign of Liam's son on his daily afternoon run, Garrett was getting a bit apprehensive. Of course, it was nothing compared to what the father must be feeling.

Liam moved to the edge of his seat, his eyes fixed on a black Ford pickup parked in front of the house. The driver's-side door ajar. "That's Wade's truck."

Garrett didn't like what he saw. "Normal for him to leave it open like that?"

Liam's eyes swept the property. "Never. Not with all the dust we get out here."

With that unsettling response, Garrett reached behind his back and pulled the Nighthawk from its holster. There was a temptation to suggest that Liam hang tight, but it was obvious that this father was ready to unleash hell on anyone who came after his son.

After putting the truck in park, Garrett pointed at the front door. "You go through the main entrance, and I'll go around the side. Don't want to spook your boy if everything's okay. But if you see anything weird, just holler and I'll come through the back. Okay?"

Liam hopped out of the truck and sprinted to the front of the house. A half-second behind, Garrett ran around the left side, stopping just short of the backyard. A quick peek around the corner revealed someone in a black hoodie standing on the deck. Garrett had just begun to take aim when Liam stepped outside.

A few seconds with his sights on target and Garrett lowered his weapon. Clearly, all was as it should be. He concealed his pistol and moved to the side of the house, finding Wade in a state of confusion at seeing the Beretta in his dad's hand. "Why do you—"

Before he could get the question out, Liam interrupted. "You here by yourself?"

"Yeah, what's going on?" Hearing Garrett's approach, Wade turned back looking nervous. "This about that guy who got shot west of town? Everybody's talking about it."

Liam wrapped his son in his arms and pulled him tight. After a solid squeeze, he let him loose. "Why the hell was your truck door open?"

Wade pointed to his muddy football cleats by the water hose. "Left it that way for like two seconds to grab my running shoes. Jeremy wanted to hit the track before dinner."

Exasperation was written all over Liam's face. "*Why* didn't you answer your phone?"

"I was in a hurry, Dad." Wade looked to Garrett, as if searching for answers to the unexpected inquisition. "Was going to call you on my way back to town."

Liam looked to Garrett, too, and shot him the universal *I'll murder him later* look that one parent gives to another. He turned back to his son. "Okay, we're going to go with my friend for a while. So, call Jeremy and tell him not today. All right?"

Wade looked to Garrett and back again. "Who is he?"

"Mr. Kohl works security. Everything's fine but we're taking some extra precautions."

"*Precautions?* For what?" Before Liam could answer, Wade responded with the line every kid of a parent that works at Pantex has uttered a thousand times before. "Oh, wait, let me guess. You can't talk about it."

Liam put his hands on his son's shoulders and looked him in the eye. "Just grab your stuff. Quickly. We have to go."

Garrett couldn't help but grin to himself at the exchange between the father and his teenage son, wondering if this is what he had to look forward to in the not-too-distant future. Asadi was already showing signs of wanting more independence. While the discussion playing out before him was probably as routine an interaction as any between parent and teenager, it was a brief moment of respite. Despite all the calamity, it felt like a return to normalcy.

Garrett was just about to head back to the truck when the phone vibrated in his front pocket. He saw that it was Kim calling, likely in search of an update. "Take it you're on your way?"

There was a little dead air, as she must have hit a dip in the road. "Where are you?"

"Out at Liam's. Picking up his son and we're leaving now." Clearly in earshot, Garrett turned and stepped away for some privacy. "Backpack is at the ranch."

"With Asadi?" Kim shot back.

Garrett could hear the worry in her voice. "Yeah. And my dad. What's wrong?"

"Call them now. Tell them to get as far away from it as possible."

"Wait. *Why?* What's—"

"Garrett, I just found out that Defense Secretary Shepard was making an unannounced visit to Pantex today. With a scheduled briefing in Liam's office."

Kim didn't have to say any more. Garrett already knew what that meant. For the second time that day he'd put the lives of the people he loved most in the world in danger. Without another word, he ended the call and immediately dialed the house— praying to God above that someone, anyone, would pick up the phone.

Chapter 30

Asadi stared down at the black Adidas backpack on the concrete floor of the barn wondering what on earth was inside. The only thing for sure was that it wasn't workout clothes, or at least not that alone. Butch inched a little closer to it, as if the thing might be playing possum, waiting for the right moment to jump up and scurry out the door. Asadi's urge to open the bag was tempered by the old man's words of caution, which sounded more like he was trying to convince himself.

Butch glanced around the barn as if someone might be listening. "Best leave that alone, I reckon. Suppose it's fine there where it sits."

Asadi looked around also in search of a better place to store the backpack, which was currently resting beside his punching bag. "I move a little?" He raised the boxing gloves to show the reason why. "Want workout before I do chores."

Butch gazed back at the horses as they lumbered up to the front of their stalls. The wheels in his mind were clearly turning over what to do next. "Okay, sonny, move it to the workbench. Good a spot as any until Kim gets here and we send it on its merry way."

Asadi hefted the backpack onto his shoulder and walked it over to the cluttered table against the wall. He'd just raked his forearm across the top to knock away a couple of greasy rags and a WD-40 can when he heard the soft *tok-tok-tok* of cowboy boots on concrete from behind.

Savanah walked into the barn wearing a big grin, which seemed to grow wider on the approach. "Well, if it ain't the champ. Never knew I was friends with Rocky Balboa."

There was that name again. *Rocky.* Asadi determined then and there that he had to see that movie. He placed the pack on the counter and then marched over to meet her halfway.

Before anything got mushy, Butch spun on a heel and made his way out the door. "Got to go check on a trough in the back pasture. Saw some standing water beside it earlier. Probably a float valve gone bad."

Before Asadi could ask if he needed any help, Butch was already out the door. He looked to Savanah, fighting off the temptation to beam with pride. "You hear about fight?"

"*Duh.* Everybody's heard about it. Sam and Craig were so embarrassed you whupped them that they didn't even want to go to class. Principal had to escort them to their desks."

Asadi wanted to jump for joy but thought he'd better play it cool. "I not feel too bad."

"Nobody does," Savanah assured. "Everybody

thinks those boys got what they deserved. That's all anyone could talk about all day. That, and how you got arrested."

Asadi was pretty sure he'd only gotten a stern warning, but given the impressed look on Savanah's face, he decided not to correct her just yet. He was no longer her safe little friend. He was tough and dangerous. A bad-boy reputation like that could get you a long way in a Wild West cowboy town like Canadian, Texas.

"Bridger came to jail," Asadi explained. "He fix everything with the sheriff. No trouble."

"Well, I wouldn't be so sure." Savanah dropped her smile. "No trouble with the sheriff, maybe, but Sam and Craig are another matter. They're really pissed. This ain't over yet."

Uh-oh. Asadi hadn't really thought about that. He assumed that since he had won the fight, the whole mess was over and done. Eyeing the old punching bag, he felt the sudden urge to get back to practicing his left-right combos. In the process of thinking of a reason to excuse himself, he heard the familiar voice of Savanah's father call out from behind.

"Looks like a whole lot of loafing on the job around here." Ray Smitty sauntered up, looking in the mood for a little playful teasing, which was pretty much always.

It had taken some getting used to, but Asadi had learned to give it right back. "Just in time for hard stuff. You ready work?"

Ray stopped in his tracks and made a big show of looking like he was turning to run. Mid-pivot, he burst into laughter and continued his lazy stroll inside. "Was headed back to the Mescalero but wanted to stop by." He got serious as he looked to Asadi. "Any updates on Lacey? Hate to bother Garrett, but me and Crystal can hardly stand the waiting."

Asadi hadn't heard anything. Of course, the only phone they had was at the house, and neither he nor Butch had been inside since they got back. "Don't know. Maybe need check." He was about to run and call when Ray grabbed his shoulder and stopped him in his tracks.

"Hold up there." Ray narrowed his gaze on the backpack. "That's the bag Lacey had with her, ain't it?"

"Garrett said bring it back to ranch," Asadi explained.

"He say what to do with it when you got here?"

Asadi shook his head. "Just said keep it until Kim arrive."

"Don't know what it is but it seems important." Ray eyed the backpack. "Maybe you ought to take it on in the house? A bit steamy out here with the thunderstorm brewing. Might do better in the AC." He raised his hands to his sides. "Just a thought."

Asadi hated to think that whatever was inside of it might get ruined. He dashed over to the bag, slung it on his shoulder, and then looked to Savanah. "Want go in and get a Coke?"

"Sounds good." Her face brightened as she turned to her dad. "Want one too, Daddy?"

"Nah, we gotta git." Ray tilted his head to where he parked on the side of the barn. "Bo Clevenger and his boy are waiting in the truck and we're due back at the ranch. Just wanted to check in and see if there was any news."

"Wait." Savanah's face scrunched together. "Did you say . . . Bo and his boy?"

"Yeah, kid about your age. Name is Sam, I think. Big chunk of Spam. Don't talk much."

Asadi caught eyes with Savanah, but beat her to the question. "Sam Clevenger?"

"That's right." Ray's face brightened. "Y'all buddies?"

Asadi didn't know what to do with that information. But the fact that his archnemesis was sitting just outside his sanctuary seemed like a horrible dream. Before he could follow up, Savanah looked over at Ray. "We'll be fine here, Daddy. Gonna feed the horses and then I'll head back to the house. We hear anything about Lacey, we'll give you a shout."

"That'll work, darlin' girl." A wink from Ray. "See you back at the house around suppertime."

After a kiss on the top of his daughter's head, Ray made a quick departure out the front of the barn. Asadi and Savanah waited in silence until the truck door slammed and the diesel engine snarled as they drove away. With the coast clear, they made their way over to the house, hopped up on the porch, and went inside.

Confirming what he thought he'd heard, Asadi ran to the phone but must've caught it after the last ring. Suspecting it might be Garrett, he placed the backpack on the kitchen table, then turned back to the phone to give his dad a call. He hadn't even taken a step when he saw a figure dart past the window toward the back door.

Ray barged through the door, stepped inside, and searched around the kitchen, looking a bit wild-eyed. "Where's that bag?"

Asadi gave it a gentle pat. "Right here."

Ray looked to his daughter. "Go outside and get in the truck."

"But we haven't fed the horses," Savanah argued.

"Just go. Right now." Ray turned to Asadi, extended his left arm slowly, and made the come-here motion with his hand. "Come on," he whispered. "Move your butt, pardner."

Asadi instinctively reached for the bag, thinking it needed to be protected. But Ray threw up his palm like a crossing guard halting traffic. His face went from fearful to frantic.

Asadi stopped short. "No want bag?"

"Nope." Ray shook his head vigorously. "No want bag at all. Just leave it right there."

Although totally confused, Asadi abided. He moved toward the door, with Ray's hand firmly at his back, and ran outside. A leap from the porch, and the trio sprinted across the yard, out into the pasture where Smitty's truck was waiting. Unfortunately, the sudden interruption and wild departure wasn't Asadi's only dilemma. Sam Clevenger was waiting there, too.

Chapter 31

Kim hadn't planned on making a trip to Pantex until after she'd retrieved the backpack, but with the potential threat against Defense Secretary Shepard she figured it was worth a detour. Fortunately, she was only a few minutes past the nuclear weapons plant. A call from Murray had alerted the facility security team, and scheduled her to give an impromptu briefing—an interesting assignment when there was little certainty about what was going on.

Of course, it wouldn't be her first time to plan an operation on the fly. It would, however, be the first one involving a member of the president's cabinet. The turf war about to ensue would be of epic proportions. Neither the agent in charge of Shepard's security detail nor the head of plant operations would want to break any established protocols. But according to Murray, they were mandated to take her counsel under advisement.

Seated at the head of the conference room table, Kim looked left to Sergeant Nathan Graham, the lead agent from the Army's Protective Services Battalion. The protective detail was essentially the

Defense Department's version of the Secret Service. To her right was Beth Madison, the head of Pantex security. Kim had only assembled the two in hopes of limiting turf battles. But the scant intelligence she was able to provide on the possible threat to Shepard was already provoking visible cues that there would be staunch resistance.

Graham fired the first salvo. "We've got a schedule to keep, Manning." He jerked a thumb over his shoulder. "If the roads aren't safe, I'll call in a helo from Amarillo to get us back to the SECDEF's plane."

Before Kim could respond, Madison jumped right in with equal vigor. "Uh-uh. Nobody flies in here until I've approved it. For everyone's safety, certain areas are restricted. Even for you."

"Ms. Madison, I don't need *your* permission to protect our principal's life."

"That's true," Madison fired back. "But you *will* need my permission to fly a helicopter over this particular nuclear weapons facility. And right now, you don't have it."

Graham pulled out a cell phone from his suit pocket and waggled it at her. "Well, I'm pretty sure I can get that in about two seconds."

Kim raised her hand to Graham. "Nobody goes anywhere, for now. By road or by air. And that includes the SECDEF." She turned to Madison. "This place is on lockdown."

"*Lockdown?*" Madison's hands flew to her sides. "Do you even know the chain of events that will cause? The disturbances to plant operations. These people here have families who are waiting for them."

Kim sighed. "I want to make sure that nobody else is at risk before we send them out there. We don't know who else might be in danger. And we certainly don't know who all is involved."

"Involved in *what*, exactly?" Madison looked unimpressed. "You mean the dead body on the side of the road? Or the wreck out by Lefors involving the local woman?"

"We just need to be cautious." Kim looked to Graham, hoping for some support. "At least until we have some answers."

Madison shook her head and laughed. "If I went into panic mode every time somebody got shot over a meth deal gone wrong around here, no one would ever go home. So, unless you've got a damn good reason to disrupt everyone's lives then I suggest you get out of the way and let me do my job. We have a process here. Protocols. Tried and true."

"I get that," Kim argued, "but with Shepard here that changes things."

"It certainly does," Graham chimed in. "It means that unless you can produce some intel showing a viable threat then you need to stand down." He looked to Madison. "Respectfully, ma'am, that goes for you, too. We'll move out at my discretion."

Before Madison could ramp up again, Kim interrupted, and directed her next comment at the agent. "I think it's better that you stay grounded, just for a while until we know what we're up against. Give us a couple hours to figure some things out." She looked to Madison. "Same with this place. Nobody leaves Pantex until we know where we stand."

"On whose authority?" Madison countered.

"Because believe me, there will be a hell of a lot of people wanting to know."

Kim stated matter-of-factly, even though she had no official directive to hand out orders to anyone, "You can tell them that the order is on the authority of the deputy director of the National Security Council, Conner Murray." She knew she was overstepping her bounds in a major way, but her gut told her to exercise extreme caution.

Graham smirked. "Since when does the Agency have any command over anyone on American soil? Thought you were acting as an *advisor*?"

Madison looked equally amused. It seemed the Pantex security chief had found an ally in the strange bedfellow with whom she was at odds with only moments ago. A common enemy among government officials of every branch could always be found in the CIA.

"Well, here's some advice for you both." Kim took a moment to look them in the eye. "Something goes wrong, I mean horribly wrong, don't come crying to me. Because I'll be damn sure your disregard for what I'm telling you goes all the way to the top."

It was at that moment Kim realized she had them. Everybody had a boss. But in the federal service that stops at one place. And the thought of a call coming from the gods on high sent a shiver down the spines of even the staunchest of career bureaucrats. With her opponents on the ropes, it was time to launch another salvo.

"What we don't know," Kim continued, "is what's in that backpack. What we do know is that it comes from an Iranian operative, and it was meant to be inside this building."

"Would've never made it," Madison shot back. "Nothing comes into Pantex without a thorough inspection."

"It absolutely would have made it in," Kim countered. "Because it was to be delivered by one of your employees."

"One of *my* employees?" Madison looked incredulous. "Who?"

"Liam Bayat." Kim gave it a moment to sink in. "He came to us beforehand to let us know he was being extorted by the Iranians."

"There's no way." Madison wore a look that fell somewhere between confusion and betrayal. "Liam and I are old friends. He could've come to me at any time."

"He wanted to," Kim assured her. "But his extortionists had made it seem that he was being watched. So, he had to go further underground."

Graham gave an understanding nod. "So, *that's* how the CIA fits in?"

In reality, it wasn't as clean as all that. Liam, of course, had gone to the derelict barman Ike Hodges at Crippled Crows first, who next disclosed it to Garrett at the Stumblin' Goat. As clandestine operations go, this one was about as sophisticated as an outhouse. But it was still better than the alternative, which could've spelled a major victory for Quds Force.

"Liam made a trusted Agency contractor aware of his situation," Kim explained. "We were in the process of enacting countermeasures when the Iranians struck unexpectedly. The good news was that we were able to disrupt them. The bad news was that someone innocent was hurt."

"Dead body found near Lefors?" Madison suggested.

Kim shook her head. "Fortunately, he was one of the bad guys."

"Then the woman in intensive care," Graham asked. "The one in the accident?"

"It wasn't an accident," Kim said. "She was on our side. Just trying to help."

Madison lost her rigidity. "She going to pull through?"

"Don't know." Kim sighed. "Just want to make sure nothing bad happens to anyone else."

"What about Liam?" Madison looked genuinely concerned. "Is he okay?"

"Liam is with my guy. He's protected. Now it's just a matter of what to do next."

Graham leaned forward and put his hands on the table. "What do you want to do?"

Feeling a little more at ease now that everyone was coming together, Kim worked up a plan that involved a floor-to-ceiling search of the plant. But she'd not even gotten the first words out when the table shook, her chest rattled, and the air was filled with an echoing *thunk* and *boom*—a sensation not experienced since her war zone tours in Iraq and Afghanistan.

It was all too clear that the Iranians were not on the run. They were just getting started.

Chapter 32

Garrett eased up alongside Smitty's white Ford and made a quick head count to confirm everyone was alive and well. Old habits die hard, and despite the assurances from his dad, this former Green Beret wasn't taking any chances. The scene upon arrival was as odd as any he'd encountered in quite a while. Not only was everyone mobbed up behind the Mescalero Ranch truck, but his old rival, Bo Clevenger, was right there in the middle of the scrum.

Garrett edged his front bumper against the other pickup, to extend the protective berm in front of the house. They were a good forty yards from the potential blast zone, which was hopefully a wide-enough space if a bomb went off. He put the truck in park, hopped out into the dewy heat, and was met by his dad and Smitty, who immediately marched over.

Butch spoke first. "What the hell we waiting on? We gotta get that bag moved quick. Thing could go off any minute."

"You're exactly right," Garrett conceded. "That's why we need to be smart about this."

"Smart *hell*!" Butch spat. "I could've tossed the damn thing into the canyon twenty minutes ago and we'd all be fine. My damn *house* would be fine."

"I know, Daddy. But we gotta wait."

"Wait on what?" Butch demanded to know. "Bomb squad? When do they get here?"

The truth was that Garrett was still under strict orders by Kim to keep things under wraps. He'd only told Smitty they were coming to keep his father at bay. Until they could track down whoever was involved in this conspiracy, the matter was to be kept quiet. One leak to the media and there'd be widespread hysteria.

Just as Garrett was about to explain this, Liam came around to the back bumper with his kid in tow. Butch, further agitated by the growing spectacle and that nothing was getting done, looked the newcomer dead-on. "Who the hell are you?"

Garrett broke in. "This is Liam Bayat." A dip of the chin to the teenager. "And that's his boy Wade. They're here to help."

Recognizing there was a kid present, Butch looked to be trying to calm himself. "Sorry for the lack of hospitality. But as you can see, I got a big problem on my hands."

Garrett looked to Smitty. "Can you take Wade over with the others for a minute while we talk? Maybe introduce him to Asadi and Savanah."

Smitty seemed to get the idea that this might not be a conversation fitting for all ears. "Just holler if you need me."

As the two walked away, Garrett tilted his head to the back of the truck, wanting a little more privacy. Once they'd moved out of earshot, he leaned in a little as he spoke. "Look, we don't know exactly what's in that bag. But as I said on the phone, we have to take every precaution. Stay clear until we can get some help."

"What help?" Butch raised his hands and looked around. "We're it."

"Kim is sending a team," Garrett assured him. "They'll take care of it."

"That'll take hours," Butch argued. "Maybe longer. And what'll they do when they get here? At some point, somebody's gotta just go in there and see what it is."

"You're right," Liam chimed in. "End of the day, someone's going to have to go in there." He looked over the truck bed and stared at the house. "Might as well be me."

"*You?*" Garrett couldn't believe what he was hearing. "Why you?"

"Because of what I did in the army," Liam explained. "Only half of being a combat engineer is blowing things up. The other half was making sure they didn't. I can handle it."

"It's not your skill I'm worried about. The problem is if it *is* a bomb, then we don't know if it's stable. And if it's on a timer, it could go off at any moment."

"All the more reason to get in there now," Liam argued. "Every second counts."

"A timer?" Butch looked distraught. "I didn't even think about that."

Butch barged past Liam, but before he'd made it a couple of steps, Garrett grabbed his dad's shoulder and held him still. "Hold on there! Where you going?"

Butch pointed to the house. "To chunk that damn bag where it can't do no damage."

Garrett held up his hand. "You're not chunking anything, all right."

"Everything I own"—Butch pointed to the house—"is within them walls right there."

"It's just stuff," Garrett shot back.

Butch shook his head. "Photos of your mother. Her wedding ring. Everything she saved from when you were kids. It's not just *stuff* and I won't let it go."

Garrett felt a little guilty for his dismissive comment, but none of those things were worth dying over. And his mother wouldn't have wanted that, either. However, that didn't mean it would hurt any less if they lost it. His collection of knives and arrowheads that he'd assembled since childhood were under the roof of a home built by his great-grandfather. The place had survived cartel assassins and foreign mercenaries. The old man wasn't going to give up now.

"Daddy, it would hurt to see all that go. I'm not gonna lie. But we can't be foolish."

Liam stepped in between them. "The bottom line is that we don't know what it is. And we're not going to know until we see what's inside that bag." He eyed the house for a moment. "No sense in us all standing around doing nothing. Especially when there might be something that helps us track down the people behind all this."

Garrett wanted to argue but Liam was right. It wasn't just about the house. There was a chance that whatever was in that backpack might contain evidence. Aside from that, nobody was coming to the rescue in the near future. There was a good chance it might be exactly what it was supposed to be—a cyber collection device. And the best person to determine if it was harmless was the engineer beside him, who'd spent his Army career working with explosives.

Letting loose of his father, Garrett turned back to Liam. "You and me then. We open the bag to see what we're dealing with. If it's a bomb, we high-tail it. If it's harmless, then at least we'll know. And maybe it will provide some clues as to how we find the ones responsible."

Certain there would be a major objection from Asadi and the others if they announced their plans, Garrett began a brisk march around the tailgate of his GMC with Liam trailing behind. Few times in his life had he felt this uncertain. But his piercing guilt over what happened to Lacey was only matched by his burning hatred for the men who harmed her. If laying his life on the line could bring about some justice, then he'd gladly take that risk.

LIAM SHOVED DOWN THE TEMPTATION to look back at his son as he headed toward the house. If they caught eyes, even for a second, he'd lose his nerve. With the stress of the risk, his brain conjured up images both real and imagined. He saw the faces of his kids—his father—a spark inside that bag, then roaring flames from a smoking crater. It was somewhere between his life flashing before his eyes and an instinctual telegraphed warning from deep within.

As Liam climbed onto the porch he noticed that Garrett lagged in his pace, naturally expecting the former combat engineer would take the lead. But his old job in the Army was a far cry from a bomb tech. Locating them was one thing. Disarming them was quite another.

If they actually did find one inside that bag, he'd be shocked if he could do anything about it. Despite his earlier claim, his skills were rusty. And he lacked the training to defuse anything more than the most basic explosive devices.

Liam made a split decision to turn around and look for Wade. He couldn't see him, at least not in that brief second anyhow, but he could envision his son in his mind. The kid would put on a brave face and play the part of the tough guy. But Liam knew better. Wade would be terrified.

Liam stepped inside the house and took a deep breath. He expected panic to set in, but instead felt at ease, as his Sapper training from Fort Leonard Wood all came rushing back. Before Garrett could point it out, he spotted the black backpack with the white Adidas logo sitting atop the kitchen table. They moved to it in silence, as if their voices could set it off.

Whatever was in that bag had been through a horrible car accident earlier, so a good jostling was not the trigger. But the big question was "What was?" Ticking time bombs, as seen in the movies, were extremely rare. In places like Iraq and Afghanistan, the preferred way was a trip mechanism or manual detonator, utilizing a signal from a walkie-talkie or cell phone.

Despite the realization that movement wasn't a factor, Liam gently drew the bag toward him, then pinched the pull tab on the zipper and gave it a tug. When it didn't budge, he gave a couple more harder yanks that yielded the same result. On closer inspection of the zipper, there was a residue on the teeth where the bag had been superglued shut.

Before Liam could even ask, Garrett had lifted his denim shirt above the waist and unsheathed the Moore Maker field knife from his hip scabbard. The glint of the razor-sharp blade plunged into the bag with ease, and Garrett dragged it parallel to the zipper from front to back. Whatever was inside was shrouded in a bundle of gym clothes—gray sweatpants, white Nike workout shirt, and a thick navy blue Under Armour hoodie.

Liam took a stab at a joke to try to lighten the tension. "Kind of reminds me of that Indiana Jones movie when they're opening up the Ark."

Garrett didn't miss a beat. "Hope it turns out better for us than it did the Nazis."

With the rest of that horrifying movie scene playing out in his mind, Liam unwrapped the athletic gear. But even fully uncovered, it didn't reveal much. The object in question had the appearance of a coffee thermos, although a few inches longer and about twice the circumference. There were no wires. No fuse. And no antenna. *Maybe it was a collection device after all*.

Liam knew what Garrett was thinking. They'd both seen their share of improvised explosive devices (IEDs) in war zones, many of which were designed by Quds Force, and this didn't have the same look.

Encased in a glossy graphite-colored plastic like an iPhone, it more closely resembled something once hawked by Steve Jobs than anything built by Iranian commandos.

Liam glanced over at Garrett. "Looks like it was what they said it was after all."

"Could be." Garrett kept his gaze on the object. "But we don't know that for sure."

"No. We don't. But it doesn't look like any kind of bomb I've ever seen. More like a casing for computer hardware."

"What makes you say that?" Garrett asked.

"Size, for one. This is too small to pack a big enough punch to do large-scale damage." Liam tapped the outside of it with his fingernail. "And this thin plastic wouldn't do much. For maximum effectiveness you want metal shrapnel. Something that can rip a person in half." He turned back to Garrett. "I'm not saying this wouldn't do some damage. But for all the effort the Iranians are going to, they'd want more bang for their buck." Liam added, "No pun intended."

"All right then." Garrett reached over and ran his thumb across the single screw atop the canister. "Let's crack this thing open and see what's inside."

"You sure?" Liam studied the opening. "If your friend has a cyber team ready to go, they may want it left untouched."

"That's true. But I can't hand something over until I know what it is. Be sure that it's safe. And right now, we're just guessing."

Liam couldn't disagree. Just because it didn't look like a bomb didn't mean it wasn't one. If they'd gone this far, then why not a little more. He pulled the Leatherman from his pocket, flipped open the screwdriver, and went to work. Four counterclockwise turns and the canister lid was loose. With his right hand he stabilized the container; with the left he pulled off the top. It only took a few inches of lifting out the contents to find the puzzle pieces he recognized.

The first was an internal antenna; the second was what looked to be about three pounds of C-4. It wasn't hard to figure out what those two things were doing together. The question was what to do next. While Garrett probably wasn't familiar with the mechanism, he was certainly no stranger to plastic explosive, having likely used something similar on direct-action assignments to blow open locks or breach barred doors.

Garrett's voice got quiet. "Just set it back like you found it. Nice and gentle."

Liam didn't move. With the contents already halfway out, there was as big a chance that it would detonate putting it back together. "Hold on."

"What the hell for?" Garrett whispered.

Liam turned to Garrett. "Nothing's changed. I still have to disarm it."

"Everything's changed." Garrett's voice rose a little. "We wanted to know what we were dealing with, and now we do. Let's get out of here and let the pros take care of it."

"What pros? You said it yourself: we don't know when they're going to get here."

"Well, at least it's stable."

"This high explosive hooked to a blasting cap." Liam turned to Garrett. "It's *not* stable."

"But it's not set to go off? No timer or anything?"

"No timer, but there's a receiver and an electrical detonator." Liam turned back and studied it again. "Fixed to some sort of comms device. Something I've never seen before. There's a frequency or something that'll activate it, but I'm not sure what that is yet."

"Like a cell phone maybe?" Garrett asked.

"Not that." Liam studied the device as he racked his brain. "Some sort of duplex communications system maybe. Hell, I don't know."

"Well, this thing can park here until Christmas for all I care. Let it sit."

"That's the problem," Liam argued. "It might not sit. A damn plane or helicopter flying over might activate it. This tech is totally new to me."

Garrett got still, and it looked like he was intently listening, possibly for aircraft flying overhead. Before he could respond, Liam interrupted. "Go back behind the truck with the others. I'll handle it."

"You crazy?" Garrett shot back. "Come on now. Let's git while we still can."

Liam wasn't crazy but he wasn't completely sane, either. What happened to Lacey, what was happening now, was all his fault. The past was the past, but the future was wide open. From here on out, his life meant nothing with the world in jeopardy. He had to undo what he'd done.

"I've got this." Liam eyed the device. "It's not complicated. It's just delicate."

"*Delicate?* I've seen this stuff go off before and there's not a damn thing delicate about it."

"Now or never, Garrett. I'm about to start working."

"What can I do to talk some sense into you?"

"You can't. I'm doing this."

Garrett let out a huff. "Absolutely sure?"

"Never more sure about anything in my life."

Garrett eyed the door, sighed again, and turned back. "Then what can I do to help?"

Liam didn't want to admit it but he was happy to have some company. "It's a little dark over here. Can you get some light on this thing?"

Garrett moved to the kitchen drawer, riffled around through the junk, pulled out a blue flashlight, and clicked the back of it with his thumb. Looking a bit surprised at the bright bulb, he shook his head and smiled. "Hate that we just wasted a miracle on good batteries."

Liam pulled out a chair and took a seat, as Garrett returned to the table, leaned over, and aimed the flashlight at the contents of the bomb. Three pounds of C-4 probably wasn't enough to level the house. It was, however, enough to make a pretty big mess. They wouldn't need a gurney to gather their remains. Just a mop and bucket.

While Liam should've been focusing on the bomb, he was still stuck on one big question. *Why?* The amount of plastic explosive was nothing to scoff at, but it wasn't enough to kill a lot of people or even inflict major structural damage. The Iranians would never take such a major risk for such little reward. Quds Force was up to something big.

Chapter 33

Kim sprinted from the conference room to the hallway to find a scene of chaos playing out several doors down. What was once the control center for Pantex security was engulfed in flames and billowing black smoke. Before she could restate her request to circle the wagons, both Madison and Graham were on their cell phones, likely calling the people they were unwilling to bother only minutes before during their meeting.

Kim sprinted outside to make her own call. She didn't know who was responsible for the explosion but had a sneaking suspicion of what was inside Liam Bayat's backpack. With the wailing of sirens filling the air, and fire trucks racing to the scene, she moved to the side of the building, hoping like hell Garrett answered his phone. Fortunately, he picked up immediately.

"Your hunch was right, Kim. It *was* a bomb."

Confused, she wondered if he heard the commotion and pieced it together. Surely news of the explosion hadn't traveled that fast. "How'd you know?"

"About the C-4?" A snicker on Garrett's end.

"We just cut the backpack open and looked inside. Liam disarmed it."

"Disarmed it?" Kim paused, finally piecing it all together. "Okay, how?"

"Don't ask me." Garrett chuckled. "Had my eyes shut the whole time."

Kim had to smile. Garrett was one of the only people she knew who could keep a sense of humor in the face of death. Of course, she couldn't condone it. If something had happened to either him or Liam, she'd live under that shadow for the rest of her life.

"Garrett, I told you not to do anything until the team arrived. You could've been killed."

"Well, I'm not one to sit on my hands. You know that. Especially when the ones who did this to Lacey are still out there."

As an ambulance pulled up along the side of the building, Kim eased further around the back so she could hear better. "I need you and Liam to get here as quick as possible."

"What the hell's going on? I hear sirens."

Kim put her palm up to her free ear to block out the noise. "That's why I'm calling. A bomb went off. Here inside the building."

"Anyone hurt?"

"I don't know. Just happened. But this place is going into lockdown."

"Okay, it'll take us forty-five minutes to get there from the ranch. A hell of a lot longer if they're shutting down the front gate."

"*Damn.*" Kim looked up at the roofs of the buildings surrounding the courtyard. "Think you could get a lift from Ike?"

"He'll fly us there if he's around. The big question is, can you get us cleared? I don't think Pantex is too keen on casual flyovers. A surface-to-air missile might ruin our day."

"I'll take care of all that," Kim assured. "Just get out here and bring the bomb, as long as you can do it safely. An explosives forensics team will be here soon, and they'll want to get their hands on it."

"I'll just be glad when it's not sitting on my kitchen table."

Kim was about to ask if he was serious but pressed on. "Did you get anything from the bag? Any evidence? Clues about what's going on?"

"Nothing really. No pocket litter or anything like that. Liam did bring up the fact that it wasn't enough C-4 to do major damage beyond the immediate area. Seems a bit strange, right?"

Kim surveyed the chaos around her. "Yeah, more like a distraction than anything."

"Unless there's more of them," Garrett suggested.

"Well, Liam didn't plant the bomb, which means someone else did. The question is *who*."

"Soon as I get off, I'll start asking. Maybe he can help to narrow it down."

Kim looked around at the scene playing out before her and realized she better get clear of the emergency personnel. "All right, I need to get a situation report to Conner ASAP. This gets to the president before he hears from me, it won't be good. We need answers pronto. That's why I need you here now. Let me know if you can wrangle Ike and I'll get you cleared to land."

"What's the plan over there, Kim? How are they going to tackle this?"

"*Plan?*" Kim let out a nervous laugh. "There is no plan. This is all just happening. All I know is protecting Shepard is on everyone's mind. But no one on earth is safer. Head of plant operations is pulling in her security officers to augment his protective detail."

There was a pause on Garrett's end. "Don't think I'd do that. Too risky."

"It's too risky *not* to rally the troops to protect a high-level official. If they don't do everything in their power to keep him safe, then someone is going to answer for it."

"I get that," Garrett said. "But if this was really an assassination attempt, it was sloppy as hell. One-in-a-million chance it ever would've worked. Something else is going on."

Kim turned again and studied the mayhem unfolding all around. It reminded her of scenes on 9/11—survivors in shock, covered in ash and debris, fleeing the burning destruction. "Maybe the explosion was meant to drive him out into the open for a separate attack?"

"Or could be sleight of hand." There was a pause on Garrett's end. "Guerrilla tactics like we used in Special Forces. Distract the enemy while you're doing something else."

"Maybe you're right, Garrett. The Iranians are clever, and given their small size and limited resources, they've always made do with less. They may have something else up their sleeves, but we have no clue what it is. An assassination plot is the most obvious conclusion right now."

"No doubt. We don't know what we don't know." Another pause from Garrett. "Just make sure that Shepard's protective detail and Pantex security do the opposite of whatever they would normally do. Throw any established protocols out the window. Mix it up."

Kim chuckled. "You obviously haven't met these people. They're not exactly *all ears* when it comes to my suggestions, especially on emergency policies and procedures."

"I hear you, Kim. But we both know that asymmetric warfare is Quds Force's bread and butter. And they do it best in chaos. And right now, there's a lot of it. I think despite the incident with Liam and Lacey, pretty much everything else is going according to plan."

Kim hated to think Garrett was right but given what she knew about the U.S. assault on the nuclear facility in Iran, there was no way they'd go to this much effort for clumsy half measures. This thing wasn't over by a long shot. Action needed to be taken. Unfortunately, she didn't have the foggiest idea where to start.

Chapter 34

Cyrus Ahmadi pushed the brake and slowed his truck to a crawl, then veered off the lonesome highway onto the gravel road leading up to a silver six-story grain silo. Per their security protocols, the Americans had pulled auxiliary forces and ordered them back to Pantex. This left only four federal agents from the DOE's Office of Secure Transportation (OST) at a disguised train-loading facility in the isolated ghost town of Kingsmill, Texas.

The OST officers were incognito, dressed like farmhands or loading dockworkers, not the SEALs, Marines, Green Berets, or Rangers that they probably once had been. Cyrus, himself, had swapped the traveling-salesman getup he'd used during the morning meeting at the motel with Liam Bayat for dirty coveralls. He'd even traded his Nissan rental car for a Dodge flatbed dually to fit the part. The only thing kept were his black wraparound Oakleys.

As soon as he parked and jumped out, clipboard in hand, two agents spotted him and made a beeline to his truck. For men who were supposed to be hiding in plain sight, they didn't play the part of auger operators very well. They looked exactly like what they were—a team of highly-skilled federal paramilitary officers transporting nuclear bombs.

Cyrus raised the phony work order and mustered the kind of embarrassed look that said *I'm lost* or *I'm late* or maybe even both. He stopped midway between his truck and the train, which was about forty yards ahead, not wanting to make the agents more nervous than necessary.

To drop it down a notch further, Cyrus decided to speak first. "This the Atterbury place? Supposed to get some measurements for a concrete job by the scales."

The agent on the left shook his head as he continued to march forward. "You're in the right spot. But nobody's around. You're going to have to come back tomorrow."

Cyrus peered around at the other two agents beside the orange and black Burlington Northern Santa Fe locomotive engine. "Would only take a minute. Just need to get some numbers and I'll be gone." As he reached into his pocket, the agent on the right moved his hand to lift up the front of his shirt, likely reaching for the pistol he had stowed in his waistband.

Before the agent could draw, Cyrus pulled out the measuring tape. "Boss is going to be pissed if I come back empty-handed."

"I get it, man. We've got a boss, too." The agent who'd made the move stopped short. "But our company doesn't own this place. We work for BNSF. Just here to load the cars."

The one on the left chimed in again. "We'd let

you in if it were up to us, but you know how it is with liability and insurance. It'd be our asses. Can't take the risk."

"No problem." Cyrus bobbed his head casually. "Don't want to get you guys in trouble or anything." He raised his arm high and thumbed back at his truck. "Guess I'll just—"

On his signal, the first bullet whapped the agent on the right center mass. A second popped the one on the left, leaving a red splotch in the middle of his chest. Their bodies had not even hit the ground when Cyrus reached for his silenced FN 509 and sprinted toward the train.

As expected, it took the surprised agents a couple of seconds to move. The one who reached for his gun went down where he stood. The other pivoted to look for cover and took a sniper's round in the back of the thigh. A third bullet pinged off the train engine's handrail and whined off harmlessly into a field. The runaway moved behind the building before the sharpshooters could get off another clean shot.

Easing up to the edge of the silo, Cyrus raised his semiautomatic pistol and peered around the corner. He sprinted to the steps and bounded upward, his aim dead center on the agent who was limping up the stairs. Cyrus pulled the trigger twice, landing a double tap between the shoulder blades. Right as the security officer reached into the crew compartment, he slumped forward, reached out, and whacked a red toggle as he fell to the floor.

Cyrus eased up the steps, barrel still pointed at the body, and looked at the button—a red light flashed below. There was no indication of what this meant, but it was certain a distress signal was sent, which meant somebody was getting the OST agents' request for help. Although Cyrus wished it had not been activated, he and his team would be long gone before anyone arrived. Once inside their rolling fortress, they'd be nearly impossible to stop.

Chapter 35

Garrett exhaled a sigh of relief. True to his word, Ike made it out to the ranch in less than fifteen minutes. Of course, it didn't hurt that he was already airborne, apparently contracted for a helicopter feral hog hunt somewhere around Lake Marvin. It was anybody's guess what had become of the passengers, as he was clearly riding solo. Ike buzzed over the Caprock, swooped around the barn by the pickups, and dropped his skids with the gentle touch of a surgeon.

Looking to Liam, Garrett gave a tilt of the head. But he had not even taken the first step when the cell phone in his front pocket vibrated. Noting it was Kim, he threw up a finger to Ike, sprinted inside the barn, and answered. "Our ride's here, we're on our way over."

"Change of plans," Kim countered. "I need you on something else."

Garrett didn't know what could be more important than a bomb going off at Pantex, but he was certainly anxious to find out. "All right, lay it on me."

"Distress signal just came in from an OST team around Kingsmill. Know where that is?"

"Industrial loading facility between here and Pantex. Why?"

"Apparently they were making a transfer right after the bomb went off here."

Garrett had his nervous suspicions but still had to ask. "What kind of transfer?"

"Five nuclear warheads. Being shipped by train to Minot."

It didn't surprise Garrett that weapons would be headed up to Minot Air Force Base in North Dakota. Quite a few of America's long-range strategic bombers were up there. What did surprise him was that nukes were being transported by rail. As far as he knew, the White Train program, which the DOE had used to move these weapons from the 1950s to the 1980s, had been shut down.

Garrett had also heard from friends in the special operations community who'd become OST agents that the DOE's new initiative, which depended on tractor-trailers, was rife with problems. Given the aging fleet of trucks and problems staffing drivers, going back to the old method of transport made a lot of sense. But a hijacked engine would be problematic. Assuming it was an updated version of the old White Train, it would be built with reinforced steel and outfitted with gun turrets for heavily armed federal agents.

"Don't like the sound of runaway nukes." Garrett shook his head, even though no one could see him. "But not sure what I'm supposed to do about that. It's just me, Liam, and Ike."

"Anybody else who could help you out in a pinch?"

Garrett looked around the corner and grimaced. "Got Ray Smitty and Bo Clevenger."

"*Clevenger?*" Kim's voice registered a mixture of shock and disgust. "How'd he get back in the picture?"

"Wondering that myself."

"Think you can trust him?" There was a heavy hint of skepticism in Kim's voice.

"Nope," Garrett answered with certainty. "But if you're looking for a guy to take down an up-armored locomotive, then he'd be your man."

"I don't want you taking down anything, Garrett. Just follow it for now and report back. Like I said, all we've received was a distress signal. Could be a technical glitch or it was hit by accident. But given what's happening around here I don't want to risk it."

"Has anyone spoken to the team guarding those warheads?"

"Not yet," Kim replied. "But they only talk on secure comms. Strict protocols. And that whole system was thrown out of whack once the bomb went off."

Garrett fully understood the fog of war, but from the sound of it, things over at Pantex were going from bad to worse. The wheels in his mind immediately started turning. There were always contingency plans in place for a *Broken Arrow*, the designated term for a nuclear weapon on the loose. Of course, sometimes the cure is worse than the disease.

"What if the Iranians have possession of our nukes?" Garrett asked. "Then what?"

"Procedures on this are set in stone. They'll scramble air assets from Cannon. If they find out nuclear weapons have been stolen, the train will be taken out. No questions asked."

Nearby Cannon Air Force Base in Clovis, New Mexico, fell under Air Force Special Operations Command (AFSOC), which meant they'd have a variety of tools at their disposal. That included access to an M-Q9 Reaper, a hunter-killer drone. With the right armament it could make short work of a train. Even an armored one. The problem wasn't stopping it. The issue was what this would look like when it was all over and done.

Garrett didn't know if a Joint Direct Attack Munition (JDAM) meeting five nuclear warheads would produce the kind of result he imagined, but it wouldn't be pretty. Even if the explosion didn't detonate the bombs, it would pollute the air and poison their water. Kohl Ranch might still be left standing, but it would never be the same again.

Kim continued: "Don't worry about the Air Force's response for now. Just get up there and get eyes on that train. We'll know more once we get a team out to Kingsmill to investigate."

"All right, I'll be in touch as soon as we find it."

Garrett had no idea what they could do about that train, or if they could even do anything at all. He only knew that letting these people destroy his home wasn't an option. Of course, detonating nukes in Kansas City, Denver, or Tulsa couldn't be fathomed, either. This was looking a lot like a lose-lose situation, as the Iranians set to deal the U.S. a devastating blow.

Garrett ended the call and moved back around the barn to find all eyes on him. His ragtag crew had questions for which he had no answers. If he was ever in need of a miracle, it was now. Shame he'd wasted a good one on working batteries for that damn flashlight.

PART FOUR

If I wasn't a Devil myself, I'd give me
up to the Devil this very minute.

—Johann Wolfgang von Goethe, *Faust*

Chapter 36

Asadi had no clue what was going on, only that Garrett had flown off in Ike's helicopter with the backpack on his shoulder and a rifle in hand. But whatever message he delivered to Butch before taking off must have been a bad one. The old man's face was etched with worry. Putting the clues together, Asadi couldn't help but think it had something to do with Lacey. What happened to her was clearly no accident and it was obvious that Garrett was out for blood.

Wanting to avoid the obvious uncomfortable situation with Sam, who'd also been left behind, Asadi looked to Butch, praying there was some important chore that had to be done on the far side of the ranch. He was about to suggest it when the dark skies rumbled with thunder.

Butch gazed out at the billowing storm clouds. "You know, after last year's drought, I never thought I'd be crying calf rope. But we're as soggy as we can get. Another gusher and we'll be walking on a sponge."

Asadi couldn't disagree. Prayers for rain had been paid in spades. The ranch was green and flourishing, which was great for the cattle and horses. But a couple of big downpours over the past two weeks had resulted in major flooding around the Canadian River. It had washed out the road leading to the highway and sent their neighbors heading for the hills.

Butch looked from the sky to Asadi. "Why don't you and your buddies go on ahead and get them horses fed? Stalls could use a little work, too." Another big crack of thunder and he tilted his head toward the house. "Gonna make a phone call for a weather report. Doppler *Dimwit* says a big rainstorm is moving in from the northeast. Might mean big waters are headed our way."

Asadi should have been more worried about the flood than the "your buddies" remark. But the idea of doing anything with Sam sent him into an immediate panic. "Uh . . . maybe it a better job for just me and Savanah."

The other kid, Wade, whose father had left with Garrett, seemed nice enough. But Asadi had a system that he and Savanah were used to and didn't need anyone gumming up the works. He especially didn't want Sam in the barn. It was bad enough having him on the ranch.

Butch looked to Wade. "Your daddy said you ain't had nothing to eat yet, so I reckon we can go in and fix you a *sammich*." He turned back to Asadi with a twinkle in his eye. "As for the rest of your futures, I see a lot of tossing horse crap into a wheelbarrow."

Asadi was just about to argue when Butch turned to Sam. "Hey, Festus! You got sense enough to operate a scoop shovel?"

Sam wore a look that fell between surprised and annoyed. "Yeah, I can shovel."

"We'll see, I guess." Butch locked eyes with the kid and marched up to him. "Didn't hear any mention of recompense for wiping your snotty nose all afternoon. So, rather than let you sit on your butt collecting dust, I figured you might help out with the chores."

Asadi could tell that Sam had never been spoken to like that before. He didn't know whether to laugh or be afraid, ultimately settling on stunned silence.

After a few awkward seconds, Sam spoke up, albeit sounding a little bit reluctant. "Well, Mr. Kohl, you mentioned a shovel, didn't you?"

"That I did, son." The old man shot Sam the kindest of smiles. "And if you're a worthy enough soul to help with my horses, you can call me Butch."

"Okay, Butch, where's that shovel?"

"Tool room in the barn." Butch gestured at Asadi. "Boy here will get you outfitted with anything else you need. Also, giving him permission to whup your ass again if you get out of line or laze on the job."

Asadi could *not believe* what he'd just heard. Fully expecting a response from Sam, he balled his fists in anticipation of the bully flying into a rage. But to his shock, there was no response at all. Sam simply gave a nod and marched toward the barn like a man on a mission. Asadi looked to a dumbfounded Savanah, then back at the old man, who stood there smiling.

"See there, sonny, just gotta keep his pudgy little

hands occupied." Butch spun on a heel and called out as he walked to the house with Wade in tow. "Holler if you need anything!"

Butch was halfway to the back porch by the time Asadi got the nerve to move. With the last of the adults now out of the picture there was no one to intervene if Sam went berserk. Of course, to this point, he'd been on good behavior, which meant the feud might be over. After all, the score was now even, as each had won and lost a round.

Savanah's expression went from dumbstruck to skeptical. "I'm not buying it. You can't believe for a second that Sam forgave and forgot. He's still gonna want payback."

Wanting to put her fears to rest, Asadi made his case: "Don't worry. I think everything okay now. He not seem angry."

"Yeah, I don't know about that." Savanah pointed toward the back pasture. "Why don't you check that water leak Butch was talking about? Just keep a little distance. I'll go in and feed the horses. He knows better than to bother me anymore."

Asadi hated the idea of ducking a confrontation. It made him feel weak. Powerless. And he never wanted to feel that way again. "No. I be fine. We both go."

Savanah didn't look convinced. "Just seems like he's backing down a bit too quick."

Asadi didn't trust Sam, but the bully seemed to have a healthy fear of Butch. "I stay on one side of barn. He stay on other. We be fine."

A slow smile rose on Savanah's face. "You sure about this?"

Asadi wasn't sure at all, but he didn't want to look scared. And he didn't want to keep running from his problems. He had faced his fears once. He could face them again. "Trust me."

Feeling a bit more confident, Asadi gave Savanah the come-along wave as he strode to the barn. But seeing neither hide nor hair of Sam as he breezed through the door raised a bit of nervous angst. And when he got the shove in the back that sent him prostrate to the floor, it was clear that bygones were not bygones. There'd be no keeping to their separate corners.

Chapter 37

As far as Kim could tell, the only good thing about the pounding rain was it helped to squelch the raging fire from the building that housed the control center. No one was killed in the blast, but if the Iranian operatives' objective was to create chaos, then they'd done that at the Olympic level. Between the flashing strobes, wailing sirens, and shouts from rescue personnel, pandemonium abounded in a way she'd not witnessed since the fall of Kabul to the Taliban.

Through a break in a huddle of Security Police Officers in military fatigues, Kim saw Beth Madison, who was barking at someone on her phone. The Pantex security chief had no doubt run through hundreds of contingencies over the years, but it was unlikely she had prepared for anything quite like this. On top of the bomb going off inside the plant's perimeter, she potentially had nuclear weapons on the loose. As bad days go, this was about as horrible as it gets.

Kim raked fingers through her soaking locks and tucked them behind her ear. Slogging across the wet asphalt there was a noticeable chill that replaced the earlier heat and humidity. She walked up for a situation report but got unloaded on with both barrels by Madison, whose eyes went fiery with her question, which sounded more like an accusation.

"You want to fill me in on what's *really* going on here, Manning?"

Kim was taken aback by the harshness of the delivery. "Fill you in on what?"

"Secretary Shepard made a comment about this being some sort of Iranian reprisal. I asked Graham what the hell that meant and he said he had no idea. But I'm sure you do."

It was obvious to Kim that the SECDEF's offhand remark had to do with the U.S. attack on the Iranian nuclear plant. Shepard was one of the few looped in and should not have mentioned a word. But the cat was somewhat out of the bag now and they'd be looking to their CIA advisor to fill them in on the backstory that led up to the bombing. Unfortunately, it wasn't her story to tell.

Kim didn't know much herself and damn sure wasn't going to tell them what she did. "Whatever it is, I'm sure it will all come out in due time. For now, my concern is keeping everyone safe until I know this thing is over."

"That's what I'm trying to do," Madison shot back. "But that's kind of hard when you're being left out of the circle of trust."

Welcome to the club, Kim wanted to say but didn't. Maybe they could commiserate over a couple martinis once this thing was resolved. For now, she had to win Madison over. "I know you're frustrated, and I don't blame you. But I need you to do a few things for me."

Madison's aggravated expression said it all. "Now what?"

"Make some changes to your emergency plan."

Madison flinched at the suggestion. "This isn't the Agency. We don't shoot from the hip. We have established procedures for what we do. I don't care what kind of *shadow war* disaster the CIA has created. That's your mess. I answer to the Department of Energy. Anything beyond the safety of my employees, plant operations, and nuclear weapons is not my problem."

"What about an *Empty Quiver*?" Kim asked flatly. "That sound like it might be your problem? A mess that has your name written all over it?"

With Kim's use of the official military terminology for a stolen nuclear weapon, the color drained from Madison's face. "What—what are you talking about?"

"I'm talking about the distress signal coming from your Kingsmill transfer station."

Madison turned even paler. "How did you—how do you know about that?"

Kim received the tipoff from Conner, whose counterpart at the DOE was giving regular updates to the president. But she wasn't about to get into that. "If you have nuclear weapons on the loose, you're going to need a big helping hand. I can provide that."

"First of all," Madison countered, "it's uncertain what's happening at Kingsmill. I sent a team over to verify. Until we know for sure, I'm not going to panic."

"Good." Kim gave a nod. "Panicking won't help

anything. I've got a team on the way over there as well. When we know, we know."

"*A team?*" Madison asked. "What team?"

Kim knew better than to reveal her CIA tactical team focusing on nuclear weapons was made up of a DEA cowboy, a bartender chopper pilot, and two ex-cons. At least mentioning the one Pantex employee was a pretty safe bet. "Group of contractors. Each with specialized skills for the job. Liam Bayat is our acting liaison officer." On the fly, she gave him an official title, just to make it sound more legitimate and hopefully mollify any concerns.

Madison looked a bit skeptical. "Given what we know, can he be trusted?"

Kim had no idea. But beggars can't be choosers. And he was the only one with any experience with nuclear weapons. "The Agency has a long-established relationship with the Bayat family. I can't say any more than that, but I have the utmost trust and confidence in him."

Madison seemed to soften. "You said we needed to make changes?"

"I think that whoever accessed Pantex may be anticipating what you're going to do next. So, I would do the opposite. Instead of going left, go right. Instead of going up, go down. That kind of thing. Same goes for Graham and the SECDEF. If procedure says to go to air, then they need to stay grounded. At least for now. Until we know what we are up against."

"And exactly when will that be?" Madison asked. "How long until your team gets to Kingsmill?"

Madison glanced at her watch. "Any minute now."

"Until then, prepare for the worst."

Kim looked around the vicinity, pondering a plan. The sixteen-thousand-acre facility that made up twenty-five square miles included 648 buildings, forty-eight miles of paved roads, and 461 miles of fence line. For the most part, it looked like any other military base or installation. But there was a part of it that made her feel like she was on the dark side of the moon.

It wasn't just the flat barrenness of the surroundings. It was the odd dome-shaped structures that looked like 1950s-era flying saucers. What went on inside those buildings Kim didn't know—didn't *want* to know. But in terms of hiding Defense Secretary Shepard and keeping him safe from a catastrophic event, there were few better places.

Looking a bit solemn, Madison glanced around also. "What do you think could happen?"

"I don't know." Kim locked eyes with her new ally. "Use your imagination."

To her credit, Madison didn't show any panic or fear, just took it all in stride. "First things first then, we need to protect Shepard." She turned and pointed to a nearby building. "We'll move him to—"

Kim cut her off. "If it's written down, don't do it. Think of something off-the-wall."

An initial bit of resistance in her look faded fast. "Okay . . . what do *you* suggest?"

There was a hint of resentment in the question, but Kim didn't have time for hurt feelings. "Find a new location where we can take shelter." She tilted her head where the SECDEF was sequestered in a nearby office building. "Set up a secure area for him and his security detail. Somewhere you'd never normally go. If possible, a place plant employees don't know exists."

Madison almost had a gleam in her eye. "Oh, I know just the spot then."

Before Kim could suggest they get moving, the Pantex security chief threw up a finger before answering her phone. "It's the OST team at Kingsmill." She answered, listened a moment, and then turned back. "We need to get Shepard underground immediately."

Chapter 38

Cyrus took a look around the train's compartment to find it almost exactly as imagined. The schematics for the railcar and engine provided by his spy within the Oshkosh Corporation, the company that built to spec the armored train for DOE, had been worth every damn penny. It made it possible for the IRGC engineering unit to construct a to-scale replica for rehearsing the assault, takeover, and operation of the engine.

Not everything had gone according to plan, but that was to be expected. In his years in special operations, most recently in Syria, Cyrus had learned to build in room for error. The first of his mistakes was trusting Liam Bayat. Of course, it was his own fault for believing the son of an apostate. Treachery was fixed within his very DNA. Fortunately, there was a backup plan, made possible with help from the Russians, eager as Tehran to bring America to its knees.

The second slipup was letting the OST agent reach the distress button, which would shave a few minutes off their escape. The Iranian deception operation had worked like a charm, and now the

Americans were stumbling all over themselves in the chaotic aftermath of the explosion. By staging a phony assassination attempt against Defense Secretary Shepard, Cyrus and his team had effectively rendered the nuclear security apparatus largely ineffective.

They'll argue, circle the wagons, and lock down the plant. In short, the U.S. government officials will fiddle while their country burns. By the time anyone figures out what happened at Kingsmill, the activated nuclear weapons will have already been transferred to secondary transport vehicles, which will disappear into the nation's heartland and be placed in strategic areas. Like a virus infecting a cell, they'd use the host's own defense mechanism to destroy itself.

For all of Washington's talk of countries with atomic bombs becoming international pariahs, the West bent over backward to appease them. Iran's possession of these warheads would change the global order overnight. Now it was Tehran's turn to do the scolding.

Glancing around the compartment, Cyrus was surprised at how similar it was to the old White Train model, which was on display in a museum. Like the old version, it was part battleship and part recreational vehicle, a devastating instrument of warfare that was an amalgam of creature comforts and ramparts. It was outfitted with a kitchen, card table, sofas, and cots with heavy partitions for sleeping agents. But there were also gunports on every side, and a hidden compartment on the roof mounted with a crew-served weapon.

Cyrus moved to the front of the railcar where two of his men were carefully making one of the bombs ready for transfer. Despite its small size, no larger than a beer keg, the weapon was capable of reducing a large city to rubble. With the process under way, he climbed to the observation deck and scanned the area through the bulletproof glass.

To the front of the train, a herd of antelope leapt across the tracks, racing across a sprawling expanse of wilderness plains that was both scarred by deep ravines and punctured with towering mesas. Looking farther out to the horizon, Cyrus studied the sky, which had morphed from a hazy gray to a blue so dark it was nearly black. A storm was brewing in more ways than one.

Cyrus reached down and grabbed the direct line to his engineer below and requested a status report. Getting the all-clear, he allowed himself the luxury of a half smile. It wasn't until he saw the black dot on the periphery that he realized they might not be out of the woods yet. But Cyrus had prepared for such an eventuality. His man-your-stations order was followed with the bomb crew leaping to their feet, grabbing their M4 rifles, and covering each side of the railcar through gunports. Whoever was following was about to meet the full force of his rolling fortress.

Chapter 39

Asadi's first instinct was to check his stinging palms. Fortunately, Sam's shove in the back that sent him skidding across the concrete floor had done no damage other than to give him a bit of a shock. But unlike the fight in the cafeteria, or at the Cat's Paw, Asadi wasn't afraid, just mad as hell and ready for payback. As he rose to his feet, Savanah stepped in between them.

Wanting to keep her out of harm's way, Asadi gave his girlfriend a wide berth, keeping a close watch on his rival. He could hear Garrett's voice of caution all too clearly. However, there was no avoiding this conflict now. Sam had seen to that with his cowardly sneak attack.

Marching forward, Asadi's vision narrowed, muscles tightened, and heart pounded like a drum. Hands raised in front of his chin, just like Garrett had taught him, he cocked a fist and moved in close enough for contact.

Asadi had just let loose when his bicep was clutched, and his body yanked backward, as if caught in a snare. Whipping around, he found Butch behind him, with Wade at his side. In the heat of the moment, Asadi had not even noticed them walk into the barn. Before he could explain what happened, Butch launched in first.

"Just talked to Sanchez. Said there's heavy rains upriver. He's evacuating folks out now. Getting them up to higher ground."

The fact that their close family friend, Deputy Tony Sanchez, was already in action meant trouble was coming for sure. Even without a single drop of rain touching their property, flash flooding miles ahead of them could send a massive wall of water rushing down the river. Two years earlier, a couple of unsuspecting fishermen were caught in a surge nearby. One dead body was recovered miles down the river, pulverized, broken, and completely unrecognizable. The other was never found.

Asadi didn't need any instructions because he already knew the drill. Their cattle herd, grazing down in the valley, would need to be moved by horseback to higher ground. He immediately looked to the stalls, wondering which to saddle up for the mission. Sometimes the old man liked to use mounts that were tried-and-true. Other times, he wanted to give the newbies a chance to earn their stripes.

"Eazy and Sioux," Asadi suggested. They were both good for roping and could use some real-world experience. "They ready?"

Butch rested his eyes on the pair as he considered it. "I think it's time for the big leagues. He turned to Wade and sized him up. "What about you? Can you ride?"

"Yessir." The teenager's face lit up. "I've been

riding since I was a kid. Learned out at my grand-dad's place and I even had my own—"

"All right, all right." Butch waved him over. "You're on the team." He then turned to Sam. "Well, I got one volunteer, and missy here is on the payroll, a top-notch rider. *You*, on the other hand, haven't proven to be anything but a real disappointment."

Before Sam could argue, Butch shut him down flat. "Sent you out here because you said you could work, but all you've done is stir up trouble. Now, do you think you can make a hand? Or do I need to keep you out of our way?"

Sam glared back. "I can make a hand."

"I hope so," Butch answered. "Because we got serious work to do."

Asadi looked to Savanah for support but got none. Before he could make an appeal, Butch was already barking orders. They each brought in the horse they were assigned to ride and started saddling up—all done double-time. To Asadi's surprise, Sam actually knew exactly what he was doing. It was a revelation that for some reason rubbed him against the grain.

ASADI COULD BARELY STOMACH THE awkward ride from the barn down to the river where the cattle were grazing. He still didn't understand why Butch had brought along Sam. Shorthanded or not, the boy was not to be trusted. Proof of that was his sneak attack in the barn. It was an act no less cowardly than a boot to the groin or a sucker punch.

Both tactics, Garrett had assured him, had their place in a survival situation but were never tolerated

in a fair fight. What bothered Asadi more than anything was that Sam's inclusion had ruined what was
otherwise an exciting adventure. Of all the ranch
duties, his favorite was herding cattle. It combined
all the skills of both horse and rider in a display
of real-world practical use. From roping to cutting,
the roundup was where the cowboy and his mount
united as an unstoppable force. All the practice and
training came together for the sake of the job.

Putting negative thoughts aside to focus on the
task at hand, Asadi looked out over the expanse of
the lush green pasture to try to get a plan of attack.
It had typically been up to Butch to think through
the plan, but more recently the old man had left
it up to him. One wrong move could turn an easy
couple of hours into an all-day affair.

Butch turned in the saddle. "Okay, sonny, how
we gonna do this?"

Asadi gazed out over the prairie to find the
brown and white Herefords spread out as far as the
eye could see. With over two hundred in the bunch,
it would be impossible to get a full accounting, but a
nice guesstimate would do. While a couple of dozen
had gathered around the water trough beneath the
windmill, others clustered behind mesquite brush
to hide from the sun. Singletons, here and there,
nuzzled through tufts of grass out in the open.

It was clear they were going to have to divide up.
Riders on each side of the herd would make a wide
circle around so as not to spook the cattle. They'd
nudge the far-flung dawdlers together and meet
somewhere in the middle to form a single drive up
to higher ground. From there, they'd make a push

from behind, cutting off any troublemakers that had a mind of their own.

Following Asadi's explanation of the plan, Butch donned a look of pure satisfaction. "Good as I'd have thunk up." He looked around at the team. "Give the order then."

For Asadi, this was a no-brainer. He'd keep Sam as far away as possible. "Me and Savanah go right for stragglers. You, Wade, and Sam go left with the big bunch."

Butch's wheels were clearly turning. "Solid idea, but I think I'll take Savanah with me instead. Not as skilled with a rope as I used to be and may need her to toss a loop."

Asadi didn't believe that at all. Butch was by far a better roper. This was just a trick to get him working with Sam. But there was no use fighting it. The old man had the final say.

Asadi scowled at Sam. "You come with me then." He half-expected the bully to balk but he didn't say a word, just moved the reins right and brought his horse behind Eazy.

Savanah wore a smirk, clearly knowing exactly what Butch was up to. She maneuvered Sioux over to his left side and shot Asadi a wink. "Hope you boys can hold your own."

As she and Butch rode left to flank the herd, Asadi turned to find Sam staring him down. Ready to get a little distance, he pointed to a mama cow and her calf on the far right and gave a command. "You take those two." He pointed in the direction of a bull. He had taken off running toward the river as soon as he saw the horses. "I'll get that one."

For the first time since the fight that morning, Sam spoke to him directly. "Looks like a big ol' boy." He added with a little smugness, "Maybe you ought to let *me* handle him."

"No way," Asadi shot back. "You get mama and baby. I take bull."

Sam held firm. "Just because that old man kept me from kicking your ass earlier doesn't mean I won't do it when we're done. What's between me and you ain't over."

Asadi thought about those words. They would have struck fear into his heart a few days ago, but not anymore. If Sam wanted a fight, then he'd give him one. Win or lose, the bully was in for a knock-down-drag-out. But for now, they had a job to do.

"Just do what I say," Asadi commanded again. "Bring cows back to herd."

Sam gave Clover his boot heels and took off in the direction of the mama and calf. But about half-way there, he veered left and chased the fleeing bull over the ridgeline. It was a clear show of defiance, and a clear sign that things were probably going to get worse.

Asadi brought Eazy into a full gallop to head them off. If the bull made it down into the flat, there was only about fifty yards to the river where the dense brush and cottonwoods ran adjacent. He was nearing the top of the rim when he heard a rumble, a dull roar, and then a rotten egg stench filled the air. As he crested the ridge, Asadi leaned back in the stirrups and tugged the reins.

Waiting on the other side of the hill was a six-foot-high rolling tube of muddy brown water, ripping a swath through the riverbed as it thundered round the bend. It looked as if the earth, once stagnant and dead, had come to life and was devouring itself whole.

Not unfazed by the eerie phenomenon, Sam sat watching in shock, as the startled bull attempted to turn around and flee. But the grinding wave of slurry gulped him up and took him under. When the bellowing beast resurfaced, his neck was girded with barbed wire.

The bull's front hooves pawed wildly but found no grip in the brew of mud. Sucked into a whirlpool, he corkscrewed a few times until submerged into the mire. His nose broke for a moment, then went back under, lost forever beneath the swirling froth of this raging tide.

Chapter 40

Ike Hodges glanced around his Hughes 500 to survey his crew. In the passenger seat to the right was Garrett, cradling his Lone Star Armory TX4 carbine, with its barrel pointed outside the open door. Crammed in back were Smitty and Bo, each with a leg on the rail, holding the Seekins Precision AR-10s he'd earlier brought for the hunters who'd been chasing feral hogs.

Liam was crammed in the middle between the two door gunners, looking a bit squeamish, likely because he had a backpack full of explosives resting atop his manhood. Ike normally charged by the hour, but with the behemoth Clevenger on board, he wondered if he ought to start charging by the pound.

Garrett turned to him as he spoke through the headset. "How quick can we catch them?"

Flying his helicopter at 150 miles per hour, it wouldn't take long. Ike had cut the distance from the Kohl place to meet the BNSF rail line, expecting to converge near the Mendota Ranch. His worry wasn't locating the train. It was what to do when they found it. These ragtag commandos might've been a helluva fighting force were they not pitted against an armored locomotive.

Ike eyed Garrett's rifle. "We'll get there in a couple minutes. What's the plan?"

There was a moment of hesitation before Garrett spoke again. "Don't really know just yet. All we're supposed to do is get eyes on the train and report back what we see."

"Report to *who*?" Ike shot back.

Another moment of hesitation from Garrett. "Kim's out at Pantex."

Ah hell. It didn't take a genius to figure out that when a CIA operations officer was out at a nuclear weapons plant, and highly concerned about a runaway train, then he should probably be worried, too.

"Observe and report, huh?" Ike chuckled. "What if we see something we don't like?"

Before Garrett could answer, Liam spoke over the comms. "I have a feeling we're going to need to stop that train."

"Figured as much," Ike replied. "But if you got any bright ideas on how to do it, now's the time." Ike pointed ahead. "We're about to make contact."

There was only an engine pulling a single railcar. It was blasting full throttle across the wide-open prairie beneath an ominous stretch of thunderheads that flickered with lightning.

Garrett spoke up. "Liam, is that the train we're looking for?"

"Ours aren't marked. But they've pulled the pin and left the other railcars behind. And these guys are looking to be going somewhere in a hurry. Has to be it."

Yet again, it didn't take a genius to figure out what was at stake here. If they were going to make a stand, then the sooner the better. Ike lined up directly with the train and lowered the collective to drop altitude and come in for a better look. He was about to ask a few more questions when Garrett raised his hand and checked a text message on his phone.

"Okay, we got orders from Kim." Garrett looked to Ike. "Says they just confirmed that the security team was killed at Kingsmill. They're scrambling air assets from Cannon to take out the train."

"Take it out?" Ike asked. "With missiles?"

"She didn't say, but if it's coming from there my guess is it'll be a drone. Maybe a Reaper or Predator. Platform with air-to-surface capabilities."

Liam spoke up over the comms. "That's protocol. If a weapon ever gets into enemy hands, then it has to be neutralized. *Immediately*."

"How long until it gets here, you think?" Garrett asked.

"From Clovis?" Liam asked. "Less than half an hour, give or take."

Ike chimed in. "This train will be too damn close to Canadian by then. They'll have to wait until it passes through open country."

"They won't wait," Liam corrected. "Drone will fire as soon as it's locked on."

Garrett was clearly taken aback with the grim news. "Why not wait until it passes through town, where it will do less collateral damage?"

Liam explained: "It's less dangerous to clean up a derailment, even with radiation spillage, than to risk letting it go and allowing the hijackers to set off a train car full of atomic bombs. In terms of destruction, it's not even comparable."

Ike shot a glance back at Liam. "Easy to make that call in Washington. *They* don't live here."

"Preaching to the choir, Ike. That's why *we* need to stop that train."

Garrett turned back to Liam. "Bound to be a way to put it out of commission without blowing the damn thing to high heaven?"

"Only if we can stop the engine," Liam replied. "Problem is that it's imperviable to almost everything but a direct missile strike. Our guns aren't going to do much unless we get inside. The engine and carrier car are made by the same company that makes the MRAP. Reinforced steel. Gunports. Even an M240 mounted up top."

As the pilot who'd be making the assault, Ike didn't like the odds. The Mine-Resistant Ambush Protected, or MRAP, vehicles the military used in war zones weren't indestructible, but the firepower on board his helicopter wouldn't make a dent on that train. Add in the belt-fed machine gun on the roof of that railcar laying down 650 rounds per minute and they were looking at a surefire recipe for doom.

After a clear moment of what was undoubtedly angst-ridden planning, Garrett turned to Ike. "Think you could get close enough to get me on top of that engine?"

"Could but won't," Ike replied.

"Why not?"

"Won't do no good. I can get you up there but

then what? You going to knock on the door, talk real sweet, and hope they'll let you in?"

"I'll be knocking but there won't be anything sweet about it." He thumbed back to Liam, who was holding the backpack of C-4. "We'll have a nice little present waiting for them."

"You know how to use that stuff without blowing yourself up?" Ike asked.

"Know a little," Garrett replied. "But the guy in the backseat knows a whole lot."

Ike glanced back at Liam. "I know you got skills. But breaching the hatch on a speeding locomotive with bullets whizzing by your head ain't exactly a walk in the park."

Liam answered quick but there was uncertainty in his voice. "Yeah, if that's the only option. Then I'll do what I gotta do."

Ike gave a nod. "Okay, I'll drop you and Garrett on top. And my door gunners here can create a little mischief while you work."

"We'll need it if they go to shooting." Garrett turned and handed the bag off to Liam. "Can you get this thing ready? Once we're on top, we'll only have a few seconds."

About four hundred yards out from the train, Ike moved the stick right to maneuver in from behind. Between his career as a Night Stalker pilot and contract security work with Blackwater, he'd pretty much flown every kind of mission on earth. But a *Butch Cassidy and the Sundance Kid*–style train assault was one he had never even imagined.

Ike had just banked left, hovered over the tracks, and was lining up for the rear attack when he got the go-ahead from Liam that the C-4 was set. Nearing the back railcar, Ike watched as the hatch opened up and a belt-fed M240 machine gun rose over the lip of the buttress on a hydraulic lift. It sat unmanned for about five seconds and then an operator moved in from behind, grabbed the cocking handle, and jacked in a round.

Knowing he should've taken evasive action immediately was a far cry from having done it. But the spectacle of watching an ordinary freight train morph into a steampunk war machine had slowed Ike's reflexes. What quickened them big-time was the volley of 7.62mm rounds that thwacked the windscreen and ripped a couple of holes in the roof.

The angle of the helicopter had thrown off the gunman's aim, but it wouldn't take long to recalibrate. And as soon as he did, bullets would be coming up beneath the floorboard. Wanting to keep his body parts as intact as possible, Ike moved the stick left until it hit the mechanical stop and raised the collective to get up and out as quick as he could.

They took three more rounds that raked across the underbelly, sounding as if they were being pelted with rocks. Breathing a sigh of relief after climbing out of the M240's reach, Ike turned to Garrett, who didn't look nearly as relieved.

No doubt he was thinking what everyone else was thinking. They didn't want their home bathed in a radioactive glow. But the only option to take out that train was with missiles, unless someone thought of a better idea. Given the countdown, they'd better do it in a hurry.

Chapter 41

The text message Kim received regarding the aggressive action taken by the Iranian operatives on the train only confirmed what she already knew. These guys were well trained and were not easily thwarted. But that was Garrett's problem now. Her immediate concern was for the safety of Defense Secretary Shepard.

Given the bomb that had nothing to do with Liam Bayat, it was abundantly clear there was a saboteur at work. Only a select few had access to the security control center, which narrowed the investigation. But that would still take time. Meanwhile, there was a conspirator among them, and she had no idea who it might be.

Scoring a hard-fought victory, Kim convinced Madison to change the so-called *undisclosed location* where Graham and another agent named Carter could take the SECDEF to hunker down and lie low. The other two members of the protective detail were dispatched to secure alternate air transport for Shepard and work up a new exfil strategy. Once the area was secure and they were given the green light by Pantex to fly in a helo, they'd be gone.

After winding through multiple layers of restricted access zones surrounded by barbed wire
and security checkpoints, they arrived at one of
the odder-shaped buildings that Kim had ever
seen. Before her was a network of old nuclear
weapons storage bunkers linked together by sub-
terranean tunnels. At a glance, they looked like
the old concrete pillboxes used by German machine gunners on Omaha Beach.

This network of dugouts had been mothballed
decades ago, but the hardened structures, capable
of containing a low-kiloton internal atomic blast,
were no less sound now than when they were built.
Should the Iranians find a way to detonate the
bomb, Kim and the others would probably survive
the initial shock wave. After that, they would be
dependent on a rescue team, assuming there was
anyone out there still alive and willing to brave the
radioactive fallout.

After Graham opened the steel door at the entrance, Carter ushered Secretary Shepard inside.
What little illumination that was provided by
blinking strobes and flickering incandescent lighting set aglow the cinder-block walls of the cobweb-
filled storage facility, teeming with junked-out
equipment that probably hadn't been used since
Eisenhower was in office. There was even a large
metal cylinder, flush to the wall, that looked exactly
like an iron lung.

Graham brought up the rear, armed with an
Mk18 short-barreled rifle. He turned back and
groaned as he threw his shoulder against the heavy
door. "Come on, you son of a—"

Kim's phone vibrated in her front pocket. "Hold up! I'm getting a call!" With a sopping wet hand, she fished it out, checked the screen, and saw it was Mario. "I need to take this."

Graham was clearly annoyed. "Are you kidding me?"

Kim looked to the SECDEF, who was accompanied by Carter about thirty feet down the hallway to what looked like a waiting area, with an old green sofa, two plastic chairs, and a metal desk shoved in a corner. They turned right and filed through an open door.

"Once we're locked in here, I'll lose signal. Don't you think it's worth a minute to see if someone might have some important information?"

A pause from Graham, who seemed to be thinking over the ramifications of *not* letting her take the call if it was something important. "Make it quick." Another groan as he jerked the handle and the door whined open to a flash of lightning that lit up the entryway.

Kim moved through the threshold, stopped short of the concrete overhang outside to keep from getting further drenched, and answered the call. "You won't believe what's happening."

"Conner's kept me up to speed," Mario replied.

"How much do you know?" Kim asked.

"Enough to know you're in desperate need of some answers."

"Got any?"

Mario chuckled on the other end. "You know how Watson's been pretty closemouthed to this point?"

Kim couldn't help but smile. She knew where this was going. "He starting to sing?"

"At least about what he knows. Which isn't much on the Iranian side of things."

"How did you get him to open up?" Kim had been given very specific instructions from Murray that they were not to touch Watson. "I mean . . . you remember our orders, right?"

"Didn't lay a finger on him, Kim. Swear on my mother."

"Then who did?"

Another chuckle from Mario. "Watson *accidentally* got intermingled in with the others. And *somehow*, they learned he was CIA. We didn't have to go to him. He came to us."

Kim couldn't help but laugh. Had it been anyone else from the Agency than Bill Watson, a traitor scumbag with blood on his hands, she would've never considered doing something like that in a million years. But *he* was the exception. She'd have loved to watch this Ivy League intellectual keep company with some of the most vicious terrorists on earth.

Hoping to get the juicy details later, Kim moved on for the sake of time. "Okay, what did he know about what's happening here at Pantex?"

"Nothing."

"And you believe him?" Kim pressed.

"Yeah, he wouldn't know the nitty-gritty on what Tehran was up to. Or the Russians for that matter, even though he was in their pocket. But he's an intel guy. It's not too hard to figure out what's going on after you get enough not-so-subtle questions from your handler."

That was true. Throughout her career, Kim had

been careful to weave fake queries in with the real
ones, just enough to throw off a double agent who
might be reporting back to the mother ship. But a
savvy operations officer can piece a story together.
Bill was a bureaucratic ladder climber and most certainly a corrupt piece of garbage, but he was good
at his job.

"So, what did he think, Mario?"

"When I got to the part about Shepard, I could
see the wheels turning. Like he knew something
was going on."

Kim knew she was getting short on time, but
didn't want to rush Mario, for fear he might hurry
through some important detail. "Okay, what does
he *think* he knows?"

"He thought there was a breach at the Pen-
tagon. Someone high-level reporting back to
Moscow. Someone in the SECDEF's immediate
circle, maybe. Or possibly even a tech op. Like his
phones, home, and office were bugged."

Kim knew a cyber intrusion wasn't out of the
question, especially with what she already knew
about the Iranians collaborating with the Russians,
and how they'd compromised the Agency's classified high-side network. But Watson mentioned
HUMINT and SIGINT. "Why did he think there
was a spy, or someone listening to his calls?"

"Information the Russians had on Shepard was
very personal. Intimate. Private conversations. Things
about his health not available to the public. Details
on his marriage, kids, and finances. It was like they
knew everything about him. Inside and out."

"Anything specific?" Kim pressed.

"Sounds like Shepard was clean. No dirt beyond a little family drama. Got a lazy-ass twenty-five-year-old who won't leave the house and get a job. A little embarrassing for a hard-charging Marine who led troops into battle. But nothing anyone could use as blackmail."

It might not have hit her had Graham not just then stepped outside the door. But no one in the world had more access to a cabinet member than his security detail. From the SECDEF's high-level meetings, travel schedule, personal health, to his family life, no one knew more than the men who guarded him twenty-four hours a day.

Kim waved Graham off. "Hold on a second. We're almost done."

"Time's up, Manning." Graham stared her down for a moment. "I'm locking the door. Choice is yours. In or out?"

Her paranoia in overdrive, Kim couldn't help but consider his words a threat. Of course, she knew that would be the response of any head of a protective detail just trying to do their job. She had no desire to potentially entomb herself with a Russian agent, but knowing what she knew now, no part of her could let it go. Like it or not, she was in.

Chapter 42

Cyrus couldn't help but smile. For an old soldier, nothing in the world felt quite as good as letting rip with a machine gun. He wasn't sure if the pestering helicopter went down, but he had certainly put a little distance between them and the train. Ducking back inside, Cyrus pulled the hatch closed atop him and sank back into his seat on the observation platform. A quick check of his watch revealed that despite the interruption they were still nine minutes ahead of schedule.

Barring any additional unforeseen issues, they would rendezvous with their counterparts in secondary transport and transfer the warheads into SUVs, where a unit of Persian expats would take the lead. Cyrus and his team would divide into pairs and make their way back to Iran via Mexico, crossing at border egresses in Texas, Arizona, and California.

Cyrus couldn't help but appreciate the irony, drawing similarities between his own mission and the Tokyo Raid in retaliation for the sneak attack on Pearl Harbor. It was thought that mainland Japan was untouchable until a bombing run of sixteen

B-25s led by Lieutenant Colonel James Doolittle in April 1942 proved otherwise. Hitting the island fortress struck a major blow to Japanese confidence and gave a much-needed shot in the arm for the Americans.

In the lineage of Quds Force operations, the hijacking of a train full of nuclear weapons was certainly the boldest. But if pulled off successfully it would cripple the most powerful military in the world and bring Washington to its knees.

Cyrus looked around the railcar at his team, who had moved from the gunports and returned to readying the warheads for the next leg of the journey. "Ten minutes!" he called out in Farsi.

The operatives below didn't take time to look up or even acknowledge. They all had jobs to do, which they had rehearsed a thousand times before. With the raise of his binoculars, Cyrus scanned his surroundings through the bulletproof glass. To his surprise, maybe even delight, the black dot was again on the horizon.

Rising from his seat, Cyrus reopened the top hatch to make ready his weapon. He would not bother his team with an interruption this time. He would exterminate these pests on his own.

Chapter 43

It took a little convincing, but Garrett swayed Ike to make another strafing run on the train. But instead of another high approach from behind the armored railcar, they'd swoop in low, face-to-face with the engine. The M240 would still have a line of sight on them, but it'd be a terrible angle. And if they timed it just right, they could take out the gunman, which would allow him and Liam to drop in without dodging bullets.

Going head-on with a locomotive careening down the tracks at eighty miles per hour in a helo doing over a hundred wasn't the safest idea he'd ever had, but the alternative to not stopping it was unthinkable. It wasn't only about the nuclear weapons. It was about justice for Lacey.

Even though Garrett hadn't witnessed it personally, the image of her clutching on to that backpack was etched in his mind. And it would be forever. His girlfriend's dedication to a mission she knew nothing about brought a lump into his throat. Her devotion had nothing to do with personal glory, or even the cause, and everything with doing a favor for someone she loved.

It was important to him, so it was important to her. That summed this beautiful woman up in a single selfless act. For this reason, Garrett wanted restitution as much as resolution.

Ike lowered the collective as he spoke into the headset. "All right, Garrett, you've managed to accomplish something that's never happened before in my lifetime."

"What's that?" Garrett asked.

"...... up with a scheme even *I* think is too risky."

Garrett wished he could've just written that comment off as Ike being Ike. But the truth was there wasn't much the old Night Stalker wasn't willing to do. "I'm up for a better one if you got any ideas."

"I don't," Ike said matter-of-factly. "Guess that's why I'm about to play chicken with a hundred tons of iron and steel."

As they approached the train, both reality and guilt set in. The *reality* was that taking out the gunner without getting shot was nearly impossible, and the *guilt* was over the fact they'd be doing it with three other fathers in the backseat. Knowing he was putting the lives of these men at risk didn't sit well with Garrett, even if one of them was a no-account derelict like Bo Clevenger.

"Call it off then." When the pilot didn't respond, Garrett looked over. "Hear what I said? We'll find another way."

Ike wore a determined look. "No, I might be convinced now."

Garrett perked up, glad to see Ike had come around. "What changed your mind?"

"Relocating would be a huge pain in the ass. I'd rather be dead than have to move."

Ike's answer wasn't the vote of confidence Garrett was hoping for, and watching the engine bear down on them about three hundred yards ahead put his plan in perspective. Come in too high and they'd be cut down by machine gun fire; too low and they'd collide with the train. Before he could argue for a better plan, Ike was barking instructions over the head...

"Okay, boys, we've got one chance. I'm here to tell you this plan involves no marksmanship. Just a matter of how damn fast you can pull the trigger."

Garrett turned to Ike. "You don't want us to aim?"

"Nope." Ike kept his stare dead ahead at the train. "I'll aim for you. Soon as I give the word, point your rifles straight down and start firing. And don't quit until you empty your mag."

At this point Garrett couldn't take his eyes off the train engine that was growing closer and closer at an alarming rate. He was just about to yell at Ike to lift up when the old Night Stalker yelled, "*NOW.*" Too late to do anything else but comply, Garrett leaned out the door, pointed his TX4 downward, and pulled the trigger rapid-fire.

It was in that moment Ike yanked back on the collective and pushed the left, shifting the bird sideways as they moved up and over the train. Garrett didn't know if the others complied, but he did as he was told, emptying every round he had into the engine and railcar.

Smitty, who had been on the back side of the

chopper and the only door gunner with a view of what happened, yelled over the comms, "Got him! Machine gunner down! Saw it!"

Garrett was just turning back to offer a high-five, even to Bo, when another sudden noise spooked him again. This one, unfortunately, was mechanical. There was a knock and sputter above from the rotor mast. Then suddenly the shrill dragging pitch of an emergency alarm sounded off in the cockpit.

Garrett looked to the pilot. "What the hell is that?"

Ike smiled. "Sound of a helicopter turning into a hang glider."

Chapter 44

Captivated by the bull's grisly death, Asadi almost forgot about the job at hand. Truth be told, the incident shook him to his core. If the wave of debris took down a one-ton animal with ease, he could only imagine what it would do to him. His heart broke for the poor cow and her calf that had found a little knoll in the river about sixty yards ahead. They were in a clear state of panic, as the milky brown waters surrounded them.

Asadi was about to suggest they return to the main herd and report the dilemma. But before he could get the words out, Sam gave his horse a nudge and took off toward the stranded pair. Expecting Clover to stop short of the dangerous current, Asadi was shocked when they kept at a full lope, crashed into the water and pushed through the muddy surge.

Asadi followed behind, hitting the river in high gear. It was evident by Sam's path he was circling around the mother and calf to ease them off the knoll, and swim them to shore. But the deeper they rode, the slower they moved. As the vicious swell rose around their horses it grew harder and harder to maintain control.

Asadi rode in behind on the left, forming a barrier to drive the cattle back to shore. He gave a solid nod, which Sam returned in kind. With the mutual recognition of a plan, they gave their horses a little kick. Slowly but deliberately, they inched forward.

The wary cow eyed them cautiously, but stepped off the knoll, into the water, and in the direction of solid ground. Content to let them figure out their own path to freedom, Asadi threw his hand up in a halting motion and pulled the reins. He expected Sam to ignore him, but to Asadi's surprise, his partner leaned back in the stirrups and Clover came to a stop.

The bovine duo made a beeline for the ridge, and Asadi flashed a grin that came out so naturally there was nothing he could do to stop it. Sam returned the gesture with equal gusto. His eyes beamed and he sat tall in the saddle.

Asadi could feel there might have been a mutual embarrassment from Sam given the fact he let his bravado slip. To reverse course, however, was even worse. With mother and calf about halfway to shore, Asadi gave a little kick to get Sioux going, then looked right to find Sam had done the same.

As Asadi crossed over the knoll and dipped back into the river, Sioux stumbled, got up, then faltered again and stood rigid. A snort and a whinny as the horse was clearly spooked. Sam noticed the frightening strength of the current as well. Whatever joy he experienced from their win was long gone. They were about to get swept away.

Feeling his pulse quicken, Asadi reached down and scratched Sioux between the ears. A *you got this, girl* later and the mare found her footing, shifting her weight against the wall of the tide, and plodded on again. Unfortunately, just ahead of them, the tiny calf was unable to hold its own and was drifting away. Asadi aimed toward the mother while Sam set his sights on the calf.

Despite the reluctance to abandon her young, Asadi was able to move in behind the cow and push her back to the shoreline. He turned back to find his partner was still in pursuit of the calf. Unfortunately, Sam couldn't push the baby back onto dry land and they drifted farther out into the deeper and faster-moving waters.

Anticipating where the calf might end up, Sam maneuvered to cut him off. But before Clover could get there, the baby's head went under and it didn't come back up. Sam dived from the saddle in search of the missing calf, then popped up seconds later about thirty yards downstream. The good news was he had the calf tucked under his arm, the bad news was he was spinning down the funnel of a swirling eddy. Sam went under for a second, then buoyed again, his mouth barely above the surface as he gulped for air.

Asadi brought Sioux into a run on the riverbank and moved up ahead of Sam, swerving from the sandbar into the water with a thundering splash. After untying his rope and shaking out the loop, he brought it over his head in a twirl and let loose of the lasso. But as soon as he released it, Sam and the calf plunged beneath the torrent. Neither boy nor animal surfaced again.

Chapter 45

Kim watched Graham with a careful eye. There was nothing in Mario's report suggesting the SECDEF's head of security was a spy for the Russians, or anyone else on his protective detail for that matter. But there was no one in the world who knew more about the cabinet members than the people who watched over them day and night. Just because they were highly vetted didn't mean they were incorruptible. Her old boss, Bill Watson, was proof of that.

Once inside the bunker, Kim took a thorough look around at the mothballed weapons facility turned fallout shelter, which was now apparently the world's most secure storage unit for the plant's leftover junk. Its catacombs, according to Madison, had at one point held weapons-grade plutonium. Now they were probably teeming with hantavirus and the rodents that carried it.

Kim couldn't help but think they were living out some old episode of *The Twilight Zone*. The office furniture, maps, and lab equipment appeared to date back to the early 1960s. All that was lacking was the creepy theme music and a little narration from Rod Serling.

Eyeing her phone as she stepped into the shadowy entryway of the complex, Kim let out a sigh when the no-service indicator popped on the screen. She didn't know if she was hoping for *immaculate reception* but being trapped in there with no hope of outside communication made a bad situation a whole lot worse.

Graham secured the lock on the heavy steel door and turned back, looking a bit on edge. Kim was a bit surprised how much his appearance had altered since they'd first met in the conference room. He and the others on the security detail had swapped their suit coats and sport jackets for battle belts and tactical chest rigs. Strapped down with extra magazines for their weapons and even a few grenades, these protective service agents, who could've passed for run-of-the-mill businessmen earlier, had transformed into commandos.

Graham narrowed his gaze, looking genuinely concerned. "You doing okay, Manning?"

Kim looked around. "Oh yeah, just checking out our new digs." She turned back and smiled. "Great place to spend the apocalypse, wouldn't you say?"

Graham took in their surroundings. "Gives me the creeps."

Not certain Graham was clean, but feeling she had no choice but to trust someone with the intel provided by Mario, Kim decided to take a chance and let him in on it. If there was a rat among them, a figurative one at least, then it had to be addressed.

"I need to talk to you about something." Kim

glanced back at the office to make sure they had some privacy. "For your ears only."

Graham looked over her shoulder, then back to her. "Everything okay?"

"I don't know yet. But I got a lead on a possible threat."

Graham looked back at her, clearly annoyed. "Well, if you got something, spit it out."

"Nothing's certain, but you might have a breach."

"*Breach?*" Graham swallowed hard and lowered his voice. "What are you talking about?"

As lead agent, Graham was responsible for every member on his detail. A leak would be traced to the top. He'd be finished.

"Your team might be compromised," Kim explained. "Someone spying for the Russians."

Graham's face turned red and twisted into a look that was somewhere between amused and furious. "*My* guys? No way. They're handpicked. There's a vetting process."

"Everyone at our level is handpicked and vetted. Doesn't mean they won't turn."

Graham seemed to contemplate the notion for a moment. "*Who* told you this?"

"Can't get into that."

"Let me guess. You heard it from some dirtbag asset, who gets paid big bucks for even bigger lies. I've been burned before."

"So have I. But this guy has access."

"What access?" There was an unmistakable venom in Graham's voice. "Access to who?"

"I told you. I can't get into that. Just have to trust me on this one."

"Trust *you*? That's a joke." Graham guffawed. "What am I supposed to do? Interrogate everyone on my team?"

Kim shook her head. "That'd be a bad idea. Best thing to do is pretend we suspect nothing."

"Then why did you tell me? Could've done a lot better if I didn't know."

Kim couldn't help but think back to Garrett's suspicion that the bombing was some kind of Iranian subterfuge. And he wasn't even aware of the Russian angle yet. She didn't know exactly what to do with this information, but if Moscow had an agent near the SECDEF, that was a problem. And it needed to be dealt with sooner rather than later.

"Look, Graham, I'm telling you this because we need to be cautious."

Kim had expected his reaction to be an unpleasant one. And it didn't disappoint. He was hit with the whole *need-to-know* information routine that riles everyone in the security realm. Sensitive intelligence was parsed out sparingly, which didn't sit well when you're left in the dark. Now Kim was wondering if Nathan Graham would want to join her happy hour gripe session with Beth Madison. There was plenty of fodder given this cross-agency crisis.

Graham moved closer. "Okay, what do we do?"

"Right now, we just need to keep Shepard away from anyone who could potentially be a threat. Fortunately, at the moment that just leaves Carter. Any reason to think he's our guy?"

"If he was a mole, he wouldn't be here. He'd be in Leavenworth."

Sometimes the signs aren't there when you don't want to see them. If anybody knew about that, it was Kim. "Dig deep for me. Really think about it. Does anything at all seem off to you about Carter? A sudden change in behavior? Personality? Spending habits? Does he have an axe to grind with anyone?"

Graham shook it off immediately, clearly giving it no thought. "Nah, he's solid."

"Nothing at all," Kim pressed. "Gun to your head, you had to find something."

Graham paused for an uncomfortably long few seconds staring daggers at her, then let out another heavy sigh. "Maybe . . . I can think of something."

Kim raised her hands, palms out. "It's probably nothing, but it's a place to start."

"I'm not saying there's anything to it. I'm just saying there *is* something a bit odd about him." Graham looked pained. "And I want to be clear. I'm not making any accusations."

Of the agents she met on the protective services detail, Kim wasn't that surprised. *Graham* was your everyman. Brown hair. Medium build. Bland personality. And so were the others. *Carter*, on the other hand, stood out. And it wasn't just because of his physical traits. He was the only one with blond hair and a bit on the taller side. But Carter had a unique kind of swagger, exuding somewhat of a California surfer vibe. He might even be described as cocky.

"So, what's the issue?" Kim lowered her voice. "Think it could be him?"

Graham looked offended. "Hell no. Nothing like that."

Kim looked back to make sure they were still alone. "Then what is it?"

Graham exhaled. "Look, you have to understand that the way we left Afghanistan left a bunch of us pissed. I mean, *real* pissed. Especially those of us who lost friends."

Kim gave an understanding nod. "I felt exactly the same. And I lost friends, too."

"But enough time passes, and you move on. You have to. Or the pit swallows you."

Kim had never thought of it like a pit, but it was a great analogy. She'd felt that way a few times at the Agency. Although she'd never particularly liked Bill Watson, she had considered him an ally. Trusted him. Being so wrong about the guy had sent her into a dark place. As long as you could see the light, you were okay. As soon as you couldn't, you were dead.

Graham continued: "But Carter never could seem to climb out with the rest of us. His resentment bordered on disturbing. Said things like our government had betrayed us. Our friends died for nothing. We'd left our Afghan allies there to rot." Graham took a deep breath as he seemed to collect his thoughts. "Anyhow, he went from rage to depression, and we kind of thought the worst. Like maybe we better not leave him alone for too long."

"If he was that bad, why did you let him stay on Shepard's detail?"

"Because we're friends. *Okay?* And we're all the guy has in the world. Kicking him off would've only made things worse." Graham shrugged. "I mean . . .

it'd be like pulling the trigger myself. I don't know. I just couldn't do it."

Kim wanted to argue that just because it was difficult didn't mean it wasn't the right thing to do. But she also knew soldiers stick together—the whole *band of brothers* bond you hear about. But Graham was anxious about something. "Then what took him off your radar?"

"Real simple. The problem went away. He got past his anger and started acting normal again." Graham looked a bit squeamish. "Kind of suddenly, to be honest."

Kim had heard too many stories just like this in the spy world and they never turned out well. "You don't buy it?"

"I don't know. I guess I wanted to believe it. We all did. But Carter talked about Afghanistan nonstop and then one day never mentioned it again." Graham perked up. "Don't get me wrong, I was glad. But at the same time, I'm an investigator. And I don't believe answers come easy. His finding of closure overnight was too good to be true. Something changed."

As far as Carter's sudden transformation goes, it was certainly weird. But Kim knew better than to presume he was a Russian agent. He could've discovered some spiritual enlightenment or gotten into the psychedelic drug therapy so many veterans were doing to cure themselves from PTSD. That said, it was all they had to go on. She couldn't take any chances.

Kim looked around Graham through the dark

corridor at the open door to the office. She wasn't able to see the SECDEF or Carter, but she could hear them talking. "Was he on the advance team that made a sweep before Shepard got here?"

Graham turned with a deer-in-the-headlights look. "Yeah. Why?"

Despite the question, it was clear by the look on his face he already knew what Kim was thinking. "Then he could've planted the bomb."

Graham looked worried. "It's possible, I guess."

"Okay, then I think it's worth getting Carter away from Shepard until we know something more. Got any ideas how we can do that without it seeming suspicious?"

Graham turned toward the voices, then back to Kim. "Yeah, it'll seem weird if I order him off by himself. But if you're comfortable, I can send you two on a recon trip down inside the complex. Make it seem random. Say I need him to escort you for your safety. *That* he'll buy."

Kim wondered what the hell she had just gotten herself into. Not only was she about to proceed farther into this pit from hell, but she'd be accompanied by a heavily armed agent who was possibly a Russian spy. Kim was tempted to ask Graham if he thought she was way off base, but the very fact he turned on one of his own was proof enough for her that Carter was untrustworthy, and quite possibly a threat to their lives.

Chapter 46

Liam had kept his mouth shut so far, but when the chopper's motor went from a healthy high-pitched howl to a low rumbling whine, he was feeling the urge to inquire about a new plan that got them safely to ground. He'd never crashed, but he had spent enough time in war zones to know people who had. Despite what some believed, engine loss in a helicopter wasn't a death sentence. An experienced pilot could autorotate in a controlled descent and use the remaining inertia to land safely. But they only got one shot and it had to be done exactly right.

As Ike worked the controls, he called out through the intercom. "We're losing power but I'm not sure why. Anybody see where we're hit?"

Liam leaned right over Smitty's lap, hung his head out the door, and looked up. It wasn't clear what went wrong, only that they'd sustained damage, as evidenced by the greasy splatter on the rotor mast. Either oil or hydraulic fluid was whirling out of the drive shaft.

Liam pulled his head back in and secured the headset. "Bullet must've hit the rotor hub or the transmission. We're leaking pretty bad."

"Okay, I'm gonna have to put her down then. She's done all she can do."

"*Damn*," Garrett spat. "With that M240 out of commission, I thought we had a real chance at stopping the train."

Liam couldn't believe he was going to suggest what he was about to suggest. "We still might." He leaned forward in his seat and pointed to where the tracks met the horizon. "Think you can get us up there a ways? Few miles ahead."

"We've got a little left. Engine goes out, I can float us a bit. But we need to land ASAP."

Liam looked up ahead. "Well, I still got the C-4. Think I know a way to blow the tracks."

Ike glanced back. "That'd make a helluva mess. Wondering if that's smart given what we know about the payload."

"There's a wreck coming," Liam answered. "No matter what. Better to hit it way out here than in the middle of town."

"He's right," Garrett agreed. "At least we can pick the spot. And hopefully, we can keep those warheads intact. They're designed to withstand a crash. But not sure what'll happen if the Air Force incinerates that train."

"All right, it's two against one, I guess." Ike looked reluctant. "What are you thinking?"

Garrett continued: "There's a place up on Red Deer Creek that floods under the trestle. Derailing the train there won't be pretty but it's better than blowing the thing all to hell."

There was a silence over the comms as everyone waited for Ike's response. "Yeah, I know it."

He reached up and bumped his fist on the ceiling. "Okay, girl, just a little further."

With those words, Ike banked right, circled back around, and cut a path over the wide-open prairie that seemed to go nowhere. "Train will go east for a while, then turn north. We'll make up some time on the straightaway."

As they shot across the plains, Liam leaned out periodically to check the damage. He didn't exactly know why because there was nothing he could do about it anyhow. Having a job though, even a pointless one, made him feel better. But the contentment was short-lived, as the bird's low rumble turned to a shimmy, and the rotor blades slowed from a whomp to a whir.

Ike came over the comms. "This is it, boys. As far as we go."

Liam had envisioned a bone-jarring, spine-pressing slam to earth, but the crash landing had been thankfully nothing to write home about, especially given the fact he was the one holding a backpack full of C-4. For his plan to work, he'd need a few items.

Liam leapt from the chopper while the others were unharnessing and studied their target from atop the knoll where they'd landed. The trestle, about forty yards ahead, was situated beside a thick cottonwood grove running parallel to the railroad tracks. On the other side was the rushing water from the overflowing creek.

Before Ike could speak, Liam interrupted. "Don't guess you have any *hundred-mile-an-hour* tape handy, do you?"

Ike looked insulted. "What kind of two-bit outfit do you think I'm running here?" He reached under the seat and pulled out a roll of silver duct tape. "Anything else?"

"Double-A battery?" Liam asked.

Ike reached under the seat and fished out a camouflage walkie-talkie. "How many?"

Liam held up a finger. "Just need one."

As Ike pulled out the battery, Liam reached into the cockpit and yanked out the headset. He studied the length of the cords and looked left to the wooden railroad trestle he would attempt to destroy. With a combined twelve feet of cable, it wouldn't give him a whole lot of space, but he didn't have much choice. It was this or nothing.

As these structures go, the old framework wasn't much to behold, just a half-dozen creosote-soaked pilings, twenty feet high, that braced the tracks above. A swirling torrent beneath it filled the channel and rushed into a spillway and flooded the overflow ditch. The slurry of mud, water, and debris had formed a violent moat beneath the tracks.

Spying just the right spot to plant the charge, Liam grabbed the backpack and supplies and took off in a sprint with the rest of the crew on his heels. He looked left down the tracks and saw the train was about a mile away, a helluva lot closer than he'd anticipated. Given the crossing and impending doom, the mission objective was almost exactly like a training exercise from Sapper school. Had Ike dropped him from his helicopter it would've nearly been perfect.

Liam skidded to a halt at the edge of the creek

and took a knee. He eased the C-4 out of the pack and turned back to Ike. "Hand me the tape and battery." Taking the handoff from the pilot, he laid them out in front of him to survey the tools at his disposal. Liam turned to Garrett, for a second time that day, in search of a blade. "Need the knife again."

Once the tool was in hand, Liam cut the ends of the cords from the headsets and spliced together the cables. Looking up and left, he saw the train less than a quarter mile away. With all the tools he'd need to blow the tracks, he scooped up the bomb and put them into the pack.

Garrett leaned over him. "If you're about to do what I think, that ain't near enough cord."

Liam didn't have much of an option. *Time for a lie.* "Not as much as I'd like, but I can get around that concrete culvert and direct the blast in the opposite direction." Of course, there was no way to do what he proposed with what was at his disposal, but Garrett would call the whole thing off if he thought it was a suicide mission.

Ike raised an eyebrow, looked at the trestle, then back to Liam. "Thinking the same. Not sure it's worth the risk."

Liam shook his head and delivered *lie number two.* "Look, it probably won't even work. So, don't get your hopes up." As a matter of fact, Liam knew it *would* work. If terrorists and insurgents with an elementary school education could do it, then he was more than capable of destroying those tracks.

Garrett knelt beside him wearing a look of concern. "I'm with Ike on this one." He glanced up and studied the trellis. "You're just too damn close not to get hit."

Liam pointed to the spillway beside the pilings. "I'll be protected behind that concrete."

Garrett eyed it, looking unconvinced. "You're sure you can do this?"

"Absolutely." *Lie number three.* "Done plenty of jobs just like it in Iraq." While he was at it, he'd throw in a fourth whopper into his string of tall tales. "And I won't use all the explosive. Just what I need."

Yeah, right. He'd hit it with everything he's got. No way Liam was going to risk his life on a plan that might not work. But there was no reason to tell Garrett now.

"What can we do to help?" Smitty asked.

"Nothing for the moment," Liam assured. "Y'all get up over the ridge and stay low. I'll be back once it's over. Want to make sure and be clear of the trellis before the train hits it."

Like any normal human being, Liam didn't want to do what he was about to do. But he owed it to his friends and neighbors to make amends. Because of his failings, lives were in jeopardy. He couldn't rescue his father but at least he could save others.

"We'll be here if you need us." Garrett rose and offered a hand. "Good luck, my friend."

Once the bomb materials were restored in the backpack, Liam hooked the straps over his shoulders. He glanced at the approaching train, now a couple hundred yards out, and told a big lie. "Thanks, Garrett, but I don't need any luck."

Liam turned and eyed the timber buttress beneath the pilings and took off in a sprint. He made a running leap to get as far as he could out into the turbulent waters, but he came up way short of the opposite bank. Immediately the current swept his feet from beneath him and he was fully submerged. In a frantic sort of doggy paddle, he battled through the debris-filled rapids and clawed his way up the crumbling levee on the opposite bank.

Soaked and mud-covered, Liam dashed to the struts and climbed the lattice of planks to a brace below the timber frame. Yanking the soaking pack off his shoulder, Liam reached in, pulled out the C-4, and placed it beneath the piling and the overhang. Using the duct tape to tamp it, he affixed the blasting caps atop the explosive and connected the headset cable.

It was at that moment when the vibration became noticeable, first in his grip of the wooden beam, all the way down to his tremoring feet. From his vantage point, he couldn't see the train, but it was close enough for him to feel it. Liam turned back to find Garrett and the others, beckoning him to come back. Their mouths were open, shouting, but he could not hear their voices for the roar of the locomotive as it screamed down the tracks.

Jumping from his perch, Liam dashed across a plank and took cover behind the concrete spillway. There was enough slack in the line to get behind the edge but not enough to shield his arm. Had Liam a moment to think it through, he never would've done it. But with his father at the forefront of his mind, he was encouraged. Emboldened. It manifested in a smile. The word *inshallah* came to him in a voice clearer than any he'd ever heard.

It came to him in the same playful way his dad used to say it. Was it a message telling him he wouldn't die? Or was it the old man's way of saying everything would be all right, even if he did? Whatever the outcome, Liam was content with God's will. With the serenity of his decision, he fished the battery from his pocket and placed it against the wire.

Chapter 47

Asadi couldn't believe how quickly he'd lost Sam in the churning floodwaters. One second he was there—the next he was gone. Thankfully, Savanah was approaching at full gallop. She slowed just short of the river's edge and eased up into the shallows. Asadi pointed to the whirlpool where Sam had gone under, but before he could explain what happened, his partner had popped back up downstream—the calf hugged to his chest.

Witnessing this, too, Savanah gave Eazy the spurs and the horse lunged forward. Within seconds, his hooves were pounding the shallow surf, kicking up a spray of water that glinted in the sunset. Asadi followed close behind them, his gaze fixed to the right, in search of Sam, who despite his best efforts lost his grip on the calf and was struggling to stay afloat.

Moving the reins to take them back in the river, Asadi called out to Savanah, "You get calf! I get Sam!"

Asadi gave Sioux the spurs to get her into high gear, but the resistance to move deeper into the river and closer to the frothing, turbulent tide made her resistant to budge. Another yank on the reins and she begrudgingly obeyed. With the lasso in grip, he raised the loop overhead. But before he could take aim, Sam went under. Only his outstretched hand jutted up from the water about six inches into the air.

There wasn't much of a target, but Asadi twirled the rope and threw it anyhow, which by God's good grace landed right where he aimed. A quick tug and the line went taut. Asadi didn't have to see it. He felt it. Sam's arm was secured in the loop.

In his zest to pull Sam out as soon as possible, Asadi yanked the reins too quickly before dallying off the lariat on the saddle horn. The sudden jolt as Sioux turned back toward shore knocked Asadi off-kilter, forcing a split-second decision—stay mounted or let go of the line.

Against every instinct, Asadi kept his grip on the tether, which yanked him from the saddle into the river. He tried to stand, but the swift current jerked his feet from beneath him. With no way to stop the momentum, Asadi reeled in the slack on the rope until reaching Sam, who turned suddenly, locked frantic eyes, and latched on to him.

Before Asadi could break free, he was pulled under by Sam, who clawed wildly in his panic to rise above the water. Asadi could see the light above, but it was just out of reach. He had nearly broken the surface when Sam's clutches found him again and dragged him farther under.

A third failed attempt and Asadi sank, battered on his way down beneath a flurry of boot heels, one which clocked him in the chin. He gasped for air but caught a breath of muck instead. With what was possibly his last attempt giving his dwindling strength, Asadi caught hold of the riverbed with his toe and dug in, giving him a little bit of fight against Sam's iron grip.

He had just made the big push when he felt an even stronger hand grab ahold of him and yank. In less than a second, Asadi was head above the water, gasping for air, as he was dragged to shore. For a minute or two everything went cloudy. It wasn't until Savanah sat beside him and draped her arm over his neck that his senses fully recovered.

With her help, Asadi sat up and looked around at an oddly tranquil scene considering the fact he'd nearly drowned. The confusion over how he was rescued faded away with the sight of an utterly exhausted, soaking-wet Butch, who had a rope cinched around his waist. Apparently Savanah had tied him off to her saddle and he'd dove in after them.

Back under the shade of a mesquite tree, Sam was on hands and knees, ridding his quaking body of the nasty brown water. A couple of ugly heaves and he collapsed onto his side, eyes focused on something Asadi hadn't noticed until now.

Butch moved to Sam, helped him sit up, and pointed at the little calf scurrying up to his mother. "You see it, son. *You* did that. You're the one saved him."

Asadi couldn't see Sam's face, but there was a change in posture. His shoulders dropped, muscles unclenched, and he leaned against Butch for support. Naturally, he'd lost a little starch through the ordeal. But it wasn't just because of his physical exertion and close call with death. What he'd shed in brooding anger he'd gained in calm contentment. He was a kid transformed. Renewed. Baptized in a river of filth, Sam Clevenger had been washed clean.

Chapter 48

The explosion that took place not fifty yards ahead was not at all what Smitty had imagined. Cherry bombs, M-80s, and Silver Salutes had been a staple of his formative years, but those were nothing compared to the fireball and shock wave from the C-4 that destroyed the trestle.

Gazing through the rising white cloud of smoke, Smitty feasted his eyes on a smoldering mash-up of concrete and steel. It took only a moment to draw the sad conclusion. No way in hell Liam made it out of there alive.

Rising from the ground with Garrett and the others, Smitty took off in a sprint toward the foaming torrent, now teeming trestle debris. What had once been the concrete bulwark protecting Liam was blasted off the overhang of the spillway and plonked into the creek.

Glancing left as he ran, Smitty tried to gauge how much time he had before the locomotive hit the gap in the tracks. If the C-4 had made a ruckus, he could only imagine the destruction produced by one hundred tons of train as it flew off the rails and collided with the earth. He stopped short at the edge of the floodwaters, but Garrett dove right in.

Survival instinct screamed at Smitty to get the hell out of there, but he inhaled and took the plunge. Through the brown darkness, they dropped a little farther, grasping around for Liam until finding him at the bottom, his legs trapped beneath a pile of debris.

Smitty grabbed hold of one arm, Garrett another, and they each gave a solid yank. It didn't take much, and Liam was freed. With a couple of kicks, their heads were above the surface and gasping for air. But Smitty hadn't forgotten about the train, turning sideways as he swam, seeing it was nearly to the point of impact.

Fortunately, Bo was standing near the water's edge. He grabbed him by the collar, and yanked him to shore. There was a brief moment when time slowed down and everything went quiet. The rush of the current, the howl of the train, and the screech of iron meeting rock made no more clamor than a whisper of air.

It was so tranquil, in fact, Smitty thought he was dead.

Unsure if he was running or being carried, he glanced down to find the toes of his boots pawing at the earth, making a trench through the dirt as Bo dragged him across the prairie. It was in that moment when the silence ended, and the mayhem began.

Immediately, Smitty turned back to find the

plan had worked. Both engine and railcar derailed, skidded along the gravel embankment, and flipped upside down into the creek. Only the underbelly, axles, and still-spinning wheels were showing— partially shrouded by a hovering gray cloud of dust and smoke.

Smitty turned to discover that the architect of this destruction had made it clear of the wreck. Liam was on knees and elbows, gasping for air. Smitty stumbled over, helped him to his feet, and draped his arm over his neck to offer some support.

Taking the help, Liam straightened up and limped alongside as they made their way to Garrett, Ike, and an equally stunned Bo, who were all standing there speechless, either in awe or horror at the mess they'd created.

Garrett spoke first. "Well, we ain't in the great beyond. So, I'm guessing the bombs didn't go off." He turned to Liam. "I've seen a lot of stupid stunts in my life, but I don't even know what to say about that one."

Liam let out a raspy hack and sucked in a breath. "How about 'thank you'?"

Smitty felt a little uncomfortable as the two faced off in awkward silence. Then Ike chuckled, followed by Bo, and finally Garrett broke into a wide grin. While each one of them had seen some wild things, no one had ever witnessed anything like this. Undoubtedly, the others were all wondering what on earth to do with their overturned railcar full of atomic bombs.

Ike looked over. "Now what?"

Garrett kept his eye trained on the wreckage. "As far as the warheads go, we just need to keep them secured. Let the experts figure how to get them out."

"What about the guys inside?" Smitty asked. "Given the gunports and open roof, that thing won't hold air for long."

Garrett gave a nod. "Yeah, we'll need to get them out of there, I suppose."

"Get them out?" Bo stepped up and faced off with Garrett. "What the hell for? Aren't these the same bastards that put your woman in the hospital?"

"Probably," Garrett shot back. "Or at least some of their buddies."

Bo was fit to be tied. "Then maybe we ought to let them suck water for a little while and think about what they done."

"It's tempting for sure." Garrett looked to be considering it hard. "But they're worth more to us alive than they are dead."

Ike got serious. "What are you thinking?"

"I'm thinking there's a bigger network than what you see here. And to find them we're going to need intel." Garrett pointed at the railcar. "Those guys are going to give it to us."

"Soon as they're in custody," Liam added after another cough, "they'll lawyer up. Won't say a word. And whoever is involved will be long gone before we can find out anything."

"You're exactly right. That's why we need to get them out. Make sure we get the first crack at asking the right questions."

Liam smiled a devilish smile. "Have a few I'd like to ask myself."

Smitty didn't know what exactly was going on. But given the edge to Liam's voice, Garrett wasn't the only one with a score to settle. Geneva Conventions be dammed.

Chapter 49

Kim was a little surprised Carter had gone along with the ruse, although maybe she shouldn't have been. Despite the civilian clothing, he was still a soldier. And not only did Graham outrank him, but he was also the agent in charge. However, it was heavily ingrained in these guys to protect their principal at all costs, particularly during a crisis. So, it seemed a little odd he deserted Shepard without making a fuss.

Carter led the way down the dimly lit corridor, just as Graham had done earlier. But unlike his boss, who kept the short-barreled Mk18 at the ready in anticipation of any danger, her new escort cradled it like he was on a Sunday stroll in the park. It could've been a difference in style, but it was also possible he wasn't in search of a threat because he knew he was it.

Carter looked around in disgust. "How far you really want to go until we turn back?"

Graham concocted a story that there might be an operational landline located somewhere within the bowels of the bunker. With cell phone service nil, it made sense they would want to keep abreast of what's happening on the surface.

As they plodded along, Kim took a crack at a little humor to see if he would open up. "What's the problem, Carter? Too spooky for you?"

"Damn right." He turned back with a playful smile. "Pretty much every sci-fi horror flick ends up in a place just like this."

Kim couldn't disagree. Down the cold, dark corridor, around every blind corner and behind each piece of canvas-draped equipment, she wondered if something would jump out and grab her. She couldn't help but feel like she was playing the part of Sigourney Weaver's character in *Alien*.

The more twists and turns they made, the more Kim understood Carter's concerns. "Just a little farther. See a big room up ahead. Office or something. Maybe there'll be a phone."

"Yeah, right." Carter turned back again, this time with a skeptical glare. "You really think that's why he sent us down here?"

Uh-oh. Clearly, he hadn't bought the deception. His skeptical response put Kim on edge. "We need comms. And there might be a landline down here. Makes sense to check it out."

Carter stopped and turned around. "That's *not* why we're on this pointless mission." He spun on a heel and marched on.

Contemplating how to address the issue without being provocative, Kim trailed in silence. It was an odd statement for an assassin lying in wait, as it could show his hand. Of course, it *was* the kind of brazen talk you might expect of a soldier who'd lost his way. *Pointless mission* certainly had a nice defeatist ring to it.

At the end of the hallway, they came to the last accessible room. To the right, the hallway was partitioned off by a metal accordion gate with a massive chain and padlock. A yellow warning sign with the black trefoil symbol synonymous with radiation danger was posted on the wall beside it. There were no emergency lights or flashing strobes in the far reaches anyhow, just the cold, black emptiness of a place where stockpiles of nuclear material had once been stored.

Carter made his way through the entry of the last room, to what looked like an old workroom, and disappeared around the door frame. Kim followed but stopped short at the threshold and peered inside. Fortunately, there were no surprises. The agent was doing exactly as he'd done before in all the other rooms along their route—lifting up old dust covers and checking the desks for what they apparently both already knew: there was no phone to be found.

After making his way around all four walls, Carter turned back. "Shocker. No comms. Just a whole bunch of rat crap. And what looks like leftover junk from Dr. Evil's underground lair."

The idea was to head back to the others after they'd exhausted all options in their search for a landline, so Kim had to stall. At least until someone from the outside came to the rescue. If she was going to do it, she might as well see if she could elicit a little intel in the process. Carter was making a beeline for the door when she called out from behind. "Hold up!"

He stopped in his tracks and turned back, looking a little startled. "I miss something?"

Kim looked around, as if giving everything another once-over. "No. I think this is it."

Carter tilted his head at the door. "Then let's get the hell out of here before a radioactive mutant shows up."

Kim didn't know exactly what to say, so she decided to get right to it. "I want to ask you something. About the comment you made earlier."

Carter looked genuinely perplexed. "What comment?"

"About why Graham sent us down here. You acted like there was another reason."

"Didn't say there was another reason," Carter argued. "Just knew it was pointless. Which as you can see, it was."

Kim could tell he was agitated, which was often a good sign in an interrogation. It meant she had hit a nerve. "But you alluded to something. And I want to know what you meant."

Carter let out a huff. "My job is to protect Shepard. Not babysit you."

"So, that's it, huh? *This* isn't your job?"

Carter broke into mocking laughter. "Ding, ding, ding! We've got a winner!"

"You don't think finding a link to the outside world might be important?"

"It's not that." Carter's face tensed. "Don't you see what's going on here?"

"No, I don't. Why don't you enlighten me."

"Graham wants you out of the picture. *Removed.*"

Kim took a moment to process what she was hearing. The knee-jerk reaction to his words was denial. He was trying to shift the blame to someone else and take the heat off himself. She took a few steps forward and locked eyes. "Why would he want me gone?"

"Surprised I have to explain this, but nobody trusts you. And nobody wants the CIA looking over their shoulder. I know you probably think we're just a bunch of bullet sponges, but we've all gone through a lot of training. Been handpicked to protect our principal. If he trusts us to keep him alive, then maybe you should, too."

It was true that nobody trusts the Agency. Kim was used to that. And with her out of the way Graham was fully in charge. *But who cares?* Now that they were sequestered, there weren't a whole lot of decisions to be made anyhow.

Playing off Carter's comment about the *CIA looking over their shoulder*, Kim started her inquiry. "Take it you've worked with my organization before."

"Over in Afghanistan." Carter shook his head and laughed. "Well, I assume it was you guys. Nobody said officially. But I got that impression."

"And what impression is that?"

"*Arrogance.*" Carter said it in a way that was more playful than biting. "Just seemed like a group of professional liars, people who weren't playing by the same rules as everyone else."

Rather than argue, Kim decided to commiserate to keep him talking. "Okay, fair enough. I can see how it might look that way. You aren't the first person I've heard it from. Have a few friends in law enforcement who give me a hard time as well."

Carter perked up. "Who do you know in LE?"

"Work with the Bureau quite a bit. Mostly

counterterrorism when I first started at the Agency, but it's counterintelligence these days." Kim decided to drop that little nugget to gauge his response. "But the guys I've been dealing with lately are in the DEA and Texas Rangers."

Carter breezed on past her *counterintelligence* admission, seemingly without a second thought. "*Texas Rangers?*" His look was somewhere between confused and intrigued. "Got to be a story there. Those guys are pretty old-school, right?"

"Trust me, there's a story. And some of these guys are straight out of the Old West." Kim gave a little more to keep him talking. "Worked with them on some border security issues down in Mexico. Cartel stuff."

"Well, I'm hoping to parlay what I'm doing in the Army into a job with Secret Service." Carter looked her in the eye. "Got any buddies you could hook me up with *over there*?"

Kim couldn't help but think Carter wasn't a guy who was looking to subvert his government. He was fishing for contacts to get a more high-profile job. Of course, if he were a Russian agent, then his minders would be pushing for better access. And there was none better than the White House. But there was something that didn't add up. No spy would be this blatant.

"Really think you could take a bullet for the president?" Kim shook off the idea. "You've got more dedication than I do."

Carter looked really pissed. "You wouldn't?"

"Hard to say. I mean, I've put my life on the line for people I work with. But that's different. They'd do the same for me. *Have* done it for me." Kim gave another shake of the head. "Don't think I could trade my life for someone I didn't know. Maybe don't like or even respect."

"That's the point." Carter stood rigid. "It's not the person you're safeguarding. It's the office. By protecting this elected official, you're *literally* defending democracy."

Feeling as though she offended him, Kim decided to back down. Still, though, she had to push Carter a little while his emotions were raw. "I get it in theory. But it's just not the same. Like Graham for instance. This is a guy you've known forever. A friend. You've had each other's backs. Would be way easier to lay down your life for him than me. Am I wrong?"

Carter looked a little confused. "Don't really know Graham. We just met last week."

His answer hit Kim like a ton of bricks. "Well, the others then. Got some longtime buddies on the detail, I assume?"

Carter shook his head. "Don't know any of them, either. New team. But I'd still take a bullet for any one of those guys. And they'd do the same for me. It's what you sign up for."

Doesn't know them? This was a completely different story than what Graham told her.

"You didn't know anyone protecting Shepard until recently?" Kim pressed. "Nobody from training? Bootcamp? In-processing?"

Carter looked at her like she was crazy. "Like I said, just met everyone the other day when I was reassigned. *Why?*"

Someone was lying here, and Kim had no idea who to trust. "Reassigned from where?"

"MacDill Air Force Base, down in Tampa." Carter looked a little downcast. "Not sure if you heard, but Graham lost someone. Hate that I got my shot this way, but there you have it."

Now it was Kim's turn to shake her head. "Lost someone? You mean . . . died?"

"Suicide." Carter shrugged. "Apparently the guy never got over Afghanistan."

Chapter 50

There was no part of Garrett that wanted back in the raging creek. But it wasn't just the fact the current was growing stronger with each passing second. It was the fact that now, potentially added to the muck and the mire was radioactive material. A string of barbed wire could slice you in two but exposure to those bombs would make for a slow and agonizing death.

Getting to the men inside there wasn't just a priority for their intel value. There was also a good chance they could be used in a prisoner swap for Reza Bayat. He was useless to the Iranians now that Liam was no longer under their control. The Quds Force operatives, however, were worth quite a lot. And their masters in Tehran would desperately want them back.

Garrett turned to Ike, who was toting his Heckler & Koch MP5K, a similar version of the one the old Army pilot used in the early days with the Night Stalkers. Garrett would normally opt for the higher-caliber AR-10s, but with the underwater swim ahead he'd need something more compact like the submachine gun. "Mind if I borrow your weapon?"

Ike unslung the MP5 and handed it over. "You're welcome to it. But I'm thinking there's not a lot of fight left in these fellas, if any at all. You really want to go down there?"

Garrett eyed the smoldering wreckage. "Not at all. But if there's even a slight chance we can get some answers then I've got to give it a try."

Liam barked out a cough. "Want me to go with you?"

Garrett shook his head. "Nah, it's going to be a tight fit. And like Ike said, they probably didn't make it anyhow. Just gonna go down for a look-see."

Garrett moved to the edge of the creek and surveyed the overturned train. The engine, not surprisingly, took the brunt of the crash, and it was unlikely that whoever was driving had survived. But the railcar was still intact, which meant someone inside might still be alive.

Before he lost his nerve, Garrett jumped back into the creek. He didn't have much of a plan except to swim to the back and come in through the rear compartment. The water level, which came up to its underbelly, was rising by the second. Only the wheelsets were visible.

Garrett slung the MP5 over his shoulder, eased it around his back, and jumped right in. He ducked a shattered plank bearing rusty nails and dodged what appeared to be raw sewage before clasping on to the back of the locomotive. With a deep inhale, Garrett dove into the brown sludge and felt his way down the metal side until reaching the latch to the door.

A turn to the right, and it opened. Grabbing the

edge of the door frame, he maneuvered to get his boot heels on the hatch and pressed. With a groan, he pushed and the hinges screeched as the door swung open. Dropping beneath the rim and pulling himself inside, Garrett wondered how in the hell a High Plains cowboy had twice in a week been in a position to drown.

Feeling rather than seeing his way ahead, he pushed through the muck, his left hand held high to feel for dry, open air. Garrett was nearing the point of panic and about to turn back when his fingers broke through the surface and scraped across the ceiling, which was actually the railcar's floor. A few frantic flutter kicks upward and his head was above water.

Garrett huffed in air and cleared his eyes as he got his bearings. There was only the faintest bit of light from the emergency LED strip running the length of floor, which cast an eerie red glow. After an unsuccessful search for survivors, he decided to head back. The three-foot open area was diminishing by the second, and in less than a minute, his oxygen supply would be gone.

Garrett had just taken in breath for the journey back when he saw a shadow move in the corner. Skimming through a jumble of debris, most of which had jarred loose from the kitchen cabinets, he pushed through the clutter until he got a better picture of the silhouette, which seemed to move with purpose, unlike the floating trash that bobbed on the surface.

Garrett looked back to find he was far from the

exit, then turned back. "Someone in here?" He tried to remain as still as possible. "No point hiding. This thing is over. Stay here any longer and you're gonna drown."

As Garrett waded forward, he reached back for the MP5 and swung it around to the front. "I can get you outta here. But we gotta move." He was beginning to wonder if he was negotiating with an upturned Tupperware container, when the shadow moved into view.

The Iranian's dead-set eyes, illuminated by the glow of the red LEDs, were the first indicator this guy wasn't going anywhere without a fight. The second, and more compelling sign, was the barrel of the operative's semiautomatic pistol leveled at his chest.

Garrett's preference was to jerk up the submachine gun and put this sorry son of a bitch down before it was too late. But that would do him no good. He would take a bullet in the process, and probably lose the only source of intel they had left. He had to talk this guy down.

Garrett eased the muzzle of his MP5 up to just below the surface. "I know this looks hopeless. But it's not. There *are* options."

Growing exhausted from treading water, Garrett reached out with his free hand and held on to the back of one of the bolted-down chairs. He was grasping for the next thing to say when the Iranian answered in perfect English.

"What options?" The operative lowered his pistol just a little. "What are you talking about?"

Great question. Garrett cleared his throat to buy a little time. "Depends on what you're willing to trade, I guess."

The Iranian furrowed his brow. "What do you want?"

For Garrett, that was an easy one. "We'll want to know everyone who was involved in this. Phone numbers. Addresses. Ops plans. A full layout of your tech capabilities. Accounting of how you got this far. We'll accept nothing less than absolutely everything you know."

The operative fixed his gaze on Garrett. "And what do I get in return?"

Garrett had no authority whatsoever to negotiate, but that didn't matter. His only objective was to get this guy talking. "Give us what we want, and you might earn a trip home."

The Iranian was silent for a moment. "Think I'm stupid enough to fall for that?"

"I know this thing is bigger than you. And there's a network of Persian diaspora here in the States on your payroll. Taking them out of operation is worth a lot to us." Garrett held up a finger. "Plus, we want our guy back."

The operative's face scrunched. "What guy?"

"We make a swap. You, for Reza Bayat."

"That traitor?" The Iranian smirked. "He's worth nothing now. If he's still alive, you can have him."

Tired of playing games and ready to end this standoff, Garrett lifted the MP5 to just below the surface and rested the pad of his finger on the trigger. With less than two feet of open air, they were running out of time. He was just about to make a move when the guy spoke again.

"What assurances do I have that you'll hold up your end of the bargain?"

"None," Garrett said plainly. "In fact, I might just kill you anyway."

The operative stared back with a curious expression, clearly confused as to why Garrett had taken the hijacking so personally. *"For this?"*

"For what you did to the woman I love. If she doesn't make it, then all bets are off."

The Iranian looked down, as if processing what had happened. "The one in the crash?"

Garrett affirmed with a single nod.

Anger flashed in the Iranian's eyes. "You can blame Liam Bayat for that. *He's* the one who broke the deal."

"I don't blame him. I blame you. So, if you're a praying man, then you'd better get to it."

The operative's face showed a look of genuine contrition, maybe even pleading. "I wasn't there. I would've stopped them from—"

"Doesn't matter." Garrett stared the guy down. "What's done is done."

It seemed odd that a man hijacking a train full of nuclear weapons would care about the life of one woman. But the inner workings of a soldier's mind were strange. Killing was often a part of the strategic objective, particularly for a special operator on a direct-action assignment. Collateral damage left a lasting scar, especially when the victims were women and children.

"One of the men responsible is dead," the Iranian

confessed. "Killed by Liam Bayat. The others are gone. I don't know where. They don't tell us, in case we're caught."

"Well, I'll settle for what you *do* know." Garrett raised the submachine gun above the water. "And for that pistol you have there. Why don't you go ahead and hand it over?" When the guy didn't budge, he added, "If I don't kill you, my friends outside here will."

The Iranian winced in pain as he passed the gun over. "It's done then. We have an agreement."

Taking the handoff, Garrett noticed the operative's shirt was soaked in blood due to a bullet wound in his left shoulder. By the look on the Iranian's face, the sting of the injury matched the sting of defeat. His mission was over, and he'd already come to the grim conclusion that *live to fight another day* was the only real option he had left.

THE UNDERWATER SWIM OUT OF the train car was a lot easier given the mental edge Garrett had of knowing where he was going this time. The only hitch was making sure the Iranian was still tagging along. They lost contact a couple of times, but a quick reach-back got them reconnected. With fresh air filling his lungs as he popped to the surface, Garrett's spirits rose.

Not only did they have a chance now of getting some intel and making a trade for Reza Bayat, but they'd also managed to take out the train with relatively little damage. Of course, it would still require a massive cleanup. But considering the fact they could've been sitting under a mushroom cloud, this was a major victory.

As they gripped on to the train car's axle, Garrett gave the Iranian a little time to rest. It was clear he was winded from the swim and feeling the effects of his gunshot wound. To make it across the waterway to dry land it was going to be a slog, and they'd possibly need help. He looked behind him to the levee, where Ike and the others had been earlier, to find them gone.

Garrett had no idea why he'd been abandoned until he heard the distant knock of automatic gunfire. His second clue was the smile that spread across the Iranian's face. He gave himself up because there was a Plan B. And it was clear by the battle going on over the ridge that his Quds Force rescuers were mounting a helluva good fight.

Chapter 51

Kim didn't know exactly what was going on, only that the SECDEF's life could be in jeopardy. She was certain now the bombing was an act of subterfuge. The intent wasn't to kill Shepard. The Russians wouldn't allow it. Given their access, they'd be losing a primary source of an intelligence. But it didn't mean they wouldn't use their spy to help the Iranians.

For Moscow, it was a major victory. They could help hobble Washington and let someone else take the blame. While piecing together the collaboration between Moscow and Tehran was important, Kim's immediate concern was protecting Shepard. Now that the jig was up, Graham would panic. The rat was trapped, and the big question was what he might do now.

He had already found his fall guy in Carter. Graham's only hope of escaping treason charges was to make sure that everyone, possibly to include Shepard, never left that bunker again.

Unfortunately, Carter was unconvinced on Kim's theory. Still a bit starry-eyed when it came to the mission and those who proudly serve, he just couldn't fathom the idea of his boss as a turncoat. Carter especially didn't like hearing it from someone in the CIA, an organization he had referred to earlier as a *group of professional liars*.

Carter stared down Kim like she'd lost her mind. "Graham working for the Russians?" He shook his head. "Uh-uh. You're grasping at straws. Just trying to come up with a reason so this makes sense."

"I'm not saying Graham is guilty. But I *do* know someone in Shepard's inner circle was spying on him. And now a bomb goes off here. What are the odds?"

"Come on, Manning." Carter smirked. "You think Graham is some kind of assassin?"

"I don't know if his intention was to *kill* Shepard. Plenty of ways to do that, which would be a lot easier. What I'm saying is he might be complicit in a much larger scheme. He's desperate. He knows he's caught. And there's no telling what he might do now."

"Don't buy it," Carter shot back. "You don't even know him. Graham's a good guy."

"I know how you feel. Trust me. I've been through this same situation with my own boss. But what about the story he made up about you? He said you were unstable. Obsessed with Afghanistan. Even a suicide risk. Don't you find that the least bit alarming?"

"Well . . . yeah, of course I do but—"

"But what? He lied about you, Carter. Basically, dimed you out. Doesn't it piss you off?"

Carter let out a huff and took a seat on the desk. "*Yeah*, it pisses me off, but there's more to the story. I mean . . . not all of what he said is exactly untrue."

Kim braced for impact. "Get to it. *Right now*. What's going on here?"

Carter hung his head, looking ashamed. "Look, I don't know anything about the Russians. I swear it. No idea about any bombs. Iranians. None of that."

"Then what do you know?" Kim pressed.

"Nothing! I'm not some kind of foreign sleeper agent or whatever you're suggesting. *Okay?*"

"Carter, you have to come clean." Kim lowered her voice, hoping he'd do the same. "If there's something I need to know, then get it out there. If you work with me, maybe I can help you. If you're lying, then you're on your own."

"So, here's the deal." Carter looked up and locked eyes. "I've wanted on this detail ever since I joined the Army. That's why I wanted to go to CID in the first place. I told you, my dream is a job with the Secret Service, and this experience is as good as it gets."

"Fine." Kim moved closer. "What does that have to do with anything?"

"What I'm trying to tell you is I really did struggle with PTSD after Afghanistan. But I got past it. For a while though I was drinking my ass off. Partying all the time to keep my mind off things. And all that led to problems with my ex-girlfriend."

Kim shot a harsher glare than intended, already knowing where this story was going. "What *kind* of problems?"

Carter pushed the air. "Nothing physical, okay. Just some unwanted phone calls and text messages. Things like that." There was a pregnant pause. "Showed up at her work a time or two. Maybe more. It's pretty cloudy." He hung his head again. "Anyhow, the last time I knocked over a vending machine. Broke some stuff in the lobby of her office building."

"Were you arrested?" Kim asked.

Carter looked up and shook his head. "No charges were filed by the building owner. He took pity because I was a veteran and I paid off the damages."

"But you *were* harassing your girlfriend." Kim laid it out as a statement, not a question. "Trying to intimidate her."

"No, it's not like that. I was in love. She dumped me. And I wanted her back. Didn't handle it well."

"You had a broken heart. Who hasn't? What does this have to do with anything?"

Carter looked genuinely regretful. "I was a drunk. My world collapsed. I'm sorry."

Kim was tempted to lay into him but let it go. "Okay, so then what?"

"Of course, my girlfriend reported this to my commanding officer. All of it went into a report and then—"

"Let me guess," Kim interrupted. "It all just disappeared."

Carter raised his hands to his sides. "I don't know how, but I was grateful to whoever made it happen. Didn't ask any questions. Just took it as a wake-up call. Cleaned myself up and got my act together.

That report would've ruined everything I'd worked for since I enlisted."

"So, you think Graham is the one who helped you?"

Carter shrugged. "He had the access and was in the right position to do it. I just assumed he wanted to offer me a second chance or something. Give me my life back."

Kim didn't want to ruin the fantasy regarding a benevolent Nathan Graham, but there was a chance he did exactly as proposed but for entirely different reasons. Carter had a history of PTSD, alcoholism, recklessness, violent behavior, destruction of property, and emotional trauma. Who better to pin a crime on than him?"

Carter pulled up his cell phone and checked it for the fiftieth time. "Still nothing."

"We're not going to have any luck with that. We have to think of something else."

"Maybe there's another way out." Carter moved back to the hallway, turned left, and stared at an accordion fence. "If we could get through here, there could be another exit."

Kim joined him and stared down the hallway at something shiny on the ceiling. "What's that up there? Silver thing?"

Carter took a couple of steps forward and eyed it for a few seconds. "Fire sprinkler, I think."

"That's what I thought. If there's one there, then there's more. Which means we might have a way to call in the cavalry after all."

Carter looked around, as if the answer might come out of thin air. "Comms are a bust, phones don't work, and the only way out of here is by Graham. And if he knows or suspects he's caught in a lie, then who the hell knows what he'll do."

Kim was worried about that herself, which meant they needed help from the outside. She turned to Carter and smiled. "You a smoker by chance?"

Carter pulled out a pack of Marlboro Lights from a pouch on his chest rig and offered it to her. "Given the late nights and stress, it's pretty much a job requirement."

Kim waved him off. "Don't need a cigarette. Just the lighter."

Carter returned the pack and pulled out a chrome Zippo. "What do you got in mind?"

"Sensors." Kim pointed to the sprinkler on the ceiling in the center of the room. "Maybe we can set off an alarm somewhere and get attention aboveground."

"Any wires to the outside have been chewed up by field mice a long time ago. Only thing you might do is get us drenched."

Kim held up a sleeve, still damp from the rain. "I'm already halfway there."

"All right." Carter chuckled. "Then what do we have to lose?"

Kim followed him into the old office and helped him push a desk beneath the silver spout. She was beginning to feel a bit silly about her plan, as if she were attempting something that had been laughably shot down by *MythBusters*. But the only alternative was to wait it out. And since Graham was tipped off, he would be suspicious, and possibly dangerous.

Kim had to throw him off his game. More importantly, she had to get Graham separated from Shepard. With little time to sparc, both she and Carter climbed atop their makeshift scaffold beneath the sprinkler and stared at each other. No words passed between them, but each knew what the other was thinking. *Is this really going to work?*

Carter flicked the lid of the Zippo open, struck the flint wheel with his thumb, and raised the flame to just beneath the sprinkler. There was an awkward moment of silence when there was nothing to do but wait. After a good half minute of staring at each other, Kim was about to call it a bust. But then a trickle of water led to a sputter, and a pop led to a spray, which ultimately sent them racing for the door to escape the downpour. Fortunately, it was contained to the office.

Carter turned back. "Now what?"

Kim had the germ of an idea for an outlandish plan, which all began with the yellow and black radiation warning sign posted in the hallway.

Chapter 52

Garrett kept the barrel of his MP5 pressed against the Iranian's back as they scrabbled up the incline of the creek bank, while Ike and the others were firing their weapons over the ridge. At the crest, Garrett looked over to find a convoy of white Suburbans about forty yards out. Five vehicles. Five warheads. It wasn't hard to decipher that these were the teams taking the handoff.

Garrett turned to Ike, who kept an eye glued to the Steiner optics on his TX4. "Looks like cavalry's arrived." He took a momentary break from firing and looked over at their prisoner. "Unfortunately, they're here for him and not us."

Garrett turned back to find the Iranian wearing an arrogant grin. A quick glance at the raging floodwaters revealed that they had risen even higher, engulfing the wreckage completely, which meant falling back was a no-go. They would fight this one out.

Smitty ducked as a flurry of rounds snapped overhead and low-crawled over. "Ammo is plum near spent and these bastards are just getting warmed up."

Keeping low, Garrett raised up just a little to get

a look over Smitty's body to where Ike, Liam, and Bo were lying prostrate, heads beneath the rim, bodies as flush with the ground as they could possibly get. "Y'all making a dent?"

Bo shook his head. "We get off a round, and they pop fifty. Damn guys are good."

Ike raised his rifle over the ridge again and scanned the area with his scope. "Just too many of them." He fired off a couple of rounds that spiderwebbed the windshield on one of the SUVs. "We take out one guy. And three jump out to take their place."

Garrett surveyed the faces of his crew to find them looking pretty gloomy. "Boys, there's no crossing over the creek to escape. Too risky. We'll just have to hold them off until help arrives."

"Hold them off with what?" Smitty asked. "Don't have more than a few rounds left."

Garrett glanced around at the vast emptiness of ranch land nothingness surrounding them on every side. With the exception of the raging creek, there were no barriers between them and the Iranian operatives once their ammo was spent.

"Who are we even waiting for?" Bo asked. "Ain't no one around for ten miles. And nobody knows what's happening. We're on our own, man."

Garrett looked back and felt the same hopelessness. There was nary a more lonesome feeling than to accept they were all alone in this fight. His only hope was Kim. He just prayed to God she was on top of it and help was on the way.

AS KIM TRIPPED THE EMERGENCY alarm beneath the black and yellow warning sign in the hallway, she actually wondered if this was the worst plan she'd ever conceived. Over the years, there'd been some doozies, but devising her own version of a Three Mile Island radiation leak at Pantex was probably at the top of the list. But PSYOPS *was* a part of her repertoire. And there was no better psychological warfare than invisible death.

The resulting sound effects couldn't have been better were they generated in Hollywood for a sci-fi horror movie. There were no wailing sirens, or alarm bells, just a long, dragging hum that moaned in unison with the glowing red orbs. Adding to the creepiness was a crackling hiss of static coming from the decades-old speaker system that sounded exactly like a Geiger counter.

Kim turned to Carter. "You know what to do, right?"

A nod in return and Kim ran back to the entrance. It wasn't hard to work up a healthy look of dread. Between the eerie-sounding chime and flashing strobes, her *fake* emergency begot a *real* shock to the senses. With a few twists and turns up several flights of stairs, they were back at the corridor near the front of the bunker. She turned a corner near the entrance to find Graham blocking their path. The SECDEF was nowhere in sight.

Dripping in sweat from the frantic run, Kim glanced back at Carter and shouted to him in a display of faux panic. "Hurry! Hurry! This way!"

Graham took a couple of steps backward and eyed her up and down. "What the hell's going on?" In his clear state of shock, he seemed to have lost any concern for the SECDEF.

"We have to get out of here!" Kim pointed to the steel door leading out of the bunker. "Let's go! Let's go!"

Graham grabbed her by the sleeve. "What happened? What triggered the alarm?"

Kim struggled to get away as part of the show. "Let go of me!"

As they rehearsed, Carter played the part of the cooler head. He raised his hands to his eye sockets and mashed the heel of his palms into them as he caught his breath. After a few seconds of huffing in air, Carter looked to Graham and spoke between raspy gasps for air. "We got into something, man. I don't know what it was."

Graham let go of Kim and moved to Carter, examining his clothes. "Why are you all wet?"

"We went into an old storage compartment and a pipe blew." Carter raised up his forearm and raked it across his face. "Burned my face, man. Can't hardly see."

Graham turned to Kim, looking desperate for answers. "Blew *what* exactly?"

Kim shook her head and looked down as if expecting to find the answer. "It was a spray. All I know is it was hot. Then all these damn alarms went off."

Graham immediately wiped his hand on his pant leg, then looked back and forth between her and Carter, eyeing where they'd been doused by the sprinkler. "Madison said their decommissioned reactors are stored down there. Locked behind a gate." He backed up a few more steps. "Weren't there any signs or anything?"

Kim looked to Carter, sounding unsure. "No, it was just some old lab equipment."

"You don't know that." Graham shot her an accusatory glare. "You don't have a damn clue what's down there."

Kim raised her hands, palms out, and moved to him. "Look, it's nothing. We're fine."

"Back the hell away!" Graham raised his left hand and pushed the air. "*Now!*"

Shepard, who'd been in the office, stepped into the hallway, clearly in a state of confusion given all the commotion. "Take it easy there, Graham. They need medical attention. Let's get out of here and get some help."

Completely ignoring the SECDEF's orders, Graham raised his rifle and pointed it at Kim. "Get back, I said! You're contaminated!"

Kim pointed to a rusted vent in the ceiling. "The air shafts are connected. If we're contaminated, there's a good chance you are, too."

Graham looked frantic, doubtlessly contemplating the consequences of radiation exposure, which included vomiting, hemorrhages, and violent convulsions. Despite the trouble he was in, his fight-or-flight instincts took over. Desperate to avoid a painful and gruesome death, his synapses were firing like mad, screaming at him to attack or flee.

From the corner of her eye, Kim watched Carter ease up his weapon. Although it was subtle, Graham detected it and switched aim.

"I see what you're doing, Carter! Don't even think about it!"

Shepard grabbed Graham's shoulder. "At ease, Sergeant."

Graham flinched, pulled away, and shuffled backward on wobbly legs. "Get away from me!" He turned his aim at Shepard for several seconds, then spun around and sprinted to the entrance. Unbolting the lock in a frenzied panic, he jerked the handle, and pulled the steel door open. A quick look back and he dashed into the darkness.

Kim exhaled and let her shoulders drop, relieved beyond measure her idea had worked. But her elation was short-lived, as Graham suddenly reappeared and was standing in the entryway. There was a flash of recognition in his eyes, and it was all too obvious that he knew he'd been tricked and they were onto him. His only out—his final chance— was to erase the last few minutes. But in order to accomplish this feat meant that everyone, including Shepard, had to die.

As Graham yanked the grenade from his chest rig and grasped the pin, Kim shielded her face. But there was no blast, no concussion, nor shrapnel— only the *check-check-check* of suppressed M4 rifles, as the Counter Assault Team stacked in behind and finished off the would-be assassin.

As if on cue, the emergency alarm suddenly stopped, leaving a momentary void filled with an eerie silence. The low murmur of hushed voices overtook the calm, then it was quiet again. The only lingering sound came from the gentle, melodic patter of falling rain.

Chapter 53

Garrett looked up from his phone to find the others' eyes on him. With not a hint of cell service, his plan to call for help had come up bust. Everyone who could assist was hunkered down beside him beneath the lip of the ridge. Looking right at his battered and shell-shocked crew, he eyed their torn clothing and muddy faces. With the relentless rattle of enemy machine gun fire, Garrett felt as though he was living out some trench battle scene in World War I.

He turned to Ike, hoping the old combat veteran had an ace in the hole. "If we can give you some cover fire to get to your bird, is there any chance you can get us in the air?"

Ike shook his head. "Too much damage. She's done for the day."

Garrett looked over to find Bo gripping his meaty shoulder. Blood was seeping between his fingers. "Dammit! When'd you take a bullet?"

"Last batch," he admitted with a wince. "No big deal."

In fact, it *was* a big deal. Bo was a tough son of a bitch, but he wouldn't last long without stanching the flow. Between injuries and their dwindling ammo supply, they were all but finished unless they could get away, or reinforcements arrived.

Escape not an option, Garrett did the only thing he could do—plan for a way to buy some time. He grabbed his prisoner by the sleeve, yanked him to his knees, and mashed the muzzle of his MP5 to the side of his head. Moving in from behind, Garrett shielded his body the best he could, keeping a ready finger on the trigger.

It wasn't a foolproof plan. He could still get shot. But even a happy-go-lucky sniper would think twice about taking the risk. Fortunately, the Quds Force gunmen ceased fire. But it was only a temporary fix. The operatives wanted those warheads. And hostage or not, eventually they'd come.

GETTING TO THE BOTTOM OF Graham's treachery was an issue for another time, but Kim suspected it had to do with his concocted story about resentment over America's departure from Afghanistan. How spying for the Russians would rectify that travesty was beyond her comprehension. But apparently Graham had his reasons, which he would take to the grave. Her only concern at the moment was Garrett's team and the hijacked nuclear weapons.

Following Pantex security head Beth Madison into the auxiliary ops center, which was set up in the back of a tractor-trailer, Kim marched up the steps to find a buzz of activity inside. Security officers either scurried about on cell phones, typed frantically on laptop keyboards, or kept their eyes glued to one of several monitors that hung on the wall.

It took a moment to adjust to the darkness, but what caught Kim's eyes first was the fifty-five-inch television screen at the front of the room. The gray picture from the Reaper drone's feed didn't show much but the empty expanse of the wild Texas plains. There was an odd hodgepodge of trees, with maybe a hillock or ravine here and there. The only consistent image was off the railroad tracks, which didn't deviate from its straight path for miles upon miles.

Madison eased up to her and stared at the display also. "Whoever took over our train knew everything about it. First thing they did was disable the tracking system."

That didn't surprise Kim at all. Given the Iranians' cyber capabilities, it was likely they had either taken it over remotely or stolen the blueprints. Either way, the Quds Force team was in total control. With the Russians now involved, it opened up a whole other avenue of vulnerability. But that was a problem for another day. Her immediate concern was the warheads.

Kim turned to Madison. "What can we do from here?"

"Watch and wait." Madison looked at a clock on the wall. "Soon as the drone locates the train, they'll fire on it. Given the rate of speed, the Reaper should catch up at any moment."

Kim was about to launch a few more questions when Madison was signaled by one of her officers at a nearby desk for a phone call. She took the handoff on the secure landline and glanced up at the monitor with a look of anticipation. Turning back to the screen, Kim watched as the drone made its way over the train—or at least what was left of it.

Madison looked to Kim. "I've got Cannon Air Force Base on the line. They want confirmation on our end that the train is no longer operational."

No longer operational was the understatement of the century. It was completely flipped upside down, and all but the wheelset was resting beneath the rushing waters of a flooded creek. Clearly the mission had changed. With the train out of commission there would be the arduous task of cleanup, which fell way outside of Kim's purview. What *was* her responsibility was hunting down the foreign actors behind the hijacking. That was just getting started.

"Can they keep their bird circling for a while?" Kim turned back to Madison. "We need to see what's going on down there."

Madison conferred with whomever she was talking to on the phone and then gave a head shake. "Strict orders. The Reaper is tasked for one reason and one reason only." She tilted her head at the screen. "If the threat's gone, the drone is gone."

"The train may no longer be a problem, but we still don't know what else, or who else, is down there. Until we get boots on the ground, we need eyes in the air."

Madison spoke a moment longer, gaze affixed to the monitor, then looked back to Kim, clearly disappointed. "Problem is the ordnance. A Reaper goes down with missiles and we've got a mess on our hands. They're launching an ISR platform now."

"*A mess on our hands?*" Kim shook her head in disbelief. Only bureaucrats could come up with a rule that obtuse. And sending an Intelligence, Surveillance, and Reconnaissance (ISR) bird or unmanned aerial vehicle (UAV) this late in the game was pointless. "We have a mess. A big one. And it's going to get bigger unless we neutralize the threat. This thing isn't over yet."

Madison went back to the phone and argued with whoever was on the other end. But it was clear she was getting nowhere. Kim had worked in enough crossover missions with the military to know you don't turn battleships on a dime. Nobody gets in trouble following the rules. They get in trouble for thinking outside the box. Of course, that was her specialty.

Kim reached for the phone in an attempt to do what she'd done before—pull phony rank. She had just put the receiver to her ear when the drone feed revealed Ike's downed chopper and six individuals huddled together by the wreckage. Five white SUVs were moving toward them.

Kim turned to Madison, who was back on her cell phone. "I think that's Garrett's crew." She pointed at the screen. "That your guys moving in?"

Madison shook her head. "Talking to them now. They're at least a half hour away."

Damn. Kim didn't know exactly what was going on, but with what she suspected was a heavily armed Quds Force team closing in on Garrett and the others, she'd have to throw them a lifeline. The only one she had was the Reaper. Now even that was getting jerked away.

AS GARRETT FIGURED, THE HOSTAGE ploy bought a little extra time, but not much else. The Iranians wanted those warheads, and would risk their commander for the sake of the op. He turned back to find the desperate eyes of his team on him, in search of answers, for which he had none. But since they'd considered one *Butch Cassidy* scene that day, then why not another?

Garrett looked to Ike. "Can't help but notice you're the only one who isn't wet."

Ike eased closer, to be heard over the gunfire. "I know what you're thinking, and you can forget about it. I'd rather be shot than drowned in a creek full of radioactive sludge."

Garrett turned and eyed the raging floodwaters. In addition to the train wreckage was busted concrete, splintered railroad ties, and jagged shards of iron and steel. He hated to think what dangers were lying beneath the surface.

"Not saying it'd be easy, Ike. But unless you want to fix bayonets, it's the only way out."

Ike chuckled, apparently appreciating Garrett's gallows humor. "Try again, amigo."

Garrett pressed more forcefully: "We move, or we die."

Ike peered over the edge again, watching the approaching SUVs. "They'll cut us to pieces as soon as we hit the water."

"This embankment is too steep for those vehicles. They'll have to get out from behind their cover, and when they do, I can hold them off." Garrett looked back to the far side of the creek. "Just leave me that rifle. I can buy some time while y'all cross."

Ike surveyed the floodwaters and turned to their prisoner. "Want us to take your friend?"

Garrett gave a nod. "This guy knows everything. No matter what you do. No matter what happens to me, just keep him safe. He's the whole key to bringing down the Iranians' network and getting Liam's dad back alive."

"Keep my MP5 and take yours, too." Ike unslung the TX4 and handed it over. "We'll give you some cover fire once we're on the other side. Bo and Liam still have a few rounds left, I think. We'll just have to pick our shots."

Garrett looked back over the ridge to find the SUVs were less than thirty yards out. "Well, pick 'em good, Ike. Kind of got a lot riding on it."

Garrett looked over at Smitty, who was mumbling some nonsense about zombies. Fighting off his curiosity to ask why, he yelled at them to run, then raised the carbine over the ledge and fired a round that thwacked the right side of a windshield. Given the glare, Garrett couldn't see if he hit the driver. But he took it as a positive sign when the vehicle rolled to a stop.

Garrett brought a gunman into his crosshairs that exited from the left. A double tap to the chest later and the guy went down. Cursing himself for using two bullets when one would do, he rested his sights on a second, who scurried for cover behind the engine block. It took a little hunting, but Garrett found some flesh and carved off a piece of shoulder. He was just feeling a bit more positive when five more operatives filed out and opened fire.

As supersonic rounds cracked overhead, Garrett turned back to Ike and the others, hoping like hell it was safe to run. But to his alarm, they were only halfway across the creek. Returning to the fight, he aimed beneath the chassis of the lead Suburban and took a couple of potshots, catching a gunman in the shins. It wasn't a kill, but the shooter was hobbled and out of the fight.

Garrett put his crosshairs on another set of legs and pulled the trigger—only to hear the awful sound of a metallic click. He tossed the empty rifle and swung up his MP5. Garrett had just found his sights when the operatives rushed, guns blazing in a stampede.

Garrett scrambled to his feet and sprinted down the embankment. He was knee-deep in the creek when the first bullet screamed overhead. Another pecked the water and a third snapped by his ear. Dreading the fourth, Garrett stopped, turned, and shouldered his weapon. He didn't as much see the operatives, as sense them, as they fired down on him from the top of the ridge.

Garrett had just let loose with a full-auto counterassault—all options exhausted and nothing left to lose—when his eyes clamped shut from the heat of the explosion. The sound of it alone should've been enough to send him diving for cover, but for some reason, he stood still. Maybe it was out of shock—or possibly out of reverence for the hand of God.

The hunter-killer drone, circling overhead, left a crater of flames, a pile of dead bodies, and a plume of smoke that billowed to the heavens. Garrett's guardian angel was, in fact, an angel of death—a sword of destruction—and quite possibly the most beautiful sight he'd ever seen.

Chapter 54

One month later . . .
Lefors, Texas

It wasn't a huge surprise to Liam that he was fired from Pantex. He had that coming and a whole lot more. Fortunately, he also had the friendship of Kim Manning, who'd waved what Garrett called her CIA magic wand and made most of his transgressions disappear. His security clearances were gone. That was a given. However, risking his life to blow the rail had bought him enough goodwill to avoid any jail time. It wasn't a perfect deal, but he'd damn sure take it.

As Liam sipped his Pondaseta beer, looking out over the pasture behind his house and watching the cattle come in, he couldn't help but smile. Modernizing the ranch with a few patent-pending inventions was the first thing he'd done since his wife's passing that truly made his heart sing. His future was on the land he'd both come to love and helped to save.

Ahead lay a combination of what the whole family could dive into—production agriculture and advanced technology. There was the cowboy stuff for Wade and the science for Robin.

Liam's daughter walked up from behind and sat by his side. "What's up, Dad?"

What could he tell her? *Thinking about a future that almost didn't exist. Wondering what would've happened if I had gone to prison or been blown to Kingdom Come.* But aside from being legally bound by the federal government never to speak of what happened again, there was no point in bringing up the past. What's done was done. It was time to move on.

Liam draped an arm over Robin's shoulder and pulled her close. "Just wondering how I'm going to do all this when you head off to Texas A&M."

Robin put her arm around him. "College Station isn't *that* far, and I'm just a phone call away. Plus, you'll still have Wade around for a couple more years."

"Let's be honest." Liam chuckled. "Probably a *lot* longer than that." He glanced at Robin, who burst into laughter.

They both looked over at Wade, too busy doing what he loved to pay them any mind. He was out by the barn with a manual post hole digger, setting fenceposts under a blazing summer sun.

Robin asked her next question, clearly in jest. "Don't you feel *awful* letting him work out there by himself?"

Liam shook his head, turned to her, and winked. "Not really. Do you?" Getting nothing but a giggle in response, he added, "*That's* what I thought."

Liam remembered Wade's warning of Robin and her boyfriend and what might have transpired. While he wanted to press for details, and quite possibly levy accusations and threats, he thought better of it. For now he'd refocus on becoming a part of his children's lives—the way he had been before their mother passed away.

While there was a temptation to launch a few more jokes at his son's expense, Liam took mercy on him. "Why don't you be a sweet sister and take the boy a glass of iced tea?"

The dutiful daughter obliged. As Liam watched a sister tend to her sibling, he couldn't help but smile. He'd been given another chance. It wasn't just the pardon. He had a new lease on life. He could be the father he'd wanted to be and the man he'd hoped to become.

Since that moment on the trestle when he was certain he might die, Liam processed the world in an entirely different way. The constant High Plains wind, which once annoyed him, now met his ear as a rustling rhythm. *Inshallah*, he'd hear the melodic crackle of cottonwood limbs and the call of bobwhite quail for the rest of his life. *This* was the sound of being home.

Liam didn't know if he'd ever move past his father's disappearance or Lacey's horrific accident, but he owed it to them to try. His life would be one of consequence and leaving the world better than he found it. And he wouldn't have to do that alone. His friends—his brothers in arms—Ike, Garrett, Smitty, and even Bo Clevenger, had all assured him of that.

Chapter 55

Asadi looked over to Bridger in anticipation of hearing what he'd done wrong. In the world of team roping, he was a better header than heeler, but his uncle wanted to make sure he was proficient at both. For the first time in a while, there was no *better luck next go-round*, just a rare thumbs-up from his perch on the fence. His partner, however, wasn't convinced.

"Half-second late." Savanah rode up on Eazy, looking unimpressed. "Let's do it again."

Asadi was tempted to argue, but let it go, knowing Garrett would be there at any moment to pick him up for dinner. "One more time. That's it."

Savanah had just spun her horse around to head back to the chute when Sam joined them on Clover and flashed a smile. "Think I could give it a shot?"

Grateful for a little reprieve, Asadi turned to his uncle. "What you say? He ready yet?"

A nod came from Bridger. "Well, I've filled his head with enough lies about my glory days and what little I know. If he feels ready, he's ready."

Sam looked a little nervous as he turned back to Asadi. "Any advice?"

Asadi figured he'd ease Sam's tension with one of Butch's favorite expressions. "If dirt ain't flyin', then you ain't tryin'."

Sam stared at him a moment, as if seriously pondering the adage, then let out a little chuckle. "All right, I'll see what I can do." He gave a little kick to Clover and took off toward the chute where Savanah and Eazy were already positioned and raring to go.

Watching Bridger give a few last-minute pointers to his new student, Asadi couldn't help but think about how far they'd come since their fight at the Cat's Paw. Sam had *made a real hand*, and an even better friend.

Alerted by the snarl from Garrett's diesel pulling up from behind, Asadi hopped off Sioux and tied her reins to the fencepost. A scramble up the slats and over the top rail, and he met his dad halfway between the arena and the truck. But the greeting was different this time. Garrett wasn't wearing his trademark wide grin, which meant something was terribly wrong.

GARRETT KNEW HE SHOULD MOVE out of the hot sun for the conversation, but there was some news in life that just couldn't wait. It was clear Asadi had already detected trouble anyhow. The dour expression on the kid's face probably matched his own. But rather than say a word, he just pulled his son into his arms, brought him in close, and held on tight.

There was a temptation to stay frozen like that forever, to avoid the discussion entirely. But it would be a cowardly move, as bad as the awful decision he'd made that had brought them here. So, rather than avoid the inevitable, he let go, knelt down, and looked Asadi in the eye.

"Well, Outlaw, I've got some bad news I'm afraid."

Asadi took a step back. "It about my brother?"

"Got a call from Kim a couple of hours ago."

Asadi's voice cracked a little. "She . . . say he dead?"

Garrett shook his head. "No. She just said that whoever it was they thought was Faraz turned out to be someone else. Kid with the same first name. Same age. Taken by the same men."

Asadi stared at him quizzically. "So, Faraz still alive then?"

Garrett didn't know what to say. He didn't want to give false hope. But he didn't want to crush his optimism, either. Maybe the best response was honesty, which was the only thing he had left. "Well, the truth is we just don't know. We don't know who he's with, where he's at, or if he's out there at all. All I do know is we won't stopping looking for him. *Ever.*"

Asadi looked down and kicked a little trench in the dirt with his boot. "What we do now?"

Garrett placed his hands on Asadi's shoulders. "We just keep living. Put one foot in front of the other. And do the best we can with the blessings God gave us."

Asadi raised his chin, revealing a couple of misty eyes. "So, we do nothing."

Garrett glanced around, looking for someone

to help. But he suddenly remembered what Lacey had told him that day on the Caprock. She'd said "*you* are Asadi's dad now. As difficult as they may be, you have to make these decisions on your own." Putting her words of wisdom together he gave his son a truthful answer.

"Waiting is the hardest thing in the world to do. But sometimes it's the *right* thing to do. We just have to be patient. And when we know for sure, we'll decide what to do together."

Asadi's face brightened. "Because we family. You and me. Team."

What could Garrett say? The kid had been paying attention after all. "Yep. For better or worse. Through thick and thin. We're a team, Outlaw."

This was typically the part where Garrett would've thrown out a hand to seal the deal. But Asadi beat him to the punch with a big ol' hug. There was no way of knowing if they would ever cross the Faraz bridge again. In all reality, the more time that passed, the more unlikely they would find him. But there was something about the hope of it that lifted Garrett's spirits. Or maybe it was simply the fact his son had handled it all like a man.

Chapter 56

She didn't necessarily want to have this conversation, but Lacey could put it off no more. The past few weeks since her wreck had been both a whirling blur and a state of soothing tranquility. It might've been the alone time in the hospital, those quiet moments of solitude from midnight to morning that really gave her time to think. To say she'd done an accounting of her life was an understatement. It hadn't flashed before her eyes. It came to a crashing halt.

Hovering between life and death, Lacey made the decision that something needed to change. She didn't blame Garrett for what happened. Nor did she point the finger at Liam, or even herself. What happened out on that country road happened for a reason. And maybe it was for the best. She wanted more excitement than her mom's little café had to offer.

Lacey smiled at Garrett from the comfort of her living room couch as he eased through the front door and closed it without making a sound. "I have a head *injury*, Garrett, not a headache. You can slam the thing shut and it won't knock me any goofier than I already am."

He eased over, practically on tiptoes, then sat down and put his hand on top of hers. "How's the patient today? Feeling any better?"

Lacey took his hand into hers and squeezed with a little oomph to prove her strength. "Definitely better with you here."

Garrett looked toward the kitchen. "Anything I can get you? Glass of water or something?"

"No, I'm fine." Lacey giggled a little. It was cute to see this hard-edged DEA agent as the doting nursemaid. "Between Vicky and Crystal looking after me I have everything I need and then some. Just sit and relax. Keep me company awhile." She glanced over at the television, where *The Office* was on. "Think I've watched every episode at least six times."

Garrett let his shoulders drop and seemed to relax. "Well, taking it easy is the plan."

Lacey looked around Garrett at the door. "Where's Asadi?"

"I let him and Savanah off at the Cattle Exchange for dinner. Ginned up a pretty good appetite today working with Bridger."

Lacey chuckled. "He's putting them to the test, huh?"

"Oh yeah, he's a bulldog. Said he's going to hit it hard this summer. Get them ready for some youth team roping events in the fall."

"Glad of it." Lacey smiled. "I wanna see Savanah give those *boys* a run for their money."

"I'm pretty sure she already is." Garrett looked

a little tense, as if he was holding back. "Look, I wanted to talk to you about something that's been on my mind. Something important."

"Garrett, you don't need an invitation with me. Just lay it out there."

He cleared his throat. "About what happened—about everything. I'm sorry and I—"

"You don't have to keep apologizing. I'm going to be all right. Surgery went fine and I'll be up and moving around in a couple of weeks. And then—"

"Not just that, Lacey. I feel like you've had to take a backseat to everything else in my life. To Asadi. Daddy. The ranch. And you know . . . all the other stuff. The missions."

The first three matters Lacey didn't begrudge Garrett one bit. It was *the other stuff* that nearly pushed her to the brink. And not just because of the danger and the secrecy, but in large part because of *her*. Kim Manning was a damsel in constant distress. No matter when, no matter what, no matter why, she always won him over with another mission.

Lacey had no doubt their relationship could survive everything but *that woman*. "Look, I always knew you had other responsibilities. And that's okay. But if you really want a future, then you've got to be home. Not just for my benefit. But for Asadi and your dad. They need a father, and a son, and I need—" Lacey stopped short before going too far. "Well, I need *you*."

Garrett eased a bit closer. "That's exactly what I want. But there's something else I haven't told you. About the ranch."

Lacey saved him the embarrassment of having to say the words out loud. "I know what's going on. I know about the bank loans. And I can tell you we'll get through it. *Together*. We'll figure out a way. All right?"

Garrett swallowed hard. "What did I do to deserve you?"

Lacey was pondering a comical retort when a knock came at the door. She looked to Garrett, wondering what he was hiding. "Who's that?"

"Well, I thought since you've been cooped up you might need some better conversation than what I've got to offer. Asadi and Savanah have been dying to see you, so I had Ray pick up some fajitas and come on over for a surprise."

It was a plan so awful that only a man could have dreamt it up. Lacey hadn't showered or put on makeup and her place was an absolute mess. But what the hell? If they didn't care, then why should she. "Well, what are you waiting for? If I've got visitors, then let them on in."

SMITTY HATED TO BRING UP business at a time like this, but Vicky had let him kick that can down the road for as long as she was going to allow it. Mescalero Exploration was moving forward, full speed ahead, and for her scheme to work they were going to need the Kohl Ranch. While Crystal and the kids went in to visit with Lacey, he kept Garrett out on the porch for what would hopefully be a quick talk. But unfortunately, his friend did not welcome the proposal.

Pondering the terms of Vicky's offer, Garrett's

anger seemed to gain both momentum and ferocity. "You mean to tell me I'd be giving up everything we have. Every precious resource. Every bit of water beneath the soil. And I'd be doing it all for free."

Smitty suddenly felt as though *he* was one of the zombies. "Not for free. She'd pay off your equipment loans, irrigation system, and the land note. Everything you owe to the bank would be taken care of and your slate would be clean. Back to square one."

"*Square one* was exactly why I went into debt in the first place. Kohl Ranch was just barely hanging on with Daddy running it by himself. For it to be a viable enterprise, I had to make some major investments. I had to take a risk. And that bit me in the ass."

"I know, Garrett. But nobody expected that wildfire to do the damage it did. Something like that would cripple anyone. But the improvements you invested in before the catastrophe made everything a whole lot worse."

"So, what's your role here?" Garrett looked skeptical. "Why did Vicky lay this on you?"

"Because you're my friend." Smitty took a moment to process what he'd just said. The word *friend* had come out so naturally he didn't realize how strange it would sound when it did. Despite the fact they'd started out on opposite sides of the law, Garrett had been his savior. And Smitty had never had a better ally in his entire life.

Garrett shook his head. "Somehow, this doesn't seem like a friendly kind of deal. Feels like I'm getting swindled. Or at the very least, taken advantage of, given the circumstances."

Smitty knew exactly what he meant. No way around it, Vicky was kicking Garrett when he was down. "You've done nothing but help me every step of the way. I hate to come to you with this kind of offer. I really do. That said, the cold, hard truth is Kaiser money saves your ranch. It ain't perfect, but it's a second chance. Maybe . . . even an opportunity."

Garrett seemed to ponder those words for an uncomfortably long time, then spun on a heel and marched toward his truck. While Smitty didn't know what his friend was up to, he *did* know when you saw that fiery look, it was highly advisable to get the hell out of the way.

Chapter 57

As Garrett entered the front door of Vicky's home, it dawned on him he'd never been inside. The Kaiser mansion, like their ranch headquarters, was the kind of place that evoked either the inspiration or ire of everyone in the Texas Panhandle. But it wasn't just the wealth. It was the flaunted *power* behind their money that didn't sit right. Mescalero Exploration wasn't just an oil company. It was a bully.

Garrett had been tormented by it not once, but twice now in his life. He didn't plan on making it a third time. As he crossed the foyer, Ted Crowley blocked his path. "Suggest you step aside, Sheriff. Won't tell you again."

Crowley threw up a hand and rested it on Garrett's chest. "Hold on a minute. You look about half-cocked. Want to make sure you aren't here to start any trouble."

Garrett stared Crowley down. "Well, there's one way to find out."

After several awkward seconds and no response, Garrett knocked Crowley's arm away, and side-swiped his shoulder passing by. He was at the threshold of Vicky's office when he heard the *tok-tok-tok* of the sheriff's boots on hardwood floors as he followed from behind. Garrett was about to whirl around and deck him when Vicky rushed to the door and got in between them.

She threw up a hand to Crowley. "It's okay, Ted, I've got it."

The sheriff gave Garrett the skunk eye as he answered her. "You sure about that?"

"Yeah, I'm positive." Vicky looked to Garrett as if getting his assurance everything would be fine. She said a bit softer, "We're *just* going to talk. Right?"

There was a moment of awkward silence that Garrett used to calm himself down as he walked farther into her office. He didn't wait for an invitation to sit, just made himself comfortable in the plush leather chair behind her desk. It wasn't meant to amuse her but apparently it did.

Appearing to wrestle back a smile, Vicky rolled a chair over and took a seat. "Guess Ray must've delivered my terms."

Garrett gave a nod. "As a matter of fact, he did."

"Sorry to do it so soon after everything with Lacey. It's just that things are moving forward, and they're moving fast. I can't wait around any longer."

Garrett leaned back in her chair and put his boots up on her desk. "Well, time is money, after all. Isn't it?"

At this point, Vicky didn't bother hiding her delight in the moment. It was written all over her face. "Lacey's looking better, don't you think?"

"Yeah, I do. Much of it thanks to your help. She

says you stop by and check in on her every day. Sometimes twice a day."

Vicky shrugged. "Well, her place isn't far. Easy to run meals over from time to time."

Garrett grinned. "All these months and not a peep. Now she's your best bud again, huh?"

"You take issue with that?"

Garrett shook his head. "You make her happy. Always did. Even back in high school."

"Then what's your problem?"

"My problem is you always get what you want from whoever you want."

Vicky looked incensed. "You think I'm using her?"

"No, actually, I don't. Honestly, I just can't decide if I should be pissed or jealous."

Vicky looked at him quizzically. "I'm not sure what you're getting at."

"What I'm getting at is with the *huge* exception of Preston, your family has never really done anything wrong." Before she could reply, Garrett continued: "I mean . . . morally questionable, and maybe even reprehensible for sure. But there's nothing they can lock you up for when it's all said and done. Kaiser's record is clean."

"Then why come storming in here, Garrett? I offered you a deal. Take it or leave it."

"I totally agree. Not a thing in the world wrong with your proposal."

Vicky brightened. "Then you're going to accept it?"

"Ah, that'd be a *hell* no." Garrett held up a finger. "But I will offer up a better one."

Any amusement from earlier was wiped clean off Vicky's face. She was all business. "What's your counter?"

"I don't want a buyout, Vicky. I want a partnership." Garrett could tell she was about to object, but he didn't let it leave her lips. "Lacey told me months ago you said you wanted the Texas Panhandle to go back to the families who founded it. The—"

"Kaisers, Capshaws, and the Kohls. Yes, I told her that and I meant it."

"Obviously, we bring the land and the resources Mescalero needs. And Bridger is the most experienced oil and gas attorney in the region. But what the Kohls also have is something even better than that. Something Kaisers will never have."

Vicky looked to be somewhere between offended and bewildered. "What would that be?"

"*Trust.* We can bring mineral owners to the table who wouldn't negotiate with Mescalero for all the money in the world. And as you know, there are quite a few of those out there who would just assume go to your competitors purely out of spite."

Just like that, Garrett had won her over. He could see it in Vicky's ravenous eyes. She tilted her head toward the hallway where the sheriff was probably lurking near the door. "It's a package deal, you know. With me you get him. He's got a stake in all this, too."

"Don't care what Crowley does. Long as he stays the hell out of my way."

"Fair enough then." Vicky rose from her chair, walked over to the desk, and stuck out her hand. "Obviously, the terms will need to be worked out.

But I think the idea of teaming up is a good one. To take on the big boys I'll need every advantage."

"*We'll* need every advantage," Garrett corrected.

As they shook hands, Garrett couldn't help but think he was making a pact with the devil. And there was a part of him that couldn't help but think this was exactly what Vicky wanted all along. Either way, he was tired of just barely getting by. But big change meant big risk. And a partnership with a Kaiser was about as risky as it gets.

If Garrett wanted to make a life on the Kohl Ranch for himself, Lacey, Asadi, and his dad, he'd have to gamble. His descendants had fought for that land, and he'd do the same. With this deal, there was a chance to set some roots and build a permanent home for his family. He could finally undo the mistakes of the past and carve out the kingdom that was stolen from them years ago. For the first time in a long time, Garrett's future had never shined so bright.

Chapter 58

Nine months later . . .
Herat Province, Afghanistan

As Kim sat in the middle of the backseat of a dilapidated maroon Toyota Corolla on the way to their rendezvous location, she couldn't help but think she'd traveled this same dirt road before. Flanked by Wazir gunmen toting AK-47s that were even more beat-up than their vehicle, she could only look forward through a dust-covered, pockmarked windshield. But with her vision further obscured by the mesh of her blue burka, her hearing became all the keener.

The crunch of gravel beneath the tires, bleating goats, and shouts from bribe-seeking checkpoint guards all seemed to amplify in the crisp morning air. Of all the places on earth Kim said she'd *never* return, this oasis city on the ancient Silk Road was certainly at the top of the list.

Garrett told her the only surefire way to get a laugh out of God is to use the word *never*. And damned if he wasn't right. But her resistance to return wasn't rooted in safety. It was that everything she'd fought for there was washed down the drain.

A cynic might chalk it up to American hubris or plain old sour grapes. But it was so much more than that. The fear on the faces of those they passed on the street was a painful reminder of all her broken promises. After the country fell to the Taliban, she had written the country off as a lost cause, submitted to the notion that Afghanistan was, in fact, *the graveyard of empires.*

Even more surreal than the reason for her return was the company in her presence. Of all the strange bedfellows who had come together, perhaps Kim was the strangest among them. She wasn't just the only female, but the lone Westerner. She decided to ditch the burka for a head scarf, which might anger their hosts from the Afghan General Directorate of Intelligence (GDI), but they weren't her concern. Her only focus was on flawlessly executing the trade.

The gathering of enemies for this provisional truce could not have been orchestrated by anyone other than Asadi's uncle, the powerful and respected tribal chief in Waziristan, Omar Zadran. While it would certainly be surreal to come face-to-face with her Iranian adversaries, it would be nothing compared to meeting the other strangers at the table.

Lying to Asadi and Liam about their missing loved ones' *unknown* status saddened Kim immensely, but she believed it was the best option given the uncertainty. Hopefully soon, her Quds Force captive, Cyrus Ahmadi, would be exchanged for Faraz Saleem and Reza Bayat, both of whom were destined for a surprise family reunion on the Texas High Plains.

Kim could have used a gunslinger like Garrett along, but she kept him in the dark as well. His future was on the ranch with family, not in a shadow war with her. While the prisoner swap seemed fated for success, Kim didn't rest easy. The only thing more dangerous than sneaking into a country run by terrorists, heroin traffickers, and warlords was making her way back out again.

ACKNOWLEDGMENTS

It takes a team to make all this happen and I have the best one in the world. The biggest shout-out goes to the ones who put up with my long hours at the computer and absences while I'm on the road. To my beautiful wife, Diana, and wonderful children, Bennett and Maddie, thank you for all your patience, understanding, love, and support. To my parents, Robert and Holly Moore, and sister, Allison Jensen, I couldn't ask for better promoters of the series. Sharing this blessing with you is one of my greatest joys.

To my literary agent and confidant, John Talbot, thank you for always being a terrific sounding board, and a consistent voice of clarity and foresight over the years. The same gratitude goes out to my editor, Lyssa Keusch, who I have come to know through the editing process and consider a friend. I'd also like to thank the behind-the-scenes team at William Morrow/HarperCollins, particularly those responsible for getting the books out there and spreading the word.

To Jason Abraham, owner of the Mendota Ranch; CW4 Boyd N. Curry (Ret.), U.S. Army 160th Special Operations Aviation Regiment; and

Jack Stewart, I thank you for sharing your extensive knowledge on helicopters and aviation.

To Joel Carpenter, (Fmr.) Army Ranger, 1st Battalion, 75th Ranger Regiment; Evan Ramirez, SOC (Ret.) Navy SEAL; CSM Lloyd E. Purswell (Ret.) Fox Company, 51st Infantry, Long Range Surveillance Company; Cody Sharpless, (Fmr.) Protective Service Officer; and Ian D'Costa, Director of Military/Law Enforcement, Lone Star Armory, thank you for providing technical expertise on weapons, tactics, and operational planning.

To my lifelong friend Cade Browning, thank you for your legal expertise and equine knowledge. To Ed Hesher, thank you for your energy industry input. A big thanks goes out to Klint Deere, Hospitality Manager, Mesa Vista Ranch, for providing great background on the area, as well as Milton Cooke, Proprietor, Stumblin' Goat Saloon and The Cattle Exchange, for helping to promote the series. I'd also like to thank Mark Erickson, Justin Garza, and Ted Evans, for all your terrific support. It's an honor to call you friends.

If you enjoyed

Ricochet

Look out for the next utterly gripping Garrett Kohl thriller, in which Garrett must find out what's truly tainted in the energy industry and uncover a deep-rooted plot in order to protect his new business, beloved ranch, and family.

COLD TRAIL

Available in hardcover Fall 2024
from William Morrow